Designer Passion

by

Dar Tomlinson

Love Spectrum/Genesis Press, Inc.

Genesis Press, Inc.
315 Third Avenue North
Columbus, MS 39702

Copyright © 1999 by Dar Tomlinson

Designer Passion

ISBN: 1-885478-79-8

Manufactured in the United States of America

FIRST EDITION

Dedication

To Mihra, who showed me unconditional love and loyalty, and finally, dignity in death.

To Zac, who is taking the sting away.

Designer Passion

Chapter One

Damn. Chandler Chesney Baker is a proverbial lady-killer.

Drawing a fortifying breath, Holly Harper told herself the blond-god entrepreneurial legend filling up her office doorway could also be the answer to saving Xtreme Ski from bankruptcy. She dredged up a smile and approached him with her hand extended.

"I'm Holly Harper, Mr. Baker. Thank you for coming."

He took her hand. On his ring finger he wore a ruby-centered signet ring instead of a wedding band. A heavy, gold watch flashed at his wrist. "Good to meet you. Thanks for working me in."

Introductions dispensed with, he glanced around the pastel-hued office, then raked a gentle gaze down her body and up again. "You're too little to fight the world of commerce." He spoke with a slow, deliberate Oklahoma cadence, a soft smile echoing in his eyes. "No wonder you need help."

She withdrew her hand from his callused grip, determined to meet his eyes. For his initial inspection of Xtreme, she had chosen her tallest heels, which elevated her to a stately five-two, and a carbon-black Donna Karan power suit with

a top-of-the-knee-grazing skirt. An antique cameo covered her
pounding pulse while holding together the collar of her creamy
silk blouse. Now her conservative attire left her feeling vulnerable.

She concluded this legendary turn-around king to be
unnerving. "I don't need help. I need money."

"For what, if you don't mind my asking?"

The pressing reasons ran through her mind. "To protect
my husband's and my father's investments in the business. To
keep the doors open until volume surpasses expense and I start
to—"

"It's been my experience that needing money is a surefire sign of needing help." Smiling, he measured her with
slate-colored eyes. "And I want you to know, Mrs. Efron—"

"Ms. Harper. I don't use my husband's name. But please
call me Holly."

He quirked a brow. "It's only fair that I level with you. I
go where my money goes. I don't fit the silent-investor type
that I hear you're looking for. I can only consider joining you
if I obtain fifty-one percent of the voting stock.

Control, in layman's language. When Lance, Xtreme
Ski's in-house accountant, had warned her that his cousin
would make a son of a bitch of a partner, Holly shoved the
warning, along with caution, to the back of her mind. Face-to-
face with Baker now, she had to keep reminding herself of
Xtreme's dire need. But Baker wouldn't live long enough to
get control.

His scrutinizing stare made her shoulders tighten; pins
and needles pricked her spine. She had made an effort to corral her mass of curls this morning, but the chignon had
mutinied on the short drive to the office. She could feel errant,
dark spirals framing her face and neck. A sneaked glance in
the antique mirror behind her desk assured her she looked like
a soap-opera vamp. She doubted her potential partner watched

those—or anything, other than Money Line.

His drawl reclaimed her attention. "As long as you're aware of my conditions, we should proceed."

Because she needed him, she prepared to listen.

She motioned to the one visitor's chair and closed the door to prevent being overheard in the cramped quarters. She rounded the circa 1800 partner's desk, repositioned a paisley pillow in the seat of her lilac chair and sat down.

Matching his brazen demeanor, she stared at him openly.

An impeccable houndstooth jacket over a black T-shirt, both most likely Armani, accentuated broad shoulders and a muscular chest. His Levi's boasted starched creases uncommon to Denver style, and stretched for miles over long, lean legs. Chandler Chesney Baker's attractiveness, his flawless stature, struck her as formidable.

"What shall I call you? Do you prefer Chandler?" She congratulated herself on achieving a detached tone.

His slate eyes darkened to soot. "Call me gone, if you don't agree with my warning." His smile, still gentle even if a bit indulgent, made her wonder if she'd heard correctly.

"Warning?"

His eyes glinted, then turned contemplative. Classical background music she had considered unobtrusive before today increased a few decibles. No one had visually measured her this close in seven years—not since the day her husband boarded a Sri Lanka-bound plane to source fabrics. His angst concerning her ability to operate Xtreme in his absence had been evident.

Her present financial dilemma validated Jules's concern.

Baker shifted his lean body and imposing height in the chair. He propped one spit-shined eel-skinned boot on the opposite knee and yawed to one side, an elbow braced on a chair arm. He wore a confident attitude well, probably relied on it, but his unlined face marked him too young for his enviable business reputation.

He surveyed the small, elegant room. His gaze calculated every detail, making her even more uncomfortable, then focused on her again. The stern line of his mouth and stubborn set of his jaw unnerved her. She rejected troubling images of working with him. He impacted her too strongly.

He continued his warning. "If I invest in Xtreme Ski, I'll be leaning over every shoulder in the place, watching where every dime goes. I'll have no choice but to question every procedure where someone mishandled the ball before I got here."

Holly doubted that. Along with pronouncing him "hell on women," Lance claimed Baker had more irons in the fire than the King Ranch. He sat on the board of three Colorado corporations and two Denver banks, had the dubious distinction of racing Thoroughbreds and quarter horses, had a penchant for Las Vegas and lived on a horse breeding ranch forty miles south of Denver. His cousin called Baker "the Renaissance man."

Lance had also divulged that, since learning of the investor opportunity at Xtreme Ski, Baker had been jetting off to Valle de Las Leñas, Yuppie America's premier Argentinean destination for ski lessons. Although she had begun to understand Lance's warnings, if a deal was struck, she was convinced her ailing company would see little of the pompous Lord Baker.

With her goal in mind, she smiled determinedly. "I don't consider your claim a warning, Mr. Baker."

"What do you consider it?"

"A promise."

His mouth formed a skeptical grin Steven Segal would have had to rehearse with a mirror. "Call me Chess."

Knight or rook? "Should we reach an agreement, when did you have in mind coming onboard?"

Her question threw mind-whirling images at Chess.

Holly Harper was a miniature quintessential female whose cultured tone mimicked a perfectly dry martini. Lance's droll remark about a "Jewish princess" had let Chess hope that she was ethnically blessed with a gift for commerce, but in no way had his cousin's irony prepared him for her dark, petite appeal.

All that well-proportioned splendor could be trouble.

He'd never had a partner, never wanted one, much less a woman. But this one needed financial help while he craved the challenge of another commercial coup. He reasoned a woman would be dependent, more inclined to take his word, not always soothing her ego by stating her two cents' worth.

Pretending to regard his warning that he'd be "running the show" as a promise was clever. He fought a smile. Her trying to out-finesse him would get them nowhere until she realized he could help her and wanted to. Or until she decided to trust him. Eventually, reaping the benefits of their association, she'd smile all the way to the bank-teller's window.

He summarized his claim. "I won't be coming onboard unless you agree to my terms."

One brow formed a minute arch. "Which are...again?"

He dredged up a take-it-or-leave-it tone. "I'll control operations and finance, with the final word on design. Simple as that."

For the first time she looked discomfited. The way she plopped off her tortoiseshell glasses made him suspect they were clear glass, employed for effect.

"You need not be bothered with design," she assured him. "Xtreme's problems stem from lack of finance only." She waved a hand adorned with a thin wedding band toward a wall crowded with plaques. "These are my awards to date. I've been nominated for Industry Designer of the Year, and *People* magazine is planning to run a feature on me and my design concepts."

She settled against the chair back. If she were a man, this was where she would prop her feet on the desk and light a cigar. He let his gaze roam the plaques, nodded, then rose and strolled to a display of custom-framed reproductions from various industry publications. The articles featured skiers wearing Xtreme Ski attire. Pacing himself, he refrained from asking if these were the innovative designs that had placed her on the brink of bankruptcy.

"Impressive." He ambled back to his seat, boot heels echoing on the scarred and neglected parquet floor.

She announced with a flourish, "I'm negotiating with Dominique Perret about endorsing Xtreme."

Who the hell was Dominique Perret? Probably, some ski celebrity. Neither celebrity endorsements nor awards would make Xtreme solvent. On the other hand, his million-dollar letter of credit would, if he kept his guard up and didn't allow her physical appeal to muddy the water. He could smell trouble a mile away. Even if it wore a cameo and a tastefully abbreviated black skirt.

"If we make a deal, Ms. Harper, I'll have the final say on what designs get turned to samples. If I don't like the samples, we'll start over."

"I presume you know a lot about fashion design, then."

"I know a hell of a lot about comfort, performance and cost control. That'll do."

Mozart permeated the stillness as she fidgeted on her flowered perch. He watched her scramble for a mental toehold while a Colorado sunset bled into her cheeks.

"You seem to have an inordinate desire for control, Mr. Baker." Her smile tempered the challenge as prettily as he'd ever seen it done.

Chess ignored a reliable trouble-signifying tickle on the back of his neck. "My MO is based on the golden rule."

Beneath arched brows, hope glittered like polished ebony

in her eyes until he finished the cliché.

"He who has the gold makes the rules."

Seeing her hope fade tapped his reluctant sympathy. She was obviously used to getting her way and considered her own paid-for press releases gospel. Her awards and favorable media had done little more than make her a local legend going broke. His tentative plans for Xtreme would result in international recognition and wealth beyond imagining for her and another entrepreneurial score for him. Attaining that meant focusing on the best agenda for each of them and not being swayed by her too-easy-to-read eyes. His hands massaged the steel chair arms as he attempted to fortify his psyche with sobering objectivity.

He extracted a mean-looking Havana cigar from his jacket, peeled off the wrapper and stowed it in his pocket. When he licked the stogie, her gaze widened.

"Do you smoke those, for God's sake?" Her glare was hot enough to light the cigar.

"Do you have a better suggestion of what I should do with it?"

Disillusionment settled on Holly; resignation seeped into her awareness, too deeply to ignore. When she stood, he rose with her, his woodsy-spicy cologne flooding her senses, underlining the futility of the situation.

She silenced her thoughts in favor of amicability, seeking to burn no bridges, as Jules Efron had taught her. Shoving down her husband's image, she lapsed into protocol. "Since you're here, would you like a tour of the facilities?"

He glanced at his watch with indifference. "I have time for a short tour, I suppose. Lance said the place is small."

Gamesmanship? Pride made her hope he couldn't see her spine stiffen. Wordlessly, she led the way out of the room. When he stopped to survey the clerical area, she became conscious of the cramped and inadequate space. Curious stares trailed her and Baker, but considering their impasse thus far, she wasted no introductions.

Sensing he lagged behind, she turned to find him peering into the kitchen.

"Pretty elaborate setup," he remarked, frowning. "Takes up a lot of space that could be used for production."

Her fists balled, nails pinching her palms. "We have a lot of social functions."

He stepped inside, leaving her no choice but to follow. She folded her arms and watched him open cupboard doors. Willfully, her gaze took in Levi's stretched over hard thighs as he squatted agilely, surveying the cluttered space beneath the sink. His easy grace screamed ex-athlete.

He turned toward her, repeating, "Social functions," as if the word were coated in castor oil. "Such as?"

She lifted her chin. "Birthday parties, potlucks, bridal showers, baby showers."

"Female things."

Irritation needled her nerve endings. How could a grin be both infuriating and charming? How could a term as ordinary as "female" reduce the activities she had named to insignificant?

"Lance is the only man who works here. His being in the minority influences the social agenda, somewhat."

"That's what Lance said."

Before she could reply, Baker swiveled on his outrageously expensive, mirror-polished boots, leaving her to trail behind. She lingered by the warehouse door while the cousins held a short, banter-filled exchange in the goldfish bowl of Lance's glass-partitioned office. Then Baker rejoined her and accompanied her to the warehouse.

Why in bloody hell had she suggested this tour?

Chapter Two

Chess was stunned by Xtreme's inadequate operating space.

A rainbow array of ski clothes hung from the ceiling, and from pegs on the wall, lined crude shelves and peeked from large generic-brown cartons on the concrete floor. Women of varying shapes, ages and attire milled about the warehouse. Some appeared genuinely busy, while, to Chess's trained eye, others only mimicked purposefulness.

In one corner a mammoth machine claiming too much space clanked a steady rhythm. He moved in that direction and stood sentinel beside a plump, sixtyish woman dressed in overalls, a T-shirt and crepe-soled shoes. Together, they watched ten barrel-like stitching apparatuses move methodically over the upper right front of what appeared to be insulated wind shirts. Sensing Holly's approach, Chess found himself gazing down into her petite uplifted face.

A disconcerting stir in his chest surprised him.

A mass of finger-friendly curls framing her face, and what little makeup he could detect, complemented her natural beauty. Precise dark brows framed warm-cognac eyes. Sculpted bone structure, skin perfect as a polished brown egg, and delicate features made his fingers twitch.

She raised her East Coast-cultured voice above the clamor of the machines to boast, "Monogramming."

Lance had revealed the menacing debt on the machine and how it kept breaking down because no one was properly trained to operate it. Maybe she should invest in hoops and needles.

"Embroidery," he corrected, using the industry term.

Holly seemed to grow a fraction of an inch taller, drawing his gaze to her sky-high heels again. Her short skirt revealed well-delineated knees, dancer's calves and slender ankles, the left one circled by a fine gold bracelet that revealed a different character facet. He felt a ripple in his groin.

"This machine monograms," she said. "My grandmother did embroidery. Women are free to accept bigger challenges today."

"At a loss, the way I hear it."

Dark eyes narrowing, she fended off his empathetic smile.

He shrugged. "Of course the loss could be remedied by hiring three eight-hour crews to get the maximum efficiency from the machine and upping the embroidery charges."

He let his gaze roam the room, conscious that her breasts rose and fell in time with her accelerated breath. That tickle played on the back of his neck again as he shot a sideways glance at this tiny woman with Titan presence. Every feature formed a perfect miniature, other than her lush mouth and full breasts, assets that pestered his undisciplined gaze. As an animal senses fire he doesn't want to risk, instinct warned Chess away, while challenge lured him to her ailing company.

Like sun darting out of a thunderhead, a smile brightened her face. "Sally, this is Lance's cousin, Chess Baker." She addressed the gray-haired woman who had turned from the machine to face them. "Sally Canfield, my distribution manager and friend."

Sally's grip could have cracked walnuts.

"You run this place?" Deciding she could use encouragement, he gave her an appreciative look.

"It runs me." Her eyes darted to Holly and then appraised him like a mother judging the clothing of a child about to enter a blizzard. "Taking a tour?"

"Ms. Harper insisted I see the facilities." He enjoyed sensing Holly's body tense. "Doesn't take long, does it?" He took his cue from Sally's hiked brow and dubious smile. "I've used up enough of your time. Horses to feed and miles to get there. Good luck with that machine," he said when Sally's wrinkle-encased smile mellowed a bit. "It can be a real moneymaker if it's handled right."

Sally turned back to stare at the revolving stitching heads as Chess and Holly walked away. From what he'd seen, the whole damn place could be a bonus if everybody produced more and watched less.

Chapter Three

Holly led the way out of the warehouse, back through the office to the front entry. When they stepped onto the strip-mall sidewalk into glaring December sunlight, she decided Chess Baker even frowned attractively. Her eyes trailed a fine gold S-link chain to the neck of his shirt. He slipped on a pair of gold-rimmed sunglasses that hid his sun-frown and covered a shallow crinkle between his brows. Feeling his brash stare behind the amber lenses, she fingered the antique cameo at her throat, cheeks warming.

Relieved, she saw him glance at his Rolex. Taking the cue, she extended her hand. He shook it graciously.

"So nice of you to come," she said. "Lance described you and your admirable accomplishments perfectly, but I'm afraid you aren't right for Xtreme."

He took off the glasses, twirled them by one curved earpiece as he studied her. "I'm right for Xtreme, Ms. Harper. It's whether you can comply with my conditions that you have to consider. My having controlling interest shouldn't keep us from working together to survive."

Survive? Somehow she didn't connect survival, or his need for it, with his self-assured image. "Actually, relinquishing control is not—"

"Those are my terms." The relenting softness about his mouth, in his tone, contrasted his words.

But words were what she must base her decision on. "Your terms are unacceptable."

He drew a shallow breath. "You could use your husband's help with all this." His tarnished-silver eyes showed compassion for the first time. With a tanned hand, he gestured toward the leased storefront space they'd just left. "I understand the two of you started Xtreme in your basement. What—nine years ago, I think Lance said?"

Caught off guard, Holly felt the piercing fangs of an old bitterness arise. But the hurt got shoved aside by the newer, more acute certain disaster of dealing with a cock-sure bastard who'd suddenly veered onto a different maneuver.

She kept her gaze steadfast. "My husband is—Julius Maurice Efron is dead, Mr. Baker."

Or he would be in two more months.

In Xtreme's kitchen, over a solitary lunch consisting of microwaved spaghetti squash, pumpernickel and Perrier, Holly reflected on her meeting with Chandler Chesney Baker.

If he knew the details of Jules's absence, then Baker's mentioning her need of her husband's help was callous. Even before he shot his remark straight into her dulled grief and thriving sense of abandonment, the man had unnerved her. She couldn't quite convince herself she'd seen leniency in his eyes, even empathy. His penetrating stare and the never-altering tempo of his easy drawl provoked her. He exuded composure while she had the sensation of scaling a skyscraper with no safety belt, her nails digging out handholds in the marble.

She wanted to believe her retrospective feelings were no

more than defiance—rivalry at worst. Yet every time he had looked at her, a carnal awareness she credited to seven years abstinence, jolted her. Strong. Magnetic. Threatening. Chess Baker was not the kind of man she wanted to tangle with at this vulnerable point in her life, and with his business pedigree and political connections, he would have no problem finding an arena bigger than Xtreme in which to compete.

Lance's pitting her and his cousin together as potential partners made her view his intentions as suspect. Her hairline bristled. She would find a different white knight.

She had better find him soon.

Chapter Four

Near sunset, Chess turned off Interstate 25 onto Happy Canyon Road, cutting across on West Colorado 85, the last wedge of the trip from Denver back to the ranch. A hell of a drive, but Sol y Sombre's serenity, opposed to city living, merited the eighty-mile round-trip. He took off the Cebe glasses, rubbed his eyes and squinted. He hadn't known the meaning of sun blindness until he moved to Colorado seven years ago and damn near had a head-on with a UPS truck along this same road.

After leaving Xtreme, he'd spent the rest of the day at the Central City blackjack tables. An afternoon of gambling had served a twofold purpose by tempering the boredom he always felt when between ventures, and he had escaped traveling half-blind into today's sunset.

He drove across a fantasy artist's palette. Hunter-green pines lined either side of the blacktop and beyond those, the Castle Pines golf course resembled a winter-gold ribbon ripped from a surprise package. Southward, the purple horizon blended azure into smoky white, changing to deeper and deeper amber as the road angled west toward a sinking fireball of sun.

He waited for the peaceful vista to console him. Instead, Holly Harper and her struggling company kept wrestling Mother Nature and winning.

What Holly lacked in stature, she made up in tenacity. Jules Efron's disappearance had evidently left her wounded, not knowing if she were widowed or rejected. That little enigma would bring a thoroughbred stallion to his knees, much less a frisky mare turned out to pasture and forgotten.

Lance had warned that Holly was a "hellcat, tough to deal with," but Chess had scoffed at the warning, figuring her for a manageable PMS case. After today, he wasn't sure.

At this stage of his life, only a turnaround, a financial score to notch his résumé gun, made him feel whole. He wanted a run at Xtreme, if his arrogant bluff hadn't scared Holly off. Lance had predicted her monetary crisis to worsen in the next few days. Chess wouldn't put the ball in her court by calling her. He would wait while studying the financial reports Lance had furnished. Meanwhile, provided she called him, maybe he could figure how to keep her in the design department and out of his hair for two years—three at the outside. Plenty of time in which to turn Xtreme around, dissolve the partnership, and seek out the next venture.

He couldn't rationalize away, however, her vulnerability, her natural dusky beauty. With bad memories lingering like the scent of old smoke, he reminded himself such frivolous criteria shouldn't be allowed to affect sound business decisions. Yet, the gut-wrenching appeal of her determination to face her problems tugged his conscience. Still, if given the privilege of taking over Xtreme, he wouldn't let Holly's physical credentials or her mettle, other than her self-applauded design expertise, factor into the overall picture.

He turned south into Sedalia and waited out a train, catching glimpses between the cars of Lance's vintage Mercedes coupe parked in front of Bud's Bar and Grill. Turmoil twisted serpent-like in the pit of his stomach, but once the train passed, he drove past Bud's without stopping. During the last five miles to the ranch he argued with himself, dredging up memories of the books he'd read on co-dependency. He couldn't hold Lance's hand forever.

According to the damn books, Lance would straighten up only when Chess quit making it easy for him, let him find a reason to stay sober. Chess was sure as hell trying and damn sure hoped he could trust those books.

Loneliness settled on him like a collapsed helium balloon as he dialed his security code, pulled through the power-operated gate, and drove down the shadowy tree-lined approach to Sol y Sombre. As he rounded the last curve, his eyes scoured the grounds and seized on an eerie blue light spilling out of the recent clapboard-covered addition to the main house. Adam was probably watching Star Trek videos. Adam Tall Horse, just a fourteen-year old kid, wiser than Chess would ever be, and not shy about passing the wisdom on, whether invited to or not.

Maybe Chess would run the story of Xtreme and Holly Harper by Adam. Or maybe he'd wait.

No sense in Adam—or anyone—knowing his getting what he wanted depended on Holly calling.

Chess slid onto a stool next to Lance in Bud's Bar. Dread poked his gut as he eyed the accumulated cache of empty bottles accompanying the overflowing ashtray on the counter.

"Drinking alone?" A few misfits and two dartboard enthusiasts made little impact on the nearly empty tavern.

Lance rallied from his slump on the gouged bar top. "Hey. How'd it go today with the raven-haired Dr. Ruth? Referring strictly to size, mind you."

Chess appraised Lance's cunning grin. "I saw your car on my way home." Hours ago.

"Why didn't you stop? I could've used some company."

"I wanted to get home—spend time with Adam. Plus a new guy showed up at the ranch. I had to orient him to the program."

"You should have brought him down for a beer."

"That might be counterproductive to the cause."

"You're a goddamned saint," Lance grudged.

The skin on the back of his neck crawling, Chess fielded the barbed remark, letting it slide. "How long have you been here?"

"Relax, cuz."

Lance twirled the empties until the labels showed. Three out of five beers had been non-alcoholic O'Doul's. Chess breathed a little easier.

Lance shrugged. "I'm not going back to rehab, no matter how good the food was. You made a believer outta me."

Reluctantly, Chess recalled the year-old intervention. "You were supposed to never touch another drop."

"I told you I'd give it a year." He shrugged. "Year's up." This time Lance's grin registered in his hazel eyes, a Baker family staple. Chess's flinty grays were a Chesney legacy. "How'd you like Ms. Harper?" Lance said. "Name fits, huh?"

"She's strung a little tight, but she's got good reason. I called Sally Canfield when I got home. I had to dig it out, but she filled me in on a few of Holly's dilemmas."

Lance's eyes glinted now. "Holly's boobs got to you, huh?"

Chess signaled the bartender, held up an empty O'Doul's bottle. "There's a little more to her than boobs." He recalled her pride in the wall plaques, the hope he'd seen in her fiery dark eyes before he'd gotten caught up in bitter memory that made him jam the needle in too far. "A lot more, maybe."

Lance laughed and clapped him on the back. "Sure. About five feet of mulishness and a hundred pounds of guts."

Chess guessed he had to laugh. It was a male thing.

Chapter Five

On Friday morning, Holly glanced up from her drawing board as Lance entered her office and closed the door. She swiveled her ergonomically correct drafting chair to face him, anxiety fisting in her stomach. "What's up?" Two calls from creditors in the last hour had rendered her suspicious.

"I saw Chess last night."

"Is that unusual? I thought you lived on his ranch." The majestic Sol y Sombre, according to Lance's word picture.

He shrugged bony shoulders. "Our paths don't cross all that often. Different interests, I guess. Chess is into careerism. His fanatic work ethic is a leave-over from his old man going busted, I figure."

That disclosure piqued her interest, but she swiveled again and took up her drawing pencil, studying a Vogue article forecasting next year's clothing trends. She would rust before she asked anything more about Lord Baker.

When Lance leaned his slender frame against her desk, arms folded as if settling in, she recalled his cousin's muscular anatomy in the revealing T-shirt and starch-stiff Levi's. Lance lacked Chess's height and blond coloring. His placid demeanor contrasted his cousin's dynamic presence, but in his own way, Lance was handsome, the only detectable family resemblance.

"It sounds like Chess has got a few qualms," Lance announced.

"About what? The price of gold, or where to get the best spit-shine on his thousand dollar boots? Or maybe where to get a bigger, blacker cigar." He had handled that one yesterday as though it had been hand-rolled by Fidel Castro.

The price of that smelly atrocity would buy Calvin Klein nylons.

"Piece of work, isn't he?" Taking a sketch from the table, Lance perused it with such nonchalance that one would never guess Xtreme's American Express card had been canceled and there were no funds to cover this week's payroll.

She glanced at the wall clock. She'd be calling her banker once he returned from his two-hour caviar and lobster lunch. She had been rehearsing her begging technique.

"Chess is interested, though. He sees a lot of potential in—"

"The arrogant bastard." The pencil snapped, sprang across the drawing board and clattered onto the neglected wooden floor.

Lance chuckled. "How's that?"

"Did he forget to mention I declined his offer?"

"Guess so." He let the sketch float back onto the table. "That won't matter to Chess. He gets what he wants, and this time he wants Xtreme." At the door, he advised, "Your money problems are over, boss. Lie back and enjoy the ride."

His advice roused her too-willing imagination and stroked her nerves like a wire brush. Chess Baker loomed a sleek, refined full-grown tiger who made her feel like a kitten. Trouble on the hoof, as they probably said in his native Oklahoma. She shuddered. She had escaped a fate worse than insolvency by rejecting his interest in Xtreme.

—※✦※—

At noon she huddled in the "elaborate" kitchen, picking without fervor at cheese lasagna Sally had brought from home. "Tasty," she murmured. "But you have to stop feeding me."

"Where's that in my job description?" Sally rose to heat a slice of French bread in the antiquated microwave. "Lucky my grandkids didn't scarf the lasagna before I could save some."

"They're still here? Annie and the kids?" Holly tried to sound empathetic—sympathetic, which the ongoing situation called for—but she could hear the phone ringing outside the kitchen. The possibility each call could be from a creditor set her nerves on end. "Did Annie find a job, or has Roy been contributing anything at all?"

"Roy's theory is he planted the seed and it's Annie's job to grow the fruit." She buttered the bread, sliced it in two pieces and, retaking her seat, placed one on Holly's plate. "Be glad you never had kids, honey."

"If I had, I wouldn't be so alone now. I think about that sometimes. If Jules and I—" She glanced up, her smile dismissive. "I'd be raising them alone, wouldn't I?"

"Sometimes that's best when you consider the alternative. It was for me, anyway. But when I see Annie following in my footsteps..." Sally soaked up the remnants of marinara sauce with bread and plopped it in her mouth, then fished a tissue from the back pocket of her coveralls. "Damn it," she wheezed. "Annie's oldest has a cat. By the time I get cleared up at work, it's time to go home and—" A light seemed to go on behind her soft blue eyes. "Enough about my curses. How're you doing, honey? Any light at the end of the tunnel? What about that guy yesterday? Lance's cousin?"

An improbable image flashed into Holly's head like an

art-deco neon sign. "What about him?"

"Is he for real?" Sally grinned, eyes crinkling. "If so, I'll take two and call me in the morning."

Holly raised her eyes. "Chandler Chesney Baker and I could never see eye to eye."

"Well, I'll loan you my ladder. If he's interested, you'd better grab him. This place is steadily oozing down the tubes, with an avalanche on the way." As if reading Holly's mind, she amended, "Sorry, honey. But it's time to face reality." She dredged up a subject of frequent discussion. "You may be against taking a lover in Jules's absence, but at least take a partner. We can't let you and Xtreme shrivel."

Holly smiled. "Baker and I would annihilate one another."

"Why do you say that? He was only here an hour. Maybe first impressions aren't lasting after all." She rose again and approached the counter. "Coffee?"

"Please."

Holly considered Baker's terms again. She understood him wanting the voting majority of Xtreme stock, but his condition of hanging around to exercise ultimate control was unacceptable. She had tolerated Jules's domineering nature because his age had led her to judge him wise. When she realized he lacked the wisdom to find his way home from Sri Lanka, she began to rethink her submissiveness, realizing it was a continuing saga. In his absence she had embraced independence.

Stirring sugar and powdered cream into the coffee Sally had brought back to the table, she voiced her thoughts. "Chess Baker is a control freak. A sexist."

Sally sipped, smiling over the rim of her paper cup. "Hunks like him can afford to be. Women stand in line for 'em."

Holly conceded a tolerant smile before offering rationale

to support her rejection of Chess. "Jules controlled me tact-
fully, and I went along with it from habit. Before him, my
brothers overpowered me. They were much bigger and older."
She attempted to paint her tone flippant. "And much louder.
You've heard the cliché, 'The squeaky wheel gets greased.' "

"People in Boston say that, too?"

"I've lived here half as long as I lived there," she reminded Sally. Almost a decade. "I'm an adopted native."

"Time flies, I guess."

Except when it dragged, as it had for the last seven years.

"Meanwhile," Sally said, rearranging a stack of paper
napkins, "back to the subject of our potential savior."

Holly shook her head. "He's out of the question."

"Because he's a control freak—never mind that he's got
the money and the smarts to keep the doors open." She sat
back, folding her arms over ample breasts. "You don't need a
lecture right now, honey, but if you're making this decision
based on a bunch of feminist crap, what about all the women
you're empowering by passing out paychecks every Friday?
Why not use Chess Baker for the cause?" She grinned.
"You're smart enough to do that without him knowing what hit
him."

The suggestion nestled into a corner of Holly's mind as
she voiced timeworn thoughts. "My father controlled me, too,
but he used indifference instead of dominance."

"How does that work? I'll try it on Annie's youngest."

"He kept me focused on him. I was always scrambling
for his attention." Not until recently had she realized even that
part of their relationship was trivial to him.

Sally pursed her lips, waiting.

"I've practically lived in Barnes & Noble's self-help section since Jules left. Looking for answers."

Sally took a quick glance at her Mickey Mouse watch,
urging, "Don't stop there."

"It's nothing you haven't heard before." Jules and her father, both rag merchants, had been close friends until Jules moved to Denver to open an Izod showroom in the Merchandise Mart. When Holly enrolled at the University of Colorado, she looked Jules up, which seemed to please her father more than anything she'd ever done. From there, marriage had seemed a logical step. "But you haven't heard my final analysis. I've decided I married Jules to get Papa's maximum approval."

Sally rolled her gaze ceiling-ward. "And you figured that out just for the price of a book?"

Holly wadded her paper napkin, dropped it onto her plate, then stacked her and Sally's plates together. "I've been so broke lately, I've been reading the books in-house rather than buying them." She had found actual therapy too painful, too static. From what she learned in the books, she compiled volumes of audiotape into a journal she reviewed periodically. To date she had concluded that she was little more than an extension of Jules until he left. Then an intelligent, motivated woman emerged, one Holly enjoyed nurturing.

"That marriage analysis is sad, honey," Sally mused. "If it's true, it might be a clue to why Jules never came back."

Weary nights of wrestling with that possibility, waking with drenched sheets tangled around her legs, backed up the commentary. Holly shrugged dismissively. "We had our good times. I never realized how much I lived under his thumb, until I wasn't. When we started Xtreme I marched around like an automaton, carrying out his wishes, never expressing my own or questioning anything." When Jules left, she had continued to run the company the way he'd set it up, at least until complications set in. "It seems he was right about everything after all."

Sally bristled, standing, shoving in her chair. "Don't sell yourself short. Jules's long business history gave him financial connections. He could get money to pump into the company."

"I know." Jules had made positive-sounding money-seeking phone calls to investors back East, then paced the basement for days until he got an answer. She had been so absorbed by design that the memory represented little more than a vague picture in her mind.

Sally bent to kiss the top of Holly's curls. "Remember, sweetie, you aren't in trouble because you're a bad operator. Give that banker hell when you call." She grinned. "Gotta get back to work. The friggin' embroidery machine is jammed again."

Holly dropped the paper plates in the trash, glanced at the clock, and refilled her coffee cup. She leaned against the counter, letting her financial quandary and Sally's pep talk chase one another around in her head long enough to give her a headache. Sally saw the dilemma clearly. Holly had needed to be set straight, yet again.

Her state of financial hardship wasn't convoluted. Jules had signed convertible demand notes that could either be called with interest due or converted to equity stock in Xtreme. When his creditors learned of his absence, they had no faith in a company run by Jules's twenty-two-year-old wife. Eventually, each note was called, with interest. Lacking an on-her-own track record, she had been unable to obtain more money. She had never quite recovered from the blow.

Even Chess Baker would find it difficult to beat those odds.

Lance stopped her on her way out at the end of the day. "I've got some bad news."

Her stomach churned, then contracted. "Let's table it until Monday. What can be done at five o'clock on Friday afternoon?"

His gaze was bolder than she preferred, and he apparently gave the question no consideration. "I got a call from
Mercer Mercantile."

She waited, paralyzed with dread.

"They got a call from the company who factors them—
Advance Capital. Advance has had Xtreme on credit watch, it
seems."

She hadn't known that, but she nodded.

"Based on our slow pay they won't honor our invoices
from Mercer anymore."

"And?" Maybe it was not as bad as she feared.

He shrugged. "Mercer's putting Xtreme on prepay status, but they'll take a letter of credit. If you can come up with
one."

A chill seized her, then seeped in, bone-deep. She could
no longer deny the severity of Xtreme's problems; something
had to be done. A face drifted into her mind. A man's claim
that they could work together for survival filtered into her
recall. The threat and promise of Chess Baker made her turn
her head before Lance could see tears pool in her eyes.

Chapter Six

Friday evening, Chess lounged on the sofa before the fire, boots propped on the coffee table, his Chihuahua, Warrior, prone on Chess's extended legs. He scratched Warrior's muscled haunches by rote as residual animal warmth seeped into his shins. He half heard the wind moaning in the pines, blowing in a front off the Sangre de Cristo range. Studiously, he flipped pages of a balance sheet Lance had dropped off before going to his cabin at the end of the lane.

Considering the Xtreme horror stories Lance had shared, he seemed to have gotten a good view of financial conditions in the month he had worked there. If accurate, the figures yielded both potential and risk, two prerequisites on which Chess put high priority. In any undertaking, he limited his wager. No more than twenty percent of his net worth and ninety-nine percent of his time. After that, he found the risk factor in any turnaround a surefire way to avoid boredom. And no question, risk guaranteed more mental bang for the buck when the adventure ended.

When married to Robyn, he had tried to justify his long grueling hours away from home with the slogan, "No pain, no gain." Robyn resented like hell being alone, but remembering his father's plight at the hands of a woman's demands, Chess bribed her with expensive trinkets and turned a deaf ear to her protests. He always told himself he'd make it up to her when he put the present venture to bed—before the next one. Somewhere along the way, she had given up on him and found someone to whom she came first. Discovering that, he vowed to never be a part of inflicting the kind of pain he felt on another man. Never to knowingly sleep with another man's wife.

Robyn had pulled out of the Sol y Sombre gate during a January whiteout, five years ago, her Cadillac piled to the ceiling with designer clothes and Steuben crystal, not stopping until she reached New York. Losing her should have taught him a lesson, and maybe it had, but he had no one on which to lavish his newfound knowledge. But he had altered his theory. More pain existed in the loneliness of the empty ranch house than in the hours he spent working, so he now focused on each venture's risk, thinking in terms of "no guts, no glory."

He tamped his musing down. He had a stockpile of grim recall stored, ready to be examined with the least provocation, but he had wallowed in self-pity enough for tonight. Thinking about his past damn sure hadn't changed anything yet.

He glanced up at the sound of quiet footsteps falling just outside the circumference of lamplight. Adam.

Chess's heart quickened.

When they had agreed Adam would be staying at Sol y Sombre, the boy had opted for a cabin, in a quest for independence. Chess compromised by adding a two room suite to the main house, providing Adam an interior and exterior entry. Adam favored the latter. But on a night as icy as this, he had used the door off the back hall, materializing across the room, a book and an after-supper sandwich in hand. Chess recalled the nearly illiterate, half-starved thirteen-year-old Navajo he had found huddled against Sol y Sombre's gate on another blizzardy morning. He had begun to think of a Colorado blizzard as a symbol, capable of shifting between tragic and good.

Deserting Chess, Warrior's nails clicked like castanets on the wooden floor as he raced to Adam. Chess swung his long legs down from the wagon-wheel table and shuffled papers, clearing a spot in unspoken invitation. Silent as smoke and nimble as a shadow, Adam eased his lanky body onto the sofa and maneuvered around Warrior to settle his sandwich and milk on the table.

After a year, Adam's fluid grace still awed Chess.

When he'd arrived home earlier, Adam and Lance had been shooting baskets, shirtless in the frigid night air, shimmying the hoop they'd bolted to a skinny pine. He had watched for a while, noting how Lance cupped his thin body around Adam's, how often the guard position turned to a bear hug, their skins contrasting like butter on ginger bread. He'd felt envious, then guilty for spending less time with Adam than Lance did. But Lance worked eight to five, a routine Chess would never embrace, one he hoped Adam understood.

"Did Lance go out?" He watched Adam's face for letdown.

"He had fish to fry." The boy sounded resigned.

Chess flipped the book that nestled in the crook of Adam's arm and read the title. *The Catcher in the Rye*. His heart thundered satisfaction, as he whistled softly. "J. D. Salinger. Heady stuff, chief."

Adam sawed off a quarter sandwich with one chomp of his flawless teeth. He chewed leisurely, his bronzed throat rippling when he swallowed. Grinning, he admitted, "When I saw it in the study, I thought it was about baseball."

Chess wasn't so old he couldn't recall a similar mistake. "Why's that?"

Adam shrugged. "Rye grass and catcher's mitts." He bit off another quarter of Swiss-laden beef wedged between two slices of Do Thi's homemade beer bread. His tongue snaked

out to catch an errant drop of mayonnaise. "I read three chap-
ters before I gave up on baseball."

"But you didn't quit reading."

"Saving face," Adam grunted.

Chess pitched the well-perused Xtreme balance sheet
onto the table alongside the not-quite-impressive inventory.
"If you wanted to save face, you would have kept your mistake
to yourself."

Wry Indian humor kicked in. "I am saving face by continuing to read and to pretend even to myself that I was not
fooled."

That had a familiar ring. "I see you're honing your
macho skill to precision."

"I have the world's best teacher."

Chess tugged on the ponytail hanging to the center of
Adam's back. "Maybe, but at least I'm not a redneck or we'd
be on the phone looking for an all-night barber to cut this
thing."

"Even you would not defy heritage, I think."

"Even me, huh?" Chess chuckled as he hauled up from
the sofa, crossed the combination family room and dining
room, going to the kitchen for an O'Doul's. "What about
you?" he called back over his shoulder. "I've got that P.I.
working in Amarillo now. If he comes up with your next of
kin are you ready for the inevitable?" Adam had no birth certificate or papers of any kind. The key to adoption was finding a relative, getting his and Chess's name on a consent-to-
adopt form. Chess didn't take a full breath while he waited for
Adam's answer. Getting none, he returned to where the boy sat
in the semidarkness, nursing a glass of milk like bourbon and
branch water. "Are you ready to become Little Adam Baker—
soon to be called Big Adam from the way Do Thi says you're
going through Levi's lately."

"I am ready to be your son. I am not ready to give up my

name and heritage." Adam wadded a paper napkin tightly, then shot it from behind his raven head, square into the center of a small empty plate.

"I'd never ask you to do that." Adoption would be a way of tapping into Chess's own Choctaw heritage, preserving it in a cockeyed, ass-backward kind of way since Adam was Navajo.

Adam took his turn at pacing, crossing to the mammoth fireplace, staring into the remnants of the fire. He seized the poker, jabbed, then threw on two more logs. "If I am not to give up my heritage and I am allowed to keep my name, we should save the time of signing white man's papers." He faced Chess, eyes hot and liquid as a tarpaper roof in August sun. "What will that do to make me more your haye' or you more the only hazke'é I know?"

Chess's lesson for tonight. "Haye', son. Hazke'é, father."

Adam's expression softened into a smile. "Cool."

Adam Tall Horse. Contrast incarnate. "Sitting Bull was big on adopting people—any body he found unclaimed. How about granting me the same privilege?"

"Sitting Bull did it with a ceremony, not a piece of paper."

The argument wasn't original. Behind a calm exterior, warring factions wrestled within Chess's nature. The part of him nursing a chronic need and the part too wise to push an inanimate object pulled, shoved, ripped. He figured three years at Douglas County Middle School with the country kids, three at Kent Denver, fraternizing with the hierarchy, and about six more in the best colleges money could wrangle would convert Adam to the Anglo's penchant for legal documents. Chess looked forward to watching Adam become a man confident enough to pass through doors he wanted to open for him.

"I'll tell you what signing those papers will do, Adam. It

will assure you no one will abandon you again. When I get my name and yours on that piece of white man's paper, I'm going to blow it up poster size and hang it over that fireplace like some guys hang hunting trophies."

Adam grinned. In spite of himself, Chess thought.

"You know why, Shallow River?" Adam's Indian name.

"Why?"

"You tell me why." This debate wasn't new, either.

"Because I'm the best prize you ever hope to get?"

"You've got it, chief." Chess clumped back to the oxblood leather sofa and nestled in, arms folded on his chest, boots on the table again. Warrior leaped onto him, curled on his shins in record time. "Now, come over here and let's read some of old J.D. so I can see what you're learning. I may start charging you for all this tutoring."

He could study balance sheets the rest of the empty week-end.

Chapter Seven

Sunday evening, Holly ended a journal entry and switched off her handheld tape recorder. She stood by the leaded glass window of her family room, absently caressing the majestic head of her Doberman, Angel. Gazing through gathering darkness onto the park-like backyard, she tried to find solace in the solid old house, in its familiar and comforting odd creaks and groans. Tonight the haven magnified a hollow feeling inside her. Past and present twined vine-like through her mind. Nagging guilt and resentment of that guilt tumbled in her head like brawling cats.

She had tried to build a new life while holding Xtreme together, but the lingering possibility that Jules could be alive kept her from bridging all the looming chasms. Jules's absence—whatever the reason—had left a ragged hole in her life, but left her haunted by a ghost she could legally exorcise in sixty more days, if she chose.

On her own, she had failed to achieve financial stability and solvency, and the slightest outside force, such as the news Lance had given her Friday afternoon, could destroy all she had struggled to gain.

Fresh, damning guilt formed a hard lump in her throat,

and dissolved to a stingy trickle of tears that spiked her lashes. Angel nuzzled her thigh and whined. Holly raised her palms to catch a residual sob. Then conclusion struck like a hammer. Before rationale could surface, she marched to the phone, chest pumping off-kilter like out-of-sync helicopter blades. A remnant spark of optimism flickered when Chess Baker's sultry drawl came on the line.

"It's Holly Harper. I hope I didn't wake you."

"It's only six-twenty."

Her optimism sputtered a bit. It seemed years later than that, but maybe not years too late. "I've had a problem since we talked."

His delayed reply broadened into a lengthy, uncomfortable silence, except for a dog yelping in his background.

She broke the silence. "Friday afternoon we got a call from the mill we buy fabric from—has Lance told you this?"

"I haven't seen Lance this weekend."

Was that good or bad? She supposed she had hoped Lance would pave the way for this call. "I'll try to be concise. When we order fabrics from Mercer Mercantile, instead of invoicing us direct they send our bill to a company called Advance Capital. Advance takes a cut out of the invoice and sends Mercer a check for the balance." She paused, envisioning the mechanics in her mind. "Then Advance Capital sends Xtreme an invoice for the total amount we owe Mercer, with directions to pay Advance direct within sixty days and—"

"I know how factoring companies operate, Ms. Harper."

Of course he knew, although he'd probably never relied on one in his life. Why had he let her run on like that? She drew a breath, fought for patience. "Advance has refused to pay anymore Xtreme invoices to Mercer. Which means—"

"You've now been put on prepay status with Mercer."

"You're sure you haven't talked to Lance?"

"No, and I've got only about two more minutes to talk to

you, if that makes a difference."

She imagined him striking out to some fabulous black-tie party, in a pewter tuxedo that matched his eyes. Mirror-shined boots. Not eel-skin, but smooth honed, pitch-black, granite-hard leather, the perfect match for his sorry soul.

With blind determination, she marched on. "I've just finished designing next season's line and I need to start cutting within the month, but I can't order fabric to cut without money or a letter of credit."

Silence used up most of what remained of her two minutes, before he inquired, "What do you want from me, sugar?"

"A letter of credit." Damnit to bloody hell. Her shaky voice would give him an edge she could never retrieve.

"Why would I do that?"

"I'm ready to do business." She spit out the surrender rather than let ego and common sense disrupt her decision to let Chess Baker own her. Lock, stock, and barrel. "Can you meet me at my attorney's office tomorrow morning at nine? Gregory Friedman. His office is on 17th and Glenarm."

"You're ready to do business." No inflection other than the cultured Oklahoma drawl.

"Yes."

"Then we agree on my obtaining fifty-one percent of the voting stock."

"Yes." A jackhammer pounded in her chest.

"I think you should know, I'll be reorganizing the board."

With people who would vote against her, but she'd find a way around that when he tired of Xtreme and failed to show up to influence his beholden board. At the moment, furnishing her sales reps with samples on time, so they wouldn't matriculate to a competitor who had product to sell, loomed vital. She reached to stroke Angel's hard slick head, making contact with stability.

"I trust your judgment," she choked out. "Will I see you

at nine?"

"I'll be there."

"You're bailing me out, and I won't forget that."

"On the street, it's called finding a white knight, sugar."

Her hairline crawled and her stomach lurched. "I won't forget that, either."

She hung up before she had to hear another patronizing word. They might both consider him her white knight, but being financially chivalrous didn't make Chandler Chesney Baker any less of a merciless son of a bitch.

Chapter Eight

At lunch the next day, Chess sliced off a bite of very rare prime rib. He eased it into his mouth, observing Holly's attentiveness to Gregory Friedman's anti-Republican diatribe. Anytime Holly spoke, Greg's eyes burned bright and assessing, as though he were forming a reply, midsentence. The pair reminded him of bookends. The same smooth olive skin, spiral-curled hair, dark, alert eyes, Kennedyesque-brogue, and assertive manner. Each carried Hermés briefcases and draped navy Burberry topcoats on their chairs, as if guarding against theft in Morton's, a posh downtown Denver steak house.

At the signing earlier, Greg had, in no uncertain terms, advised Holly to rip up the one-sided partnership agreement, a precedent for how much cooperation Chess could expect, he figured. Seeing them with their sable heads together now made him wonder if an alliance had been formed against him. He also wondered what conditions governed the private union Holly and Greg already enjoyed. Greg wore his ardor on his sleeve, but her feelings were harder to detect. For reasons Chess neither could nor wanted to label, he hoped the attraction was one-sided.

Abruptly, Greg lounged back in his chair, announcing

conclusively, "Newt Gingrich is a wormy rednecked peach. That's my final word on the matter."

Holly's throaty laughter floated above a background of softly clinking silver on china and polite luncheon conversation. Chess wondered how much she would protest replacing Greg with Chess's longtime legal counsel, Karsh and Fulton.

Greg turned his attention to Chess, pinning him with his gaze, eyes big behind thick-lensed, silver-framed glasses. "So you played for Oklahoma under Barry Switzer—conference champions, no less. What? In the eighties?"

Chess nodded.

"Halfback, right? I remember some big lateral-pass runs."

Greg had done his homework. "Yeah. I couldn't make quarterback, but that's probably best. I turned my obsession for calling signals to business, the ultimate place to quarterback."

Out of the blue, Greg switched topics. "Jules Efron was a smart businessman."

That remained to be seen. "Is that right?"

"Once Holly gets Xtreme squared away, Jules will be able to take up right where he left off."

Holly concentrated on spearing a green bean from alongside her vegetarian omelet. Eyes fixed in the distance, she washed it down with the Dom Perignon she'd suggested they order.

Chess asked, "When's this?" That Jules would "take up right where he left off."

Greg's eyes narrowed. "When he gets back."

"We'll see." Chess stole a glance at Jules Efron's stunning wife. "Timing is everything." So far, Jules's timing, whatever the reason, proved lousy.

Greg's shoulder vibrated from the nervous jiggling of his foot beneath the table. "So, cutting to the chase, what are your plans for Xtreme?"

Chess sipped Dom. "To turn it around in two years."

"How?" Greg sagged forward, fingertips on the table edge.

Holly watched, listened, eyes childlike, large and round with a fringe of paintbrush lashes needing no eyeliner or mascara. Chess had never seen a woman with more natural beauty, and those eyes gave away her hopes and fears. So he might as well get his cards on the table, maybe clear up some fear.

"I'm going to grow the company by aligning every screw and tightening every bolt till it strains—in layman's language, torque it and everybody working there until they're doing more than their share."

Holly flinched, and the sardonic grin vanished from Greg Friedman's face. He and Holly exchanged looks.

"Some people aren't capable of performing two jobs," Greg warned.

"Then they need to find another kitchen to cook in."

"Does Holly know your plan? She never mentioned—"

"Yes." She did now. Chess pushed his plate away and wiped a napkin over his lips. He reached for a silver bucket perched on a leggy stand by his chair, the placement an indication the waiter had marked Chess to pay the tab. "More champagne, Holly?"

Her quick refusal signified her reaction to his disclosure.

"Time is the factor here." He kept his tone casual. "The ski apparel business is peaking. We'll get in bigger, then get out before the down cycle."

Interest glinted in Greg's eyes. "What are you basing this time-factor theory on?"

"I'd rather not say. You know how a prairie fire can get out of hand."

"If the industry's peaking, how will you grow the company?"

"By cutting cost and raising market share and profit in the international market. Especially South America."

"Big undertaking."

"I'd do that anyway, peaking or not."

"How?"

"I'll discuss my strategy with Holly first. If she feels you need to be informed..." He shrugged, his voice trailing.

Greg grew taller abruptly, squaring his shoulders. "I did some research. As strung out as you are in your other...interests, seems you'd let Holly worry about Xtreme. A man can only stretch so far." He added grudgingly, "Even an entrepreneur."

"Worrying is my job, not hers." He smiled at Holly and got nothing back. "I'll handle it."

Greg looked dubious, then daunted. "Just where does all this energy come from, Baker?"

"I'm not married, and I don't chase women." He settled against his chair, shifting his long legs from beneath the table, directing his closing remark to Holly. "Saves a hell of a lot of time and puts me in perfect control."

Holly's tiny fingers, tipped with extravagant red nails, gripped her water glass as if it were a life preserver. He imagined those nails running down his back, gently, teasingly. More likely, she'd sink them in his face, if given a chance.

A cellular phone jingled. Greg and Holly's hands hit their briefcases in rapid unison before their gazes riveted on Chess's jacket pocket.

"Excuse me." He rose and left the table.

Chapter Nine

Holly watched Chess cross the room, admiring the graceful movements of his athletic body. He stood in the entry, talking on the smallest cellular she had ever seen. Rearranging her future, probably, and she couldn't even vote.

Greg wadded his napkin and tossed it on the table. "You can bet he bleaches his hair."

Her eyes stole to a shock of wet-wheat hair falling unrestrained across Chess's wide brow. No blow-dryer, gels or sprays employed by Lord Baker. Soft to the touch. "I doubt that, Greg. Where would he find time?"

"I guarantee you, he's gay. You can put money on that."

His familiar jealousy reared its head. Only his peeved expression kept her from laughing. "I don't sense that at all."

Greg rolled his eyes. "Any thirty-four-year-old guy who looks like that—neither married nor chasing women—is gay."

She watched Chess gesture, take a few steps as he talked. He possessed an arrogant grace that could easily arouse a man's envy and a woman's excitement. "I doubt he has to chase them."

Greg shoved back his chair. "You're already waving a white flag."

"That's asinine. We aren't at war."

"I'll remind you that you said that." He stood. "I've enjoyed all I can take. Tell the cowboy I said thanks for lunch."

Holly's gaze shifted again. Chess's well-tailored charcoal pinstripe, impeccable pearl gray button-down Nicole Miller signature tie, and glove-soft Italian loafers labeled him "all city." But the lonesome wrangler drawl was intact.

"Call me tonight," Greg said. "Give me a blow-by-blow of dessert." He pivoted on his heel and, with little more than a nod, brushed past Chess returning to the table.

Holly dragged finesse and determination from the depths of her being as Chess slipped back into his chair. "Greg said thanks, but he had to run."

He smiled tolerantly. "Reminds me of a banty hen my grandmother had."

"Rooster, you mean."

"I mean hen." The line in the sand.

She signaled for coffee. When they were alone again, she stirred in cream and sugar. "Lance told me about your glory days at OU."

"You had to get it from Lance?" A flaxen brow arched. Score one for her.

"Well, being from Boston—and a few years younger, I guess I missed all the furor."

"Maybe Lance will show you the scrapbook." He grinned lazily, a new and appealing attribute.

"He likes to brag on you."

His eyes quickened, then clouded with an expression she couldn't grasp. Surreptitiously, she took in his classic cheekbones, granite jawline, perfect nose and smoldering eyes framed by lashes as thick as her own. A potential minefield. Her body betrayed her, even as her mind sent up warning flares.

"Playing football is how you got that scar." Shallow but pronounced, jagging just below one heavy brow, the scar contributed to, rather than marred, his masculine appeal. "Your helmet flew off during an OU/Nebraska game." Lance had painted the tale vividly.

"Like you said, glory days." He sipped coffee, studying her over the gold-rimmed eggshell cup. "Let's talk about the task at hand, darlin'."

Rancor shot up her spine, but a dozen other sensations gurgled up like tainted water from a sewer, emotions she hesitated to analyze. "I hate false endearments. You need to understand that."

She might as well have waved a red flag in front of him.

"That's nothing but a compliment. You are darlin'. Who's ever told you otherwise?"

Her father for one, when he didn't know she existed, and Jules, when he'd failed to come back, ultimately deserting her to this backwoods millionaire sexist fiend. Chess Baker was playing a game of paddleball with her psyche, bouncing between his staunch business role and condescending good-old-boy act. Diplomacy having failed, she asserted her resolve and explored a different approach.

"Tell me how you plan to make Xtreme profitable."

"Why? Is Friedman waiting for a report?"

Her cup clattered in the saucer, sloshing coffee on the pristine tablecloth.

He held up a manicured hand, palm out, the gold band of his signet ring gleaming in soft light. "Let me preface what comes later by saying the turn-around will be quick. I won't be staying any longer than need be."

She thought of Jean Arthur gazing longingly after Alan Ladd in *Shane*. She substituted her own face into the vision, wearing a joyous expression as she waved at Chess Baker exiting Xtreme in all his gorgeous glory. Yet his two-year turnaround projection contrasted her opinion of "longer than need be." Conflicting images roared in her head like debris caught in a tornado.

"On what do you base your sense of urgency, if I may ask?"

That shallow furrow between his brows deepened. "You can do what you want with this information, but if you repeat it, it becomes a rumor and rumors have a tendency to spread like—"

"Prairie fire. What's the rumor?"

"It becomes a rumor only when you repeat it."

Exasperation blurred her vision, clanged in her ears like that damned inferior monogramming machine. "Which do you prefer? To hear me promise or to hear me beg?"

His mouth twitched. "It's simple. The snowboarding craze is encroaching on the ski industry. Right?" When she nodded, he said. "Do those people wear Bogner? Descante? Xtreme Ski?"

Her mind darted to the slopes, to the rag-tag snowboarding enthusiasts with their buzzed hair and body jewelry. Most importantly, she visualized cutoff baggies, holey sweatshirts, denim jackets and army-navy surplus duds. Her scalp crawled and her face flushed. "It's only a trend."

"Right, but a trend Xtreme is going to beat."

She reverted to Greg's unanswered question. "How?"

"I have a long-range agenda, but first we'll cut expenses to the bone by firing half the people who work there."

All women but Lance, a major concession to his expertise. "They're like family. I don't have the heart to fire them."

"You won't have to. I'll do it."

Lack of a heart apparently didn't bother Chess Baker. "I won't agree to that. By employing women I keep them off welfare rolls where they would have ended up after being deserted by some lazy—" The women depended on her, trusted her. She couldn't fail there, too. "By employing women, I empower them."

"Not at the expense of the company."

She folded her arms under her breasts. When his admiring gaze fastened there, she quickly lowered her hands to her lap. "How will we operate with half the workforce gone?"

"Like I told Greg, anybody who's left will do a job and a half. Including you and me. Those part-time menial jobs that draw full-time pay will get absorbed throughout the company."

"There are no menial jobs, only menial attitudes."

He let that slide. "I'm bringing in some Vietnamese to run three shifts on the embroidery machine. They're clean, hardworking people who still take pride in what they produce."

"Women, I hope."

"I've already hired a man to head up the crews. We'll see who he recruits. Family probably. They stick together."

Already hired a man? Probably while she stared out the window the night before, agonizing over whether to turn over the reins of her life to Chess Baker. His expedience rankled.

She stretched for a foothold. "Did you major in business?"

"Communications."

She felt her mouth twist, quashing a sardonic laugh. Evidently, he had obtained his degree through athletic merit, not grades. "Interesting."

His eyes softened with retrospect. "I planned on going into sportscasting when I got too old to play ball. An injury that healed wrong kept me out of the pro draft."

His vulnerable expression, a tinge of humility, rendered him human, stirring something close to sympathy that left her wary. Then tenderness exited his eyes, casting her onto a more familiar shore.

"I got my business acumen by watching my father go broke. I saw all the things not to do—not to let happen, actually."

One brow crept up involuntarily. "Such as?"

"Such as feeding somebody's ego or watching out for their self-esteem when I know I'm the one who's right." He signaled for more coffee. "Which brings us to design."

Damn him. "You have no design expertise."

"I have design knowledge." And no qualms about the waiter hearing.

She watched him take a slender metal tube from his inside pocket, one bearing an elaborate gold imprint she could easily detect as Portofino and in smaller print, Macanudo Imports. He opened the tube and shook out an ugly black cigar. She recoiled a bit, in spite of an urge not to. He placed the object where it encroached onto her half of the table, breaching common courtesy but not enough to issue license for complaint. Wondering what he sought to prove, if anything, she attempted a return to the issue at hand.

"Design knowledge such as?"

"Such as, older skiers won't buy what I saw coming off the machines last Friday. Too flashy. Trendy."

She tapped the cigar with a nail, inched it back toward him. "Our line is designed for the young extremist generation, not the Ensure crowd."

He shrugged. "The sixties generation is the one with time to ski and money to pay top prices."

He took up the cigar, tapped it lightly like a fragile pencil against the table and then aligned it with her coffee cup. Invading her space as he had her life. She tried to ignore the strong, sweet aroma, the rich texture, the tapered tip.

"Xtreme is designed for a younger crowd," she said.

"Not anymore. The price is going up. In the time we have left we're moving into a more elite market."

That appealed to a latent desire, but she aimed her tone at indifference. "What else?"

"We'll take the money we save on salaries and stage an advertising blitz, hire a publicist. Xtreme in every major industry magazine, ads in *Colorado Lifestyles* and *Denver-Boulder Magazine.* And we'll sponsor entries in every racing event that gets television coverage." He leaned back in his chair, thumbs hooked behind his alligator belt in a satisfied, conclusive manner. "We'll imprint our shipping cartons with the company name in big red letters." He signaled a hovering waiter for the check.

"That makes no sense. Imprinted boxes cost a fortune." Jules had adamantly saved money by using generic supplies.

"The cheapest form of advertisement. I've already called Dixon container. We'll be flashing the Xtreme logo on those cartons all over the country by next week."

"Just when did you have time—"

"I get up early, sugar, and a cell phone means no down-time."

Although he was mesmerizingly attractive, she under-stood his state of singleness. Who could stand to live with him? He had probably given up chasing women because once word that he was an insolent, mercenary bastard got out, they ran too fast.

"Well, you certainly seem to have control of everything."

She whacked the cigar down on his side of the table and dusted her fingers on her napkin. When she stood, he shot up like a geyser. "Please, don't get up." She should have stood several times before, just to watch him pop up and down like a Chess-in-the-box.

He remained standing as he gouged his name in bold, unreadable script across an American Express Gold Card voucher.

She managed a grudging, "Thank you for lunch."

"My pleasure."

He retrieved the cigar, ran it under his exquisite nose,

then stood it on end in his coffee cup. He wrangled her coat from her floundering grasp and held it low, the perfect angle for her to slip into. Managing to retrieve her briefcase and handbag before she could, he tucked the case beneath her arm and hung the strap of the oversized Louis Vuitton bag on her shoulder.

Glancing up, she obviously misinterpreted what she had thought to be gentleness in his eyes. He stood close enough for her to sense radiating heat, smell his woodsy cologne, enjoy the silky glide of his sleeve against hers as he lowered his arm. She half expected him to, half wished he would, button her coat against the January cold and kiss the top of her head.

Chapter Ten

When Holly walked into Xtreme, she immediately noted Toby, the receptionist, filing her nails while engaging in a lethargic phone conversation. Chess's vivid description of aligning screws and tightening bolts vibrated in Holly's mind. She considered which additional half-job she might delegate to Toby, provided she even survived the inevitable "torquing" of Xtreme Ski.

In the warehouse, Holly and Sally stood observing mutely as the factory representative, who regularly serviced the monogramming machine, put a Vietnamese man through training. The enthusiastic bob of the man's dark head matched the rapt attention in his soft black eyes.

Sally smiled gently, murmuring, "Cute, isn't he? Name's Dinh Quange. He showed up this morning in an old Dodge beater with a handwritten note from Lord Baker. I quote: 'Dinh works here now.' "

Holly nodded. "I got the word at lunch. Apparently they'll be arriving en masse."

Sally struck a Statue of Liberty pose. "Give us your torn, your tired, your poor..." She grinned. "Paraphrasing, but you get the message."

"I'm getting the full message. Loud and clear."

"How'd it go this morning? Is Baker a genuine sexist?"

"A genuine sexist tyrant." She caught her unruly curls in her hands, slicking them to the back of her neck for a moment, as lunch conversation played on her mind. "You may be getting some extra responsibility, but, if so, consider it a compliment."

Puzzlement corrugated Sally's already lined face.

"According to his excellency, half the staff will be fired and the other half will be doing two jobs."

Sally frowned, her gaze running warily around the warehouse. "That's scary, even though it sounds feasible. You mean you, the mother of all females agreed to it?"

She shrugged, shoulders heavy. "Might makes right."

For a moment Sally cocked an ear toward the instructions being given Dinh, then brought her attention back to Holly. "You know, honey, Baker's not all wrong. A lot of bogus time gets punched into the clock around here."

"Sometimes we're busy enough to need everyone."

"Ever considered temps? I hear they're life savers."

"I'm going to bury myself in design, and—"

A hand grasped her arm. She wheeled anxiously. Toby looked down at her, grinning wryly, emery board in hand.

"Toby, you can't leave the phones."

"Lesser of two evils." Her grin broadened as though she watched a movie no one else could see. "Thought you might want to know you've got company in your office."

"Who?"

"I think I heard you call him Lord Baker after he left last week. Tall, blond, devastatingly—"

"Toby!"

"I think he's moving in. Better check it out."

Dammit to bloody hell. Stalking away, Holly imagined Toby's name topping the list of dispensable employees.

Just as Toby had claimed, suit coat off, sleeves turned back, Chess Baker squatted near a large Mayflower carton, unloading its contents onto her scarred parquet floor—thus far, a laptop computer, a small television, a lamp with a base depicting a horse in full running stride, jockey on board, and a huge dictionary. He glanced up, casting those stormy eyes upon her length and breadth before continuing his chore.

An unfamiliar combination of anger and relief left her queasy. "What are you doing?"

"Moving in." His pants leg clung to a hard thigh as he stretched to place a photograph of a blond woman holding two dogs on the corner of the old partner's desk.

"With me?" Incredible.

"I asked—Toby, right?—for directions to my office, but she couldn't find the map." He took a pair of running shoes and a sweat suit from the carton and placed them on her visitor's chair. According to Lance, Chess ran religiously every day some time between rising and going to bed, varying with his schedule. Apparently he planned to spend enough time at Xtreme to have to sandwich running into his work agenda.

She assured him, "There are no offices—besides mine." And Lance's fishbowl they had hurriedly concocted when he became a part of Xtreme.

Holding a bronze plaque, Chess swiveled gracefully in his squatting position to look up at her. "That's what Toby decided. Lucky for me, you have a partner's desk, huh, partner?"

He rose, placing the plaque beside the photograph. Holly retrieved her glasses from where they hung by one stem thrust through the opening of her blouse, secured by her cleavage. Boldly she perused the plaque. Sedalia 1998 Mini Roper Champions. A favored trophy? When his entrepreneurial accomplishments had been touted by *Time* and *The Wall Street Journal*? She looked back at him.

"Maybe I could hang that little award with yours. It won't stand out enough to deflect attention from the overall true picture."

She ignored the barb. Verbally. "I have a partner's desk for good reason. I use both sides."

"Impressive." Was that actually a begrudging smile? "But why's that?"

She inhaled deeply, paced herself. "I use one side for dealing with design and the other for managerial purposes."

"You really have been wearing all the hats, haven't you, sugar?"

His humoring tone raked a rusty currycomb down her spine.

He opened a bottom drawer, rifled through crammed files, then closed the drawer with an exquisitely shod foot. "You just proved my point. This half of the desk seems to house your managerial efforts, so I'll take it, since all you'll be bothered with from now on is design."

"I don't consider design a bother."

"That's good. Since I consider kicking butt a pleasure, we'll make a great team." He strode around the big desk and dragged her chair to his commandeered side.

"That's my chair."

"I'll borrow it until I can have one delivered."

"You can't—it's lilac, for God's sake."

"I don't have a problem with that. I also eat quiche." He handed her the pink paisley pillow. "Here. You'll need this."

She jerked the pillow away from him and clutched it to her breasts. Her gaze careened around the already cramped office, fabric samples piled in one corner, sketches haphazardly thumbtacked to the pink linen-wrapped wall. She had relished the privacy once she'd gotten over the shock of Jules not being there.

Apprehension coiled in her stomach like a copperhead.

"I can't possibly share this office." She tossed the pillow into the corner with the samples, punctuating her statement. Hands on hips, she waited for him to show any sign of rationale.

"Well, I'm sorry you feel that way." Turning away, he rearranged the phone to his liking, then placed the photograph of the woman and dogs more to the center of the desk. Curiosity raging, Holly paced to the plaque-laden wall, arms wrapping her breasts, then paced back.

"There has to be a better solution." She detested the wavy timbre of her voice.

He turned to face her, settling one trim haunch onto the edge of the desk, his foot resting on the sweat suit in the seat of the visitor's chair. "I have a suggestion." When she waited, brows raised, he said, "Why don't you take your crayons and tracing sheets home and work there—where you started out. Maybe when we see some profit we can lease a little extra space. Looks like there's plenty sitting empty next door."

A flush seared her skin like wind off the Mojave. "Don't hold your breath."

Stone faced, he said, "You don't think we'll make a profit to lease extra space?"

"Don't hold your breath waiting for me to go home." Her nails nipped her palms. "I'll see you ride into the sunset first. You can take that to the bank, cowboy."

"Good." His voice turned gentle. "If there's anything I like, it's looking at a beautiful woman while I do my damndest to make her rich and happy."

Holly spun on her spike heel and stalked from the office, a trait she feared she'd hone to perfection in the next two years.

—≈≋❖≋≈—

Cocked back in Holly's chair, feet propped on the managerial side of the desk, Chess studied Robyn's picture, fighting a flood of marital memories. He observed the cramped little office, reliving Holly's panic and ire, regretting his remark about her crayons and tracing sheets. In fact he regretted the majority of what he'd felt compelled to tell her today, and all of what he'd volunteered gratis.

In the restaurant, he had tested her by placing the cigar in her unconsciously staked-out space. Penetrating that space more deeply the second time invited her to assert herself. She had acted on cue, her pretty throat pinking up, signaling her agitation. When they parted, her hands shook as she slipped into her coat and grasped the strap of that too-big handbag she toted around. Recall of a short, stiff gait and elevated chin as she abandoned Morton's in favor of a blizzard, assured him their association would be a rocky ride.

It didn't take a Rhodes scholar to see they were getting off on the wrong foot, most of it his fault. Holly shouldn't be held accountable for his wary stance with women, a theory formed long before he knew Xtreme existed. Or barely existed. At least he'd been truthful in telling her he looked forward to having her across the desk from him. He could relieve her of her burdens, give her back her stability. Tomorrow he'd be on his best behavior, make up for the trials he'd put her through.

But what the hell would that accomplish, other than prolonging her agony? She'd be happy when he was gone. End of story.

"You a drinking man, Chester?" Sally stood in the doorway, coat in hand.

Swinging his feet down, he admitted, "Not really, but I do make exceptions."

"I've got an extra ten bucks and an hour until I watch *The Simpsons* with my grandson," she announced with a kindly smile. "How about I buy you one for the road?"

"Sure. Let me bed down the horses and I'll meet you at

the door." He arranged a few personal items, snapped off the light on Holly's half of the desk, taking a last quick survey of the little office. Under these cramped conditions, he could only hope Holly would keep those wounded doe eyes on her designs and not deter him from a plan she already resented him for devising and would hate him for consummating.

Chapter Eleven

On Wednesday, a blizzardy, daunting morning anyway, conscious of the aftermath of Bijan cologne, Holly surveyed her surroundings. A maze of electric cords stretched across Chess's commandeered side of the big desk. The wires continued briefly along the floor before plugging into a multi-outlet, industrial extension cord with a glowing surge-suppressor light.

Yesterday, technicians had appeared unannounced to install television cable while the phone company installed a dedicated modem line. As Holly had attempted to work in the hubbub, she relinquished any thoughts of Chess not taking a hands-on role in Xtreme.

Now she sat doodling, contemplating the memo she'd found on her desk announcing his latest brainstorm: Computer Assisted Design, or CAD, as he referred to it. According to the memo, CAD would revolutionize Xtreme design. Up to now, Lance had the only computer at Xtreme. His expertise warranted it. Hers would arrive soon, along with a dreaded instructor.

She glanced at the plaque wall, then picked up an engraved invitation to the Industry Designer of the Year

Dinner and examined it. Again. In her state of upheaval, she questioned the need for change. What had hell wrought in the formidable form of Chandler Chesney Baker?

Sally stuck her head in the door. "Coming?"

"Coming." She found a legal pad and followed Sally across the hall to gather with the Xtreme department heads in the cramped combination conference-showroom for an early morning staff meeting called by Chess.

Sally, representing distribution, Helen Trent, order entry, Rhonda Sullivan, production, and Lance, accounting, lined both sides of the oblong conference table. Holly and her design assistant, Janine, crowded together at one end, facing Chess and Toby at the other.

Chess's stiff white shirt, turquoise and silver string-tie, western-cut corduroy jacket, boots, and the cream-colored Stetson resting brim up on the table, allowed Holly to hope Xtreme was not his final destination for the day. She suspected Lord Baker had bigger prey to rope and hobble. Just as well, for she had fabric orders to place, now that she had been financially endowed.

"Should we get started?"

All heads swiveled, gazes riveting on Chess.

He took the time to place a metal-cased Portofino cigar on the table in front of him. "I want to cover a few points this morning to acquaint you with my plan for—"

"Excuse me," Holly interjected.

Chess looked up from the papers in his hand, his steel-gray gaze locking into hers as if magnets were imbedded there.

"Since this is Mr. Baker's first official day, something needs to be settled."

His brows hitched, bringing the familiar furrow into play.

She donned her glasses, then removed and stowed them. "Something I feel will make everyone more comfortable."

He slipped his sleeve back, consulted the Rolex. "Shoot,

princess."

Holly saw Rhonda and Helen exchange covert smiles.

"You may not have noticed, Baker, but no one wears cologne at Xtreme." Based on his disbelieving expression, she savored the small victory of striking a nerve.

"Why's that?"

"For various reasons that have proven—"

"Name one." He sank back, broad frame straining the chair. His eyes lit with energy both sensual and challenging.

In her side vision, Lance's smile seemed triumphant.

"Allergies."

"Whose?"

"Sally's. She's miserable in close quarters with anyone wearing fragrance."

Chess looked at Sally, who busied herself picking up a report Holly wanted to throttle her for dropping. He waited for Sally to right herself, his mouth threatening a smile when their eyes finally met. "Sorry to hear that, Sally," he said so intimately Holly could barely hear. Then to her, "Name another."

"Well, no one else, but—"

"Another reason, sugar." Surprisingly gentle.

Her perturbed mind darted to the single other reason. "It—perfume—we can't have the odor attaching to the fabrics."

He placed his Mont Blanc pen on the table. Gripping the table edge, he balanced his chair on its back legs, eyes assessing each face in indolent sequence. Janine squirmed beside Holly. On her right, Lance slouched, eyes averted. Chess's gaze ended its journey with her and stayed there. She fished her glasses from her cleavage, donned them with purpose.

He picked up the cigar, shook it from its case and ran it beneath his nose, then patted his jacket pocket absently. "Toby, would you please get me some coffee?"

He patted a different pocket. The six people surrounding

herself and Chess held their collective breaths.

"Black." His gaze holding her prisoner, he placed the cigar back on the table.

"Actually, that's not Toby's—"

Toby shot up and bolted for a thermos and cups on a near-by counter. Holly visualized inscribing the girl's name in the book of traitorous survivors.

Chess lowered his chair to the floor, eyes brooding over the rim of the white paper cup Toby handed him. He appraised Holly before treating her to a grin charming enough to settle a riot. "I think I have a workable solution. Sally is excused from this meeting and any in the future, and I'll swear on a Bible to touch no fabrics."

"I'll survive," Sally murmured with a chastened grin. "I know where my bread's buttered."

He appraised her kindly. "You're sure? I wouldn't want to cause any suffering."

Holly managed, "Then you should consider not wear-ing—" before Sally's quick, warning glare silenced her. When Holly stood, Chess rose as though they'd rehearsed, giving Lance no choice but to lumber upward. That left her no choice but to try and save face. "I've been informed on the topic Mr. Baker is about to share." She spread honey on her tone. "If you'll excuse me, I'll take care of a high-priority matter."

Head high, she made her exit, then spent the next half hour in her office straining to hear his deep, seemingly lowered voice as he addressed the meeting across the hall. Guilt hung on her like a shroud. Janine's job was being eliminated, and although no one else in the meeting would be fired, half their departments would be and when Chess announced the changes, she should be there to lend support. An hour of soli-tude lent ample time in which to wonder what saving face had cost her.

Chess's footsteps outside the door at midmorning alerted

Holly of his return. She ceased murmuring into her tape recorder and switched it off as he stepped into the shared office.

His eyes and ears had missed nothing.

"Keeping a journal?" How did he manage such a pleasant and detached demeanor?

Finding his perception assuring, yet maddening, she stuffed the recorder into her Vitton bag on the floor. Attempting to look discouraging, she donned headphones and pretended to adjust the volume on a silent radio. She busied herself with "crayons" at her drafting table, a soon-to-be discontinued item, in deference to a computer. Chess's occasional tapping of the laptop keyboard accompanied the low drum of *Inside Opinion* on the financial channel. When she circled him for an unneeded trip to the bathroom, a glimpse at the stock market report filing across the television screen assured her he favored overkill.

He was a creature of excess.

Between attacks on the keyboard, he used his cellular to talk to a broker named Keith and gestured with a newly uncased cigar. Holly listened to names like Brassie Golf, Sport Haley, Sony, Apple and GE, as Chess reiterated the buy and sell orders he had placed by modem. She begrudged him credit for leaving nothing to chance.

Concurrent with his endeavor to fatten his personal fortune, he fielded six calls from Xtreme creditors. His remarkable desk-side manner, the various winsome ways he promised, "the check's in the mail," stirred her reluctant admiration. How would it feel to be the recipient of that soft persuasiveness?

Shortly before noon, he donned the Stetson and checked his appearance in an antique mirror above a barrister's bookcase. He tossed the virgin cigar in the trash, gave her a dazzling smile and exited wordlessly. Holly took off the silent headphones and stared at the door, the empty quiet and the woodsy aftermath of his cologne haunting her.

She went out to console Janine.

Chapter Twelve

Chess glanced up from *The Wall Street Journal* as Lance entered the back door of the ranch house just before midnight. Nestled into a ball on Chess's outstretched thighs, Warrior stirred and growled low in his sleep. Chess smelled beer and cigarettes from across the room and hoped the beer was O'Doul's.

"Hey," Chess said. "How do the grounds look? Do I need to take a stroll and check it out?"

"Your sanctuary's secure," Lance quipped. "I saw a light in number ten. I thought that was being used for storage."

"I thought so, too. A woman and a little girl showed up around suppertime. Do Thi gave them the keys to the kingdom." He grinned at the mental picture of woman and child snuggling down in warmth instead of sleeping God knew where. "How was Bud's tonight?"

Lance shrugged. "Same ol', same ol'. I thought you'd stop by."

He adjusted his boots on the table to make room for Lance's sock feet. "Adam's enthralled with diagramming sentences. I didn't want to disappoint him by not doing my part."

"How's the tutoring going?"

"He'll be ready for summer school."

"That's progress, considering—"

"I know." Chess didn't want the word *illiterate* associated with Adam. "He's brilliant beneath all the rust."

"How was the stock show today? Buy any prize studs?"

Chess folded the paper, pitched it onto the wagon wheel table. "The usual extravaganza, but I picked up rodeo tickets. I'm taking Adam this weekend. You want to come along?"

"Sure." Lance studied him. "I've been thinking about Holly's perfume speech this morning. She was testing you."

No damn joke. "You think so?"

"I told you she's a bitch."

The term proved bothersome. "Hellcat, the way I remember." That term had appealed to him, challenged him.

Lance shrugged. "What's the difference?"

Chess considered the marked dissimilarity. "She feels threatened, is all. After what you've seen in life, I'm sure you can relate. She's protective of her territory and her little brood." That probably hinged on feeling deserted, which had left her gun shy. He'd had hell since Monday with creditors. Once she realized he'd taken that off her, she might calm down. He compared it to gentling a spirited filly, a matter of gaining trust. "She'll settle down," he concluded with false conviction.

"Either you're going soft," Lance said, grinning, "or the boobs are getting to you. Which is it, cuz?"

"I'm just trying to cut her a little slack."

"It's the boobs."

Lance's base grin activated that tickle at the back of Chess's neck—the one that signified something out of kilter, something he couldn't yet identify.

A week later, Chess waited at the conference table for a

scheduled meeting he dreaded.

Lance appeared at the door, official-looking data in one hand. He slipped into the chair to Chess's left. "Where's the midget shrew?"

"Talking to Gregory Friedman." Greg's expression had turned incredulous as he glanced around Chess and Holly's shared office. Greg and Holly's conspiratorial voices had echoed behind him as he exited the space, granting them privacy. "She's late."

"She and the Jewish Clarence Darrow have a thing going. They'll stretch the visit out as long as possible."

Chess mulled over Lance's comment, thinking of a photograph Holly kept on her desk. Her and an older man, both dressed in ski clothes, linked arm in arm. He assumed the man with the robust build, a shock of dark gray hair and Holly's same dusky coloring, to be her father. The fact she kept no picture of the mythical Jules pleased him in a way he was reluctant to acknowledge. Before he could reply to Lance's comment, he heard Holly's quick, distinctive steps in the hall. She rounded the corner and slipped gracefully into her favorite chair at the opposite end of the table.

"Waiting for me?" She smiled as though she'd just come from the dentist with a lip full of novocaine.

"Some things are worth waiting for, sugar."

The smile vanished. She sat taller in the chair. The appealing rise of her breasts when she took a deep breath almost tempered the ugly possibilities that had triggered the meeting.

She pilfered the neck of her sweater for her glasses, slipped them on and shuffled papers, murmuring, "I hope this won't take long. I'm meeting Greg for a drink."

So she wanted to play hard ball. Her attitude was unchanged since their meeting last week, unaltered from the aloofness she'd shown since then. Unchanged indefinitely, he had begun to think. Why not? She'd gotten her money, whether by hook or crook.

"I'll be brief, Holly. It doesn't take me long to detect a cracked horseshoe."

From the corner of his eye, he saw Lance sit up straighter, execute the Baker frown.

"My Zane Gray is rusty, I'm afraid." Her hot-coffee eyes glinted with mock confusion.

He knew no diplomatic way to tell her. "At my request, Sally and Dinh's family checked hard goods against the inventory sheet Lance had given me." Stress lines had gathered around her mouth when he mentioned Sally's name. Without doubt, Holly felt betrayed by his and Sally's developing friendship. "There's a hell of a discrepancy between the old and new accountings."

He got silence from both parties.

"For days I've dealt with creditors trying to collect bills I couldn't find on the review statements Lance gave me. Plus I've been signing checks covering invoices that fall into the same category." Holly's quizzical expression led him to explain. "Accounts payable that weren't included in the initial statement I based my buy-in decision on." He waited for that to penetrate. "Can either of you explain that?"

A simple question as loaded as a primed and pumped shotgun. The way Holly gripped her hands in front of her, her chin tilted, told him his subtle accusation had rattled her. A temple pulsed. Her teeth raked color into her plump lower lip before she lifted her head. A perfect portrait of spirit and fragility made him want desperately to be wrong.

She took off the glasses and stored them again. "I'm sure Lance can explain. Accounting is his department."

With a nod, Chess gave Lance the floor.

Lance flipped pages bound into a folder, closed it, pushed it aside and cleared his throat. "The figures on this report were prepared by Lois, Holly's former accountant. Only being here a month—recognizing the potential of the company—knowing you were hot to find a turnaround—" His voice snagged. He took a breath and began again. "I didn't want to hold out for an audited statement before I told you about Xtreme, so I took Lois's word the figures were dependable."

"When did you realize you were wrong?"

"I was down here on a Sunday night—I like to work when it's quiet. When I went over the figures again—hoping to talk you two into a deal—a sixth sense told me something smelled, so I got into the computer and checked inventory."

Holly's lips pursed deeply enough to hold a six-karat diamond before cognizance lit her eyes. "I donated a batch of seconds to the Good Shepherd resale store. I never got around to deducting them from inventory."

Chess looked at Lance, wishing it was that simple.

"I planned to tell you on Monday," Lance said. "When I stopped by the house, you were out running—had no way of knowing you two were signing papers that morning." He shrugged. "I know how you operate, Chess. You get hold of the bull and wrestle it to the ground, whatever the odds. So I decided to see what happened."

"Why?" Chess asked.

Lance glanced at Holly, then clamped his lips. She didn't speak, but nothing she could have said would have touched Chess the way her searching, forlorn eyes did. She was either innocent or a gifted actress.

"Do you think Holly purposely doctored inventory?" Chess prompted

Stunned, Holly looked at Lance. His face reddened.

"Not exactly."

"Have you given those statements to anyone else? Like the bank?" Chess probed.

Lance nodded. "Holly was trying to talk them out of

more money. They asked to see some figures."

Chess's heart hammered. He extracted a crimped stack of invoices from a file and pitched them on the table before Holly. "I found these in your drawer. What's it mean, partner?"

She looked ill. "I didn't cheat you. I'd never do that."

"Then what happened?"

Her chin hiked. "Something you can't imagine."

"Try me."

"I had no way to pay all the invoices flooding the mail every day. So I developed a system." When he nodded, she explained, "I'd open the mail and take half the bills into my office, give the rest to accounts payable. Every day, I'd take an invoice from the drawer, depending on which creditor gave me the hardest time, and pay it out of my personal account. Money Jules left me when—money that Jules left."

Her soulful expression wrung his heart, making him wonder which he wanted to do more, hold her or spank her.

"That story will hold up in a court of law about as long as a kite in a tornado, sugar."

She pounced on that like a cat on a fallen bird, negating any tender thoughts he'd had. "Are you threatening to sue me?"

"I'm not." He'd figured out long ago, winning with a woman hinged on forgetting to keep score. Still, he resented the hell out of not being dealt a full deck. "The bank might, though. You're flirting with jail when you try to get a bank loan by submitting falsified statements."

She rose to pace, arms wrapped below her magnificent breasts. "It was unintentional—an oversight."

A judge just might believe her. A man, confronted with the same circumstances, would be doomed. "Well, as Lance said, it's water under the bridge. I'll deal with it, but I don't think I'm obligated to stay with my first plan."

She stopped pacing. "What are you saying? You aren't torquing the company now?"

He easily detected her relief. Her joy. "That has to be done anyway. I've decided to take Xtreme on the public market."

"Sell it?"

Her evident distress made him say, "Not exactly. Going public means—"

"I know what it means. What do you take me for?"

"A Barbie doll who plays games with invoices?" He followed up with a grim half-assed smile.

"Damn you." Her eyes glittered, near tears.

"Look, Holly—I'm doing what's best for both of us. I don't intend to feed money to a tiger that can't be satisfied. I explained the snowboard issue to you. That and the false figures I relied on calls for additional money now, and who knows how much after that." He gauged her understanding but detected little beyond disagreement with the going-public issue. "I've taken two companies public in the past. I have a lay-down formula, but I've got to activate it immediately." He addressed Lance, whose eyes glowed with surprise and interest. "You think you're up to the task? It'll be grueling to put it all together—but worth it."

"I don't have any public offering experience."

"We'll hire a consulting firm to walk you through. Then you'll have experience to go anywhere when you leave Xtreme." Lance had drifted from job to job since college, accumulating nothing, putting down no roots. "Or maybe you won't want to leave here. No reason you'd have to. Are you with me?"

"Sure, cuz. I'm always with you."

"I'm not with you, in case you care." Holly leaned her palms on the desk, straining toward him. "I don't want to lose this company—"

"You'll be wealthy, sugar. You can start another company."

She considered for a moment, then frowned. "I don't want—Jules started this company and he trusted me to run it. That's what I'm going to do until he comes back."

So that was it. He admired her loyalty, yet something about hearing it voiced made him feel cold and cheated. "And if he doesn't come back?"

"Then I'll keep Xtreme. It's mine. It's all I am. I won't give it up." She pivoted on her spike heels. "You're a traitor, Lance." Her voice trembled. "The two of you probably staged this charade. I'm sure you had this in mind from the start, but you knew I wouldn't go along with it. I'd fire you, but what good would it do? Lord Baker would hire you back to execute his plan." She gathered her bag and briefcase, then faced Chess. "You two deserve one another, but you'll need to team up, because it won't be easy to take Xtreme away from me."

Her heels clipped down the hall before Chess heard the warehouse door creak, then close softly. A lead weight sank in his chest. He labeled the sudden emptiness he felt as shock. Nothing else computed, but the profound sense fell barely short of pain. Her resigned determination made him consider going after her, telling her they'd give it a while, maybe implement another plan. Instead, he thought of investments he'd seen go sour before. The only way to sweeten this one was to bow his neck and execute.

Lance interrupted Chess's reverie. "Ever heard that joke about Jewish husbands, cuz?" When Chess remained quiet, Lance stood, gathering the financial reports in question. "Why do Jewish husbands die before their wives?"

Chess had heard the crude joke. "Because they want to," he said quietly. Could that be it? Jules had left Holly because he wanted to? Or was he off somewhere wanting to get back to her as badly as she wanted him to return?

Chapter Thirteen

Sally stuck her head in Chess's door long after the outer office and warehouse had cleared of all but the embroidery crew.

"Burning midnight oil? How's the view from the little boss's chair?" She stepped into the office, appearing weary, brandishing two shot glasses full of dark liquid and a fifth of Jack Daniel's Black Label under her arm. "You still a drinking man, Chester?"

Chess swung his boots down from Holly's side of the desk, drew his eyes away from the enigmatic photograph she kept there. "Still not much. But I'll make another exception."

"Well, from what Holly told me before she blew Dodge, this could be the best exception you'll ever have."

She passed him a glass, tapped it with hers, sank into his chair and swung her Reeboks onto the desk. Her deeply lined eyes invited him to do the same. He accepted, kicked back and sipped straight bourbon.

"Who's this?" She nodded to Chess's one photo.

"Robyn, Rachel and Rita. My ex-wife and my ex-dogs. In that order." He took a long pull of Jack, studying the picture of Holly and the mystery man.

"Only nice guys keep pictures of their ex-wives." Sally grinned. "'Course, you probably do it to scare women away."

"It's the only picture I have of the dogs."

She laughed. "Want to give me your version of what happened here tonight?"

"A fifteen rounder. I could have used some help."

"You had Lance."

"Fuel for the fire. Minnie Mouse thinks he and I teamed up on her to steal the company."

"Did you?"

"I'm going to make her rich. That's a hell of a lot better than what she did to me. Intentional or not." He read Sally's eyes, but didn't get much, other than reserved opinion. "I guess you know about the falsified reports."

"Falsified is a strong word."

"Erroneous reports." He dredged up a smile. "I don't believe in sinking my money into a sow I now suspect I can't make into a silk purse."

"You'll never convince Holly to let go of Xtreme."

"Why not? She needs to learn not to marry any company. With the profit from her stock, she can do anything." The sales pitch registered on his own ears. "Running the same company day after day, year after year, is a sure ticket to boredom."

"Not to her. Xtreme is her security blanket. Her identity."

"She told me. In explicit terms."

"Then there's Jules. By the grace of God, he gave her his power of attorney before he boarded that plane. To Holly it was an executive decision. Xtreme and all their assets had always been in her name anyway—"

That pricked his interest. "Why's that?"

Sally looked hesitant. "Something to do with avoiding liability—you know, lawsuits. Jules had been around the pike, seen some scary business practices in New York, I think."

Chess nodded, mind-filing the information.

"Her mission in life is to keep Xtreme together until he comes back," Sally said. "Complicated, but there you go."

"Why does everyone around here assume Jules Efron is coming back?"

"Only Holly assumes that. Pride, I think."

Or hope, he figured. "How long's it been now?"

"Six years, ten months and counting."

"She could rot waiting."

Sally laughed. "Anyone with Holly's energy won't rot." She urged tolerantly, "So she's pissed at Lance, huh?"

"Yeah, and he's the innocent victim."

"He's a big boy. He can probably take care of himself."

Chess wished for Sally's confidence. "I'm used to watching out for him."

"How did that happen?" Her gaze swept around the office, taking in Chess's trappings. "Looks like you have all you can say grace over."

He drained the glass. "Habit I guess. It started when we were kids."

Popping up, she tipped the bourbon bottle over his glass. A glunking sound broke the quiet. She filled her own glass and settled back into position, smiling encouragement. "What started when you were kids?"

"You sure you want to hear this?"

"If I go home I have to bathe grandkids. Go, big boss."

Chess shrugged, grouping his thoughts. "Lance was born in Japan and grew up there. His dad—my father's brother—worked for Sony. The year before Lance would have been a high school senior, his dad took early retirement and moved back to Oklahoma, to his roots, where my family lived. He invested his life's savings in my father's trucking business."

Sally nodded, rolling the glass against her bottom lip.

"Right off, I could see Lance knew zip about American culture. I attended a fancy private school in Oklahoma City— Casady." He shrugged again. "Football captain, class president—overachiever." He grinned. "I figured Lance would join me at Casady, so I decided to show him the ropes, ease him into the adjustment."

"Nice guy."

"It didn't work. Lance failed the entrance exam. That kind of set a precedent for our lives."

She nodded again, eyes sharp above the rim of her glass. "If I give this to you straight—"

"I won't hold it against you, and I won't repeat it."

He mulled that over before giving in. "He went to public school and hung on the fringe of my crowd, never really belonging either place." He let himself examine that. Even at that young age he had seen the damage the experience dealt Lance. "We migrated to OU in our freshman year and I slipped right into my role. Football. The right fraternity. I made the Dean's list majoring in communications." Memory brought a smile. "I dated only campus queens."

"And Lance?"

"I think the term is, 'lived vicariously.' "

"I get the picture. So you got used to trying to make sure things happened for him."

"There's more."

"Always. Let's have it."

"Mom finally got enough of being a workaholic's widow and divorced my dad when I was a sophomore. Dad did okay until he remarried—a younger woman who balked at watching sitcoms while Dad worked. She gave him an ultimatum, and he took her and the party scene. He's an alcoholic now. Bankrupt."

Making installments in Aaron Baker's behalf had become Chess's life goal. When he attained financial security he'd wanted to pay the debt in full, once and for all. Aaron, stone-broke and liquor-addled, believed in hoarding your fortune in interest-accruing accounts, doling it out to creditors. He couldn't rationalize that debt interest washed out drawing bank interest. Nevertheless, Chess still honored his father's old-school theory by complying with his wishes.

To Sally's quizzical look he offered, "Remember I told you Lance's dad had invested—"

"His life's savings in your dad's company."

"My aunt divorced him and—"

"Crap." She took a long drink.

"He killed himself—a gun to the mouth."

"Jee-zus."

Chess nodded. "Lance had to finish school on student loans he's still paying off. Over the years he's shown the Baker propensity for addiction. He's an alcoholic and a gambler."

"You survived the mess. Why not him?"

"Like I said, I'm an overachiever." He threw back the last of the bourbon, recalling how he'd felt he was scrambling up a sheer granite cliff with the odds stacked against him until... "My maternal grandmother was half Choctaw."

A light snapped on in Sally's eyes. She observed his pale hair and olive-hued skin. "That's why you always look like you just got off a plane from Florida." She grinned.

Used to comments like hers, he smiled wryly. "I got just enough Indian blood that I can live on the reservation if things get too rough in the outside world." Some days he considered that an ace in the hole. "When I was a kid, I spent summers with Grandma Chesney in Tishomingo. I could barely tell a Tomahawk from a claw hammer, but the other kids—full bloods—called me Two Colors." He forced this grin. "I spent lots of time rutting around, looking for an Indian princess who'd accept my being a freak, no questions asked. Over the years, I stopped dwelling on my physical makeup and focused on accomplishing something."

Sensing Sally's scrutiny, he looked up. Her tender smile jump-started more story. "Anyway...my Grandma had been drawing oil royalties for years, never cashing the checks, living like a pauper. She called out of the blue—when things were toughest—gave every cent to me. I parlayed it, and here I am."

"And Grandma?"

"She died in luxury five years ago. But you can see where I felt guilty about Lance. Still do. There, but for the grace of God... It bothers me when Holly accuses him of rooking her."

"Then you trust him."

"Sure. Why wouldn't I?"

"You can't buy loyalty, Chester. Remember I told you that."

"Apparently I can't buy Holly's trust or cooperation." Just as he couldn't buy his wife, or a baby to save his marriage. He swung his feet down, rose and flexed. "What can a man buy, Sally, that he gives a damn about?"

"How about my dinner? You look like a hearty eater. Why not take me down to Charlotte's Web and let me watch?" She stood, placed her palms on the small of her back and arched. "Lance says you're womanless. Dinner out beats an empty house. Unfortunately, I wouldn't know about an empty house."

Chess went to the coat tree for his leather jacket and pulled it on. "Sounds like Lance keeps everybody informed. Did he tell you about Adam?"

"Not yet."

"In that case, it could be a long dinner." He circled the desk, shut down the laptop and snapped the computer lid closed. When he leaned toward the desk center to turn off a two-sided banker's lamp, his hand bumped the photograph Holly kept on display. He picked it up and turned to Sally. "She talked about protecting her father's investment." Another good reason for going public, he reminded himself. "Are they close?"

"Not at all." Sally gathered the glasses and the half-empty bottle. "I'll run these back to the kitchen."

Chess replaced the photo and switched off the lamp. "They look close."

"That's not her father. That's Jules Efron."

—⟨⟩—

Chess tossed in bed, listening to the north wind howl through the pines and the two-thirty Burlington coal train pass through Sedalia. In his mind he could see her pushing through the mist, banking a curve and hugging a stream. This time of night, right on schedule with the train, he allowed himself thoughts unfit for daytime. In the dark he could dwell on them, dissect his memory with razor-sharp edges. But tonight he thought of Holly Harper, the little bundle of contradictions who stirred his protective instincts. In spite of the fight she put up, innocence and vulnerability clung to her. Though he acted like a bastard, a user, he was actually a man caught between what he knew he should do and, for the first time, the hesitancy to do it. It surprised him, that after all this time he could be vulnerable, a sucker for dark, wounded beauty.

Robyn hadn't been a fighter. She had suffered what she imagined to be Chess's injustices silently, then gone behind his back to retaliate in a way that should be criminal and was.

At least with hair-trigger Holly he knew where he stood.

He flipped heavily in the bed and pulled the pillow over his head to shut out the mercury vapor stream lighting the grounds. A mystery surrounding Jules filtered through

Chess's petition for sleep. In all her diminutive, volatile splendor, had Holly been too much woman for Jules?

Would she prove too much woman for Chess?

Chapter Fourteen

Holly bustled around Xtreme's kitchen, putting together a tray of food while Sally drank her morning coffee and watched.

"I talked to Greg last night, after my bout with Chess. Greg assured me going public's not a fate worse than death," Holly announced. "It's possible I could stay on as CEO, but with enough money to operate. If I play my cards right."

Sally eyed the burgeoning tray as she filled her coffee cup. "Is this your deck you're shuffling now?" She straightened a yawing supermarket daisy bouquet in a mock-crystal vase.

Holly smiled, lips stiff. "My mother used to say, `You can catch more flies with honey than with vinegar.'"

"Not exactly a feminist stance or a Jewish homily."

"My mother was neither feminist nor Jewish." A blonde shiksa, Cynthia Harper, had adopted only the Jewish traits she admired before she divorced Holly's father when Holly was five. Even though Holly had been allowed visits with her paternal grandmother and aunts, the divorce had deprived her of a Jewish heritage. She had taken Jewish women's studies in college, but recognized no personal Jewish characteristics, which left her feeling part of herself had been lost.

She found a small dish in the cabinet for the strawberry cream cheese. "I've converted her advice to my own doctrine: There's more than one way to skin a fat cat."

Eyes rolling, Sally made her exit, murmuring over her shoulder. "If we're talking about the same cat, altering one hair on his sleek body would be a sin."

Holly filled a chrome thermos with steamy Gevalia Kaffe. As she screwed the top on tightly, and poured cream into a tiny glass pitcher, the echo of Sally's words triggered a nagging concern. In characteristic motherly fashion, Sally needlessly reminded Holly of Chess's superior physical appeal. She crammed Sally's not-so-subtle chiding to the back of her mind, searching for the butter in the crowded refrigerator, pursuing her newly adopted plan.

After talking with Greg, she'd woken in the night even more riled, determined to survive this turnaround. Of the strategies they had discussed, she preferred going public least. Not everyone had the stomach for Wall Street's relentless pace. Once Xtreme became driven by Wall Street, it would no longer be the small entrepreneurial company she loved.

She stirred frozen orange juice into a pitcher of mineral water and reiterated her personal strategy in her mind.

Based on the honey-and-vinegar philosophy she had shared with Sally, before her mother divorced her father, Holly had never seen her challenge him. Regretfully, Holly had followed tradition, allowing Jules to orchestrate every phase of their lives. In his absence she had learned women are not compelled to embrace the world's expectations—or in the present milieu, Chess Baker's edicts. She was neither obligated to kowtow to his agenda, nor to be grateful beyond recognizing Xtreme's regained state of solvency. In language he'd understand, she planned to "take the bull by the horns." She would research and obtain superior fabrics, and by using CAD, produce designs innovative enough to triple accounts. She anticipated no problem, since he had opened up the international market, something she had only dreamed of.

Xtreme had been built on design. She would use the prestige of the upcoming award she was sure to receive and the build-up from the public relations firm Chess had hired to make Xtreme so superior, so profitable, even he couldn't consider selling.

Somewhere in the remainder of her sleepless night, she had been forced to admit that her original goals for Xtreme had shifted. Her primary focus no longer centered on holding the company together for Jules, seeking that pat on the head from both him and her father. More than anything, she wanted to prove her ability to act on her own merit, to maintain her professional identity and provide jobs for the women—and men, now—depending on her.

Working with Lord Baker would be a challenge, but she sensed additional change in the air. Referring to Chess by that name no longer roused ready agreement from the Xtreme staff. In the weeks he had been there, employees—both administration and distribution—had evolved past suspicion to respect. If joining the ranks of respect furthered her chances of regaining independence, she would either master or fake the homage.

She grasped the tray and exited the kitchen, her conclusion to comply offering as much solace as surrendering to a root canal.

When she came through her office door, Chess glanced up from his laptop computer. His gaze, gray-blue smoke this morning, settled on the tray with a mildly aggravated expression. Then cognizance lit his eyes and an indolent smile complemented his face so appealingly her mouth felt cottony.

As he rose and came toward her in a cloud of Bijan, she maneuvered the door closed with her foot. The finality of the latch catching resounded in the room. "I hope you haven't had breakfast." She relinquished the heavy tray to him. "Lance told me you run instead of eating most mornings." Running had rendered his lean, carved facial features as hard and delineated as her skier's calves. "I hoped we might declare a truce."

"By breaking bread together?" His brows arched.

The hair on her nape sprang to life. He had the gall to be amused by her peace effort. Proof lay in the depths of his eyes, in his gorgeous, insolent smile.

I can't do this.

She cleared a space on his section of the desk, easing the picture of the blond woman aside. As he lowered the tray there, she skidded sideways, but not before their forearms brushed.

Her heart responded with a pronounced thump.

He presented a picture of western elegance. In the weeks past she had learned to judge his daily agenda by his attire. If he would be leaving the office on business, or had an in-house visitor scheduled, he wore magnificent suits, white shirts so flawless she suspected he wore them once and discarded them, and signature Nicole Miller ties. If merely passing by Xtreme on his way to only God-knew-where, he wore Levi's and boots. Somewhere in the weeks past, her reaction to his casual attire on his just-passing-through days had changed from elation to disappointment.

She realigned her priority, fixing a smile in place. "I hope—do you like bagels? If not, I have croissants."

He scrutinized the tray. His gaze, one that could quickly turn as piercing as diamonds drilling into rock, was gentle. "I won't go hungry." He settled into his chair with the lazy arrogance of a prince waiting to be served. "You could spoil me, sugar. I might start to expect this." A signature Chess Baker compliment.

No one had ever talked down to her with a more charming delivery. She had come to realize that Chess liked women.

He was capable of treating them well, but he saw them through a sexist veil. His self-centered male ego prevented enlightenment.

Focusing on his benevolent good humor, she swallowed a rejoinder. According to an article from *Psychology Today*, regular nonreactive communication could retrain a brain and set a more "loving" tone for future discussions. Interesting.

Holly was bent on testing the theory.

Focused on her purpose, she poured Chess's coffee. Glancing surreptitiously at the photograph, she allowed herself a visceral fantasy. Would waking in his arms, having breakfast with him every morning, resemble heaven or hell?

Chess's mind grasped the efficiency with which Holly dispensed her peace offering, noting the erect posture of her perfect little body, the sultry pursing of her full mouth and the way she kept her eyes focused on the task at hand. Rather than a subservient attitude, she displayed a hostess's demeanor.

The way she positioned the filled plate before him and lined up a glass of juice with his coffee made his pulse quicken. The cadence raced off the charts when she tucked a napkin into the neck of the mock turtle he wore beneath his flannel shirt. While her long chianti-stained nails teased his skin, he kept his hands on the chair arms, returning her smile. Considering the closed door, he wondered what she'd do if he drew her onto his lap and negotiated peace more pointedly.

She picked up a cigar from the desk, dangled it from her fingertips, and then replaced it, eyeing him curiously. He tossed the Macanudo in the trash basket and bit into a bagel.

"I never see you smoke those." She eased into her chair across the double desk. "I only see you waste them, and I know they're expensive."

So she'd been researching his habits. He smiled tolerantly. "How do you know?"

Silently, she looked at him from beneath a fringe of black

lashes, her expression gentle in the lowered lighting. He had concluded she liked the room dim, with lamplight filtering onto work surfaces. He was finding the arrangement soothing.

"I used to be hooked on cigars," he admitted. "Now I'm down to smelling and touching. Tossing's a small price to pay for near freedom."

She chewed a bite of croissant and took a sip of orange juice. "When you get past your sensual indulgences you can donate all that money to cancer research."

"I'm kind of partial to my 'sensual indulgences,' but if it would make you happy, I could begin matching the amount I'm spending with a donation."

She shrugged, breasts rising within her soft V-neck sweater in a familiarly appealing way. He had become fond of seeing her fish for her glasses, and wondered where she had stashed them.

"Whatever soothes your conscience." She chewed delicately now, seeming to break her train of thought to savor the food. After washing it down with orange juice, she picked up the conversation, nodding toward the upside-down Stetson on the antique bookcase. "So you're bound for the north forty today?"

He tried to catch the shade of her tone but failed. "Lance and I are catching a noon plane to Ruidoso to check on one of my horses, then on to Vegas for a couple days."

Her compact body tensed at the mention of Lance's name. "I've heard he has a gambling problem. Do you think it's smart to encourage that?"

He drained his coffee, stood to reach for the thermos. When she made a quick move to rise, he motioned her down. "I'm trying to convey the moderation theory to Lance."

"That's an Episcopalian concept. Are you Episcopalian?"

He laughed as he settled back into his chair. "Are you an

Orthodox Jew?"

"I'm Jewish by descent. Jewish father, Catholic mother. They fought constantly over religious beliefs. I've never been in a synagogue in my life, or to mass. So...point taken."

Her pixie smile led him on. "Vegas loses its power when you decide what you can afford to lose and don't violate the agreement you made with yourself—and the limit you set with the cashier before the first card is dealt."

"Do you practice that theory?"

"Definitely. I've seen horror stories." His cousin among them.

"Does Lance practice your theory?" Her beautiful lips released the name with disdain.

"He does when I'm there. He doesn't go alone, any-more."

"You're baby-sitting." Above the rim of the juice glass, her eyes pinned his.

It didn't take metaphysics to see her resentment of Lance escalating. "I like his company."

She veered to a different topic. "What about the ski out-ing Saturday?"

The public relations people had set up the outing, but he knew Holly could carry it off alone. He planned to pick a snowy area in Xtreme's parking lot for the "photo opportuni-ty," then let the office staff and Holly board the charter bus for the slopes without him. "President's Day weekend at Vail will be crowded enough. I won't be missed."

Did he see or only wish for disappointment skittering across her gaze before resignation settled in?

"Instead of Vegas, it seems you'd spend your gambling money in Central City or Cripple Creek, so Colorado could benefit."

Maybe Lance was right about the name Harper fitting, but Chess tried to credit her with healthy curiosity. "Stakes are

too small." His turn to shrug. "I hoped that proposed legisla-
tion— raising the five-dollar limit to a hundred—would pass,
but since the House voted it down...."

She latched on to that like she'd discovered ice in hell.
"Then you prefer high risk."

"Controlled high risk."

"Is there such a thing? Seems to me control would eliminate—"

Enough. "Actually, I like the cheesecake they serve in
Vegas." He settled against his chair back, placed his napkin on
the desk. "New York cheesecake. If you'll overlook my out-
of-state gambling preferences, I promise to bring you a slice."

She eased her chair back, rose and approached with the
juice pitcher. When he held his glass out to accept her offering, she poured with her eyes on Robyn's photograph.

"Holly—"

She jerked back just as the glass ran full, juice dribbling
onto the leather desktop. Her gaze swung from the picture to
his face. She murmured, "Sorry," as she dabbed distractedly
with an extra napkin. "Your wife could be your twin."

"Ex-wife." He'd bet the divorce hadn't been omitted
from all of Lance's tale bearing. Was this little hellcat capable
of being coy? "You're right. Robyn and I were a pair—voted
the couple most suited to marry, class of '88. How could we
go against that prediction?" He drained the juice, dabbed his
mouth and tossed the crushed napkin onto his plate. Standing,
he jabbed his fingers into his back pockets. "Unfortunately
ratification by the whole class couldn't keep us together."
Hearing his own words caused his spine to stiffen.

"Too bad. The resemblance is remarkable." Eyeing the
photograph, she sat back down, and he followed suit.

They ate in momentary silence. He watched her blot her
lips and imagined tasting orange juice raveled with red-wine
lipstick. When she leaned across the space to deposit her plate

and glass on the tray the sweater strained against her chest, and her upward glance trapped his. Color rose in her cheeks. She'd caught him. Again. Her body was proving to be the perfect tool to stoke his baser needs.

He tried tramping down his tingling nerve endings with pragmatism as he added his plate and glass to hers and refilled his coffee cup. "How're you coming with CAD?" He nodded to the computer rig that had replaced her hallowed drafting table.

She rummaged on the computer table, her face a placid mask. Then, in answer to his question, she placed a printout on the desk. He studied the rendering, raking a hand through his hair. In deference of the moment, he postponed his design critique.

"Looks like you're becoming computer literate."

She studied the printout, too, or pretended. "I'll be moving this afternoon."

Damn. The remark about taking her crayons back to her basement had returned to haunt him. "Why's that?"

"You need privacy."

"Not really." He needed to look across the desk at her, incentive for figuring how they could both win this game.

"Have you read Virginia Wolfe's *A Room of One's Own*?" She cocked her head, eyes oversized in her face, topaz nuggets in the gentle lighting. "It stresses the importance of having your own space—especially women. I'm taking the advice to heart."

"How's that, sugar?" The room had already taken on an empty feeling.

"I've cleared a space in the warehouse. We have some glass partitions and an old metal desk in storage. I'll move my computer out there."

She lifted the tray with finality, but he seized it. She seemed a little startled when the weight transferred from her hands. He set the tray back on the desk and placed his hands on her shoulders, looking down, feeling her searing warmth through fine wool. She tensed, then he felt her tremble. Skittish. Was she afraid of him? He hadn't sensed that before.

"Don't move out, darlin'. I won't be here long, and I'll try to give you space till then."

She shook her head. "I should be closer to production."

When she didn't break his hold, he wrestled with an urge to close the gap between them.

"I want to try to make up for the invoices," she said. "I owe you that."

His heart twisted a fraction. "Just being willing to is enough."

"I want you to know, I'd never cheat you purposely."

"You were under a lot of pressure. I've been there."

She looked skeptical. "Are you sure you believe me?"

"I've got nothing to gain by lying to you."

Her body gave a feeble backward shrug, and he released her. "It's settled, then. We'll go on cohabiting."

He crossed to the door and opened it. Their gazes clung as she walked toward him bearing their breakfast residue.

"If you're going out, honey, be careful. The streets are slick. If you start skidding, keep your foot off the brake. Just steer and ride it out."

She tilted her head, murmuring, "Just like life."

"Just about." When he bent to peck her cheek, she jerked, turning just enough for him to meet her mouth. A grave accident. She tasted of cream cheese, coffee and a poignant sweetness he tried to ignore. Did he see the same fire that leaped to life in his belly mirrored in her eyes?

"Thanks for the breakfast and the truce, darlin'." He smiled. "Deep down, I'm a lover, not a fighter."

She fixed him in an impish gaze. "That could be hazardous to your dictatorial reputation."

With a toss of her dark head and a sultry smile, she left him to ponder her abrupt change of heart.

In the car, on her way to a dental appointment, Holly let the scene just played run across the screen of her mind.

I'm too aware of Chess Baker.

When he came close, she felt emotional panic, her heart racing, pulse quickening. The kiss, his heat, his full, soft mouth tasting of coffee and buttery croissants, a platonic gesture gone askew, had sent her reeling. Even though she detested his relentless machinations involving Xtreme, her body betrayed her, rebelling against a long celibate hiatus.

For seven years she had lived in a sensual vacuum, forming no more than friendships with men passing through her life, feeling married, though sexually starved. Merely encountering Chess made her feel she had walked into a tiger's cage. His charismatic strength, arrogance and male beauty menaced, yet mesmerized her. Based on their different agendas, common sense goaded her to back away, just as she would from any wild and dangerous animal. Yet a part of her wanted to see the same hunger in him she felt every time she saw him or thought of him, to see longing swirl in his stormy eyes. Thinking of his eyes now, the possibility of piercing their secrets, triggered a flutter between her thighs, followed immediately by a disturbing thought. His gentle kindness and the congenial eagerness she had seen in his cloud-gray eyes this morning could be hazardous to her original impression.

She was dangerously susceptible to him, while he was wildly unpredictable, wanting nothing more than a profit and quick exit from her and Xtreme. Her mind embraced her father's emotional desertion and then Jules's defection. Controlling her feelings for Chess would avoid more pain.

Chapter Fifteen

While waiting for the blackjack dealer to shuffle a new shoe, Chess kept a watchful eye on Lance at a bank of dollar slot machines. After Lance had extinguished his limit in short order, leaving the table in sullen boredom, Chess had requested the table be closed and played head-up with the dealer. His luck had been hot for the last hour, as the stacks of black chips before him signified—not a good time to leave the table unless luck changed with the next round dealt, as it easily could.

He took off his hat, ran his fingers through his hair, stifling a yawn. When the dealer shoved the tight stack of newly shuffled cards toward him, he placed the fawn-colored Stetson on an empty chair and cut the deck. Catching Lance's eye, he motioned him over. As Lance approached, Chess signaled the dealer to wait, then scooped handfuls of chips into the Stetson and held it out to Lance.

"How about cashing me in? I'll go through this shoe and we'll have dinner, catch Seinfeld's show, maybe." If Chess were alone, he would play around the clock, or at least until he grew too exhausted to keep track of which cards had been dealt. "I'll meet you at the cashier's cage."

"Got it," Lance mumbled and shuffled away, hat in hand.

Ten minutes later Chess slipped off the stool, stuffed more chips into his pockets and made his way through the crowd toward the cashier's cage. In the near distance, still holding the Stetson upside down, Lance engaged in animated conversation with a young, immaculately dressed Japanese man. As Chess drew into earshot, he realized they were speaking Japanese, Lance's second language. Even though they'd never met, the man's eyes quickened as Chess approached.

Lance turned, lapsing into English.

"Can you believe this, Chess? Meet Koichi Mihatsu. We went to school together in Tokyo." Lance's face beamed, uncharacteristically. "Small world, as they say." Then to Mihatsu, "My cousin, Chess Baker."

Mihatsu bowed nimbly. When he straightened, Chess offered his hand. Mihatsu's sturdy grip contrasted his frail stature.

Chess looked down, meeting his eyes. "Nice to meet you."

"It is my pleasure, sir. I am very pleased to find your cousin here, though I am surprised." His eyes disclaimed his smile. "Our meeting is not as great a coincidence as it appears to be, however. I have an office in Los Angeles and often come here for weekends."

In Chess's side vision, Lance continued to grin, eyes alive with green fire. Chess sought a way to prolong that satisfaction. "We were just about to have dinner. If you'll join us, I'll cash in and we'll make a dent in my winnings."

A small dark hand lifted, palm out. "Oh, no. I cannot impose on your kindness. The two of you must be my guests."

Chess relieved Lance of the Stetson. "Twist his arm. I'll be right back."

He stood in line behind a frazzled couple with a cup full of red chips to collect his winnings, then stuffing his pockets with hundred-dollar bills, made his way back to Lance and

Mihatsu.

"Get this," Lance called out when Chess reached hearing range. "The world's getting smaller. Koichi's in the ski industry."

The back of Chess's neck tickled senselessly. He credited the feeling to the coincidence of Lance finding Mihatsu. "That's a hell of a note."

Mihatsu smiled, adjusting his tortoiseshell glasses, eyeing Chess gently. "You are to be commended."

"How's that?"

"You produce goods. America has become a land without substance. You do not make things anymore." He spoke quietly, his voice overshadowed by the surrounding casino din. "Manufacturing ads value to raw material and creates wealth, but Americans are fascinated with Wall Street and junk bonds. They make money by manipulating paper. Paper profits do not reflect real wealth."

The little man had gall to volunteer that speech, even if it had merit. Before Chess could frame a rejoinder, with a grin as self-deprecating as his words, Lance agreed.

"That's me, Koichi. A friggin' paper pusher. Chess'll verify that."

Chess's scalp tightened. "I might be able to shed a different light on your theory, Mr. Mihatsu. I had the cashier make dinner reservations. We can compare stories."

Mihatsu half bowed, dark eyes stern. "I agree only if I am permitted to buy champagne."

Unable to restrain the reaction, Chess's eyes locked with Lance's. Lance smiled wryly, shrugging, eager to forego a thus-far sober weekend.

"Chess'll probably arm wrestle you for the bill, but as far as I'm concerned, you're on, Koichi." He clapped Mihatsu's slender shoulders. "Special occasions cry for champagne."

Over appetizers, Chess listened as Lance questioned

Mihatsu in depth. Mihatsu signaled the hovering waiter to pour more champagne, then disclosed modestly, "I am head of Nakamoto Industries. Perhaps you have heard of my company."

"You manufacture skis," Chess said. "Damn good ones. I keep a pair strapped to my Jeep."

Mihatsu smiled and tipped his head. "You are kind. I admit they are of superior quality and our business is lucrative, but you are the fortunate one. Urayamashii ni!!" Again his head bobbed forward, eyes lowered for a second.

Chess glanced at Lance.

"He envies you, cuz."

"What the hell for?"

"You manufacture ski apparel. You are in the business I wish to be in."

"Why?" Lance spoke around a mouthful of cognac-seasoned pheasant sausage. "Apparel's trendy, and trying to stay ahead of the competitor's design is a pain in the ass. Nakamoto puts out state-of-the-art equipment and the consumer grabs it, a new pair every year."

"That is very true. Yet Xtreme has no issue with trend, for your superb design goes beyond the confines of trend."

The observation cast Chess back to the printout Holly had shown him yesterday and a flaw that wouldn't stop nagging him. If intuition proved right, altering that detail could push them over the cutting edge. He hoped.

"Thanks for the compliment, Mr. Mihatsu. I'll pass it along." But not until he had convinced Holly of his idea.

"Please. You must call me Koichi, if we are to share stories."

Chess nodded, despite how little he wished to share.

Lance grinned as he drained his glass. "Let's get back to your envy. I like the ring of that." Looking around distractedly, not spotting the liveried waiter, he reached for the bottle.

Mihatsu's eyes, observing Lance's breach of etiquette, bore the frown his disciplined face would not allow. "Among Nakamoto's Tokyo holdings is a fabric mill. Much fabric is produced and sold. Yet some machines sit idle. Our goal is to obtain maximum return on our investment by finding a way to utilize the amount of fabric we are capable of producing."

Chess and Lance waited.

"You are the established clothing manufacturer Nakamoto desires to be. I envy you this, but I do not covet." He held his champagne glass aloft, smiling. Chess couldn't douse the feeling Mihatsu's toast bordered on condescension. Mihatsu turned his gaze to Lance. "Shall we speak of things more conducive to digestion? I must hear of your life in America, my good friend. I have thought of you often."

Remembering the hot table he'd left and feeling he should give the friends privacy, Chess excused himself the moment protocol permitted. Once Mihatsu had risen, bowed, then shaken hands, Chess slipped his arm loosely around Lance's shoulder.

"I'm going back to the tables. Come by and cash me in when you're finished." Their devised arrangement, cashing in periodically, worked to his advantage. Not allowing chips to accumulate made it more difficult for pit bosses to keep track of house losses and eased dealer pressure.

"I'll be a while. If you're on a winning streak, better not wait for me."

Chess painted his tone congenial. "Fine. But you'd better go easy on the grape juice. We've got an early conference call."

"Give it a rest, cuz." Surliness pervaded Lance's fictitious grin.

Mihatsu's pitiable expression assured Chess concern was justified, yet hopeless as mucking out a horse stall with a spoon.

⟶⊱❖⊰⟵

The cards had cooled. Or maybe he'd lost concentration, broken stride. He left the table, threaded his way through throngs of people and took the elevator to the top-floor complimentary suite. In the shower, he gave in to the notions that had badgered him throughout the siege of lukewarm card hands.

He now had a new theory on why Jules had left Holly. Instead of being too much woman, Chess had begun to think she was too delicate for any action other than protecting. She deserved to be taken care of until all that aggression she had put aside to make his breakfast got permanently squelched. Until she puffed up with confidence, not from fear. But she'd never allow that from Chess, and maybe Jules hadn't been up to it, or hadn't recognized her need, or, worse yet, didn't care. Anything involving Jules Efron hinged on genuine speculation, but lately Chess found his mind haunted more and more with wondering.

He turned off the water and reached for a towel bearing the Mirage Hotel monogram. Deep in thought, he rubbed his body with the luxuriously thirsty material. Holly had looked so damn cute standing on tiptoe, leaning across the desk to pour his juice. He smiled, remembering how she had spilled it while eyeing Robyn's picture.

Gripping the towel on either end, he rubbed his buttocks dry, indulging in images of how she'd look in a frilly apron and not much else—or a negligee, redolent with their dried body fluids and mingled early morning smells.

His body reacted on cue to the picture his mind painted.

True, he got too much pleasure out of watching her bristle when he called her "sugar," watching her slow, camouflaged burn once he worked up to "darlin'." The southern male tradition had proved unacceptable in today's gender conscious society, but he didn't put much stock in political correctness. He could almost see her nerve endings come alive, curls snapping as she squared her shoulders. The way the very air around her crackled with life, reliably stimulated him, making him imagine other, more intimate, volatile reactions she might have.

Had this happened to his father? Had the woman who worked alongside him every day, the woman who became his second wife, gradually mesmerized Aaron Baker? A woman who changed after marriage, just as Robyn had. A woman whom Chess's father had followed down a path to financial destruction.

Like Aaron, Chess was finding too many reasons to ignore the danger signs, too many excuses to focus on what might please Holly, downplaying correct business decisions. His altered feelings hinged partly on her vulnerability, coupled with tenacity, and partly on her vitality. The guard he had sworn to never lower now dangled at half-mast, and he wavered dangerously between jerking his defenses back into place or tossing them like an eight-dollar Macanudo.

He seized the bathroom phone and pushed a button.

"Good evening, Mr. Baker."

The Mirage beat hell out of the Holiday Inn. "How're you doin'?"

"Fine, sir. How may I assist you?"

"By arranging to ship a cheesecake to Denver. Tonight."

"My pleasure. May I please have the recipient's name?"

He pictured Holly's face and past characteristic expressions he had witnessed. Hope, that day they met. Later he'd seen anger, resistance, suspicion. Defiance. Then, yesterday morning, repentance and restored hope. He let the accidental kiss, her taste, fill his mind before he settled on that last sultry smile she had awarded him, her last cheeky challenge.

"Send it to my partner. Ms. Holly Harper."

"How would you like the card to read, sir?"
"Let's just say, 'A promise is a promise.' "

He dried his hair, did a quick pass with a razor, slipped into fresh Levi's and a clean turtleneck. He pulled on his boots and exited the vacuous suite. In the casino he took an end stool at a blackjack table near the front entry for a threefold purpose. He would give the casino a fair shot at his winnings, considering the comped suite, be prepared to salvage Lance when, and, if, he returned, and eventually pass another lonely night.

Chapter Sixteen

The night before the ski outing, the phone rang as Holly stepped from the shower. Balancing the receiver between shoulder and cheek, she filled a palm with Anaïs body lotion, hoping to take advantage of moisture clinging to her body.

"It's Henry Chastain." The investigator she kept on retainer.

She listened to his story of how Jules might have been sighted in New Delhi as she spread the scented balm on her lower torso, avoiding her eyes in the mirror, now and then murmuring, "I see. Yes...I see." Clearly, Henry had left no stone unturned to verify or eliminate the possibility of discovery.

"Probably nothing will come of it, but I'll call the minute I know something, Mrs. Efron." He was allowed to call her that to save confusion, since, for him, Efron had probably become a household word in seven years. "Don't get your hopes up."

The warning pricked her mind like nettles. Strands of memory gripped her as resentment and guilt for the feeling warred in her soul.

—❖—

Hours later, she bolted out of a nightmare in the middle of the night, shaking, cold, skin slick with sweat, her heart pounding. She could not quite recall the dream that had woken her, other than Jules's presence—an ill, emaciated, strangely attired Jules. A stranger. Her stomach knotted with anxiety. She left the bed to change her soaked nightgown, then stood staring out the window at her snow-packed backyard, internally cursing her vulnerability. Angel's warm body against her calf eased Holly into reality, then gratitude that Jules's vision had been only a dream. Grief, once twisted around her like choking vines, no longer existed. Tonight, her innermost emotions in no way resembled getting her hopes up.

She dialed Janine's number and anxiously waited out four rings for voice mail. "Hi. I desperately need to talk to you."

She talked to her journal while awaiting Janine's call, then finally surrendered to the urge to call Greg, seeking the insight and caring she knew she could count on. She woke him but heard no resentment in his tone, which stirred a cache of guilt, concern that her dependence on him might foster illogical hope.

He was quiet for a time after she told him about Henry Chastain's phone call. Finally, he asked her, "Exactly what do you want here, Holly? Concerning Jules."

"I know what I'm supposed to want."

"That won't carry much weight for staving off nightmares."

"I know. Sometimes I feel I'm going mad." She listened to the house creak, to Angel's tags jingle from the foot of the bed.

"Does not being able to follow your conscience have

anything to do with Baker?" His flat tone hinted that he knew.

She sat up against the headboard, straightened covers and smoothed them, reluctant to examine or answer the question. "I don't want anything terrible to have happened to Jules, but—"

"Anything terrible that could happen is water under the bridge, Holly. Either you want him back or you don't."

"I've changed so much since he left." The painful metamorphosis flashed on the screen of her mind. "I've made a lot of mistakes, but they're mine. I'm not ashamed to claim them. If Jules comes back—if he's alive—I won't have the freedom to make mistakes."

"If you've changed enough, you will."

"That's my biggest...dread." But not her clearest conclusion. "If he's alive, that means he deserted me by choice. I wouldn't want him back under those conditions."

Greg's sigh carried through the wire. In her mind's eye she saw his familiar frown, the harassed look in his dark eyes, eyes that would look strange in the middle of the night without thick-lensed glasses.

"Then why do you have Henry turning over every rock in India? Why don't we just assume Jules is dead, or doesn't want to come back, and get on with our lives."

Verbally, she ignored the suggestion in his words. "I have my reasons." Closure had become paramount. The clock was ticking, her decision concerning that closure looming in the foreground now, rather than far into the future. "This conversation is redundant, isn't it?"

"Nothing about you is redundant."

"What would I do without you, counselor?" She strove for levity in her tone.

"That's one problem you won't have to face. Trust me."

"I do, Greg. Implicitly."

—◦⋘◇⋙◦—

Holly swung her seven-year-old Saab into the Xtreme parking lot before daylight the next morning. Cars, Sally's and Toby's among them, dotted the snow-packed setting. She had passed a mini bus displaying a Charter-Vail sign when she turned off the interstate a few blocks back. As she got out of the car, headlights from Chess's smoky-gray Grand Cherokee flashed across her body. The immediate banging in her chest—elation scrambled with surprise—left her winded.

She worked purposefully at unfastening her skis from the roof of the Saab, listening to the Jeep motor cease and a car door slam. Powerless, she glanced over her shoulder to see Chess's form, backlit by the virgin dawn, advancing. A man who possessed his cock-sure walk needed little else to turn a woman's head, especially on a morning after a phone call that had left her life's axis spinning out of balance.

She strained to reach the last latch holding her skis in place, trying to ignore the woodsy aroma floating toward her, his body warmth closing in. Wordlessly, he retrieved her skis and stood them on end before her.

"Good morning. I thought you weren't coming." She stomped her après-ski boots in fresh snow.

"You thought or you hoped?" he murmured without looking at her. He resnapped the ski-rack latches, his nylon ski suit rustling in the snow-shrouded quiet.

His powerful presence overshadowed her disappointment and curiosity for his gruff demeanor. "When we had breakfast, you indicated..."

"I figured I shouldn't leave you to shepherd the crew alone." He looked at her, eyes softer than his tone.

She squared her shoulders. "This is not Xtreme's first ski outing, believe it or not. I would have managed."

His brow furrowed. "I should have stayed in bed, you

mean."

Against her will, her mind's eye pictured him in bed.

"Considering the publicity pictures, you should be here, but it must have been hard to get up in time to run first." When he didn't return her bantering smile, she averted her eyes to unnecessarily tighten the strap around her skis. "Thank you for the cheesecake. The special courier was a bit showy, but the cake was delicious."

"No problem." Sun shot over the horizon, lighting his face, flawless, except for a shaving nick on his strong chin. His eyes took on a dour cast, his mouth a bit grim, as he nodded behind her. "The bus is here. Let's get the show on the road."

Before she could shoulder her skis, he grasped them and crossed back to his four-by-four for his own gear. As she watched Lance disembark from the Jeep, stretching indolently, and light a cigarette, she wondered what had displaced the affable demeanor Chess displayed when they'd "broken bread together." Most likely, it hinged on spending a mandatory day with her.

She shared a seat with Sally on the hour-long ride, Sally's grandchildren chattering animatedly across the aisle. Additional shrill, young voices came from the back of the bus.

Sally leaned forward toward Chess where he and Lance occupied the seat behind the driver and raised her voice above the din. "Where's Adam? I was looking forward to meeting him."

Holly's curiosity piqued when Chess answered, "He woke up sick this morning," the regret in his voice detectable. A frown line appeared between his brows. "Thanks for asking."

After that, he fingered a cigar and talked continuously on his cellular, making call after call, his face never losing its grave expression, while Lance slept, curled against the window.

Holly was unable to defeat her curiosity. "Who's Adam?"

Sally's grin told her she'd failed at feigning indifference. "Ask Chess. It's quite a story."

Holly leaned her head against the cold window and pretended to doze. She would ask him when hell froze over.

—≈≫❖≪≈—

The bus turned onto Vail Center Road, drew to a stop and belched its load. The photographer waited nearby, equipment ready. Skis in hand, Chess stood next to Holly as they waited for the driver to dole the remaining skis from a gaping hole in the side of the bus.

When she reached for hers, Chess said, "I'll take those."

"No." Chafed by his earlier testiness, she seized the skis and stepped backward into a clearing large enough to allow her to shoulder the burden. "You might spoil me, and you might not be here for the next outing."

"You can count on it, partner."

Her head jerked up in time to catch his sketchy smile. With mixed emotion, she recalled the note enclosed with the cheesecake. *A promise is a promise.* She unshouldered the skis.

"In that case, here. What harm can a solo performance as a member of the so-called weaker sex do?" As she surrendered the skis, their hands brushed; current shot through her gloves and up her arm. She painted her face placid.

The cameraman herded the staff, decked out in a colorful array of Xtreme's best offering, into place at the mouth of Vail's celebrated covered bridge. Gore Creek rushed in the background.

As Chess dictated who should pose with whom and

orchestrated the shots as though he possessed photography expertise, whatever had been bothering him seemed to dissipate. Holly suspected his lighter mood hinged on taking the control she would normally have assumed. The aftermath of last night's nightmare about Jules had rendered her passive enough to follow Chess's directions.

When they posed together and his arm slipped loosely about her shoulders, she fought the urge to nestle against him. Senseless tears blurred her vision. Confused, she drew away, commandeered her skis and strode across the bridge.

He caught up and wrestled her equipment from her again. Over her shoulder, Sally and Toby watched with interest as they trudged along together amidst the Xtreme crew and their families. Lance hung to the back with the cameraman.

"What's the matter, princess?" Chess smiled down at her, one brow expertly cocked. "Having a bad day?"

Her spine prickled. "I could ask you the same thing."

His slightly apologetic look did little to hide the storm in his eyes. "Don't ask. No sense in both of us worrying. But you'd better smile, or you'll spoil the day for your devoted followers."

She considered his earlier sullenness. "Why is a woman expected to be nice, even when she's suffering?"

His brow corrugated, a muscle ticking in his jaw. "You're too much woman, Holly, to try to operate like a man. That's my role. Tell me what's bothering you. I'll fix it."

She shook her head. How would he fix it? By ceasing to exist, thereby erasing her erratic attraction to him? By proving Jules actually had abandoned her, something she'd never been able to accomplish? As they neared Pepi Sports, she tried to rid her mind of the skeptical expression Jules had worn that last day.

A dim light glowing and movement inside Pepi's shop brought her up short. She turned to the group, hand aloft, palm out, addressing the cameraman. "This is one of Xtreme's biggest accounts. Let's get a shot here beneath the shop sign. I'll see if by chance that's Pepi Gramshammer inside. If so, he'll pose with us." She turned away, then pivoted back to Chess. "Want to come inside and meet Pepi?"

He grinned wryly, eyes crinkling at the corners. "You're back in control. If he's there, rope him and drag him out here. I'll con him out of a bigger order."

The early riser inside the shop proved to be Kelly Dexter, Pepi's merchandise manager. When Holly returned to the group gathered on the wooden porch, Kelly in tow, Chess had migrated across the street and struck up a conversation with a blonde in a black catsuit. As the cameraman staged the Xtreme group, leaving a vacant spot between Kelly and Holly, she tried not to watch Chess's animated gestures and brilliant smile.

Posing arrangements complete but Chess still absent, Lance offered, "I'll get him or we'll be here all morning. He's got a thing for blondes—probably comes from looking in the mirror."

As she tried to ignore the cat-suited blonde pirouetting now for Chess's scrutiny, Holly's "No," came out too adamantly. "We'll shoot without him," she ordered, closing the reserved gap. "He won't be missed."

In her side vision, she saw Sally's eyes roll skyward.

The picture session over, Holly tromped past Chess wordlessly, the blonde's throaty laugh grating her nerves like concrete scraping tender knees. His penchant for control evidently kicking into high gear, Chess caught up to the group where the street came to a dead end, ski rental and lifts on the left, ticket window and ski school on the right.

He raised his mellow voice to drawl, "Anyone who needs skis, fall in at the rental shop. How many people need skis and lessons?" He took a head count. "Okay. Get fitted, then I'll walk you over and get you set up." He paused, eyeing the group. "Toby, you look ready to roll, so you take my credit card to the ticket line, get lift tickets for the group. Ten adults, twelve children."

He unsnapped the top of his suit and fished in an inside pocket, then as if remembering Holly, nodded toward the crowd gathering at the Vista Bahn. "You go ahead, darlin'. No reason both of us should hang around taking care of business. Your worshippers will catch up to you out there somewhere, maybe." He smiled, white teeth flashing in his tanned face, hair tumbling onto his forehead like spilled gold in the early morning sun. "Maybe not, though. I hear you're a hot dog."

She pushed her sunglasses to the top of her head and looked up at him. "Will you be able to fit skiing into all of this managerial procedure, cowboy?" Would he be catching up, too?

"Yeah, but you're way out of my league, partner. I'm taking Lance to the green runs to impart my newfound ski knowledge."

He had assumed correctly that she preferred not to ski with Lance, but did she see challenge or resignation in his eyes?

She turned to the dispersing group. "Have fun, guys. If I don't see you on the slopes, we'll meet at the children's fountain at two o'clock and then head for the bus. Remember— party at my house at six o'clock. Save some energy."

Threading through the crowd toward the Vista Bahn, she attempted to hold her head and shoulders in such a way as to camouflage her disappointment at being dismissed. Then she saw the blonde lurking on the sun porch at Los Amigos Café, sipping coffee, face turned sunward, gaze glued to Chess's machinations. Hurt and fury propelled Holly into the lift car, and fear of those emotions accompanied her climb to the top of the mountain.

Chapter Seventeen

Chess and Lance were the first to arrive at Holly's. She greeted them fresh from the shower. Her scrubbed face shone makeup-free, rosied by the early spring sun, her natural beauty intense enough to make Chess ache. A hot-pink ribbon caught her damp hair in a kinked ponytail high at her crown. Ringlets had already escaped around her temples and on the back of her marble-smooth neck.

An oversized, cropped pink sweater exposed her lean, brown middle, and second-skin shiny white leggings she could only have found in the preteen department sheathed her legs. Cute summed it up. Damned cute, as usual, until she opened her opinionated, though highly kissable mouth. Yet, he had to admit, now and then jewels of commercial wisdom tumbled from that mouth. The difficulty lay in fighting an urge to acknowledge her offering, thereby modifying his Xtreme agenda, prolonging it. Maybe indefinitely.

When Holly returned to buzzing around her food-strewn kitchen, Chess helped himself to an unescorted house tour while Lance watched an Avalanche game in the study. The room containing a big-screen television apparently had belonged to Jules. And still did, Chess reminded himself.

Masculine trappings underlined by framed sales awards, golf and fishing trophies, a scuffed and scarred leather chair, a standing ashtray hosting a well-chewed Sherlock Holmes pipe, proclaimed as much. Visited with a ghostly sensation, Chess spent little time in the room before heading down a long hall he hoped would lead to Holly's bedroom. Her Doberman, Angel, tagged his heels.

When he stood in the doorway, mission accomplished, the massiveness of the space impressed him foremost. Especially when compared to Holly's diminutive stature. This imposing scale followed the general structure of the old house.

Angel leaped gracefully onto the elaborately dressed bed and curled her sleek body into a contented ball. He visualized Holly swamped in the big bed, tossing, reaching out to emptiness. The probability of her loneliness, based on his own nocturnal ordeal, rumbled around in his mind. An intimate vision of Holly and Jules, the phantom in the picture she kept on her desk, settled behind his eyes, irritating raw nerve endings like fingernails on a chalkboard, forcing him to turn away from the bed.

He moved to a bookcase between two leaded-glass windows to examine the contents. If they were not decorator's props, she read the classics, from Homer to Hemingway, and had threaded her way through an impressive number of bestsellers. He noted Nicholas Evans's *The Horse Whisperer* on her night table. A smile tugged his sun-chapped lips. Did the novel represent Holly's idea of a western?

Her taste in music, according to the crowded shelf of alphabetically filed compact discs, ran from opera and new age to rock, heavy on vintage Eric Clapton. No Vince Gill or Garth Brooks allowed. He imagined gnashing teeth, dark eyes snapping intolerantly should she ever be subjected to his favorites on the sixty mile round trip between Sol y Sombre and Xtreme. Not a likely possibility. He pivoted on a boot heel and went toward a door he imagined would lead to a closet.

Opposite an elongated rack housing Holly's adolescent-size wardrobe hung the most impressive display of men's clothing Chess had ever encountered, Cerruti and Hugo Boss be damned. Shirts, jackets, slacks, suits, overcoats. A perfectly color-coordinated assortment arranged in that order, waited for the owner's reclamation. An extravagant number of shoes, perfectly aligned by style and color, waited for the master of the house to step back into them, just as the mistress apparently awaited his re-entry in her life.

Knowing for certain, now, what he had only feared, Chess turned from the proof of his discovery and went toward the sound of the party, his goals for Xtreme reaffirmed.

Confusion and conflict flooded Holly when Chess strolled into the crowded kitchen. After the pains he had taken to ignore her on the slopes, she had not expected him tonight. Lance's presence was an even bigger surprise.

As she dished crepes onto a warming platter, observing Chess and Sally's animated conversation, for the hundredth time, she envisioned the blonde who had waited for him on Los Amigos' sunporch. Catching her own dusky reflection in the steel range hood, she thought of Robyn, hearing Lance's divulgence of his cousin's propensity for blondes.

Chess, who had migrated to the sitting area of the country kitchen, bent from the waist to stoke the ebbing fire, his form nicely etched against leaping flames. Holly imagined cowboy elves employed for the sole purpose of pounding his Levi's in a rocky creek bed to get that perfect faded and frayed effect. Then they were shrunk to perfectly mold his hips and thighs so her eyes would be drawn where they had no right to be looking.

When he straightened and turned, his gaze catching hers, she experienced another of those irrational leaps in her midsection. He smiled like a cat, a flaxen Siberian tiger about to pounce on his prey, then turned away when Toby tapped his shoulder.

Holly clattered plates and flatware onto the counter. In her side vision, Chess focused his attention on Toby, leaning a shoulder against the mantle as though it were a corral fence, thumbs hooked into his waist, directly above his pockets. His extended fingers drew Holly's eyes downward. Heady desire sluiced through her, then popped out to dampen her flushed brow.

"Dinner is served," she called shrilly enough to cause Toby's head to snap around, a knowing smile escaping.

Once satisfied her guests were fed, Holly gave in to her helpless urge and went in search of Chess. In the formal living room, a group gathered in a circle before a second fire, but she found Chess at the far end of the room, alone at her French desk, as though assuming the throne of command. Angel curled at his feet, her chin resting on one boot. Somehow, the feminine nature of the desk complemented Chess's masculine grace, the amber glow from the desk lamp highlighting his sexuality like an aura.

He glanced up at her footfalls on the oriental carpet, making a move to stand, but she motioned him down.

"You did good." He nodded at his plate, wiping his lips with a pink napkin. "You look right at home in the kitchen. Maybe you missed your calling." His lazy drawl contrasted a distinct tension around his mouth. That stirred her curiosity, maybe even her sympathy, but failed to erase her pique over his cleverly camouflaged refusal to ski with her.

"Today's woman has many callings." The taunting edge of her voice betrayed her. Hands full, she hooked a ballerina slipper around a chair leg and dragged the chair to the desk. "Women are up to the challenge of multiple callings. In fact, we employ our female strengths to outdo one another."

"Unfortunately, you don't always compete with women."

Her hairline tickled as she thought of the blonde in the catsuit. "Oh, women no longer bother to compete with men. Winning over them is a lay down. Pun intended."

He held her gaze, let the silence build until she realized she was out of line and had to fight the urge to apologize for her bitchy attack.

Finally he spoke. "I'm a pragmatist. I've seen people— even the weaker sex—screw up everything they set out to accomplish, by stretching too thin."

"The opposite seems to be true for you." She took a bite of chicken crepe, washed it down with Jordan Chardonnay.

"I'm a man, sugar. I can stretch and reach farther. God made us that way."

In truth, he was an improbably beautiful, cynical, chauvinist bastard. No getting around it. She wished to God she were big and strong enough to pound that infuriating arrogance out of him. As long as it remained intact, her longing for him would go unrequited.

"What's your opinion of today's outing?" she asked.

He put down his fork and flexed his shoulder muscles. "I'm sore as hell. How about you?"

"Hotdoggers don't get sore." Somewhere she found a smile.

He sipped wine, his stormy eyes narrowed, pinning hers over the glass rim. "Today showed me our designs need work."

One brow eased upward, as she urged calmly, "Why do you say that?"

He shrugged, pushing his plate away. "I spent most of the day observing the competition's product."

The dreaded image of the blonde's skin-on-a-sausage suit imploded in Holly's mind like a blown-out tire, snapping the thread of tension thickening inside her since early morning. Since last night's phone call. "Did you research beyond your friend's K-Mart catsuit?" His faintly pitying look said she was out of line, but she couldn't seem to stop. "Catsuits were last year's news."

He hesitated a moment before warning quietly, "Hidden snaps are about to be this year's news. We're going to zippers. Big, brash, gold ones, with an abstract X for the pull. Xtreme signature zippers."

He had done in-depth planning while she skied alone and then cooked crepes for her followers who were slowly, but steadily, switching over to his camp. She shook her head, pushing back her own plate. "No zippers." She sensed sudden quiet at the opposite end of the room where the majority of the staff made up an audience. "The elegance of design needs no adornment."

He smiled, eyes maddeningly tolerant. "I think your problems might stem from believing your own propaganda, sugar."

"I wasn't aware I had a problem."

She might as well not have spoken. "We're going to play up the man's angle more in the coming season. Women will follow suit. No pun intended. Just predicting the ongoing scramble for equalization." He offered a disarming smile, leaning forward in his chair, warming to the debate. "Men hate fumbling with snaps. They like zippers."

"That's because they're always looking for an opportunity to lower them," she said quietly. "Convenience and brevity are major considerations with men."

He sank back in the chair. "For God's sake, Holly. We're talking design. Can we just keep our eyes on the ball here?"

Angel started and whined as Holly came forward in the chair, folding her arms on the desktop, forgetting to lower her voice. "Balls, don't you mean? Since that's what your proposed design change is obviously all about. The balls and brains debate."

Too late, Holly sensed their audience's reaction to her unlowered voice. Tension, like electricity, flashed through the room, tightening skin, raising short hairs, and freezing breath. She caught Sally's warning glance.

Chess swung his boots to her polished desk, crossed one ankle over the other. Inwardly, she fidgeted beneath his unwavering gray gaze, felt its probing power. "Well, now that you brought it up, darlin', our women's line needs work. It's garish. Puts me in mind of hookers."

He might as well have struck her. Design and her identity were synonymous. She thought of what she stood to lose. Or had she already lost?

"I'm sure you've researched that market thoroughly."

Deadly silence assured her she had hit a nerve. Finally, he shoved to his feet, sending Angel scrambling.

"Hell's bells," he mumbled.

Sudden desire to hurl herself into his arms and plead forgiveness for her bitchiness jolted her. Yet hurting more, she twisted the serrated edge of the blade she had injected. For his ears only, she whispered into the thick silence. "Someday you'll go too far, cowboy. Hopefully you'll stay there."

Bewildering her, he lifted her discarded wineglass, placed his lips on the imprint of hers and drained the contents, but she caught his troubled expression just before she walked away.

Only tenacity kept tears at bay until the house emptied and she voiced her painful confusion in her journal. Then she cuddled Angel against her, warding off the loneliness of the big empty bed, and cried herself to sleep.

Chapter Eighteen

Chess dropped Lance off at his cabin, did a quick check of the grounds to satisfy himself all paddocks were sufficiently latched and premises secure. Then he let himself into Adam's outside entry.

Hearing the even breathing in darkness interrupted only by the sliver of moonlight through the window, Chess crossed the room and lowered his form gingerly beside the bed. A hand to the forehead assured him Adam's temp was down. Apparently, the recurring aches and pains had subsided, just as Do Thi claimed when Chess had called home on the way back from Vail. He had hated like hell to leave Adam out of the ski outing and hated going to Holly's party more, leaving him alone for the evening. Hindsight intact, he considered the volatile party scene. He should have adhered to his antisocial nature, made his excuses and come home.

He crossed to the window, cranked it open a fraction, then stayed there. Braced by one forearm, he surveyed the grounds and stables, lost in reflection.

A hell of a day. First, Adam turning up too sick to go. Then Do Thi had reported him sneaking off, even though he felt like hell, to talk to some guy down by the gate—staying there, until she'd gone after him in Chess's Corvette. Who the hell was the guy, and how did it affect Adam's claim to be orphaned?

On top of this curious dilemma had come news of the dollar fluctuating on the international market, a minor detail that could turn Chess's fortune from grand to mediocre in a matter of days. The three-day President's weekend robbed him of a course of action other than worry. How would the downturn in the dollar affect his decision to sink enough extra capital into Xtreme to secure the new warehouse lease he had committed to?

And damn it all, he'd taken his concerns out on Holly. Because of the asinine way he'd baited her, their clash had crossed the T in trouble, as far as days go.

He put off examining the residual effect of the fight and thought of her house, what it revealed. He'd never seen a more inviting home. Masculine appeal with feminine influence. How would she like to try her hand at redoing the ranch house, get Robyn's stamp off it? But why? He could hire that done, not that she would consider it in his lifetime, anyway.

Holly Harper represented an amazing piece of work, an ultrasonic alarm system set to go off if he blinked. Just as Lance had said, she was giving him a test he couldn't even consider failing. Winning was paramount, so why did he feel like an ogre for baiting her tonight, for loving and hating her rage?

At last he let himself face the cut-and-dried situation. He wanted to get Holly's unpredictable volatility beneath him, ride her and gentle her, expose the priceless spirit and beauty she kept hidden behind all that frustration. He could do it, too. He saw evidence in her telltale eyes. She needed it, wanted it, whether or not she realized. But a barbed-wire fence might as well stretch between them, one capable of tearing irreparable wounds. The barrier bore Jules Efron's name and face. Even though Holly claimed she chose to think of him as dead, Chess lacked assurance of that. He sure as hell wasn't sure Jules was dead. He probably never would be sure.

Based on that conclusion, he had no choice but to disregard his desire for Holly, do his time and get the hell out of Xtreme.

In the middle of the night, he welcomed a revelation.

Holly's tirade was symptomatic, based not on his suggested—dictated—design change, but on the blonde in the catsuit. Finally, startling realization of Holly's jealousy afforded him a long-overdue night of restful sleep. The next morning, not quite trusting the significance of his nocturnal conclusion, he tucked the knowledge into his psyche, hiding it like a rare jewel he would unwrap and examine later.

Chapter Nineteen

The moment Chess and Warrior stepped into Xtreme's darkened reception area, Warrior's ears pricked, his tiny muscular body tensing. Chess locked the door behind them, watching the Chihuahua from the corner of his eye, attuned to his low rumbling growl.

"Stay," Chess whispered, also freezing.

Distant, high-pitched whining floated on the quiet and lodged in his awareness. Angel? He turned, scrutinized the parking lot through the glass storefront, spotting neither Holly's car, nor any he recognized. Still, it sounded like Angel, and if she was here, Holly had to be, as well.

He rehashed the night before: Holly leaning on the desk, stiffened arms framing her beautiful breasts, perfect emphasis for the upbraiding she had issued. He scooped Warrior up, held the warm trembling body against his chest, fighting the urge to turn on his heel and avoid the issue.

As he stood there listening to a thin, clanging sound he couldn't identify, along with the distinctive rustle of nylon, his curiosity won. He crossed the ghostly order-entry domain and proceeded down a long narrow corridor to the executive area, carrying Warrior, sneakers silent on the tile floor.

Holly didn't wear signature perfume, but there was no need. Her signature fury wafted out when he rounded the corner and appeared soundlessly in the open door to the conference-showroom. Abruptly, he understood Angel's pitiful whine and Warrior's empathetic trembling.

The clanging sound he'd heard proved to be Holly ripping hangers from the sample display, as Chess watched her do now. An escalating mound of samples on the floor produced the rustling noise. He wanted to laugh when she stomped the last hot-lime discard with a hiking boot, but regret and a strong desire to appease her quashed the urge. He placed Warrior on the floor, watched him race beneath Angel and sniff her sex with tail-wagging joy.

"Holly?" He advanced into the room.

Holly whirled, her name reverberating in her temples heart racing, rage burning like flash fire. Their eyes met and clung. Intent on her mission, she reached for a lipstick-red-trimmed-in-silver jacket, jerked it off the hanger and tossed it on the floor. Somehow she managed to restrain stomping the garment. "What are you doing here?"

He came forward, breaching her space, her anger and hurt. "I didn't see your car. How'd you get here?"

"I walked."

He looked down at her shorts, bare legs and slouch socks.

One of those touted Denver days that could follow on the heels of a blizzard had boosted temperatures into the sixties, melting last night's storm residue with incubator warmth. She had set a new record, hiking furiously in hopes of burning off frustration. And failed. "I want to know what you're doing here."

"Shouldn't I be here?"

"It's Sunday, for God's sake." Was nothing sacred? She reached for a blurred, electric-blue something on the rack, but he moved in and clamped her wrist. She struggled. He held on. Frustration mounted as her warring emotions raged. She considered kicking him—better yet kneeing him—rendering debilitating damage.

"I needed a file." He nodded to the pile of discards on the floor. "What is it, Holly? What's wrong?"

She laughed bitterly. "Obviously, I'm making room for your zipper fetish. But I suggest the zipper pulls should be replicas of cowboy boots, not Xs for Xtreme."

"You're taking this personally. It's not. It's business."

"Of course." She wrestled away from him, turned her back, managing to rake a purple windshirt with her. She clutched the item, biting her lip, tasting blood. Angel's sympathetic whine brought the senseless threat of tears that congealed into a throat lump. Disgusted by her weakness, she groaned loudly, kicked senselessly at the stack of clothes on the floor. Her foot snarled, and she pitched forward. She landed on her knees, yawing sideways onto her folded calves. Angel raced forward, Warrior on her heels, insinuated her body between Holly and the floor, and licked her face.

Chess moved behind her now, so close she could feel his presence. She sensed his overpowering body lowering, his warmth, the scent of dried sweat on the workout clothes he wore— not wood-spice cologne, but headier. Dizzying. The smell penetrated her senses. Then his arms went around her, crossing over her breasts from behind. She squirmed. He dropped one arm to circle her waist and drew her to him, clamping her against an erection scarcely harnessed by knit-jersey coach's shorts.

She gasped as raw sexual heat swept through her.

Ceasing to struggle, she gave Angel a warning look, then looked over her shoulder, searching. Desire curled through her, as sinuous as smoke. His palm splayed across her stomach to draw her against him more tightly. His other hand cupped a breast. His eyes fogged, then stormed with desire she abruptly realized she had hoped for. Coveted. Craved.

He smiled, the expression so sweet, so appealing she felt a stranger was mauling her. "Right, sugar. You're driving me crazy. You didn't know that?"

She shook her head.

"I don't give a damn about that blonde. I want you."

He relinquished her breast to plunge a hand into her hair, to twist her head around until their mouths met. His unshaven chin chaffed hers, pricking and searing. His lips were full, moist, his tongue hot and deliberate. Jagged, delicious pain jetted along a path from her mind, through her torso, and settled in the cove between her thighs. She swiveled to face him. Moaning against his mouth, she rose to her knees and aligned her body to his, squirming against his rigid sex. Her arms circled his waist, molding her to him. His hands framed her throat. Thumbs beneath her chin, he tilted back her head, his mouth working hers, his tongue matching the pulse in his groin.

She pulled back.

How could this be happening? How could she resent a man so much and want him so badly? Arousal and misgiving grappled for control, twisting, shoving inside her. Then she remembered his resigned smile earlier, heard the echo of declared want that matched her own bewildered craving. She moved her mouth to his, seeking to relieve the churning at the core of her soul.

He tugged her sweatshirt from the band of her shorts, both hands diving beneath to search, find and caress. She broke the kiss and sat back from him, shocked and gratified by the intent in his eyes. His smile put her in mind of a child who had gotten his undeserved way.

He caught her shirt by the hem and worked it over her head. None too gently, he peeled it from her arms and flung it away. His hands about her waist, he lifted her as if she were weightless and buried his face against her breasts, faint feral noises escaping the back of his throat. Just as quickly, he lowered her. His hands found the camouflaged front clasp of her bra as easily as if it housed a homing device. He ran splayed fingers from the erratic pulse in her throat, downward, forefingers trailing through her deep cleavage before his hands parted to caress her breasts. Passion spanned pleasure to pain.

"God, Holly, you're beautiful." His hushed, husky voice held a reverence unheard before. His eyes were satiated, mellow, yet sheathed in desire.

He stripped off his shirt, revealing a sleek, muscled chest crowned by amber fleece that lined his breast bone, circled his nipples, brush stroked his hard stomach and trailed behind the band of his shorts. She stared at his bulging crotch as she reached to savor a thicket of burnished gold curls covering a muscular forearm.

When she moved against him, he lowered her onto the stack of rustling nylon, his facial muscles taut, his smoldering gaze raking her bared body. His hand explored inside the loose leg of her shorts, then ran down the back of her thigh to grasp her calf and tuck her leg over his hip. His erection gouged her stomach. He kissed her deeply, purposefully as his hand worked her canvas belt, tugged the snap open at the waist of her shorts. The sound of her zipper lowering tapped some distant concern she lacked the will to explore, allowing her to ignore ensuing doubt. She heard his shorts unsnap, felt him shove them down, then ease back from her, breaking their embrace.

Jarred back to her senses, she opened her eyes and lay back, watching him balance on an elbow to search his back pocket until he came up with a thin leather wallet. Her eyes seized on the telltale ring etched beneath fine, smooth leather. Guilt, shame, and a dozen other emotions twisted in her chest, tightening around her lungs like tentacles.

She reared onto her elbows, chest heaving. "What are you doing?"

One brow quirked. He smiled that lazy, tantalizing smile. "Hush and I'll let you help me."

Reality as caustic as poison penetrated her reason. She tightened every muscle against the desire to let go, to give in. Her belly quivered, the juncture below aching. What the hell had possessed her to lie down with a man who dangled her future off the end of his whims? Why was she giving in to a hunger kept buried for seven years? Giving in for what? Less resistance toward Chess Baker's schemes?

Her forced-down need, her craving, turned her chest into an overinflated balloon. Pressure closed her throat, pushed hard at the backs of her eyes, dizzying her. When she tried to sit up, he pushed her back gently, the wallet clasped in his hand. His mouth, sweet, wet, coaxing, claimed hers. She went rigid.

Even as desire rose beast-like inside Chess, Holly's sudden resistance penetrated his senses, allowing him to half release her. She lay small and delicate beneath him, her breasts flattened against his chest with every sharp breath. High color mottled her sculpted cheeks. Heat seared his veins and pooled in his groin. He wanted her sleek, bare legs wrapped around him, wanted to watch her face, her eyes, when he filled her, wanted her in a way he had wanted no woman since Robyn.

"You thought of everything, didn't you?" she breathed.

"What are you talking about?"

She worked her hand up, seized the wallet and ran her thumb over the raised circle within the leather, her eyes chastising. "You're a machine if you fear commitment this much."

In his distracted state, grasping her meaning was difficult. "There are factors other than pregnancy to consider, sugar."

"Is that what you think of me? That I roll around on

floors with any man who comes along for recreation?" Her eyes flashed. "Who are you protecting? You or me?"

Recalling his actions the first couple of years after Robyn left, he told himself the condom was for Holly's benefit, but suddenly separated from his carnal goal, he began to understand what had happened. In his reckless need, he had ignored common sense and coerced her to do the same. She had regained equilibrium sooner than he, but chose to blame her recovery from passion on his thwarted attempt at safe sex.

Regardless of who had recovered first, the issue was Jules.

She squirmed, but he pinned her, raked his palm over her brow, and smoothed back her kinky black hair. "I'll protect both of us, Holly. This won't happen again. You have my word."

Her eyes quickened, then acquiesced as she turned her head to the side, the fight gone from her. He moved off her, adjusted his clothing and looked around for hers as Angel and Warrior moved in, sensing their restored rights.

He found her bra. She swiveled from the waist, turning her back to slip into it. In the intense pall, he heard the plastic hook engage. She shrugged her sweatshirt over her head and scrambled to her knees, eyes accusing still.

He grasped her beneath the arms and rose, bringing her up with him. His gaze holding hers, he snapped her shorts and buckled her belt with finality. Then, aching, he ducked his head to kiss her. Tenderly, he moved his lips on hers, seducing her into softening, responding. A selfish act, but he had battled for his mind, his soul, in a war he'd lost the day he walked through Xtreme's front door.

He had to know he hadn't imagined she wanted him, too.

She whimpered in denied need. Satisfied, he released her and pulled on his shirt, his eyes averted. He scooped up Warrior and left the room, a vision of Holly standing amidst the zipperless ski apparel engraved on his conscience.

In her office, Holly shakily rolled her chair close enough to prop her hiking boots on the desk. Head pressed to the back of the chair, eyes closed, she stroked Angel's sleek head, listening to the ghostly creak of the building. Angel whined.

"I'm all right, baby," she crooned, wanting the words to seep into her own intellect and erase the void within. "I almost let that cowboy rope me in, but I recovered my senses."

Her anger over the condom had been irrational, but he had flaunted his pragmatism in the face of her seven years of abstinence, enraging her. Seven empty years, in which she had continued taking birth control pills in anticipation of just such an attraction as she felt for him. She wanted and needed to be loved without stipulation; his caution had pushed her over the edge of logic. The powerful magnet that jerked them together had been restrained by his machinations.

Still, she had reacted illogically.

She touched her lips with her fingertips, then tried to banish the memory of Chess's skillful mouth. She crossed her arms and tucked her hands beneath her armpits, powerless not to relive the look in his eyes when he caressed her, or her desire for him. Stopping their coupling, ending the insanity, had been almost more than she could do.

"Love of any nature is a woman's worst option," she whispered. "Remember you heard that from me, Angel."

When she arrived home, her voice mail contained the promised message from Henry Chastain.

"Sorry, Mrs. Efron. Just as I feared, that report on your

husband didn't hold water. Some guy who looked like him, okay, but not him. I'll keep trying. You call me, or the missus, if you feel like talking."

Helplessly, Holly thought of Chess again, rethinking the greatly overrated virtue of restraint.

Chapter Twenty

On Tuesday Chess paced the floor of his Ruidoso A-frame. Beyond a mammoth expanse of glass, a wailing blizzard matched his agitation. Majestic Sierra Blanca Peak towered in the distance, but the storm and darkness denied him the normally calming view of the mountain range.

He checked his watch. Five past one in the morning—or more significant, five past eight, London time. Where the hell was Peder Andrews? Finding him never presented a problem when Chess wanted to add money to—

The cordless phone in his robe pocket jingled. He jerked it out and stabbed the talk button. "Chess Baker."

"Good morning, Mr. Baker. Crown Equities returning your call. I have Mr. Andrews on the line." Then she crooned, "One moment, please."

The chipper, but proper, English dialect did little to soothe Chess's nerves. Waiting, he padded barefoot across the cold wooden floor to his desk and replaced the cordless with the desk phone just as a voice came on the line.

"Peder Andrews, here. Is that you, Chess?"

Although he had never met the man or seen his picture, Chess kept an imaginary likeness in his mind: gray hair, blue eyes, milky skin, steel-framed glasses and bow tie. A banker's image. "It's me. How're you doin'?"

"Up a bit early, hey?" Heavy on the "t," "hey" dangling.

"Actually I haven't seen the sack yet. That's next on the agenda. What can you tell me, Pete?"

"How's that? Tell you about what?"

Chess waited.

Peder finally said, "About the dollar, you mean?"

Knowing Peder had understood the question all along affirmed Chess's concern. "That's what I mean."

"Not to worry, old boy. These trends can turn back as quickly as they start up." The matter-of-fact tone gave Chess an added image of Peder shuffling papers, lining up a day of playing God with other people's money. Then came the hedge. "Or at least, not to worry yet."

Months back, Peder had employed assertiveness in persuading Chess to put the majority of his offshore bankroll into foreign currencies, betting the dollar would appreciate. The strategy had appealed to Chess's patriotism, but now, instead of that assertiveness, he detected an edge of doubt in Peder that turned his gut to sandpaper. He tried shutting off the kaleidoscope of commitments he had made, and continued to make, to Xtreme. Commitments necessary to protect his initial investment. He had swum too far into a raging stream to turn around; he had to keep swimming for high ground.

A vision of Holly on her back, staring up at him, tangled with dollar signs, the thwarted use of a condom whose shelf life had probably expired anyway, and a vain vision of ripping up already signed contracts and leases. Beyond the window, wind howled. A wall of heavy glass waved like an American flag on Election Day.

"Chess?"

"I'm here. Just thinking."

"If you're concerned, I can take you out now. Put you

into something other than currency."

"At a loss." Unanimous with the way his life had been drifting as of late.

"Well, yes."

"What do you recommend? Stay in or take the hit and run?" Why ask? The verdict was his, no one else's. Life always came down to that.

"I'm afraid that's your decision."

Afraid? "And it's my money, but let's play 'what if?' If it were your money, what would you do?" Ninety days ago, Peder Andrews had been willing—eager—to play this game.

"It's not my money, Mr. Baker."

Interesting shift in manner and tone. Chess waited, putting the ball in Peder Andrews's court. A phone buzzed, ripping the staid British background.

Andrews cleared his throat. "I recommend you wait it out. Ignore the loss for now. It's only a paper loss until you cash in. It might prove quite handy, come April fifteenth."

For the first time since Las Vegas, Chess thought of Koichi Mihatsu. The little man's lecture on America's fascination with paper profits echoed in Chess's mind. Normally, slow-playing a loss wouldn't merit such agonizing consideration, but that was before Xtreme had sapped any normality from his life.

"Okay," he said at last. "Let it ride, but fax a full accounting of assets to my Ruidoso number."

He hung up. Feet propped on the desk, he hugged his chest, head tucked onto his shoulder, inviting sleep. He shivered from the nearness of the icy window, but anything beat taking his turmoil to the even colder empty bed awaiting him.

The next afternoon, Chess stood outside Apache's stall

with his trainer, Wayne Chino. Man and horse watched a curvy redhead representing Ruidoso Downs Racing Relations strut the length of the barn toward the exit. Lush hips swayed within the sack of a long wooly sweater topping girdle-tight red stirrup pants. Apache snorted, pawed ground and tossed his head, tugging a laugh from Chess. He stroked the elegant muzzle, then scratched behind the steed's ears.

The trainer eyed Chess. "Well, that gal's pissed."

"She sure as hell is." Damn it.

Wayne shoved callused hands in his front pockets, rocked a little on manure-crusted boots. "How'd you rationalize turning down that tour of The Museum of the Horse, guided by no less than last year's Miss Ruidoso?"

"I've got things to do."

"When'd you change your mind?"

"About what?" Chess hiked a brow, knowing.

Wayne spit a brown stream, raked hay over the mess. "About Jeanie. I watched you prime her pump when you were through here last week. All's you had left to do this trip was to pull the handle."

Exactly what he had intended when he left Denver on the heels of Sunday's fiasco with Holly. Somehow, when he faced the artfully painted, perfume-doused statuesque redhead, the need to assuage his ego had waned. He shrugged. "I guess my theory on mixing sex and business clicked in."

Wayne's brow corrugated in turn. "What theory?"

"Don't, under any circumstances. Women can even screw up a wet dream."

"Is that one of them oxy-moron statements?"

Chess laughed. "What's the story on Apache? Is he coming around?" Apache had won his heart by going lame in the final claiming race last season but missing the show position by only a nose. Adhering to some primal part of his brain that measured a man's worth in horses, Chess bought Apache.

He'd waited all winter to see if gambling on the quarter horse would pay off.

"I haven't had much chance to work him this winter," Wayne grumbled.

"How much of a chance?"

Wayne grinned. "Just enough to let that ankle heal proper. He'll be ready for the Futurity Trials in May. You comin' out?"

Who the hell knew? The way things were going, Apache might be on the auction block by then, along with the stock at Sol y Sombre. Chess crammed the thought back, labeling it over-reaction. Weathering this storm called for no more than getting his ass back to Denver, then keeping it off the show-room floor. He only had to practice the women-and-business theory he bragged about.

And he had to get Holly the hell off his mind.

Chapter Twenty-one

Holly exited the CAD software and shut down the computer. Zippers. She switched off the lamp, braced her elbows on the table and buried her face in her palms. Exhaustion ran across her shoulders, down her spine, but she rallied to dial the phone.

When Janine answered, Holly said, "It's me. Damn it to bloody hell, Chess was right about the zippers. The new designs are extraordinary."

"I thought they might be." Resignation marked Janine's tone.

"If you're going to be there, I'll bring a printout by. I'd like your opinion."

"I'll break out the mocha almond fudge. Yogurt, of course."

"Deal." Holly hung up and scanned the designs again. Zippers. She could win next year's Designer of the Year award, too, and owe it to Chess for opening her eyes.

After last Sunday's wrestling match, continuing the partnership was an impossibility, but she had to give him credit for being right about some things. A lot of things. For one, trimming employees to bare minimum had made Xtreme run like a well-oiled machine, like the man himself. Although not in the black yet, the company had been cleaned up and steered in a new direction she could handle, if she could somehow wrangle Xtreme back from him. Now that her motivation had changed—

She heard a rustle and swiveled her chair to find Sally framed by the doorway and darkened hall beyond. She held two glasses of ice, an ice bucket and a fifth of something that glowed a warm amber color beneath her arm. Holly rose, made it to Chess's side of the desk and sank into his cold empty chair.

"Still at it, sweetie?" Sally progressed to Holly's side of the desk and lowered her burden.

"I thought everyone was gone. Annie's probably waiting for you to bathe kids." Somewhere in her dejection, Holly found a smile.

"What do you mean *probably* waiting?" Sally unscrewed the bottle top, poured Johnny Walker Red without invitation. She looked at a stack of printouts by the computer, then back to Holly, eyes soft. "Seems like Toby would have some time to help you with this design load."

Holly slipped out of her shoes and curled her feet beneath her, tucking her short skirt around her thighs. "She doesn't know CAD and Chess has her scouting Neiman and Saks in her spare time to filch ideas we might incorporate into ski gear." Her throat broadened. She supposed that in his absence, she should amend that to, had her scouting.

Sally passed her a half-filled glass and hiked a hip onto the desk. "Speaking of the beauteous beast, where is he?"

Holly took a long sip of Scotch. She looked at Robyn's picture and the idle laptop, then averted her gaze. "I haven't heard from him."

Sally feigned incredulity. "It's been a week."

"Who's counting?"

Sally guffawed. "Well, is solitude heaven or hell?"

"Both."

"How can that be?"

Holly let the week run through her mind, all the things she had accomplished. Some were life altering. "I love the quiet, the peace, the lack of scrutiny. Reminds me of my pre-Baker days, when I was a naïve but free, take-charge woman."

"I guess you're talking about the heavenly part."

She nodded, took another, longer sip. "I miss him."

"Imagine that."

Holly's throat lump graduated to pain. She smiled around the ache. "I was getting great tips on the market, too. Like learning how to use good ol' boy charm to con brokers out of unattainable stocks. I had just learned what a basket of stocks is, and I was ready to parlay that into independent wealth." She drained the Scotch and reached for the bottle, catching Sally's frown. "The son of a bitch picked a hell of a time to dump me."

"Without reason, too. Cruel, heartless bastard."

Holly closed her eyes, considering all the reasons.

"You want look round?" The small Vietnamese woman, who identified herself as Do Thi, wiped her hands on a brightly flowered apron as she looked anxiously at Holly. "Mr. Chess not mind bit. He be very happy you like house."

Was she so obvious? "Well, maybe a little, while I wait? Are you sure?"

Sparse black brows inched up. "Sure look round?"

"Sure he's coming back."

"Oh, very sure. Come back. He very, very good always come back when get hungry."

She turned Holly, steering her away from the glass-and-leather appointed grand salon where she had camped for the last hour, watching Warrior maul Angel on priceless Persian carpet.

"Start there." Do Thi nodded toward the end of the hall. "Mr. Chess bedroom and study. You much like. Wait see."

Dogs on her heels, Holly made her way down a hall exhibiting a pastel array of southwestern watercolors bearing unfamiliar signatures.

Sol y Sombre, understated on the whole, had been a surprise from the moment the imposing gate halted her, then, when she gave her name, admitted her with a flourish as though she was expected. She had parked her car in visitors' parking out front and walked around the house, where she spotted small gray cabin-like structures dotting the well-kept but unpretentious grounds that surrounded an aging two-story white house. Gray shutters and a carved mahogany door completed the picture. A well-equipped children's playground and a horde of Vietnamese children roaming the grounds with adults, some of whom she recognized from Xtreme, posed the greatest enigma, thus far.

The quarters Do Thi directed her to were roomy and masculine, with a lived-in appearance. An assortment of ill-matched, heavily worn furnishings could be either flea market finds or priceless antiques. Chess Baker was that unreadable. His color preference ran to browns and grays, the window coverings, bed dressing and chair fabrics rough and nubby. A corner housed an intricate weight machine that explained his muscular build in his lean runner's body.

A study small enough to have once been an oversized-closet jutted off the bedroom, offering a view of the stables through an oversized window. The space held an oak roll-top desk topped by state-of-the-art computer equipment. A cabinet filled with books also hosted complicated media equipment. Indian rugs and short, coarse white dog hair decorated a worn suede chair.

As Do Thi had claimed, nothing about Chess's quarters proved unlikable, but Holly's throat pained and her eyes burned. Which did she want most? To flee or to climb between the covers of his turned-down feather bed. She trailed her fingers over a rough linen pillow slip, thinking of the prickly feel of his unshaven face. Her palm stroked a plaid wool blanket as she tried to purge her mind of further imagery.

His doorless bathroom had a beckoning effect. Thirsty black bath towels, a gray flannel robe on the back of the door, a large bottle of Bijan on the vanity, and a horsehair rug on the wooden floor. A double-headed shower and an over-sized black marble tub sported brass fixtures. Imagining the blond woman in the picture on Chess's desk, smiling as she lay back against the sloping tub, Holly turned away.

While the dogs tussled in the center of the bed, she took mental inventory of Chess's bulging bookshelves. Meanwhile she kept a watchful eye on stables and grounds cloaked in a warmish winter day so like that sunny Sunday a week ago.

His taste in literature ran a ragged gamut but leaned heavily toward Elmore Leonard, Tony Hillerman, and Tom Clancy. On the nightstand, she had seen Jack Kerouac. He favored country music, but had a penchant for Linda Ronstadt and movie soundtracks. Jean Claude Van Damme weighed heavily on the extensive movie collection, yet her eyes settled on *Dances With Wolves* and *Sense and Sensibility*. Chess Baker was chameleonic.

Voices echoing on the still day turned her toward the window. From atop a huge brown-and-white spotted horse, Chess leaned sideways to unlatch the corral gate for a companion on a pale horse with blond mane and tail. A big-billed baseball cap hid the stranger's face, but the slender, graceful form, a black ponytail pulled through the back of the cap, and Holly's thudding heart allowed her to identify the figure as a young woman. Shoving down disappointment and resignation, she gave fate credit for making her mission easier.

She pulled on her fleece-lined jacket, slipped out a side door to a wooden porch and stood watching for a moment. Then, with Warrior and Angel butting her calves, interrupting her deliberate stride, she made her way through the late February afternoon toward her astonished host.

Chapter Twenty-two

Loosening Geronimo's saddle cinch, Chess watched from beneath the shadow of his hat as Holly approached wearing a take-no-prisoners expression. The distance prevented him getting an accurate reading other than her purposeful stride and body posture. Should he duck? Or should he follow a powerful urge to throw her kicking and screaming over his shoulder, haul her back through the door she had exited, drop her on his bed, and end the turmoil in his gut and groin.

Reacting typically to any occasion that involved Chess being out of pocket for twenty minutes, Warrior left Holly and raced through the open corral gate. He yelped and zipped around Chess's boots like a pissed-off bee. Chess dropped to his knees and deferred his befuddled reactions from Holly to the Chihuahua. Warrior leaped into his arms, managing to knock the Stetson askew as Chess surrendered to a bath of hot kisses.

Aware that Adam watched curiously while unsaddling his palomino, Chess reset the Stetson low on his brow and massaged the scruff of Angel's neck when she sidled alongside.

The smallest pair of boot-shoes Chess could fathom appeared in his lowered vision, then parted slightly, affecting a sturdy stance in the sandy corral. He released Warrior and stood, meeting Holly's eyes, wondering if memory of last

Sunday reverberated in her mind, too. Searching her face, he found it rosy and glowing, from the rarified winter air, he guessed. He could only hope the flush didn't indicate temper. He hated the thought of Adam watching him get flogged by a banty hen.

When Holly looked at Adam, light flickered within the sable depths of her eyes, then settled into a kind of satisfaction Chess failed to grasp.

She looked back at him, face solemn. "If Mohammed won't come to the mountain..." She shrugged. "The mountain has come to Mohammed."

"I appreciate the gesture, but through my bedroom?"

Her perfectly formed brows arched. "You're not only obstinate, but territorial, I see." Then miraculously, she smiled.

Chess executed a shuffle-step around Warrior, moved back to the Appaloosa to work on the cinch again, eyeing Holly across the horse's broad back. "Do Thi routes all visitors through my bedroom, including the Culligan man and the farrier. I'm just hoping I didn't leave any dirty underwear lying around. As for obstinacy, that's family legacy." He heaved the saddle off Geronimo's back and slung it across the top fence rail. "Nice to see you, Ms. Harper." He grinned over his shoulder, then turned, drawing Adam forward with his eyes.

Adam hiked his own saddle next to Chess's, then removed the ball cap as he approached. Chess hugged the boy's shoulders, sheltering him beneath an arm. "This is Adam Tall Horse. Adam, this is my—"

"Holly Harper." Eyes curious, she extended her hand.

Brandishing a wise-ass smile, Adam cut his obsidian eyes Chess's way, then back to Holly. "You're Chess's partner. I've heard all about it." He shook the offered hand.

Holly drew a line in the dirt with her boot, eyes diverted.

Chess tugged Adam's glossy ponytail, then gave him a gentle shove. "How about putting those saddles away, chief, and tackling that math project we talked about?"

"I need you to help me."

"I've got company. You start, and I'll catch up."

Adam grimaced, then grinned at Holly as though not holding her accountable. "See you later."

"It's nice to meet you." She cast a curious look at Chess before moving to the corral fence and climbing a couple of rungs. Forearms hooked on the top rail, she stared across a pasture of grazing Arabians into the Sangre de Cristos. Skin-tight jeans packaged her backside attractively, and skier's calves bulged when she balanced on the balls of her feet. She had managed to capture her unruly hair at the back of her neck with some kind of band the color of claret. Predictably, worm-like curls inched over the corduroy collar of a denim jacket. He figured she'd made a concession to him and Sol y Sombre with the jeans, even if they boasted a designer label. A nice gesture.

He removed Geronimo's bridle, looped it over the horn of the saddle Adam had left for last and joined Holly. Planting a foot on the lowest rail, he hooked his arms tightly over the rough wood fence to keep his hands off her. That urge—to touch her, and so much more—had almost made him throw away his vow never to mess with another man's wife.

"Where'd you find those?" he said.

She shifted her gaze from the mountain range. "What?"

"Those Barbie Doll jeans."

"I have my sources."

"Well, you're shopping in the right places." When she laughed softly, he urged, "How'd you find the ranch?" And, why? Their gazes, level for once, locked across her shoulder, her eyes sultry.

"I stopped at a nursery in Sedalia—The Garden Patch."

She waited for his nod. "Someone named Karen seemed to know every little twist in the road." Did he hear an accusatory tone? "She was kind enough—"

"Karen does Do Thi's herb pots every year," he offered quickly. "Plus the houseplants." Holly seemed to want more. "And the beds around the house."

"Talented." Her mouth pulled into a smile before she tilted her face to the sun. "It'll soon be that time again, won't it—to plant, I mean."

He took his hat off, ran a hand through his hair, then dangled the battered straw Stetson in his hands. "Don't let a day like today fool you."

"Or you."

He laughed. "What the hell are you doing here, Holly?"

"We'll get to that." She confiscated his hat, turned it in her hands, examining the sweat stain beneath the beaded band. "Scruffy." She squeezed the pattern of the overcreased brim. "Not in keeping with your normally projected character."

When she passed the hat back, he noted the absence of her thin wedding band.

"It's Saturday attire." Donning the object of discussion, he tugged it low over his eyes, then tilted his head to observe her. "What gives, partner? Don't tell me you were in the neighborhood and decided to drop in. Not after our last little scuffle."

She averted her eyes and called, "Hi," as Dihn Quang ambled past, headed for the house. "What is he doing here?" she asked without turning her head. Still smiling, she waved again. "And Suong...and the rest? Who do all those children—"

"They live here."

"In those cabins?" Her tone was incredulous.

"A few adults live in the house—Do Thi's helpers."

"I'm sure Lance lives in the house."

His and Lance's discussions on the subject, and Lance's unrelenting preference, ran through his head. "No. His cabin is the last one on the lane. Close to the drive."

"And Adam?" She cocked a brow.

"He has his own quarters." He motioned. "That addition to the side of the house."

"Is he Native American?"

"Navajo. His Indian name is Shallow River. Shallow River Tall Horse."

"I saw a black man on a mower down by the gate. Are you running a rainbow coalition sanctuary here?"

"Not by design." He shrugged. "It just happened."

She climbed the remaining rungs, twisted lithely to sit on the top rail, her hand briefly grasping his shoulder for balance. Fire shot through his body and settled in his loins. Her eyes mirrored the sensation as she jerked her hand away and gripped the fence. Surreptitiously, she inched her thigh away from where it brushed his forearm.

"Do you want me to keep asking questions?" she asked.

He damned sure did, if that would prolong her stay, regardless of her reason for being here. "The Vietnamese are a long story." He shrugged, watching Adam gracefully hoist the second saddle off the fence and stride across trampled ground to the tack room. "Complicated."

"I'm listening." She waved to another familiar passerby. "Are you hungry?"

"Not as hungry as I am curious."

"I'm starved. On Saturday we serve breakfast at ten. Do Thi gets to skip making lunch in favor of an early supper. Adam and I rode out long before ten." The crease in her forehead deepened, and he realized he'd only confused her further. "How about some lunch in Sedalia? We'll call it breaking bread."

Her head snapped up a little, eyes quickening, but she

almost smiled. "Then you'll answer all my questions?"

"Maybe."

He let go of the fence and reached in one motion, grasped her waist and swung her down. Her belly bumped his semi-hard crotch before her feet touched the ground. She danced backward, slapping imaginary dust from her jeans. He waited for her to settle and look at him.

"Sorry." He grinned.

She looked away, hugging herself.

"Do you like greasy hamburgers?"

"I haven't had one in years."

"That settles it."

"What about Angel?"

He chanced a glance to where Warrior circled the Amazon canine worriedly, seeking a way to mount her. "She's obviously being entertained. Warrior doesn't get many female callers."

"I can see why," Holly murmured dubiously. "I suppose he's harmless."

Chess laughed, drawing her into step beside him. One hand resting lightly on her shoulder, he steered her toward a vintage black Corvette parked next to a clump of naked scrub oak. "Trust me. Unless Warrior locates a ladder in the next couple hours, he's harmless."

As they pulled through the ranch gate onto a two-lane highway, Holly belted into the passenger seat, Chess allowed his father's bankruptcy to nudge his recall. The football scholarship had covered his tuition, but he'd had to sell the 'vette, a high school graduation present, to stay in the fraternity house. Once he was financially secure, he had spent months tracing the car across three states in order to buy it back and restore it. Today, that obsession made sense.

The 'vette had been created to transport Holly to Bud's Bar.

Chapter Twenty-three

When Holly stepped into the bar she blinked rapidly against the sting in her eyes. The anti-smoking movement had yet to make inroads in Colorado ranching country. A blue haze hung over the crowd, along with the pungent scent of burning tobacco, body heat, cheap perfume, spilled beer, and meat frying. Dim lighting revealed a packed room. Thronged shoulder to shoulder at the long bar, circling hackneyed tables, and overflowing booths, patrons laughed and drank, and stuffed themselves.

As they paused inside the door, scouting for seats, Holly was aware of a nearby table of men eyeing her. Then they exchanged looks boys learn in kindergarten and spend their lives honing to perfection. Chess's touch fell lightly on the small of her back. He threaded her through the room to a ragged two-seater booth sharing a corner with a jukebox boasting an out-of-order sign.

A Dolly Parton cloned waitress wearing moccasins, Spandex jeans and a long-sleeved T-shirt lauding the Colorado Nuggets ambled from behind the bar, order pad in hand. Holly noted the woman's ability to maneuver through the crowd without ever taking her blue-shadowed eyes off Chess.

"Hey, Jerri. How's it goin'?"

"Not much has changed since last night," she grunted, eyes surveying Holly on the sly. "You get your cousin home without endin' up in the bar ditch?"

"Yeah. Thanks for calling me." Eyes somber, mouth grim.

Jerri poised the pad. "What'll you have?"

"Hamburger or cheeseburger, Holly? No decision hassles."

"Cheeseburger, hold the beef. A double order of fries."

Chess fished a dilapidated cardboard menu from behind the napkin holder and angled it toward her, forefinger pointing to a bold-print warning: NO FRENCH FRIES DAMMIT!

"Sorry, honey. Thurman—the owner—hates fries. Selfish bastard." He grinned at Jerri as she shifted her weight, sighing.

Flustered by his intimate tone, Holly doubled the cheese on her meatless burger with an acquiescent smile.

"Double burger for me, and two O'Doul's, Jerri." Sliding the menu back in place, he advised Holly, "You have to go through the motions of drinking beer. It's an unspoken rule." He removed the beat-up Stetson and his wool vest, placing them on the dead jukebox. After tousling his string-straight yellow hair vigorously with his palm, he finger-plowed it. "Bad hair day."

He wouldn't live long enough to see a bad hair day. In the week's business hiatus he had cultivated an amber jaw stubble which gave him a more rugged than ragged appearance, and his hair, although always shaggy in back, now played tag with his collar and spilled in long heavy fringe onto his forehead. Chess Baker's unrestrained beauty should be disclaimed as criminal.

His hard leg crowded hers when he stretched to reach into his jeans' pocket to produce a coin. "Heads or tails?"

"I'm not much of a gambler. How about Dutch treat?"

"Not while I'm alive. Heads or tails on who sings first?"
Reading her confusion, he elaborated, "Your reason for the
visit or my multi-ethnic boarder story?"

She stared into a storm cloud of implacable eyes.
"You'll have to sing first. My reason for coming has gotten a
little murky." She had begun to suspect that hearing his tale
might convolute her original aim even more. "Tell me about
Adam."

His eyes warmed, danced a little with uncustomary light.
"He swears he has no family. If I can prove that, I'll try to
adopt him." Reading her curiosity, he explained, "Dealing
with the Bureau of Indian Affairs can be touchy. I've got
Choctaw blood, so I'm hoping...for now, we're keeping a low
profile regarding our plans."

She searched his features for evidence of Indian blood,
settling on olive-hued skin she had assumed resulted from a
predilection toward the outdoors. "How did you find him?"

She could only guess what passed his mind's eye as he
said reverently, "He found me."

"That's all you're going to tell me?"

He smiled. "For now."

"Still my turn?"

He cocked a fist, forefinger jutting out. "Shoot."

"Why do all those foreigners live at Sol y Sombre?"

Jerri swished by, depositing the mock beers on the table.
Chess gave her a quick, engaging smile, then tapped his
sweaty bottle against Holly's.

"I said it was complicated, but it's actually one of those
situations that materialize while you're taking care of other
things."

She waited, sipping O'Doul's.

"Robyn hired Do Thi through a state agency that places
immigrants. A few weeks later, she learned Do Thi's brother

could come over if he had a job waiting."

Holly nodded, smiling, getting the picture.

"The brother turned out to be Dihn. Dihn was engaged to Van." He shrugged, smiling. "Van now works the middle shift at—"

"I know. They've salvaged the damn monogram machine."

He looked pleased. "News that Robyn and I were soft touches traveled fast. All the way to Vietnam, without a hitch. Soon Van's mother showed up, then Dihn's cousin." He shrugged again, made a resigned gesture. "I found jobs for them or put them to work building cabins. You saw that stack of lumber out by the barn?" She nodded and he said, "When we know someone new is being processed, we start building. It all works out."

"We?"

He grinned. "I've been known to drive a nail or two."

"No wonder you wanted to buy into Xtreme. Now you've got all your boarders bringing home paychecks."

With a smile guileless enough to unnerve her, he said, "Yeah, that damned embroidery machine cinched the deal. It came down to Xtreme or trying to get child support out of Robyn."

Jerri reappeared, shoving two paper-lined plastic burger baskets onto the table. She clanked down a small bowl of pickles and onions and dashed away, arms full of Miller Lite.

"No lettuce or tomatoes," Chess apologized.

Holly poked pickles between the buns, into squishy cheese. "So you're crediting Robyn with your benevolent act?"

He lifted the top of his bun, squirted mustard on a patty, then padded the burger with pickles. "She kicked it off."

"You kept them all when she...when you divorced."

He took a bite, eyeing her as he chewed, eyes sobering.

"Maybe I thought she'd hear I'm a nice guy and come back."

A rock formed in Holly's chest. "That's sad."

A smile avoided his eyes. "It was a joke."

Recalling the picture on his desk, she doubted the validity of his comment. With her beer bottle, she sketched a circle on the wooden table, then proceeded like a traveler cautiously setting foot in strange territory. "I'd like to hear about Robyn."

He nodded toward her basket. "Aren't you eating?"

She ripped open a bag of chips and nibbled one, smiling when he donated his unopened bag. "Will you tell me about your marriage?"

Beneath his heavy lashes, his gaze was tornado-dark, but rocksteady. "What do you want to know?"

"Whatever you want to tell me—why it didn't last." There had been a time, not long ago, when she would have sworn she knew why. Now, after what she'd seen today... Affection for Adam, patience with Warrior... His generosity.

He pushed his empty burger basket away. After rummaging in the pocket of his jacket, he placed a small black cigar on the table. With his empty bottle, he signaled the bartender. "We were young and dumb." He unwrapped the cigarillo, put it in his mouth, then spoke through clamped teeth. "Our marriage was like undertaking a Lego project without instructions."

"Don't light that." She kept her voice level, eyes focused.

"I don't carry matches."

His voice poured over her like sun-warmed caramel, but his intense brooding look, and all he had told her, made her think of him as two different men. She wanted to look more deeply behind this new door. "Tell me about it."

He shrugged, sipping new beer. "Robyn and I were Big Man and Big Woman on Campus. Everybody's all American and the queen of everything going. She majored in marketing, ambitious as hell, just like me. I thought we'd have that in common, but she changed after we married. After I made some money."

"How?"

"She quit work, started reading *Southern Living* and *Cosmo*."

"Strange combination."

Pensively, he twisted the signet ring on his finger. "She wanted to make home comfortable enough to get me there and be alluring enough to keep me there. Meanwhile, I read *Barrons* and *Money* magazine. I lived my work—the game, the challenge. The rush. Whatever I got into, I pursued it dawn to midnight. Making money was everything." He shrugged. "Still is, I guess."

She nodded, knowing the power of getting caught up in a goal, even though her case differed from his. She'd been driven by demons from the past. She also knew what guilt felt like, recognized it in Chess's demeanor. Throat closing, heart tumbling like a stone in rapids, she observed a telltale shadow in his eyes as he stared past her shoulder.

"Once we moved to Colorado, to the ranch, Robyn couldn't take the isolation. She left me."

Somewhere Holly had read that workaholics actually aimed at cutting themselves off from relationships, feeling safer to connect to their work than to people. His resigned tone, however, prompted her to forgo the lecture. "It sounds as though you've forgiven Robyn."

"I never forgave her, but I understand. Former Big Women on Campus can't tolerate being ignored." He forced a smile. "I went a little crazy for a while. In South Denver or Douglas County, no unattached woman over the age of eighteen was safe. I guess I thought I had something to prove."

Holly nodded, the last seven years skidding across her mind. She had reacted in the opposite vein. Atrophied. Or so she'd thought. "Because she abandoned you."

He snapped the cigar in half, tossed it into his empty basket. "There was a little more to it than that. Robyn got pregnant when we'd been married a couple of years, but she miscarried. She wanted a baby badly. I did, too. I thought that would pacify her, I guess. When she didn't get pregnant again, I had some tests done." He took a long, pointless drink. "I'm sterile, always have been."

Holly's mind darted to Adam and a thousand other questions.

"Before I calmed down enough to tell Robyn I knew she'd cheated on me, she got pregnant and miscarried again."

"That broke up the marriage," she said quietly.

"Maybe—yeah, I guess. I never told her I was sterile. I just stayed away more. Ultimately, that broke up the marriage."

She covered his hand with hers for an instant, then clasped her hands in her lap. "I'm sorry, Chess."

"I got over it. After my sexual binge, I had an HIV test and cleaned my act up—started taking precautions."

"Where did the urge to change come from?"

"Adam." His reverent tone underlined the name. "He gave me reason to stop feeling sorry for myself and take responsibility."

She found a smile. "You take your white knight image seriously, cowboy."

He folded his arms over his chest, cocked his head and eyed her with a familiar insolence. "So, you see, you had nothing to fear from me last Sunday. As Shakespeare put it, 'Mine honor is my life. Take it from me, and my life is done.' "

She shook her head. "I wasn't afraid. I was angry." Their gazes collided, serving up a mixture of good and bad memory. "I don't know what happened to me."

"You don't? I sure as hell do." His eyes bored into hers.

Again she examined last Sunday's anger. It had stemmed from his assumption that she indulged in a lifestyle opposite what she had chosen. She had no history of sexual encounters and no string of past lovers, such as he spoke of, from which to draw experience. Just Jules, and intimacy hadn't been enough to keep them together. She feared leaving herself vulnerable again. Chess Baker, a true chameleon, capable of changing at will, was not a man to rely on. "I don't know how it happened, but it can't happen again."

"That's my line."

"We're like oil and water."

He gave her his honed Earl of Arrogance smile. "If you throw a match on that combo it burns like hell."

Until it burns out. "Nevertheless, I expect you to keep your promise."

A muscle pulsed in his jaw; his mouth tensed. "Your turn to sing." His tone backed up his expression.

For a moment, she debated revealing the era of her marriage to him, even in fairness for what he had shared. Part of her wanted to withhold the past, the same way she guarded her body and emotions. Yet part of her wanted him to know.

"It's a simple story. I came to Colorado to pursue my passion. Skiing. Jules lived here. He was an old friend of my father—Jewish. I married him for all the wrong reasons. Maybe those reasons are why he left me." She watched Chess's jaw harden, saw his eyes cloud empathetically. "Jules has been declared legally dead. I could have done it weeks ago, but—"

"Legally dead?" His eyes quickened.

"I couldn't find a solid reason, and I kept thinking he'd come back. Then when we—after last Sunday—I realized I've been waiting too long. I'm alive and too young to be loyal to a man who's either dead or wants me to think so." Whether Jules had left her or gotten himself killed, she had waited long enough.

Chess shredded half the discarded cigar into the basket. "Tough decision, I guess. Like filing for divorce, maybe."

"It is a divorce. The marriage is legally over, too, just as when the death of any spouse occurs."

His eyes narrowed. "If he does come back, what then?"

"We're no longer married. We never will be again, even if he comes back." She sat back against the tattered booth, gripped the table edge. "This may sound ghoulish, but I'm in the mood to celebrate."

"I'll buy you a glass of cheap wine," he offered quickly. "Bud's Bar has the guaranteed cheapest and worst."

She nodded and watched him work out of the cramped booth, saunter to the bar, order and start back. With self-will, her eyes took in his worn Levi's. Faded at the crotch, they fit his frame snugly, clinging to his thighs like a bad reputation. His shirt looked old and soft from many washings, the flannel appearing fragile against his rugged body. She forced her eyes away as he slid back into the booth, set a short tumbler of pale yellow liquid before her, and clicked glasses.

"To freedom," he murmured, taking a healthy drink. "No regrets, though? No second-guessing, like I did my divorce. Still do sometimes."

"No regrets. The marriage was in trouble when he left. Maybe that's why—"

"What kind of trouble? If you feel like telling me."

She embraced the memory. "Subtle trouble. When I made the bed in the mornings, my pillow was always hanging off the bed on my side, his next to it. In the night, I'd pulled away and he had chased me."

Chess smiled indolently, nodding. "Yeah?"

"Jules is—was—twenty-three years older. That's not old, really, but we were developing different needs, ones we never discussed."

"Different needs sounds familiar. I hope you—good luck, Holly, with what life hands you." He tapped her glass again. "If you can drink that wine, sweetheart, you're tough enough to face whatever comes along."

Holly drained the glass.

—◦❖◦—

Back in the car, Chess mulled over what Holly had told him about Jules. The legal action she'd taken had made her husband's death official, but no more real. She evidently felt the same, since she continued holding Chess to the pledge he'd made while she lay half naked in his arms. She wanted a platonic relationship, and he would do his damndest—

"You asked why I came here today."

A mini blizzard had developed while they'd eaten. He chanced taking his eyes from the road to look at her wordlessly.

"I came to tell you—beg if I had to—I wanted out of the partnership. No matter what it took."

He cocked a brow. "You've changed your mind?"

"Yes."

"Why?" He felt the car fishtail and jerked his gaze back to the road, easing into another vehicle's deep tracks.

She relinquished a smile. "You aren't what you pretend, Chess Baker. Any woman would be crazy not to want you for a partner."

He grinned. "I'm not sure which is the real me, but I put on my black hat every morning before I pull out of the Sol y Sombre gate. You know that old saying about the best defense being a tough offense. It's a hard world out there."

"The offense theory worked for me, too, until you came along."

"Well, God made men tougher, honey. What can I say?"

Mild irritation marred her calm demeanor, but she spoke without ire. "I've thought of going public and it's what I want. I owe Jules nothing now, and I trust my ability and your expertise to protect my father's investment." She stared out the window for a while. Too long. Finally she looked at him again, saying, "I want what's best for me. I've decided that includes trusting you and learning all you can teach me before you leave Xtreme." She seemed to falter, but then picked up her speech. "If I can make a good enough showing, maybe I can stay on after we go public—at least as director of design. Greg says working for a public company would be the best of both worlds. Maybe you could set that up for me."

Hearing her so easily dismiss him from her life and realizing Friedman had a free shot at her with Jules supposedly out of the picture made Chess's gut clench. Still, considering his prior claims of a quick exit, what choice did she have?

"We'll strike a bargain." Getting an interested look from her, he went on. "I'll do my best to get you situated, if you'll give Lance a chance to prove himself. He had no ulterior motive when he introduced us. You have to believe that."

Watching her stare out the side window again, he clutched the wheel to keep from testing a finger-friendly curl. "Are you game, Holly?"

She addressed the blizzard. "Something about Lance bothers me." Lengthy silence ensued before she acquiesced. "I'll try."

"Fine."

And he would hope like hell nothing came of the rumor he had started about Xtreme being up for sale, being placed on the auction block. Available to the highest bidder.

Chapter Twenty-four

Bundled in a Clint Eastwood duster and a hat more beat up than Chess's, Adam approached the Corvette as it pulled into the yard. An anticipatory smile flashed in his brown face.

"Can you stay for supper, sugar?" Chess cocked a brow at Holly, smiling his invitation as he braked and slipped the gearshift into park.

She eyed the ranch house. A dim light spilled out his bedroom window. Thoughts of the self-imposed exile of her empty house made her ache, but staying here would only encourage the impossible. She shook her head and got out of the car.

Adam and Chess engaged in a hearty greeting their two-hour separation hardly merited. While Holly tried not to listen, they held a muffled, mysterious conversation involving fever and chills, aches and pains. Then Adam went to find Angel while Holly and Chess waited in the frosty twilight.

She tucked her hands beneath her armpits to ward off the cold. Chess leaned against the Corvette fender, arms folded across his chest, legs crossed at the ankles, wind-swept snow accumulating on his hat brim. Snow bit her cheeks. Overhead, wispy clouds writhed and curled their way across a shroud of slate, and in the pines frigid wind mimicked the ocean's roar in a seashell.

"What happened to spring?" She trembled.

He uncrossed his ankles, holding his hand out, palm up. When she frowned, rooted to the spot, he said softly, "Get the hell over here, woman. I'll keep you warm."

A warning pulse thrummed in her throat, but rejecting a mental image of last Sunday, she felt herself closing the gap between them. Nerves tingled along her spine. Her gaze dodged his, avoiding the appeal of snow-dusted lashes. The manner in which he drew her against him and wrapped his arms loosely across her back screamed propriety while it kicked her pulse up ten beats. Even the way he pressed his mouth to her hair before tucking her head beneath his chin maintained a modicum of etiquette. However, the way his crotch bulged when their bodies melded, the pleasure she took in the reaction and that pang of pleasure in her sensual core, represented nothing genteel.

He rocked her in his arms, murmuring, "Better?"

More like ecstatic torture. Rattled by his gentle nearness, their telltale reactions, she wished for the safety of his familiar insolence. He was big and strong and warm; she could stay in his arms forever. But Chess didn't think in increments of forever. She couldn't get caught up in running to him, depending on him or believing she meant more to him than a disposable end to a means. A time would come when she needed him, like she had needed Jules, and Chess would be gone.

At the sound of Adam and Angel approaching, he eased her back, hands on her shoulders. "Thanks for coming all the way out here. It was a nice gesture."

Her lips tugged. "Not if you consider my original intent."

"Screw details." He smiled indolently, fingertips kneading her flesh through the thick jacket. "We're going to score with Xtreme, honey, and, we'll do it together. You have my word."

Then why did that furrow appear between his beautiful eyes?

"Score, as in 'a promise is a promise'?"

Angel's snout bumped Holly's butt, and she stiffened to keep from colliding with Chess. He tightened his hold for an instant, then accompanied her in the direction of the Saab, an arm looped loosely about her shoulders.

"Trust me, Holly. A promise is a promise."

Reluctance to be alone prompted her to stop by Xtreme. She would clear her desk and review the new designs for fabric selection. Getting a headstart toward the workweek would free her mind for tomorrow's ski trip to Aspen with Janine.

She found her key by the vapor glow from the empty parking lot, opened the storefront office and held the door for Angel. A light inadvertently left on in the kitchen lit the reception area. At Toby's desk, she examined Saturday's mail and extracted her own before proceeding along the darkened corridor.

She flipped on her office light and froze in the doorway.

Angel's ears went back. A growl rumbled in her throat.

"Lance!" Damn it to bloody hell. What was he doing sitting in the dark at Chess's desk? "You scared the hell out of me. What are you doing here?"

He swung his feet down and rose, shuffled papers on the desk, hands awkward, face scarlet. She easily detected alcohol on his breath.

"Hey. I thought he'd keep you at the ranch all night."

How did that relate to his being here on a Saturday night? "How did you know I went to—"

"Spies. Did you get a ride in that featherbed? How'd you like it?"

Anger surged, but she struggled for will over her tongue. She edged inside the office, behind her own desk. Trepidation lay like a dead weight in her stomach. She found her glasses, slipped a letter opener inside an envelope flap, then perused the contents, her eyes refusing to focus. All the while the unnamed "something" bothering her about Lance, other than being with him in close quarters when he'd been drinking, raged.

"What are you doing at Chess's desk?" she murmured, pretending to read.

He shrugged. "Looking for a market report he asked me to analyze. Guess he took it with him."

Looking in the dark? "Your car's not in the lot."

He gathered a sheaf of papers, tapped the edges on the desk. "It's at the back entry. I unloaded some files I've been working on at home." Apparently recovered from surprise, he eyed her, green eyes cold as a frost-glazed pond. "What's with the twenty questions? You have another fight with Chess?"

She whipped off the glasses. "None of your business."

He grinned. "Clever bastard, isn't he? He'll dangle you till you're begging for it, but I hear he leaves satisfied road-kill." His eyes narrowed appraisingly. "You might want to do yourself a favor. Give in sooner, rather than later."

Rage flared so violently she felt as though she lunged forward even as she sat down and rolled her chair to the desk with purpose. She reached for the phone. "I'm not going to take this, Lance. I'm calling Chess."

He shrugged. "I'll tell him you asked me to meet you here, then changed your mind."

"Why would I do that?" she demanded.

"Maybe you didn't like it that I'd been drinking when I showed up." He grinned crookedly, swayed a bit. "He'll believe me, not you."

Holly berated herself for remaining in the room, but Xtreme was hers. If she ran from Lance she'd be proclaiming a damaging weakness.

"Get out." She managed a calm tone. "Don't make a practice of hanging out in this office in the future. Nothing here concerns you."

Angel's ears pricked higher, her growl deepening.

He laughed. Malevolence echoed in the quiet. "Afraid I'll find another surprise for my cuz? Like stray invoices, maybe?" He started toward the door, then stopped. "You need taking down a notch, Holly. Chess'll do that. He'll even make you like it till you figure out what's happening. The outcome won't be pretty."

"I'm sure you'd enjoy that."

He made a move toward her, but Angel came to her feet, teeth bared, throat rumbling. Holly opened a file drawer. Hands trembling, she tucked a letter only God knew where.

"I don't like you, Lance, no matter whose cousin you are. If you don't leave this building I won't be responsible for Angel's actions." She met his insolent gaze. "That won't be pretty, either."

He laughed, a bitter snort. "You shouldn't blame me for Chess's action, you know." He gestured dismissively. "But what the hell. I'm used to it. 'Night, babe."

Evil lurked in the aftermath of his exit. Even though she lacked understanding for what she sensed, dread plagued her. She surveyed the room, eyes settling on the computer, on her chair. The lavender paisley pillow had been tossed aside, the monitor and keyboard left uncovered.

What could he have been looking for? And why?

Elbows on the chair arms, she lowered her face into her palms. A violent inner tremble surfaced, quaking her body before determination vaulted her from the chair. She checked the back alley for Lance's car, then went hurriedly into his glass office. She snapped on a glaring light, eyes canvassing the perimeter. His desk lay bare as a marble grave slab. She tried the drawers. Locked. Every one. What did she hope to find? If she didn't know, she couldn't recognize it. To assume Lance would leave a trail for her to follow was foolish.

She moved to the phone, then recoiled. What could she tell Chess, other than she had surprised his beloved and trusted cousin working on Saturday night? Should she bear tales of Lance treating her shabbily—or his disparaging remarks about Chess? Would he really take Lance's word over hers, believe what Lance had threatened to tell him? Considering the agreement she and Chess had made only hours ago, any unprovable suspicion she aired would label her a whiner looking for an excuse to welch on their agreement.

For now, she could say nothing.

As she exited the office, an incoming fax left in Lance's machine caught her eye. He had apparently missed the arrival or thought it not important enough to read. She skimmed the wavy print. The origin, Tokyo, and the heading, Mihatsu, gave her no clue. Then, she read the message again, to an attentive Angel.

"Transmission received and employed, for now. I await your further accomplishment. Good job, old friend. K."

What little she knew of Lance's Japanese background badgered and fueled her suspicion. His conducting personal business at Xtreme's expense annoyed her, but agitation went beyond that to some enigmatic plane. She read the fax again, discerning nothing new, only underlining her disquiet. Carefully, she replaced the fax and went back to her office, the name Mihatsu and the initial K indelibly engraved on her mind.

Chapter Twenty-five

A week later Chess looked up from his laptop to study Holly across the wide desk. Since her visit to the ranch, he had kept his distance, adopting a polite but detached air as they conducted business in the shared space. Today, circles beneath her eyes, rounded shoulders that made her look even more petite and uncommonly vulnerable, challenged his feigned indifference.

"Something bothering you, Holly?"

Even as she shook her head, huge, hot-looking tears poked to the ends of her lashes. His gut twisted.

"You want to tell me? If it has to do with Xtreme, I might fix it."

She shook her head again and ran the pads of her fingers across her cheekbones. He gripped the chair arms, resisting the urge to rip their platonic arrangement to shreds. She leaned across the desk to pass him an engraved invitation to the Industry Awards Dinner.

"I know this is short notice, but would you like to be...are you free to escort me to the awards ceremony?"

Her voice lacked its usual verve. She kept her wounded-puppy eyes focused a notch below his chin. He fished for a

Macanudo and shook it from its can while he examined the invitation. In the interest of not molesting her again, he should refrain from spending an evening in her company. As he wavered she beat him to the punch.

"I saw your picture in the *Post*—at the Anchutze party. I know you own a tux." Her soft smile looked painful as hell.

"I couldn't get out of that extravaganza gracefully."

She fixed her gaze to his, dismay obvious. Apparently she didn't consider an evening of drinking, dancing, close confines of a car—maybe being asked in for brandy—counterproductive to a platonic association.

She strained to jerk back the invitation. "Fine, Chess," she murmured. "I assumed you'd welcome another photo opportunity—for Xtreme's sake, this time."

He ran his tongue along the tobacco seam, wanting a match as badly as he'd want a snow cone in the Sahara. "You're the photogenic half of this team, honey. I wouldn't feel right horning in on your glory."

Her shoulders squared, chin tilting. "Fortunately, Greg is not so humble. He'll take me."

Over Chess's petrified body. He made a big production of thumbing a pocket-sized Day-Timer. "On second thought, looks like I'm free. If you'll allow me to change my mind, I'll be glad to take you."

Her eyes burned, then watered. His sudden reclaim of his senses had proved as useful as a rulebook at a riot.

"I wouldn't want to risk that, cowboy. You might change your mind again. I prefer sure things."

Having sealed his fate, she rose wordlessly, slipped into her little Burberry coat, shouldered her big bag, and left the room.

He gave her time to exit the building, then made a dash for the warehouse. "What's wrong with Holly?"

Sally examined a completed logo too carefully, eyes

focused. "Didn't she tell you?"

"If she'd told me, would I be out here begging you for information instead of sitting glued to the market channel?"

Sally filed a windshirt in the stack of rejects and reached for another. "If she wanted you to know, she'd tell you."

"That would probably go against some damned gender code she operates by. You're above that crap. What's wrong with her?"

Sally sighed. "She's been getting hang-up calls. All hours of the night, and a few at the office. It's getting to her."

He relived the defeat in her eyes when he'd so callously turned down her invitation. "So she thinks the calls are from Jules." Bud's Bar, the hollow sound of clinking glasses and the taste of last Saturday's cheap wine, burned in his recall.

Sally smiled, equitably. "Jules is dead. Haven't you heard?"

He chortled bitterly. "Jules will never be dead."

"Maybe with time and the right incentive—"

Overhead, the tinny intercom vibrated. "Chess, line three."

Chess hugged Sally's meaty shoulders. "Thanks for sharing. Use your phone?" He moved across the warehouse to take the call at her desk, Holly's tears and Jules's face whirling in his head. "Chess Baker."

"Hold for Peter Andrews, please."

As he waited, his gaze roamed a warehouse stuffed to the rafters, every inch of space allocated, woefully inadequate. Mentally, he reviewed the lease he had signed, the contractor waiting for the go-ahead to draw refurbishing plans. His crowded mind ricocheted between Xtreme's dwindling bank account and Holly's wet eyes, then riveted on yesterday's phone call from a ski-pole company in Los Angeles. Their inquiry into Xtreme being for sale could be either his salvation or worst nightmare.

The hand to be played depended on how Holly cut the deck.

"Andrews here." He sounded winded.

Chess kicked back in Sally's rickety wooden chair and plopped his Bally loafers on the desk. From a nearby inspection table, Sally watched, smiling, then resumed her chore.

"Chess Baker, here. How're they hangin', Pete?"

Short silence while Chess imagined him consulting language-translation software. "Very carefully, these days, I'm afraid."

"I hear you." So much for levity. "I've been reviewing this breakdown you sent yesterday. Seems we're a little heavy in Banomex Bonds."

"Well, yes you are, but that decision was made—"

"Before the rumblings out of Mexico. Nobody's blaming anybody. Just tell me how that situation is likely to affect my position." He knew, but he had some warped desire to hear it voiced. Or some asinine hope of being wrong.

Silence. He watched Sally stretch to hang a windshirt.

"Look, Pete, normally I wouldn't hassle you over this, but I've got complications of a different nature." Rapidly the California disaster played through his mind. Based on a tip he'd gotten in the Bronco skybox a month back, he bought stock in Meridian Oil, which had since suffered a spill off the coast of Santa Barbara. Meridian had plummeted, and now the company paid clean-up bills instead of the dividends he had banked on to offset his Xtreme investment. Some days he felt backed into a box canyon by a flash flood. Other days he sensed his fortune being eroded by a slow flowing river of bad judgment.

He drew himself back into the hands-on scenario. "Just give me a brief rundown of how you see this Banomex thing."

"I won't pretend the devaluation of the peso isn't serious, Mr. Baker, and will most certainly create multi-defaults." The

Englishman's detached inflection and marked formality smacked of printed copy, making Chess wonder how many other disgruntled calls Peder Andrews had received today. "The Mexican stock and bond markets are sure to plummet."

The reliable tickle on the back of Chess' neck exploded into a flaming rash. "Will it recover, or do we sell now?" He heard a phone in the background, then another.

"Would you excuse—"

"Let it ring." Hackles rose on his spine. "We're talking on my nickel. I want the whole deflated five cents worth."

Sally's head jerked up with his elevated voice.

Andrews resumed a monotone. "Holding your investment is high risk, to be sure, but if the world—mainly the U.S., of course—comes to Mexico's aid, this could be a buying opportunity, rather than a disaster. Especially if you go for the convertible eleven percent coupon issue, which matures in the year two thousand three." Peder Andrews paused, the buzzing phone creating a tense backdrop. "However, if Mexico gets no financial assistance, then it's—"

"Chaos."

"Precisely."

"Yeah. That's about the way I figure it." Asking what Andrews would do in Chess's shoes would be plowing the same furrow from the opposite end. He swung his feet down, rose, stretched and massaged his lower back. The decision resembled a Vegas crapshoot, or splitting tens when the blackjack dealer had a face card showing. A blind gamble, nothing more. "I'll hang on for a few days and call you with my decision."

"I know from the wire that the U.S. Senate is debating— if you could get a feel for what they have in mind, it would be advantageous."

Advantageous to Peder Andrews and Crown Equities, as well. As Andrews said, a possible buying opportunity.

Chess didn't want more cheese. He wanted out of the trap.

"Better answer that phone, Pete. Might be a live one." He hung up and dialed Washington. Time to call in the contribution favors he had assumed he'd never have to rely on.

Back in his office, while he waited for the Oklahoma Senator to return his call, he tried to focus on that last million his grandmother had given him. The million she'd called reseed money. The million she had made him promise to sock away in an Okmulgee bank and draw interest on, no matter how many high-risk investment opportunities arose. He had honored her wisdom. That money remained there to fall back on, but today's in-your-face failure gnawed his gut.

He seized the phone when it rang. "Chess Baker."

"Mr. Baker, this is Senator Nickles's assistant. He asked if he could return your call after his meeting—in about an hour, hopefully. Will you be available at this number?"

Chess wrangled a verbal smile. "Count on it."

As he settled in to wait, he thought of his roommate and co-captain at OU. Kevin's mother, Anita Richardson, was now the attorney general. Chess had gotten to know her well during his glory days at OU, their rapport based on Chess's helping Kevin achieve and maintain a 3.8 grade average. Kevin's mother, a congresswoman then, had stressed repeatedly that should Chess ever need anything....

Thank God, he'd never had to ask for that favor. Yet.

His mind drifted to Holly. Her tears had made him feel like dull razor blades were scraping little slivers off his crusty heart. Given her state of mind, she would oppose what he eventually had to tell her, but putting it off would do nothing to soften the blow.

Chapter Twenty-six

Holly worked at wrapping and stuffing Jules's trophies and memorabilia into a carton. She trained her eyes on her work, wrestling with Chess's unnerving presence in the close confines of the study. That and his undisclosed reason for being there. He filled the room like a stallion in a stall.

"I'm sorry to be a bad hostess, but I still have the closet left to go, and the moving company is due in the morning. Whatever you have to tell me..."

He took Jules's pipe from the smoking stand, cupped it in his palm and studied her, gaze penetrating. "Are you giving his things away—donating them?"

She snatched the pipe and rolled it haphazardly in newsprint and crammed it in the box. Just when she thought her anger toward Jules had died, it would seize her, silent and intangible as fog, but every bit as blanketing. As suffocating. Although the wound was scarring over, it remained sensitive to probing. Guilt nagged her for taking it out on Chess, but she still smarted from his reaction to her invitation to the awards dinner, senselessly associating his rejection with Jules's desertion.

"It's going to storage," she murmured.

"You still think he's coming back?"

"Not to this house. I'm sure of that." She ripped a framed certificate from the wall, plopped it on the desk in the center of a *Denver Post* sports page, then, hands on hips, faced Chess. "You said you had something to tell me. Knowing your crowded schedule, I suggest you begin."

"Holly, about the awards dinner..."

"Water under the bridge." She swiped an errant kink of hair. "I hope you're not here to rehash that."

With Angel on his heels, he paced to the study door and leaned against the arched frame, arms folded on his chest. Then, like palace guards, man and beast paced back. "Ever heard of America Ice?"

"They make ski poles."

He nodded amiably. "I got a call from them last week. They've picked up on my involvement with Xtreme, and—"

"How?" Her heart fluttered, though she didn't know why.

"Industry hype, I guess. Anyway, they asked for performance figures and a proforma—you know—like you gave me before I joined you." He executed his affable, crotch-stirring grin. "Well, not exactly like you gave me."

"Why?"

He kept smiling. "The stuff you gave me was doctored."

Her cheeks singed. Hackles raided her spine. "Why did they ask to see figures and a proforma?"

"Could we sit down? Have some coffee—a drink maybe?" He looked around, back at her, brow furrowed, then gave up and braced against the desk. "They're interested in Xtreme."

"Interested how?" A pulse thudded in her ears.

He took a cigar from his blazer pocket, clasped it dagger-like. "Actually, partner, going public's not the all to end all."

"It was a few weeks back. What's changed since then?"

"Well..."

"Yes?"

"Ever heard of extenuating circumstances?" He flashed his blond-god grin. She struggled to field it, blank it out.

"What are you trying to tell me, Chess?" Her upturned palm made a sweep of the room. "I've got miles to go here, before I sleep."

He sighed, wrapping his chest again. "America Ice is initiating an expansion program. They've got their eye on several smaller industry-related companies. Xtreme's one of them."

"Precisely what does that mean?" She lowered her suddenly infirm body to the arm of Jules's favorite chair. "In non-entrepreneurial terms?"

Thoughtfully, he unwrapped the cigar, sniffed it, stuck it in his mouth, then removed it. "Holly, do you trust me?"

"Is that an issue, here? Damn you, Chess, get to the point."

"If America Ice likes what they see, they're looking at merging Xtreme into their parent company. They might be open to you remaining head of design. You'd have a staff. You could hire Janine back, if you wanted."

She bolted up, attempting to ignore all but one word. "Merging? Is that anything like sucking the life out of any little company they take a fancy to?"

He straightened. For a moment, she thought he was going to reach for her. He shoved his fingertips in his back pockets. She credited him with honoring her edict of no sexual involvement, but why was she so wounded by his concession?

"It's nothing like that," he said. "If I thought so, I wouldn't be considering..."

Considering? Hope sprang to the forefront. But what could she actually expect, other than a misleading tactic, from a man hell-bent on having his way? "Then you mean you haven't made a decision?"

He looked grieved. "I wouldn't, without talking to you."

"Or telling me, you mean. I gave up the right to be consulted long ago. What do you mean, you're considering?"

"They've asked us to come to New York to meet with them."

"I won't go."

She crossed to the trophy wall and took down another framed document. He moved alongside and took it from her hands. Their arms brushed. Their eyes locked. She felt she'd encountered heat lightning. She willed her eyes away and he resumed his distance, his own eyes troubled.

"Why are you so opposed to this, Holly? You haven't even heard the details of the offer."

Could he really not know, after the way she'd shared her goals with him, after the bargain they'd made just a week ago? The question of what had caused him to change his mind plagued her before she realized he'd known about the America Ice inquiry then. "Why didn't you tell me about America Ice when I came to the ranch?"

His eyes clouded. "When I saw your enthusiasm to go public, I decided to tell America Ice we weren't interested."

"Then you changed your mind. Why?"

He shrugged. "More of those extenuating circumstances."

Such as strong desire to be rid of her sooner. Yet she sensed something reserved in the machinations of his mind, an addendum he deemed her unworthy of hearing.

He ran a hand through his hair. "You have to roll with the punches, be flexible, if you want to make money."

"Money is your god, not mine." She stalked out of the study. He and Angel followed, Angel whining. In the kitchen, she leaned on the hackneyed, time-tested butcher block, grasping for stability, for composure. "All this amounts to your having another change of heart. Nothing more. You got control of my company, and now you're bored, so you're selling me out. You're sacrificing me and my desires."

"Honey—" She glared. He amended, "Holly, you don't understand. Once we went public, Xtreme wouldn't belong to you anyway. There's no difference in a public offering and selling—merging—with America Ice. Think about it."

"You said you'd help me to stay on. It's easy for you to ride off in the sunset, cowboy, but I'm the schoolmarm in this little scenario. I need a job." She hated her sense of vulnerability. Even more, she detested revealing it to him.

"You'll be rich, ma'am." He grinned, but with little assertiveness. "You'll want for nothing."

"I don't care, damn you. I want the security of being attached to something." She dislodged from the counter, paced to a leaded glass window and stared. A harried, frazzled woman stared back. "No, that's wrong. I don't want to be attached to something. I want to be attached to Xtreme."

"I'll take care of that."

She addressed her reflection. "Just like you promised to take care of me if we go public."

He reasoned gently from behind her. "If this deal goes through, taking care of you is a lay-down. I won't be staying on, so they don't have to factor my high salary into their offer. They have to have a designer, and with your prestigious reputation—especially after you win the award next week—they'll be jumping at the chance to keep you."

He fell so silent that she turned around. He stepped back when her folded arms brushed his chest. Their gazes locked.

"I've got my reasons for wanting this." His gaze caressed her. "All I ask for is your trust. I'll take care of you. I swear."

"Another worthless promise," she whispered.

He flinched, frowning, but he didn't relent. "Will you go

to New York with me? We'll listen to their offer. If you don't like it, I'll..."

She supposed he had run out of promises. "You'll what?"

"Will you go, Holly?"

Crossing to the sink, she turned off the light with finality, sealing them in semidarkness. "I'll let you know."

"When?"

"When I decide."

His expression indicated he had more to say, but changed to resignation. "Fine. Want me to help you with Jules's things? 'Many hands make light work,' as Grandma Baker used to say."

She watched her bitter laugh hit its mark. "Just go, Chess. I can fight my demons alone."

As of now, Chess Baker was one of her demons.

Chapter Twenty-seven

Two days later, Holly slit a creamy envelope bearing the gold-embossed return address of Phillips Philadelphia, a high-end woman's clothing line headquartered in New York. Based on no more than a hunch, her heart beat in her throat. The concise letter proved her perception correct. Her designs had caught Phillips's eye. The body of the letter consisted of a proposal. Phillips wished to license Holly to design and Xtreme to manufacture and distribute an exclusive line of aprés-ski wear to be marketed under the Phillips label.

Brian Zuckerman, CEO, would await her reply.

Holly read the letter again, then once more. The proposal validated her worth as a designer. Where did the offer fit into Chess's sudden penchant to merge Xtreme with America Ice? How could she use Phillips Philadelphia to thwart the merger?

She seized the phone to dial the number in the letterhead.

When Holly walked into the Industry Awards cocktail party on Greg's arm, a magnet-like force drew her gaze across

the room to Chess. A cerise and cobalt Colorado sunset mat-
ted his athletic stature while an expanse of glass overlooking
the after-hours calm of 17th Street served as a frame. A black
tux and white shirt played up his fair hair and perennial tan.
Her chest felt clamped in a vise. Longing swept through her,
settling between her thighs in a rhythmic throb that mimicked
the jazz quartet across the room.

The physical repercussion of seeing him did nothing to
ease her angst over America Ice.

Toby, Lance, and Sally made up the rest of Chess's four-
some. In the distance, Holly assessed Sally's tulle and lace
mother-of-the-bride frock. Once Chess had asked Sally to be
his date, a search for the dress had thrown her life into chaos
and left it in financial strain. As Holly witnessed Sally's days-
on-end furor and anticipatory chatter, even realizing Chess had
tried to change his mind and escort her failed to quash her
envy.

When Sally waved, beckoning Holly, she smiled but
shook her head, halting Greg in mid-step. "I don't feel like
shop talk," she explained, veering in the opposite direction.
"Let's get a drink, and I'll introduce you to Danna Lewis-
Gordon from *Powder Magazine*. She's over there with Pepi
Gramshammer."

Greg's gaze followed her nod to a group across the room.
"You must be dueling with Wyatt Earp again." He smiled
wryly.

She struggled to keep her eyes off Chess. "Constantly."

"Glad to hear it. What is it about a woman in a one-
shoulder, slit-up-the-side, black velvet dress that turns a man
into an animal—not to mention an ankle bracelet?" he said, as
they waited at the crowded bar for their drinks. His specula-
tive smile did little to hide his wistful tone.

She recalled her image in the cheval-glass in her bedroom—the form-fitting dress she'd spent weeks searching for,

black moiré spike heels revealing toe-cleavage, her hair sleeked into a chignon that thus far hadn't rebelled, the diamond studs her Jewish grandmother had given her, and multi layers of mascara dramatizing her eyes. She had aimed for stage presence.

She smiled her acceptance of his compliment. "You look nice, too, Greg."

"Me and all the other penguins." He grumbled, glancing around.

Willfully, her eyes stole back to Chess's distinctive form. "Your hot-pink cummerbund sets you apart."

He angled his body between her gaze and subject. "But does it nudge your feral instincts?"

She nodded toward the attendant. "We're next. I'll have white wine."

When they had attained their drinks, Danna Lewis-Gordon welcomed them into her small gathering and made introductions.

"We were talking about you, Holly," the editor of a local magazine announced. "Seems we all voted for you to receive the award, so if that's a trend, I'd say you're a shoo-in."

"Thank you." The stranger's analysis made her temple thrum. She sipped her wine, eyes lowered, attempting humility. "Xtreme is doing well."

"Based on design, do you think?" A shop owner, one of Xtreme's smaller accounts, pulled her gaze back from Chess and addressed the group in general. "I hear you have a new partner who's turning things wrong side out and upside down."

A shaft braced Holly's spine, but she found an ingratiating smile somewhere in her agitation. "It's too bad the industry doesn't give an award for creating chaos, isn't it?"

Soft, polite laughter rippled through the gathering as Pepi remarked, "I met him. He seems knowledgeable."

Danna said, "I read an article in *U.S. Business* about

Chess Baker. They called him a wunderkind—a turnaround prince, crediting his bravery to Choctaw blood, or some ethnic thing. I can't quite recall."

Holly dismissed that, recalling Sally's amusing statement that Chess claimed to have barely enough Indian blood to know a tomahawk from a claw hammer.

Danna fastened her in her gaze. "You're fortunate. Baker thrives on growing small companies into prosperous conglomerates."

Except for Xtreme, which couldn't hold his interest.

After cocktails, Holly located Xtreme's designated table. A three-across arrangement provided dining for six. She took an end seat nearest the podium, preparing for an unencumbered walk to the stage when the award announcement came. Lance and Toby occupied the opposite ends. After attentively seating Sally across from Greg, Chess took his place across from Holly. She ignored him. While liveried waiters served dinner, she made an attempt at conversation with Greg while she picked at her vegetarian plate. Pent-up anxiety kept her hand returning to the wine as her eyes strayed to Chess's graceful hands manipulating his rare roast beef.

Once dessert materialized, the ceremonial speeches began. Coinciding with coffee service, the presenter took the podium. Holly jerked when she felt Chess's socked foot caress her calf beneath the narrow table. She inched her leg away, eyes riveted on the speaker.

Last year, in this room, spurred by hearing a name called other than her own, she had promised herself—and sworn to Janine—this year the award would go to the Xtreme team, and Janine would have the honor of accepting. Her absence tonight reiterated the onslaught of changes since then, changes orchestrated by the man across from Holly now. Her tyrannical, implausibly handsome, sometimes tender, white knight.

She forced her mind off Chess and away from America

Ice. Away from the design disk she had discovered missing that morning, the enigma of Lance, the uncertainty of her life. Sipping scarlet Clos du Bois from a shaky glass, she tried to focus on the speaker.

"Now it's my pleasure to announce this year's Industry Designer of the Year Award goes to..."

Holly placed her glass on the table as the envelope containing the winner's name ripped, echoing through the room.

"...Patrick Hanson of PolarSki."

Her face seared. Shock waves ravaged her body. A frantic urge to bolt seized her at the exact moment Chess's feet shackled her ankles, welding her to the chair. Across the table, his gaze captured hers, a magnetic beam that held, steady and unblinking. Rage slammed her. She searched his face for gloating but found none. Instead, tender, smoky eyes drained hers, absorbing the hurt and shock that his tenacious foothold prevented her revealing to the entire room. Numb, she somehow managed to join him in applauding the winner, easing the discomfort of peers who had come to celebrate her victory, encouraging them to follow suit.

Forcing back tears, she allowed Greg to hug her and acknowledged Sally's empathetic smile. Numb, vaguely aware of an orchestra beginning to play, Holly watched Patrick Hanson accept his plaque. In a dressed-up corner of the ballroom, Patrick posed for pictures, then returned gracefully to his own jubilant table, dance music paving his way.

Chess eased his hold, his body contorting to replace his shoes. He stood, extending his hand. Like an automaton, Holly accepted and preceded him to the dance floor where she moved into his coveted, distrusted arms, locking her eyes on a ruby shirt stud.

"Smile, Holly." His lips were warm and close to her ear, his voice soothing. "Next year's voters are watching to see how graciously you lose."

"Thank you," she murmured, resting her face against his chest. "For saving me from myself."

"No problem." His voice vibrated against her cheek, his hand caressing the back of her neck briefly. "White knights were put on earth to save princesses."

Chess had never seen her looking more sensual or more vulnerable. As he guided her listless form around the floor, he indulged in a fantasy of bundling her up, carting her to the ranch, making love to her and turning the vast wasteland of his bed into fertile ground. He wanted to yank her out of the ass-nipping world of commerce, make her pregnant and keep her barefoot and beholden. She would be there, safe at Sol y Sombre, round and happy, when he came home every night. Do Thi could teach her to make ram gói and laqué duck, and Holly would spend her time reading pseudo westerns, content-edly growing his baby.

What the hell was he thinking? He couldn't make her pregnant, and although tonight might temporarily daunt her, she wanted to be God's gift to commerce. None of his fantasy would ever work—and hadn't that been one of his disappoint-ments in Robyn? That she had dropped out of the business world to collect marriage royalties, leaving them little in com-mon?

What the hell did he want, anyway? Did he think lock-ing Holly up in some remote outback would insure machismo, or keep him from going broke, maybe? He hung in limbo between reality and desire, a man damned tired of being alone, while all Holly wanted from him—all she'd ever wanted—was to get herself re-entrenched in a fat and healthy Xtreme. Somehow, she had convinced herself a public offering held the answer. For the moment she rested pliably against him, soft and warm and grateful, but the moment would pass.

He could save himself grief by remembering that.

Chess noted Greg watching them intently. Finally Greg

rose and crossed the crowded floor with purpose. Chess delivered Holly into other eager arms, resentment buried in his heart, safe from detection.

——※❖※——

When the bedside phone ripped the midnight quiet, Chess's hammering chest proclaimed the caller. Or maybe the pounding represented rampant hope.

"It's Holly. I'm sorry to wake you."

"No problem. I fall back asleep easily." A prideful lie.

"Are you going to New York?"

"I'm supposed to go tomorrow afternoon. I haven't told them differently." He'd been sweating going alone, which senselessly felt like betrayal. At the moment he debated going at all.

"Would you still like me to go?"

He waited for his pulse to quiet. "Only if you want to."

"I do. Can you get me on the flight at such short notice?"

He'd get her on if he had to buy the damn plane. *Yeah, with what?* With the remainder of the fortune that had begun diminishing the day they met. "No problem, partner. I'll pick you up around one o'clock."

"That's not necessary. Give me the time and flight number and I'll meet you."

He listened to sleet pepper his windowpanes, pines moaning, the old furnace pump, the electric blanket hum and click. If she were here, would she be cold and want him to hold her through the night? Or musky warm as she had been when they'd danced? Was she cold now, in her big, half-empty bed? Or did the bed host Jules's ghost, the same apparition that ran defense against his thoughts of having her in this bed?

"Look outside. We're having a blizzard. I'll pick you up."

Chapter Twenty-eight

On board the plane, luxuriously settled in first class
with club soda and caramelized nuts, Holly allowed Chess's
close, comforting warmth to penetrate her consciousness.
What would it be like to truly be his partner, to trust and
believe he wanted all the right things for each of them and
not only for himself? What comfort would she find in
believing he would be content to stay with her, instead of her
certainty that their "small potatoes" company bored him?
The time it would take to go public would thwart his sudden
urge to abandon Xtreme and her, but her failing to win the
award gave him less bargaining power with America Ice,

so—

"What are you reading, sugar?" He stretched his long
legs as far as the bulkhead would allow, swiveled in his seat
and closed the laptop lid, masking a market analysis.

She kept her eyes on the papers in her hand. "The list of
questions our suitor is likely to ask." He had requested she
study the projected questions days ago, be ready with the
answers he'd written out. Back then, she had thrown the
papers at him, swearing he'd never get her name on a Xtreme-
America Ice contract.

He grasped her chin gently, his hand warm and smooth.
"What changed your mind about coming, Holly? Not that asi-

nine award, I hope." Slate eyes searched her face. "You can't throw in the towel that easily."

She pulled her head back, her skin icing up without his touch. "It's not asinine to me." Fixing him in a mock glare, she warned, "Don't think I'm beaten, cowboy. Maybe I'm only changing horses in the middle of the stream."

"Why does that scare the hell out of me?" He traced the rim of her ear with his little finger, a caress so light she might have imagined it. "Why'd you change your mind about selling?"

"For a gambler, you aren't very smart."

He grinned indolently, arching one brow.

"Never count your winnings before you leave the table."

He kept grinning. "What changed your mind?"

"You asked me to hear the deal." What he'd done last night, keeping her seated at that table, saving her from humiliation—no matter how unorthodox his method—convinced her she owed him something in return. The feeling got tangled with the result of her call to Brian Zuckerman two days ago. She'd been assured Phillips Philadelphia would hire her to design the new après-ski line whether or not Xtreme was included. If she announced at the America Ice meeting she refused to stay on as Xtreme's designer, would that sway their decision, leaving her with both Xtreme and Phillips Philadelphia? An anticipatory chill pebbled her arms before guilt rushed her. Momentarily, she contemplated telling Chess about the missing disk containing the new zippered designs. The hope she had simply misplaced the disk, along with the realization she soon wouldn't have him to depend on, kept her quiet.

"I'll listen," she said. "If I don't like what I hear..."

With controlling interest in Xtreme, he owned her. She must remember that and not be swayed by the false concern he so capably doled out when it suited his purpose.

—≍≍≍◈≍≍≍—

In a dimly lit corner of the Four Seasons Hotel's Fifty-Seven-Fifty-Seven Lounge, Holly gave in to Chess's spin for the club's celebrated martinis.

"Two," Chess told the waiter. "And an O'Doul's chaser."

She smiled wryly, knowing he wouldn't touch the martini. They clinked glasses, murmuring, "Cheers," their fingers brushing. She jerked her hand back but not before heat raced up her arm, and spread through her awareness.

His blond magnetism turned to bogus innocence as he swigged the nonalcoholic brew from the bottle. Conservative bankers'quality attire, complete with a rep tie replacing the Nicole Miller ritual, portrayed him a bit vulnerable and out of character.

She looked around the bar, observing the paneled walls, lush brass and leather appointments, anything but the man across from her. Finally she gave in, and felt one of those now familiar queer little jumps in her middle when she found his stormy gray eyes awaiting her.

"I'd like tomorrow's agenda. Time and place." Her voice reverberated softly within the privacy of the booth.

"We'll meet with them in the suite. Ten A.M." He lifted the martini, set it down untouched and searched his jacket pocket absently. "I've got room service set up for coffee, then lunch, in case the meeting runs long." He uncapped a metal Portofino tube and dumped a sweet smelling Macanudo into his palm. "Our flight's at six. We should easily be squared away by then."

"Expedient." Barring complications.

"What about tonight?" He smiled fetchingly. "I have some pull with Maguy Le Coze at Le Bernardin that should get us a table. We're together so rarely, we shouldn't waste it."

His words aroused her like deceptive caresses. She

thought of high teak ceilings and soft blue walls, Le Bernardin's intimate atmosphere. She forced her mind to the surroundings at hand, her smile a mild rebuke. "We've never been 'together' from the start—on anything. Tonight is merely an addendum to the real issue."

He settled against the booth, his long legs stretching, brushing hers before she could shimmy sideways. "Addendums come at the end, Holly. This is now."

Her hairline rippled, agitation and fantasy tangling. "Tonight is a coincidence—a prelude to tomorrow's business." Sighing, suddenly weary, she pushed her glass away. "I'd love to debate you, but I'm tired, Chess. I didn't sleep well last night." She crossed her arms, massaging them.

He studied her face, then lowered his languid gaze to her shielded breasts as he rolled the cigar between his thumb and forefinger. When he raised his eyes again, he looked decisive, as though poised to plunge off a high dive.

"Fine. We'll consider this a strategy-planning drink. I have an appointment at eight. You can get to bed, if that's what you want."

"With whom?" She felt weighted down by fatalism. What right did she have to ask?

"Robyn came to OU from New York. When she left me, she moved back—off the park, a few blocks away." His tone bordered on apology that discounted her earlier rejection. "I called and asked to see Rachel and Rita. The dogs. I haven't seen them—" He pulled up short, returning her painful, skeptical smile. "Right. I guess I want to see if Robyn's sorry yet. For leaving me."

At least he'd opted for honesty. A picture whirled in Holly's mind like fractured bits of glass in a kaleidoscope, every image more disturbing than the one before. Every possibility too painful to examine. She examined them anyway. Robyn moving familiarly into his arms, the dogs yelping and circling, sealing a family unit he still longed for.

"You evidently want her to be sorry, and you're determined to have your way." She slipped into her coat, then clinked her martini glass against his. "Let's drink to perseverance, cowboy."

He sipped beer, reading her down the length of the bottle. "Want me to walk you upstairs?"

Dismissed. "I wouldn't want to keep you from the dogs." She maneuvered decisively from the booth, but a listless ache tempered her normal stalking departure.

Chapter Twenty-nine

After Holly left, Chess sat thinking how she had looked in her fur, a black-and-white spotted concoction that made her resemble a pregnant panda. Compact and cuddly and vulnerable. After seeing Jules's closet, witnessing his impeccable taste, Chess would bet, Jules had bought the coat. Chess envisioned ripping it up, using the scraps to polish tack.

Holly could pack and store Jules's possessions until eternity, but she'd never be free of his hovering spirit without the fortitude—why the hell mince words—the desire to give the residue of her marriage away, or burn it. Just as she wouldn't be free of Jules until she desired someone else enough to vanquish the ghost.

Chess rested his head against the back of the booth, picturing their cab ride from La Guardia. When they crossed the Queensboro Bridge, Holly had exclaimed over the sprawling metropolis. A hard, hollow lump had lodged in his throat and robbed his air. Even glorified by diffused sunset and emerging twilight, the Big Apple paled compared to her petite classic beauty.

When they'd entered the hotel from the limo and waited at registration, looking at her, pretending they actually represented a team, had left him longing. Her cheeks had pinked from the cold they'd scurried through. Rain had crimped her hair into wiry-looking curls he knew were actually silky soft, like the dark, downy tuft guarding the treasure he had yet to seize.

Here in this booth, he had been painfully aware of every part of her, her breathing, the lift of her shoulders, breasts moving beneath cashmere. Her petite gracefulness stirred his groin, reminding him just how feminine she had felt beneath him two weeks ago. That memory endowed him with an erection that would have kept him from seeing her to the suite, even if she hadn't rebelled so rigidly.

He signaled for another O'Doul's, thought of asking for a match. Instead, he whiffed the Mac and stowed it in the tube. Thanks to the troubled dollar and Banomex bonds, his days of trashing eight-dollar cigars had been placed on hiatus. Make that cigars, first-class airfare, and limos.

He sipped the acrid martini, realizing he didn't want to see Robyn, or even Rachel and Rita enough to delve into the unchangeable past. Nothing would ever quash the sting of Robyn's infidelity, or his guilt for having driven her to it. His mouth twisted in a grim smile. *Let sleeping dogs lie.*

He wanted Holly, wanted to love her. His heart ached for that, desire settling on him like hot lava. After all this time, all the hard lessons, realizing that he remained vulnerable to such emotion surprised him. He should be able to steel himself against it, know enough to back away. Giving in meant he'd be risking pain again. But he wanted so badly to hold her, take comfort in her camouflaged sweetness, scrape away his calluses, and give back comfort.

In childhood, the way his father withheld approval if Chess failed—at anything—had taught him winning was everything. A desire to win had made him an aggressive competitor, willing to mow down anything in his way. Even his marriage. Maybe Holly presented a chance at the biggest prize of all, a second chance at the joy of life: loving someone more than he loved winning. If he wanted her, he had to ignore contingencies, screw consequences, and apply himself to win.

How tough an opponent could a damned dead husband be?

He let himself into the suite quietly, then spent some time gazing out a rain-splashed window onto a wet and glittering 57th Street. He entertained an urge to investigate the sound of running water, tinkling glass and soft music seeping from Holly's open bedroom door. His sex grew warm and heavy with the thought. Desire gathered like granite pebbles in his groin. He turned from the window and shed his jacket and tie, going to stand in her doorway.

She had managed to turn the room into a seductive haven. Bouquets of fresh flowers sprouted from water glasses and an ice bucket, while beside the bed, candles of varying heights flickered, filling the space with the scent of...peach, he thought. Raspberry, for sure. Faint classical music drifted from a clock radio that any woman not as superiorly feminine as Holly would have used for a morning alarm only. The open door of the adjoining bath emitted more intimate sounds that propelled him trance-like to that second, sacred door.

She whirled, hands darting frantically to breasts and crotch. Only the gut-wrenching sight of her sheathed in a sleek peach-hued nightgown kept him from laughing. The smooth satin fabric supported by two thin braided straps outlined her nipples, clung to the shallow suggestion of her belly, sheathed her hips, inviting him to behold the treasure beneath, drawing him into the room.

"Damn it, Chess." Her cheeks burned, eyes stormy. She

looked around frantically, one arm folded across her breasts, fingers splayed over the hint of shadow between her thighs. He took the negligee robe from a hook on the door and offered it to her. She appeared frozen.

"Turn around." He struggled like hell to sound calm, to keep his voice from jumping like his psyche, but her eyes widened as prettily as a doe's. He smiled, holding the garment open, lowered like a fur coat. Finally, she turned her lush backside to him and slipped into the robe. As she hastily wrapped and tied, he took mirrored voyeuristic pleasure in the precious weight of her breasts straining the fragile fabric.

She faced him, looking saccharine yet sultry now that her nipples imprinted dark circles against satin. He ached to dig into her wild wet curls as his gaze ran down her body and fastened on open-toed satin pom-pom slippers. His eyes seized on the gold bracelet around her perfect ankle.

He forced his eyes back to hers, attempting to pace himself.

Chapter Thirty

Holly's senses reeled. Confused and conflicting emotions clogged her throat. "You scared me," she murmured, mouth grim.

He rewarded her accusing glare with a broad, guileless grin. "In that nightgown, you scare me, sugar."

The counterplay set off a chain reaction that ended in a low, warm flush. "Obviously, I thought I was alone."

He shrugged, settling a haunch onto the vanity, fingering her hairbrush. "Well, God works in mysterious ways."

And the devil worked overtime. "Did you forget something?"

"Actually, I remembered something," he drawled.

His eyes shifted to the undisguised pucker of her nipples. "What's that smell?" His brow hiked. "Not perfume, surely?"

"Anaïs. Body lotion."

"Interesting." He smiled triumphantly.

"What did you remember?"

She watched him do a mental shuffle. "I want to coach you on the questions list," he said, tone casual, eyes intense.

Turning to the mirror, she ran her fingers through her damp hair, fluffed it off her face, trying for her own detached tone. "I studied on the plane. Remember?"

"I've thought of possible new questions. I don't want you to embarrass yourself. Partner." He grinned with boyish appeal.

She made a point of glancing at her watch.

"I'm not going to Robyn's."

She met his mirrored gaze. "The dogs will be disappointed."

He crossed to the door that led to her room, then turned back, one tanned hand shooting through already tousled hair. "I'll wait for you outside with the new questions. I wouldn't last five minutes in here." The seductive pitch of his voice, the way his eyes skimmed her body before he exited threw her senses into pandemonium.

Searching her own eyes in the mirror, she willed her breath to calm, her heart to steady. It was her call. She could close and lock that bedroom door. Did she want that? Before she could smother the answer it flooded her mind, then pooled in her breasts and belly. What could happen, out there where he waited for her, canceled all she had asked him to promise. For the moment, need overwhelmed wisdom, robbing her of strength to care.

He had actually spread the question-and-answer sheets onto a heavily carved square table. She slipped into a chair. Their forearms brushed as she reached for a query sheet, but she kept her eyes lowered to his hands.

He took the paper from her, pitched it and cocked back, Cole-Hahn loafers on the table. "You know those," he said. "I'll ask you the new ones."

She braced her elbows on the chair arms, leaning forward. Daring to meet his gaze proved to be a grave error in judgment. His unguarded hunger stunned her.

"Look, Holly," he said huskily. "Let's cut to the chase. If they ask you anything about finance, just say, 'I defer to Chess.

That's his department.' Flower it up, like, 'that's why we make a great team.' Or 'made,' since I won't be staying on."

She sat back, hands on the chair arms, her eyes boring into his. "Is that how you're going to answer the design questions?"

In one motion, he jerked his feet down, rolled back his chair, wheeled her away from the table, and squatted before her. "Screw what I'm going to say. You're driving me crazy and you know it."

She laughed. "Score a round for me."

He laughed, too. Softly, beautifully. His hands smelled like cologne and rich tobacco leaves as they stole to her face, thumbs stroking her cheekbones. The caress moved to the sides of her throat, then inside the neck of her robe, easing it back, along with the straps of her gown. He whispered, "It's hard to keep a cowboy on the range, once he's seen Paris."

She feigned a confused look, murmuring, "More Zane Gray?" as he eased her clothing from her breasts. Her blush started at her nipples and stained her chest like red ink. "Chess..."

His smile slow and intimate, he knelt before her. The heels of his hands inched up her rib cage. Gently, he pressed her breasts together, running his tongue along her shadowed cleavage. Desire streaked through her and blended with the heat in her groin. He raised his head to meet her eyes. Willfully her hands went to his brow, brushed back his pale hair, then circled his neck to twine in the fringe edging his collar. The golden hue had prepared her for the feel of straw. Finding the texture soft, resilient, she felt she had reached the end of a long, harried journey

"Do you know how long I've wanted to do this?" she said.

He caught her hand, kissed her palm. "Not as long as I've wanted you to."

She smiled a challenge. "How about from the first day?"

"How about from the moment I heard the warning that you're a hellcat? I like tests."

Like a blind man trying to see with his fingertips, he reverently, tenderly traced the contour of her breasts. His eyes, a bit glazed, sought hers again. "Do you want me, Holly?"

"So much," she whispered.

"Show me," he whispered back.

She leaned into him, her fingers tangling his hair. She ran her tongue over lips she had craved endlessly, darted into their corners. He tasted yeasty-bitter after the O'Doul's. She savored, nibbled, drank. Passion coursed down her throat, straight into her being. As his mouth parted to take hers, her body fragmented, then throbbed with new life. She pulled back, staring into his smoldering eyes.

"That much, huh?" He smiled, breath ragged.

"More."

He stood, bringing her up with him. Gently possessive hands circled her waist and lifted her onto him, twining her legs about his hips, her arms around his neck. He massaged her muscled thighs, grinning devilishly, as if he'd scored a coup. She clung to him, her hair flying out behind her, as he danced in triumphant circles. When they stopped spinning, his hands clasped her buttocks beneath the gown and robe, pressing her lower body to his. He was hard, rigid, primed with passion.

Legs tightening, she cocked a brow and whispered against his mouth, "Did I do that to you, cowboy?"

"Yeah." He smiled evilly. Angelically. "In the bar."

She tilted back her head in laughter and his warm mouth sought her throat.

"Did you light those candles for my pleasure? And buy those flowers and play music and wear Anaïs?"

"For my pleasure. You weren't supposed to be here."

"Feel like taking on a partner? Sharing the wealth?"

She shrugged. "Sure. But I'll keep controlling interest."

Laughing huskily, his heart thudding against her breasts, he carried her to the bed, assuring she would not spend another lonely night wanting him.

Chapter Thirty-one

She loved the gentleness with which he lowered her to her feet beside the turned-down bed, the way his mouth hungrily sought hers as his hands tugged the belt of the robe loose. He worked robe and gown until they skimmed downward and puddled at their feet.

She whispered against his mouth, "Turn off the light."

He switched off a nearby lamp. When she turned to an arrangement of candles, mouth pursed, he drew her back to him, hands voracious on her lower back. His fingers splayed on her buttocks then roamed upward to ravel her hair.

"You're beautiful. I want to see you."

Although confident in her body, thoughts of laying her sensual emotions bare made her cringe.

"Tell me what's wrong, sugar? I'll fix it." His tolerant smile flashed white-hot in the candlelit room. While one arm circled her waist, preserving their bond, his hand manipulated shirt buttons. He pulled the garment from his pants and worked it off. His arms crossed behind her, he lifted her, sealing their bodies, skin to skin. His dusting of hair scratched her upper chest, as his smile became a moan against her throat.

Carnal impulse shot the length of her body like a heat-seeking device, then congealed into an ache, a craving. "I've been with no one since..." Just as she had prayed it would be when this moment came, she could speak no name, nor recall a face other than that of the man holding her. "There's been no one for seven years."

Hands on her shoulders, he searched her eyes, his own incredulous and urgent. Then understanding dawned. His fingertips at her throat drew her face to his, and he whispered against her mouth, "Then thank you for this honor, darlin'."

His reverent tone gave her courage to admit, "It's been so long, I'm almost scared."

He drew her hand to his waist, guiding her fingers to release his belt, lower his zipper. "How long since you've ridden a bicycle?" Eyes tenderly mischievous, he released her, stepped out of his shoes, shed his clothing in one graceful move and got rid of it with a careless kick.

Her body began to warm. Slicken. Throb. Her eyes rapacious, she feasted on the bunched muscles of his arms and legs, ridges of his chest, pale hair shimmering on bronzed skin. A silky patch above his navel narrowed to a downward stream of fine gold. Rooted in a nest of amber, his sex sprang hard and splendid, bruising and searing her thigh as he lowered them to the bed. Soft yet frantic desire came to her in the form of a gift, a memory-free onslaught of craving. Like fine wine, she wanted to sip and savor the moment, and yet, to gulp greedily, spill and splash it over her parched, starved body.

His hands and mouth moved to her breasts, destroying the last of her reticence. His tongue circled, cheeks flexing as he worked gently, coaxing. His lips, a hot caress on tender flesh, led her in an intricate dance of trust and freedom. Need pierced her mind, then permeated her body, edging her too quickly toward the brink of release until he brought his mouth back to hers. Their kiss was almost violent, an explosion of desire gone rampant, but she welcomed the frenzy. Beneath his hands, she was a butterfly bursting from a dreary cocoon, a former captive finally allowed to relish life's glimmering light.

His eyes holding hers in the golden, aromatic light, he trailed kisses down her body. Plunging her hands into his hair, she clasped tight handfuls when his mouth nuzzled her curly tuft then moved to the hollow of her thigh, his teeth nipping tender skin. At last, prompted by her soft moans, he covered her, fitting his hips between her legs. Their mouths joined, his seeking, hers eager to give. To take.

She reached to guide him, curving upward to receive him. He introduced his body to hers, entering gently, leisurely. He kissed her, pacing his thrusts with his tongue, transporting her to a distant spiritual and physical realm. Then he grew still and for an eternity, stared into her eyes. When he began again, she cried out, her quiet gasp reverberating in the night.

Wanting desperately to be filled by this man, as she had wanted no other, she circled his lean hips with her legs, craving, yet wanting to prolong the inevitable. His guileless and feral celebratory moan pushed her beyond control, over a guarded brink into helpless resignation. The first shimmering implosion rocked her, granting a riotous joy of surrender, more intense than she'd ever known. She arched frantically, her internal muscles regaining memory to clinch around him, drive the pleasure on and on to blinding fervor, to suck him in, imprison and then set him free.

His body concentrated strength for one last thrust, propelling him into his own spasm as abandonment moved in waves across his face. Fulfillment mounted, then exploded and rushed through her. Hot and wet, it spilled into sweet abundance onto her thighs, as her tears spilled into their joined mouths.

He eased off her, then curved his body around hers, one leg across her hips, a calf aligned with her thigh. He whispered, "Did I hurt you, princess?"

She shook her head, the back of her hand struggling to her wet cheek. He tasted her tears, then framed her face with his palms, his fingers combing her hair.

"Tell me why you're crying."

She turned her face away. "For so long I've needed...someone."

His finger on her chin turned her face back to his. "Someone?"

He waited for something she couldn't yet give, his gaze bathing her face, his breath a warm, sweet vapor on her cheek. At last he kissed her tears, swallowed them, working her mouth until she fitted her body to his.

"You taste so good." His hands at the backs of her thighs melded their bodies. "Sweet, sweet, Holly."

She pushed back to see his eyes. Now that she had surrendered to him, she needed to see the mouth that spoke the affirming words she craved to believe. Most of all, she needed him to fill her, to let their union take away life's uncertainty. Desire swelled within her, negating sanity, surrendering to an innate craving. She moved onto his newly burgeoning penis, grasping his hair, seeking his mouth. He raised to meet her as they fed once more a hunger too long ignored.

Somewhere in the night, he eased his arms from around her to leave her bed and stealthily gather his clothing. Like a compensated thief, his nude form stole gracefully from the room. Quietly he closed the door behind him.

Stunned, she listened to the latch engage, then rolled into a tight coil, feeling deserted, wanting to believe she was wrong. She fought back tears until they constricted her throat. She had shared her fear, trusted him with a fragile damaged part of her. Had he used her vulnerability against her? Had he, with shameless expertise, hell-bent on winning, seduced her to guarantee the AI sale?

Or would he return, hold her as she slept, allow her to wake in his arms?

She lay alone as dawn crept in, reality forming a jagged, bottomless chasm in her awareness.

Ruthlessly, she denied herself the privilege of tears, vowing to pit America Ice against Phillips Philadelphia to thwart his plans. Yet she failed at denying the factor she hadn't counted on.

She was deeply, helplessly, in love with Chess Baker.

Chapter Thirty-two

Chess stood in the open terrace door, still clad in sweaty running gear, the cellular pressed to his ear droning a hollow, summoning buzz. A run through frigid deserted streets sure as hell hadn't wiped out the fact of what he'd done. Goddammit, he knew better than to let wanting her enter into the grand scheme, but he had lacked the balls to stand his ground. Culpability had already begun to circle his conscience like a starved rat stalking a baited, well-oiled—

The ringing ceased.

"Good morning. Crown Equities." The breathless but still prissy English voice assured Chess he'd accomplished his goal of being this morning's first caller. Although he'd never seen the woman, he always pictured her as Moneypenny from the Bond movies.

He chose to forego the usual pleasantries. "Peder Andrews, please. This is Chess Baker."

"Good morning, Mr. Baker," she crooned. "I'm sorry, but—Oh, I believe he's just coming in. Could you hold, sir?"

"Not for long." Not when fate had chosen to personally deliver his friggin' world to hell in a hand basket while the government debated on whether or not to bail Mexico's ass out of the sling. Certainly not with visions of Holly writhing beneath him and questions of how to right the night's blunder pricking his brain like a bur under Geronimo's saddle.

He cut to the chase when Andrews came on the line. "Where do Banomex bonds stand this morning?"

Andrews cleared his throat and Chess heard him take a sip of something—coffee or nerve tonic. "I regret to say the bonds are yielding about fifty cents to the dollar."

"What about Teléfonos de Méjico?"

"You don't own any Mexican telephone stock, Mr. Baker."

"Right." His mind scrambled to shape even a tentative plan as he watched toy-like cars navigate a distant thoroughfare, their lights pin dot-sized beacons in the vastness.

Andrews cleared his throat again. "Teléfonos de Méjico has plummeted to six. An extremely good buy at this time."

Chess's sardonic chuckle hurt clear to his bare toes. If only America Ice had materialized months ago, or long enough ago for the merger to have been negotiated, putting closing at hand. Money could have been wired to London to refurbish his tapped-out accounts in time to take advantage of today's golden opportunity. Water under the bridge, but if AI wanted to coincide with their own rapidly approaching fiscal year, maybe he could still negotiate an immediate closing. Stock for Holly, but none for him. He would demand cash, even if he had to take a discount, even if he stood to lose a fortune when news of the AI-Xtreme merger hit the wire. He hated that solution, but had no choice.

Visions of Holly raveled his mind, how they'd never gotten round to rehearsing AI's sure-to-be-asked questions.

"Thanks," he said at last. "Just getting the lay of the land. I'll be talking to you."

He hung up, entertaining a vision of taking the Okmulgee million to Vegas, putting it on the crap line, and letting it ride once, win or lose. If he won, he could replace the stake before his grandmother rolled over in her grave and have another million to take advantage of the chaos in Mexico that could either make or break him.

Visions of losing the million on a gambling table gave him grave doubts about his sanity.

In the shower, he turned his thoughts to Holly. Tight, tentative, almost virginal, fragile as old glass. He had bought her trust with his hands, his mouth, yet months of speculation had left him unprepared for her response. Now he understood that his attempt to protect her with the condom had labeled her wanton, when in truth, she had been starving. His insensitivity and her justified anger had deprived each of them.

Again, he felt her shudder beneath him, heard her muffled cry. A moment after his own release, he had wanted to be inside her again, willing her to say he was the "someone" she needed. He bid the balmy water to ease the shock of the nightmare he'd had while she slept in his arms, a dream that Jules had returned. Beneath the pelting stream, stark reality tempered his urge to return to her bed and drive the dream into obscurity. No matter how long that private investigator had looked for Jules, nor how many legal papers Holly had signed, Chess couldn't dismiss the feeling he was cheating a ghost. Since it hurt like hell to try to rationalize the inane foreboding, he settled for it, avoiding justification. If he went back to her now, in his mind he'd be the third person in her bed.

Five minutes before ten that morning, Holly came out of her room. She wore the same prim black suit, cream blouse, cameo and signature sky-high heels from their first encounter, looking even more fragile and exuding more heart-wrenching appeal today. She had managed to slick her mass of curls into an arrangement controlled by a large clasp at the back of her neck. Circles beneath her eyes, visible from his conference-table vantage, pecked at his conscience like ravens in a fertile field.

"Good morning, princess." He wrestled a yearning to go to her, hold her and share his complex, rueful thoughts.

A wary look, her up-tilted chin, told him her mood equaled his turmoil. When he rose and went toward her, unable to resist, she turned her back and busied herself with coffee.

He placed his hand on her shoulder, finding it as knotted as his belly. Her involuntary jerk sloshed coffee onto the tile counter, her cup clattering in the saucer, but her face was composed. He withdrew his empty, aching hand.

"If you left Robyn in the middle of the night...after..." Her throat moved as she swallowed. "No wonder she..."

She spoke so softly he strained to hear, but he understood her meaning. His wife had left him because he'd been a selfish, anesthetized bastard, behaving no differently than Holly thought he had last night. "I had to make a phone call, honey."

Too calmly, she nodded, murmuring, "Which meant more to you than waking up with me."

"A call to England. The time difference screws things up."

She moved out of touching distance, then faced him, tiny gold hoops glowing against her jawline. "Your reason for being gone when I woke up—I don't buy it."

"The call was in our best interest. Both of us." *Tell her the truth, that you're in trouble. You owe her.* "I know how it looked—what you're thinking."

She made another try at the coffee. Raising it to her mouth, she sipped, meeting his eyes over the cup. "I doubt you've ever known what I'm thinking, and I fear you never will."

Her declaration propelled him toward her. She held up a hand, palm out. It trembled almost imperceptibly, like a feather rippled by a sigh.

"You knew, though, just how to calm the savage beast and guarantee what you wanted."

"That's not true. I want what's best for both of us."

Door chimes shattered the raging quiet. He reached for her. She shrugged away, crossed to set her coffee on the bar, then turned with deliberate calm, cocking a perfect brow.

"Ever the white knight, aren't you? To insure what you consider best for each of us—regardless of what I want—you mercifully took the starving widow to bed. But any mercy was for you, to make sure I'd say the right thing to AI this morning."

Her dead calm intonation made him wish she had screamed the accusation.

"You used the only method left to get me beneath you, and that's been your aim from the beginning—to put me in my place."

His gut coiled. "Jesus, Holly. Don't talk that way."

She seemed not to hear the repeated chimes and then the light rapping at the door, but the untimely demands vibrated in his cluttered mind.

"Your chivalry is slipping a bit, Chess. You were gallant enough to bed me, even in deceit. You just didn't have the decency to let me wake up in your arms."

Deceit was the word all right, and the duped husband was not here to defend himself or fight for her. Immersed in a nightmare he couldn't shake, watching her cross the elegant room and open the carved door, he whispered, "I love you, Holly," too softly and too late for her to hear.

—⋙✧⋘—

In the beginning, Chess cringed when the two America Ice executives fired questions at her. He tried to catch her eye to give her an encouraging smile. She wouldn't look at him. She put on her glasses, kept them on, as though hiding behind them.

"Your profit margins were low in the beginning, Ms. Harper, and then slipped miserably in the last few years. What do you attribute that to?"

Without pause, she said, "Lack of operating capital. Without my husband's financial expertise, I had no extra money with which to expand. When Chess joined me, we were able to open the international market. Sales can only escalate now."

As the session continued, Chess fingered a worn-out Macanudo, allowing her perfect performance, her composure, the ease with which she had slipped into business protocol and jargon to mesmerize him. His confidence soared and his roiling gut quieted somewhat.

"Then you feel confident Xtreme can maintain the present margins without Baker's input?"

She nodded, then like a trial witness, said, "Yes."

"Anything in the future picture that would change that?"

"In Chess's absence..." She took a breath. "According to Chess's plan, I'll add more sales reps, here and internationally. At his suggestion, I've begun a more innovative unisex concept design. When we get moved into the larger space we've leased, I'll be able to broaden the line by adding headgear and I plan to conduct a market search aimed at adding aprés-ski wear."

The last disclosure surprised Chess. Of course she had assumed the money for any new venture would come from his inexhaustible fortune—wealth he arrogantly continued to let her believe in while his pride kept him from divulging his true financial status.

As the interrogation continued, the AI execs nodded and exchanged glances. She had evidently studied the questions on her own after he'd left her last night. Her expertise in fielding the inquiries, the accuracy with which she recited the answers, enhancing them with ideas of her own, eased his dread and sent his admiration soaring like a comet. Hot damn! She was brilliant. He would never again doubt her claims that Jules's disappearance had thrown her into unmanageable financial straits.

Yet, he was acutely aware of her distress beneath the composure and perfect performance. The wounds he had inflicted plagued him far beyond the relief of knowing they had bagged the AI-Xtreme merger.

Instead of counting his winnings at the table, as she had warned him against, his mind kept going to the feel of her in his arms, that hallowed space between her thighs, the sensation of drowning in warm, liquid silk. He had experienced the supreme sexual encounter: ultimate love for a woman who trusted him with her very being. Then he had denied them the luxury of—

Holly's sudden move to stand, her announcement that she had no more to say, brought him from his reverie and to his feet. The AI representatives stood in rapid unison, offering her their hands across the table.

Chess willed her to look at him, petitioned her with a soft, intimate tone. "Stay, Holly. There's more to discuss."

She smiled, eyes focused somewhere beyond his shoulder. "I'm taking an earlier flight than I planned on. I'm sure you'll do what's best for each of us."

A pall fell over the table and invaded the opulent room as she made her exit, quietly closing the bedroom door behind her.

The two men shuffled papers, cleared throats, snapped and unsnapped briefcases, interrupting the otherwise eternal silence. Finally the older of the two spoke.

"Reynolds and I need to confer in private a minute, Baker, in order to present an offer."

Holly's announcement of "an earlier plane" reverberated in Chess's head. He heard a stranger's voice answer. "That won't be necessary. I've decided I'm not interested." The words came from a man he liked better than the bastard who'd inhabited his soul as of late.

The younger executive blanched. The older, more seasoned negotiator smiled grudgingly. "Shrewd, since you haven't heard an offer. But no sense in finessing. I'm impressed with what I see and with Ms. Harper's apparent ability. I'm prepared to—"

Chess stood so abruptly, his bad knee caught. "I don't mean to be rude, and I'm sorry to inconvenience you, but I'm uninterested in any offer. Xtreme is no longer for sale."

The younger man stared at the hand Chess offered him, releasing his breath. "You can't be serious, man. You're leaving too much on the table."

An ironic understatement, considering Chess had planned on borrowing against the agreed-on merger to take advantage of the Mexican crisis. Maybe commitment to Holly, the sacrifice, would salvage more than this man could imagine. "I'm sorry I took up your time, but trust me, I'm serious."

He waited as they collected their wares, then preceded them to the door and opened it with a smile. "Nice almost doing business with you." He restrained himself from closing the door before they'd cleared it.

After listening to rustling sounds from within Holly's room, he bolted for the phone and dialed London while praying the Mexican market fiasco had Peder Andrews working late.

He answered on the fifth ring. "Andrews here."

"Chess Baker. Glad I caught you."

"Just." He sounded harried. "Do you have news, Mr. Baker?"

Chess shrugged mentally. "Congress is meeting, and from my sources it looks favorable, but I've made a decision on my own." One with about as much logic as drawing to an inside straight. "Load me up on Banomex—the eleven percent convertible offering. And Teléfonos. Five hundred thousand each."

"Excuse me?" Banker language for, your funds are non-existent. Your account is empty. You're broke."

"Increase my position first thing tomorrow. You'll have to trust me until additional funds arrive to cover the trade."

A slight pause. "I see. What shall I tell my people to watch for, in the way of additional funds?"

"A bank wire from First Bank of Okmulgee, Oklahoma."

Chess hoped that by the grace of God he could balance the broken promise to his grandmother by keeping his original pledge to Holly.

A promise of their mutual survival.

Chapter Thirty-three

Holly managed a separate cab to the airport. Chess appeared moments before take-off, looking more familiar in boots, Levi's, Stetson and a shearling jacket. She hid out in the ladies' room until she heard the boarding announcement. A final stop by passenger check-in assured her Chess had some-how wangled a seat next to hers when she had been told hers was the last in first class. Enduring the dubious stare of the ticket agent, Holly opted to sit in coach, even though she'd paid first-class fare.

The Denver airport proved more of an obstacle. Chess wordlessly trailed her from the plane, on and off the under-ground train, up the escalator and into baggage claim, where she engaged a porter. She turned over her claim checks and requested a cab. Awed and angered, she watched Chess engage the same porter, fish for his bulging money clip and bribe the man to take her arriving bags, along with his, to the Cherokee.

As Holly stalked behind, burrowing into her fur, head bent against frigid wind and peppering snow, the porter dropped back, matching his long stride to her short steps.

"He said you all wuz tiffin' and you wuz jest mad. I dint

see no sense in that. Anyways...it's too cold for you to be ridin' in no cab."

"Thank you, Cupid." She climbed into the Cherokee, leaving the traitorous porter with the blond Judas.

Joining her, Chess directed, "Buckle up, sugar. It's going to be a rough ride."

As if it hadn't been already.

He started the engine and switched the heater to defrost. An icy blast shot out of the dash. Looping a wrist over the wheel, he stared straight ahead. "We're not leaving until you buckle up."

With a huff, she engaged the belt and folded her arms. She rested her cheek against the frosty window and closed her eyes, closing out his revered and disturbing profile.

After an hour of her silence and a multitude of phone calls from his side of the truck, he pulled to a curb in the snow-plagued twilight, a block from her house. He kept his eyes on the street, foot on the brake.

"The AI deal is off."

Her head jerked round before she could fake indifference. "Why? Didn't I convince them for you?"

His brow creased. "You more than convinced them, sugar. They begged for Xtreme."

"Interesting."

"What?"

"Interesting to imagine what new scheme could appeal to you more than selling me down the river."

He slammed the gearshift into park, turned toward her and hurled the Stetson into the back seat. "You don't get it, Holly."

She whirled to face him. "Enlighten me, Chess."

He reached out. She pushed his hand away. She knew him too well to label his expression as pain. Manipulation, most likely.

"I care about you, sugar. A hell of a lot." Softly.

Ire boiled up, spilled over. "Don't you dare use that on me."

His hands closed on her forearms, fingers digging through the thick coat, dragging her across the seat until only the console kept them apart. Her head snapped when he shook her, then he pressed her face against the soft suede of his coat, his hand caressing her neck, lips pressed to her hair. "It's true."

Voice muffled, she insisted, "You shouldn't. I went to New York with plans to sabotage you. Surely you know that." Pressed against him, she sensed his surprise.

"But you didn't," he murmured, breath warm against her temple. "And I didn't sell you out. I care. I know it's hard, darlin', after the way I've behaved, but try to believe me."

Care? Euphemism for feelings he chose not to admit? Her heart quickened, even as scenes of the night before and questions twisted her mind. She pushed back. "Then why did you leave me in the middle of the night?"

"Jules." It sounded like a half sob. "I can't get rid of the feeling you belong to him."

"You got rid of it long enough to—"

His hand clamped her mouth. "Don't ever say that to me. It doesn't apply. We made love. That's why I let America Ice go." He tilted her chin, touched his mouth to hers in a chaste pledge. "Say you believe me."

She wanted desperately to believe, to trust, to curl against him and end the war. "Jules means nothing to me, Chess. All I feel, when I think he might have abandoned me, is anger. Anger for the hell he's caused. When I think he's dead, I feel only dull sorrow. Mostly, I feel defeated by the mystery of it all—regret that I'll probably never have the answers."

He touched a fingertip to her lips, drew it across the corner, along her throat. "You're sure that's all you feel?"

"Very sure. Jules was a father to me, nothing more. Never a husband or companion, never a lover, even though he's the only other man I've slept with." Images of last night descended, rippled in her breasts, then ran downward into a dark, sheltered ache. "I never loved Jules. I know that now."

His eyes searched hers in near darkness. "How do you know?"

"Because of the way you made love to me." She ran her hand into his hair, onto his neck, ruffling the soft fringe. The result left her kitten weak, longing. "Jules and I aren't married. We never will be again. If he came back tonight, I'd feel nothing."

He caught her hand and pressed his warm lips to her palm. "Do me a favor, sugar."

She smiled. "I guess I'm game. Do I have to memorize questions and answers?"

"Say you want me. Memorize it."

"Come home with me, cowboy. We'll talk about it there."

When they turned onto her street, she spotted a white car parked in her drive.

Fresh, man-sized footprints led to her darkened front door.

Chapter Thirty-four

A honed inner sense told her the identity of her visitor even before the ghostly figure stepped from the study into the shadowy foyer. Her heart tripped against her rib cage like a nervous hummingbird. Blood rushed in her veins, a river on a rampage.

"Jules! My God!" Her hand flew to her throat, her mind sprinting between relief and anger that he was alive. She had a sense of stepping out of herself to dredge up niggling, senseless details. She heard her curt demand, "How did you get in?" before she recalled Sally was dog-sitting Angel.

The harsh greeting stung him visibly. His denying gaze focused on Chess, then back on her. After fishing in his pants pocket, he flashed a small metal object. "I still have a key."

His voice pricked familiar memories; his reply answered a multitude of questions and enforced suspicions she had harbored for years. Musky cologne and uncommon dishevelment trickled into her consciousness. A tie she recalled, unfashionably narrow now, hung loose on a wrinkled shirt. He hadn't shaved recently.

The sound of her luggage being lowered to the marble floor ricocheted within her grief. She glanced at Chess. His nearness, their ruined plan, all she'd postponed saying to him, jarred her. Chess's body howled protest as he eased back, allowing the intruder to hold her. She kept her arms at her side until guilt raised them in a feeble, obligatory half hug.

The moment propriety allowed, she moved away from Jules.

"This is Chess Baker." Eternity passed before she trusted her voice, trusted her eyes to meet Chess's. "Jules Efron."

"Nice to meet you." Chess's hand might have been weighted. She scarcely recognized his voice, or registered his obligatory greeting.

Jules's hand was even slower to act, his handshake a parody, his eyes haunted with inner anxiety. "You, too."

At last Chess broke the ensuing silence as he bent toward the luggage. "I'll put these in the bedroom, Holly."

"I'll do it, Baker." Too quick. Too emphatic. "It'll get me back into a husbandly role."

Holly exchanged looks with Chess, hers denial. She couldn't read his. She didn't want to believe she saw sick satisfaction. He straightened, his back rod stiff, the innate furrow materializing between his pale brows. His teeth clamped so tightly a white rim formed around his mouth. Holly tried but failed to catch his gaze, for he studied Jules now. Chess's expression, anger tinged with acquiescent resolve, made her stomach fist.

"I wouldn't want to stand in the way of a husband's duties." He looked at her. "Any of them."

She felt the blow of his words. "Chess, that's not—"

His eyes cut her off. "You two have catching up to do." Tone remote, he snapped the shearling coat, adjusted his hat, shoved his hands into his pockets. "Adam's waiting for me."

Adam had not been a factor before. She felt sick. Sentenced. "I'll walk you to the car."

Before she could object, Jules's arm circled her waist.

Chess's gaze, shape-shifting emotional clouds, focused there. She drew back, blood racing. What the hell was Jules thinking? Was he trying to step into her life where he had stepped out?

The three of them stood mentally circling one another, Chess's eyes cold as icicles. Silence persisted until she opened the door and stepped into the frigid night. She picked her way down icy steps to wait for him on the walk. He caught up to her, grasped her arm and ushered her back up the steps and onto the porch. She balked, skidding backward before he could open the door and manhandle her inside. Their gazes locked.

His voice hard, he confessed, "I left your bed last night, because I dreamed Jules came back. I hoped it was a nightmare." He waited for an indication that she understood. "It wasn't. Jules is no ghost."

"To me he is. I told you if he came back, I'd feel nothing." Her breath frosted up. "It's true. I feel nothing." Except regret for how the reappearance was affecting Chess.

Down the street, a car sloshed into a drive, a child's greeting rang on the stillness. Holly breathed the feral smell of suede, aching to run her hand inside the jacket's shearling collar. She wished he would open the coat, fold her into its wooly pile and let her absorb his masculine warmth.

"Will he be staying here? With you?"

"I don't know." Her mind raced through possibilities. "If he does, that, too, will mean nothing."

"To me, it does." His eyes pinned hers in the muted porchlight. "Come home with me."

Her mind dissected the invitation, came up with one answer. "I can't. Jules and I have to talk. I have to have closure."

He folded his arms over his chest and looked at the Cherokee. "You told me you'd created you own closure."

A one-sided resolution. "I need to know he under-stands."

He reached as if to touch her cheek but dropped his hand. "Good night, Holly. It's been interesting." He opened the door, guided her inside, then firmly closed the door. She stared at the carved hardwood barrier. Jules breathed intrusively. The grandfather clock hammered, echoed, hammered. She had wanted to tell Chess she loved him, but he'd given her no opportunity.

She prayed he'd come back.

The Cherokee engine fired. Hope died.

"Who is that guy?"

She faced Jules, staggered by change. His face had slack-ened, surrendering to his fifty-four years. Wiry hair, once raven like hers, appeared shot with pewter and on the verge of receding.

"Chess is a complicated story. I need to hear yours first."

Deep brackets ringed his mouth. "I see he knows where the bedroom is."

Quaking, she moved past him, through the arched door into the living room and crossed to the bar. "Would you like a drink?"

"That's all you have to say? After all this time?"

Her hand went to the Scotch—his drink of choice—vac-illated, then seized the Courvoisier. After pouring two jiggers and adding ice, she crossed to the sofa and struck a waiting pose. "There's Scotch. If you'd like some." Glenlivit. After learning she preferred it, she no longer kept Chivas.

She hated the fire he had built in her absence. She hated even more the way he stoked now, then familiarly tossed in wood from the battered brass tub. Resentful déjà vu sprang to life.

He sat down next to her, running his arm along the back of the sofa. His face appeared anxious, gaunt. His hand rested too close to her shoulder, and she stilled her body from burrowing into the sofa corner. He had once been her life, the man she counted on. Tonight, he seemed more like an adversary.

"I've had amnesia, Holly."

She fought not to scream. Laugh. Sob. "Until when?"

"A few months ago."

"You expect me to believe that?"

He looked shocked. "It's true."

"But you chose to let me go on wondering." To go on struggling with Xtreme. Go on agonizing in amnesia of her own, until she inventoried her life, canceled it, and began anew.

"I needed some time to get myself together before I came home. You wouldn't have liked the man who woke up."

She had never regarded amnesia as sleep. "I need more than that, Jules. I lived in hell after you left."

He shifted his weight, curving one leg onto the sofa, facing her. His rheumy eyes glinted with possible reprieve. "If you missed me so much that your life was hell—"

She shrugged off his reach, rose, paced to the fire and stared into its depths. Chess stared back at her from the amber flames. "A different kind of hell. Every last one of your friends demanded payment on their notes."

"I didn't expect that." His tone revealed unconvincing incredulity. "I assumed they'd convert to stock."

He expected? Assumed? "I lived through financial desperation. Rejection. Looming failure." She glanced over her shoulder, finding self-satisfaction in his anxiety. "I lived with fear I'd been abandoned." Imprisoning, lingering, life-altering fear. Fear that had affected her relationship with Chess.

He started toward her, dismissing her logic with a wave of his hand. "That's ridiculous. We were never apart from the moment we met. Why would I abandon you, if I had a choice?"

His cavalier demeanor cut like a serrated blade. "For seven years I've asked myself that." He stopped midstride, flinching at her tone.

"I've stopped asking." Stopped caring. "Tell me more about the amnesia you suffered."

His blanched facial tone blended with his hair. "I'd rather not. Too many bad memories."

"I thought amnesiacs had no memory."

"You know what I mean."

Did she? "I need to know if you simply woke up one day with no identity."

He ambled to sit on a sofa arm, palms braced on his thighs. When he met her demanding stare, he jerked.

"The third day there I was mugged—lost all my papers."

"How do you know, if you couldn't remember any-thing?"

"I didn't know, until later, when I regained my memory." He expelled breath, eyes milking hers. "I woke up in the gut-ter with a young girl leaning over me. She took me home, and her family took care of me."

Better than she had? She had catered to his wishes, often shelving her own. She had worked with him. Had sex on his schedule. Run his home to his liking. At his request, she had learned to cook flanken in his kitchen and eaten countless meals at his table while feeling like an alien.

Now he was the alien in her house.

"There's no record of your calling on any fabric sources." His reason for going. She adopted a skeptical look. "What did you do those first two days in Sri Lanka?"

Wordlessly, he drifted to the bar, splashed vodka over ice and sipped, before echoing, "Record?"

"I had a private investigator looking for you for seven years. He found nothing to indicate you existed after the plane landed." No hotel records, long distance calls, or credit card charges. Nothing. She had assumed he'd been killed soon after disembarking, in some scenario resembling the mugging he described. When no proof materialized, she had begun to doubt. "What did you do for the two days, Jules, since it was only to be a three-day trip?"

"I was sick—some kind of bug I got from plane food." He yanked his tie loose, then stood with one hand in his pocket while the other clutched his quietly rattling drink. "I knew I'd have to hump that third day to make up for lost time. I got careless, cut through an alley and ended up half dead without a clue."

His memory appeared flawless now. She gave him an I-want-more look.

"The family I mentioned—a dirt-poor widow and five children—nursed me back to physical health and helped me find a job in a spice exporting business." He issued his cajoling rag-merchant smile. "Curry, of course."

And while he contentedly shipped spices, Xtreme's lenders were calling to demand their notes be paid in full. She shivered, massaging her arms. "That's all? You shipped spices, adopted a new identity and forgot about everything else?"

"I had no choice, Holly—no memory of another life." His voice lilted, as though he'd achieved a coup. "It wasn't easy. I went to the embassy, assuming I was American because of my accent-free English. They had no record of anyone missing who fit my description."

Unlikely. She had contacted the embassy before hiring Henry Chastain. Once he had investigated all other sources, she'd contacted the embassy again. "You went there only once?"

"Three times. I went a second time to see if a missing person report had been filed yet. When none appeared, I stayed away. In fact I kept a low profile in order to get Indian papers from the underground. When the amnesia left and I knew who I was, I returned to the embassy for American papers."

A cache of unsavory images rushed her mind. "Who sent you underground?"

He shrugged, mouth hardening. "My new peers."

She found it hard to imagine Jules operating covertly. Or had that been a trait she'd overlooked in her youth and naïveté? "And you never tried to determine your identity after that?"

He slumped onto the sofa. For the first time, defeat crept into his posture. He released his breath. "Try to look at it this way, baby."

Her spine crawled as he rushed on, unaware.

"I didn't know who I was—know about you or what kind of life I had back here. The simplicity of doing menial work, returning to a bare little room with a cold shower and a straw mattress on the floor had a certain appeal. I drifted into it."

And when he'd "woken up" with a memory, he had been unmotivated to contact her for months. Beating a dead horse held no logic, considering his earlier explanation of pride motivating him to regroup before coming home. Pride. A catalyst for such decisions as hers to have him declared dead and gain her freedom, if not peace of mind.

He must have read her thoughts. "My biggest regret is you seem not to believe me."

She took a breath and plunged in. "I've had you declared legally dead. Just as if I had buried you. We're no longer married."

He seized on that fallacy. "I'm alive. We're married."

"I also got a conventional divorce, based on desertion."

He grimaced. "I don't like you saying that."

"I hated feeling it."

"Now you know those grounds don't apply."

She knew little more than she'd known at the beginning

of this discussion. "Wait here. I have something to show you."

In the study, she closed the door, hastily dialed the phone and waited while a droned message played out.

"Greg, it's Holly. If you're there—"

A click. "I'm here. Just catching a *Highlander* rerun."

She released a choking, pent-up breath.

"How'd it go in New York? Will Wyatt be riding into the sunset soon? Are you a richer, wiser, and free woman?"

"Jules was here when I got home. He's here now."

"Holy shit. I told you he'd come back. Is he staying with you? Considering the divorce, I mean?"

Her hairline tingled. "You mean will he be sleeping with me." Being asked the question a second time forced her to examine the issue. "He looks down on his luck. He can use the guest room for a few days." She got only silence. "He claims he's had amnesia."

"How do you feel about that?" Greg asked cautiously.

"My feelings are...complicated."

"Want me to come over? It'll take five minutes tops."

And have Jules think she was running scared? Was she? "How legal are the papers I signed?"

"You haven't seen him in seven years. Legality is your big concern?"

"I don't need a lecture. I need legal advice. At least until I decide if he's telling the truth." She crammed back thoughts of the months that had passed since he "woke up."

"He's dead, Holly. If he'd shown up before the ink dried, he'd still be dead." Greg fell silent. She heard the Highlander theme in the background. "But if he's telling the truth, will you take him back?"

"I'm talking about Xtreme. I need to know my legal standing there." Images of Chess, Jules, Xtreme, and the question of whether or not Jules told the truth, whirled in her mind. Answers got lost in irresolution.

"Legally you always owned Xtreme. Nothing's changed." He expelled breath. "But it's complicated. I'd better come over."

"No."

"I won't bill you."

The laugh he sought from her wouldn't come. "If I handled the last seven years, I can handle tonight. Call me tomorrow."

She opened the safe, extracted the death certificate and returned to Jules, determined to ensure her freedom.

Chapter Thirty-five

Chess pulled the Cherokee to the curb a block from Holly's house, near the same spot they had parked earlier. He rested his brow against the steering wheel, fighting a wave of acid churning in his belly. Finally, he raised his head and stared into the darkness, coming face to face with raging guilt. He tried but failed to find comfort in Jules's legal death. Instead, he settled for Adam's wise disregard for legal documents.

Never mind that Jules was more of an asshole than Chess had pictured, or that he'd obviously left Holly floundering for seven years. He was alive and had returned to claim his booty, and Chess had broken a self-promise made in the throes of Robyn's adultery.

He had slept with another man's wife.

Fear wrestled guilt, emerging as dread. Dread of losing control. Now that his adversary was no longer a dead man, would he take Chess's place with Holly and take her place at Xtreme? With his finances and emotions in chaos, was he up to fighting a live adversary?

One certainty flashed in his head. In New York, lust had defeated his sense of right and wrong. No amount of regret could erase the fact he'd made love to Holly. Only by staying away from her, granting her and Jules a chance to reconcile, could Chess make amends.

Giving in to yet another weakness, he straightened in the seat, fished a limp, worn-out Macanudo from his pocket and waited for the dash lighter to pop. He touched the glowing tip to the cigar, puffed mightily and drew acrid smoke into his lungs. He cracked the window and pulled away from the curb, one last question tormenting him.

Why did he have to love Holly so goddamned much?

And why hadn't he told her?

His heart pumped spastically when the Cherokee's headlights flashed across Adam's quarters. A lone figure stood in the shadows between the clapboard add-on and a towering pine. Chess doused the lights. He watched the glow of a cigarette lift upward, flare, then plummet to the snow. The figure turned in profile and Chess recognized his cousin's lank form. A quick glance at the dash clock resurrected the tickle on the back of his neck. Lance should be polishing leather on the end stool at Bud's, lining up the night's action.

What the hell else could be wrong in the existing maelstrom?

He approached the dimly lighted appendage, fresh powder piling over the tops of his boots. Lance huddled without a coat, hands in pockets, coughing quietly.

"What's wrong here, Lance?"

"Not much now. Welcome back. How'd New York go?" He rummaged for a new cigarette, snapped his lighter, sucked deeply.

"Something's wrong with Adam. What?"

"Let's get a drink. I'll tell you all about it." Lance's alcohol-free breath revealed just how bad things had to be.

"Suit yourself on the drink. I'm going in to see him."

A hand seized his upper arm, the grip frail.

"He's finally asleep, cuz. Let's get some coffee."

In Do Thi's warm aromatic kitchen they faced across the small oilcloth-covered breakfast table in near darkness.

Lance stirred cognac into his coffee. "So, I get this call around three this afternoon from Do Thi, hysterical as hell. She's crying and babbling about some woman being here and Adam freezing to death. Sure enough, when I get here he's shivering and jerking and chanting—"

"What do you mean, chanting?" *Some woman?* Chess's gut knotted.

"Raving, maybe. Dancing around in circles—twisting, dipping, singing the same words over and over. Clean out of his head, for sure."

"Yei-bi-chai," Chess murmured.

Lance cocked his head.

"It's a Navajo chant. A healing dance. He was trying to accomplish his own healing." He cursed himself for not being there, grateful Lance had been. "Tell me about the woman."

"Do Thi says she called herself a shaman. Buckskin and feathers. Drove an old truck. Claimed she was here to get Adam." He took a swig of coffee. "By the time I got home, Do Thi had chased her off with the double barrel from your bedroom."

"Christ!" Chess pounded his shirt pocket. No Macanudos. He eyed the cigarette pack bulging his cousin's pocket, then tore his gaze back to his face. "Tell me about Adam. How'd you get him calmed down?"

"I couldn't. I got him onto the bunk but he was too cold—and achy. He kept shaking and muttering how the Navajo created the sun from a slab of quartz crystal and how the sun could make him warm if he could just get to it."

The Navajo emergence myth. Jesus... "I should have been here," Chess said, thinking aloud.

"It scared hell out of me."

"Why didn't you call? You could've run me down somewhere."

Lance's eyes hardened. "What could you have done by long distance?" He grinned finally. "Anyway, I figured you had your hands full of Tycoon Annie."

Lance's troubled eyes helped soften his crude and ignorant rendition of what had really happened in New York.

"All of a sudden he seemed so skinny and helpless. I stuffed him in the car and took him to the Castle Rock Emergency Center."

The tickle on the back of Chess's neck evolved to full-fledged hackles along his spine. "What'd they tell you?"

Lance gave a cursory grin. "That he had aches and chills. I wanted to punch the bitch."

Chess attributed that claim to the cognac. "Yuppie flu."

"What?" Lance eyed him in the pale light from the cooktop.

"Yuppie flu—chronic fatigue syndrome. Adam carries the virus." Chess had looked it up on the Internet, studied hard.

Lance laughed, one brow cocked. "Adam with yuppie flu?"

"Getting upset—stress—triggers it." He waited for Lance's nod. "What did the clinic do for him?" He braced.

"Nothing. Since I obviously wasn't the next of kin or the legal guardian and had no friggin' idea who is—"

"I damn sure hope to hell you didn't tell them that."

"They wouldn't treat him. Told me to put him to bed and give him Tylenol." He made a dismissive gesture. "I did. Then I told him football stories till he dozed off. End of story."

Chess wished that were true. He clomped to the refrigerator for a Coors, crossed back and laid his hand on Lance's shoulder. "I'm going out there for the night. I owe you, cuz."

Lance glanced up, eyes quickening, lax smile spreading. "Anytime. He's a good kid, sweet, kinda. I hate like crap to see him hurting." Squinting, he studied Chess. "Who the hell do you think the woman was? What does she want?"

"Name's Shimasani," Chess said. "She wants Adam back on the reservation."

Chapter Thirty-six

When Holly entered her office the next morning, a cigarette butt in an antique Limoges bowl grabbed her attention.
The smoker had crushed the stub among the brass paper clips
the bowl held.

Had her intruder been defiant or simply a slob?

With a map pin, she fished the residue from the bowl and
examined it. Marlboro.

Her arms blossomed with goose bumps as her mind
reeled. Only a few of Xtreme's employees smoked. They
shared smoke breaks outside the building, in fair and inclement
weather. Skin clammy, suspicion skyrocketing, she rummaged
in the back of her center desk drawer looking for a small silver
key. Gone. She jerked the drawer open, ransacked the contents. No key.

Like a cleanliness fanatic who had found a roach in her
kitchen, Holly felt ill. Sinking against her chair, she told herself nothing could be pilfered from a locked computer, and she
must have dropped the key into her handbag before going to
New York. A change of handbags had failed to transfer the
key.

She rose, prepared to return to the house, to her closet.

An inner voice urged her back into the chair. She swiveled, then flipped the computer's power switch. A green light blinked, steadied, glowed. Her caller had unlocked the machine, taken what he wanted, and left it unlocked to taunt her, instead of covering the transgression. Hands trembling, she shoved in a blank disk, copied her latest design concept and deleted the file from the screen. She cast about for a place to hide the disk.

War. She stood alone. No generals. No soldiers.

Except Chess. She could no longer delay revealing her suspicions about Lance.

Two days later Holly wheeled into Xtreme's parking lot and spied the Cherokee for the first time since Jules's return. The absence Chess had maintained since then was over. Inside the building she found their shared office empty and cornered Sally in the warehouse. She had to shout over the clamor of the sewing and embroidery machines.

"Have you seen Chess?" Over Sally's shoulder, she gave Dihn a dutiful wave and a forced smile.

"Hi, sweetie." Sally hefted a heavy box of ski caps onto a conveyer belt. "What's up? How'd you shake Jules today?"

Holly considered the aptly phrased term. "He dropped me off and kept the car to get a haircut and run errands." Her stomach contracted fist-like as she estimated how much time she had before his return. "Where's Chess?"

Sally braced her ample hips against a counter. "He was like a caged animal, pacing up and down the hall and wearing out that cellular." Her face looked pinched, as though backing up her description. "He went for a run."

Holly headed for the front office where she camped inside the glass door until she saw Chess enter the lot from a side street. She sprinted without a coat into the frigid spring day to wait next to the Cherokee. When he spotted her, surprise flickered over his features. Her heart thumped arrhythmically. He checked his pace, then slowed to an endless walk. She watched his chest heave. Memories flew past her eyes like a carousel spinning out of control, replaying his same telltale body motion from a previous, less painful encounter.

He stopped in front of her, breath soughing in his lungs, eyes brooding. "What are you doing out here? It's cold."

"The mountain has come to Mohammed again."

His eyes took on a haunted sheen. He looked west toward the snow-crowned mountains, paced in a small circle, hands on hips. Willfully, her gaze lowered to his bulging thighs and calves beneath his running shorts, then back to savor his sinewy shoulders and upper arms revealed by a tank top. The heavy, onyx-faced Rolex gleamed among the amber hairs lining his wrist, tiny diamonds glittering in pale sun. Perspiration, pungent in the cold air, drenched his hair, streamed down his neck and beneath the shirt. He loosened the jacket tied around his waist and pulled it on.

Longing acute as pain swept through her. "Why didn't you return my calls? Didn't Do Thi tell you?"

He stopped pacing and met her eyes, standing so still now he could have been a statue but for the latent energy he emanated. "I took Adam to Ruidoso for a few days."

Visions of the cigarette in the Limoges bowl flashed in her mind. She relived the lonely panic of discovering the tampered-with computer, her feeling of need. "Why Ruidoso?" Why now?

Within the frame of pale lashes, his eyes darkened, brooded. He moved to the driver's door, unlocked it, jerked off a headband bearing the Xtreme emblem and tossed it inside. He unfastened a mileage counter from his ankle, tossed it. When he fitted the keys into the ignition with purpose, she moved alongside. He closed the door and turned back to her.

"I've had some problems with Adam. Lance handled it while I was in New York, but I needed to spend time with Adam. Alone." He added, "I've checked in with Toby every day. She had my number."

His homage when he spoke of Lance stepping in, "handling it," assured her now was not the time to voice her suspicions. "Toby finally told me you were calling." The girl's reluctant demeanor had led Holly to believe Chess had sworn Toby to secrecy concerning his whereabouts. "I was in the office. Why didn't you talk to me?"

His eyes went flat as worn-down river stone. "What's to talk about?"

Shards of fear and resentment tingled her scalp. "We're running a business here, in case you forgot, partner."

He was skilled at aloof expressions. "I've talked to the department heads every day. I rely on Lance to keep me informed of any problems."

She bristled, but kept quiet, her eyes demanding more.

He rubbed his forearms briskly, as though starting to sense the cold. "Every time I called, they told me Jules was here. I figured he was back on top of things."

Instead of voicing an expletive, accusation or plea, she jerked open the Cherokee, hoisted herself beneath the wheel and closed the door. Their eyes locked through the window glass. Finally, he crossed in front and climbed into the passenger seat.

His scent, cologne laced with soured sweat, permeated the enclosure. He trembled from the cold. The need to embrace him warred with the urge to punch him, now that she fully understood his abstinence agenda. But, then, he'd never said he loved her, only that he cared; Chess cared for everyone, an emotion that often came packaged with control. Considering his show of indifference, feigned or real, now seemed the wrong time to confess her love.

She turned toward him in the seat. "Are you punishing me?"

His brows torqued. "For what?"

"For Jules. Are you staying away to make me suffer?"

"Four months ago you lived for the days I didn't show up."

"Damn you, Chess." Her eyes smarted.

His expression softened. "I'm not punishing you, sugar. I'm taking the cure. Like quitting smoking, or drinking. Staying away from you removes temptation."

"And forces me to take the cure."

Expelling breath, he drew one leg into the seat and jiggled a well-defined knee in out-of-character agitation. "I'm trying to make things easier. For both of us."

"Chivalrous bastard." She bit her lip, hugged her rib cage, her arms framing her breasts.

He kept his eyes on her face, dedicated to the cause.

"I've got problems that go beyond Jules coming back." He ran his hand through his hair, fished the headband off the floor, fingered the logo. "And you need time to rethink your divorce, with his input. I don't want to influence that, but I'll sure as hell be around to see the outcome."

She seized the headband, crumpled it, then smoothed it against her thigh. "I made that decision on the seven-year anniversary of Jules's disappearance. Why do you want me to make it again? Are you sadistic or just insecure?"

A painful-looking smile worked the corners of his mouth, then faded. "It's a little more involved than that."

"Then what? I have a right to know what you're thinking."

"How about me, Holly? Do I have the same right?"

Hope surged. "Jules is sleeping in the guest room until he finds his own place. I haven't let him touch me, and I won't. "

Looking mildly appeased, he habitually touched his chest, patted lightly and came away empty-handed. After rummaging in the center console with no result, he raised his eyes to hers. Then he took up his cause. "I'm not sure who my partner is now. You or Jules. Since I turned down America Ice, I have to rethink a public offering. If we go on sleeping together, and if you remain my sole partner, I worry that I'd be cheating Jules out of what might rightfully be his. His wife and a fair share of Xtreme."

She was unsure of the moral and ethical boundaries governing Xtreme, uncertain of anything beyond wanting Chess to hold her, tell her they'd work it out together. Abruptly, she realized how thoroughly he'd been taking care of her since he walked in Xtreme's door. Today she felt alone again.

"I'm working on all that," she said.

"I would never have signed on...invested in Xtreme and taken on a male partner."

Had he even heard what she'd said? "But a poor defenseless schoolmarm was fine." Her voice quavered. She hugged herself fiercely.

"You needed me. I like being needed."

"I still need you, cowboy." The tears slipped over, slid down to invade the corners of her mouth. She swallowed against the pain in her throat, tasting salt. She dotted her face with her sleeve. "Don't desert me."

Arms folded on his chest, he leaned his back against the door. "The most I've ever hurt in my life was when I found out Robyn cheated on me. Or in plain terms, slept with another man." His face twisted, underlining his confession. "I swore I'd never be a party to—I know the hell that cheating causes. I promised myself I'd never sleep with a married woman. I screwed up in New York, but I've got my head on straight now."

And now she was going to pay for the wounds Robyn had inflicted. His vulnerability and senseless guilt left her with a bleak wintry sense. His determination to hold his ground, give her up, scared her. "Your morals are intact. You still haven't slept with a married woman. Jules and I are divorced. He's dead. I don't love him. I never did."

He watched, waiting for more, she thought.

"Until I know he didn't have amnesia, that he actually left me, that he's only back to reap the benefits of Xtreme, I won't know how to deal with him. Your theory of avoiding me is asinine." Now she waited for concession that didn't come. She took a breath, regrouped. "Why are you doing this, Chess?"

He remained silent, his look tender yet remote.

"What kind of problems?"

He cocked a brow.

"You said you have problems that go beyond Jules." She placed her hand on his knee; his skin seared her palm before he eased away from her touch. Her heart clenched. "What kind of problems?"

"It's personal." His mouth formed a grave line. A deep groove appeared between troubled eyes. "I'll handle it."

"I thought that's what partners are for. To share."

He shrugged, a gesture she seldom witnessed, a showing of having no answers.

"What about the ski show in Vegas next week?"

"What about it?"

"I was planning on you...on us going together." Being together, joined at hollows and angles, in every way possible.

He stared out the window, studying a passing car. "You can handle it. You did it long before you knew I existed." He turned back smiling, eyes somber.

She mauled her bottom lip, seeking pain to ease pain. "All that's changed. I'm very much aware you exist now."

He straightened in the seat. "I have to go, Holly. I dropped Adam off at Cherry Creek Mall to see a movie. I want to be there—"

Her letdown was almost palpable. "What about your things?" She'd seen documents and market reports scattered all over his side of the desk. "Your clothes?"

"I'll pick them up later."

When she wasn't there. "Fine."

She straightened as though liquid steel shot through her spine. Her hand went to the door handle, eased it up. His gaze rushed there, then away.

"I always knew you'd be riding into the sunset. I just didn't know it would be so soon."

As though he hadn't heard, he yawed sideways, ran his palm into the space between the seats and came up with a cellophane-wrapped cigar. Eyes fixed, he zipped the thin red starter tab and unsheathed the object. He shoved in the dash lighter, pressed it, his fingertip whitening, not nearly as detached from their debate as he'd led her to believe. Before he could poke the cigar into his exquisite mouth, she grabbed and snapped in one motion, then threw the pieces in his lap.

"Suffer, damn you." She slid down from the truck, ran across the parking lot and into the building.

"Jules called," Toby announced over the clatter of computer keys. When she glanced up, getting a look at Holly's face, she sank back in her chair. Her hand froze near the pulse in her throat. "Jeez, Hol."

Holly swiped tears frantically. "What did he want?"

"I put the message on your desk." Toby returned to clacking keys, eyes averted, cheeks flaming.

In her office, Holly curled into Chess's big leather chair, legs drawn beneath her. She glanced around the room, taking in her plaques and his roping trophy, his humble contribution to the memorabilia wall. She stared at the traitorous computer and Robyn's picture, the aftermath of his cologne plaguing her. Emptiness settled like a shroud as she read the note Toby had left for her.

"Jules found that Indian wine he told you about. He'll start dinner, then pick you up. Call if you want to talk to him before then."

Jules refused to believe reconciliation was impossible, and the longer she allowed him to stay, the further away she drove Chess. The realization overrode her patience. Yet, until she knew if Jules was lying, past loyalties and commitments complicated their association.

Images of going to Sol y Sombre, making Chess understand, nagged her. An intimate dinner with Jules would be a distasteful substitution. She crumpled the message and closed her eyes, leaning her head against the chair.

A movement in the door brought her forward with a start.

"What are you doing here? What do you want?"

Lance waved the papers in his hand. "Thought I saw Chess outside. Where'd he go?" Cigarettes bulged his shirt, but languidly he fished in his pants pocket and removed a small plastic and foil square. Eyes and movements indolent, he split the pack with a thumbnail and popped a piece of gum into his mouth. The fool was chewing nicotine gum while continuing to smoke. She pushed judgment away, seizing on the possibility of gaining insight into Chess's behavior.

"What's wrong with Adam?"

His laugh turned to a wheezy chuckle. "Chess is blaming his absence on Adam, huh?" He leaned against the doorframe, arms folded, ankles crossed. Chewing. "You moved into the roadkill category pretty fast, Holly. Faster than most. You must not be as good as Chess thought you'd be."

She tried leveling him with a look. He didn't flinch.

"I'm not quite as spoiled as my cuz, though. I'm used to his leftovers." His twisted grin patronized. "I've been analyzing the situation. I'll bet Greg Friedman's taken a powder now that your old man is back, but I'll also bet the old man can't satisfy you. Looks like I'm next in line, boss."

The Limoges bowl loomed in her side vision. She thought of Chess, the seclusion of the Cherokee, how she'd forsaken the opportunity to reveal her suspicions about Lance and his actions toward her.

"Crawl back in a snake hole, Lance. You make me sick."

His laugh bordered on maniacal. "You need a good screwing, Holly. I'd be glad to perform the task."

Bile ran along her throat, burned in her chest. Wanting to retch, she seized a stapler and heaved. The missile bounced off the wall near his head. He never moved. "You won't live long enough to even touch me."

He shrugged crookedly, then straightened and tossed the papers on Chess's desk. "Don't bet on it." He gave her a rancid smile as he ambled out the door.

She longed to scrub herself in boiling water.

Chapter Thirty-seven

Chess turned up the shearling collar of his denim jacket as crisp, jagged air scraped his face and neck. Beneath him, Geronimo plodded steadily down a draw and up again, then settled into an even walk. His head kept time to the rhythm of his stride, breath clouds billowing from his nostrils. Further up the trail, Adam's palomino, Gigi, left prints in a shallow, late April snow. The fresh fall had already begun to melt in the incubator warmth of the sun edging over a distant stand of oaks. A biting wind brought a sensual moan from the hovering pines, lifted Adam's unleashed hair off his neck and rippled Chess's hat brim.

As they passed beneath the branches of a low-hanging spruce, a fine sprinkling of dislodged snow settled on their shoulders and on the horses' manes and rumps. The mist changed Adam's jet hair to polished granite. He appeared no burden to the palomino, but an extension. His supple body adhered to each rise and fall of Gigi's gait as though some mysterious spirit bound boy to animal.

Chess looked away, troubled by the uncertainty of maintaining this morning ritual, wondering how long he would be privileged to witness Adam's grace and natural abilities. He buttoned his jacket at the throat, telling himself the chill on the back of his neck had nothing to do with losing Adam.

The icy lump in his chest wouldn't dissolve.

He redirected his thoughts, only to have them fill with Holly. She'd be leaving for the airport about now, the first leg of her trip to the Vegas ski show. She hadn't mentioned the trip again, but he had pilfered a copy of her itinerary from the ticket envelope left on her desk. As late as yesterday, he had kept room in his schedule for Vegas, senselessly, hoping—hoping what? That he'd wake up and find Jules's existence really was a nightmare? Or would he find instead that Jules had accompanied her to the ski show, as he'd done all those past years, according to Sally. Most likely he'd see his way clear to go this year, considering the wide berth Chess had given him.

Abruptly, the perfume of peach and raspberry candles and Anaïs replaced evergreens, leather and horseflesh in his senses. He relived Holly's New York hotel room, her compact, searing body, her raspy cries. A hollow ache shot from his groin into his chest. Left center, where he'd wrapped his heart in barbed wire in a too-late attempt to keep Holly out of it.

Adam pulled up short and reined around to face him, making Chess realize how far he'd fallen behind, a victim of musing.

"What are you thinking?" Adam queried as Chess caught up.

His mind shimmied away from Holly. "About how late your light burned last night." Seeing the Mercedes pulled close to Adam's outside entry meant Lance had stopped on his way back from pillaging the Sedalia bars. "Were you and Lance playing poker again?" When Chess learned Adam was going along with Lance's penchant for strip poker, he had put a stop to that. He hoped.

Adam nodded, a cagey light playing in his eyes. "What else were you thinking? It looked more serious than matchstick poker thoughts."

"About you, chief. About why the hell you won't level with me."

Adam looked to the west, beyond the trees where a green and white meadow sloped gently to a frozen stream. Saddles creaked in the hush. Bits clanked almost soundlessly.

Adam lapsed into his Navajo voice. "My lips cannot speak."

Chess took a long breath. "Don't you want to stay here, Adam? If you'd level with me about life on the rez, I could start looking for reasons why they might let you."

The boy chanced a glance, eyes somber. "They who?"

"The tribal court. Or the BIA. Big Brother. If there's a reason you shouldn't go home—wherever the hell home is— they'd be fools not to let you stay with me. I'm Indian. We've got that little ace in the hole, don't forget."

Too fast for Chess, a dark hand shot out to rake this morning's yet-to-be-shaven amber beard. "Yeah, right. A freak Indian." Adam issued a tight-lipped grin.

Chess dodged sideways, staggering Geronimo a bit. "Never mind the genealogical screw-up. I've got papers."

He watched the boy massage his upper arm, snake a bony brown hand beneath a mass of silky hair to rub the back of his neck. When they ventured onto this topic, Adam's aches and pains were so immediate they appeared faked. Chess knew better. Adam didn't practice deceit. He had only mastered omission.

Half a mile later, Adam said quietly, "I've been thinking."

No damn joke. "Well, that's different."

The chiseled aquiline profile eased into another stingy grin that soon died. "I don't want to go to school."

"Get over it, pal." Chess reached to cuff a lean shoulder, massage a muscle. "School's a given—summer school in fact.

You'll be enrolling in a couple weeks."

Chess studied the sharp profile. Stone. Lips grim. As Adam's hands held the reins loosely, one eased to where the other rested on the saddle horn. Covertly, he massaged a frail wrist. Chess felt the boy's pain in his own joints. Flu-like symptoms, he had read.

"You'll ace school, kemosabe. You're a brain."

Adam took up movie jargon. "The white man's school could be bad medicine."

"There'll be a long line of white man's schools." He thought of the planned progression that ended with Harvard. "It's a white man's world, Adam, and you've got to be prepared to participate." The resistance in Adam's expression tightened Chess's hairline. "Just where the hell should you go, then?"

Adam flexed in the saddle to rub the back of his waist as he turned a signature smile on Chess. Full, artfully carved lips spread over flawless teeth. "I should learn at your knee all you have to teach me, wise, yellow-haired one."

Chess slapped Gigi's rear with the flat of his hand and spurred Geronimo to keep up with the palomino's sudden bolt. He raised his voice over pounding hooves. "You might pull that charm crap on Do Thi, chief, but mark my words. Your brown fanny will be warming a chair at Castle Rock Middle School this summer."

Chess glanced at the Rolex again as the house came into view. Holly could be stowing her baggage in the Saab's trunk, backing from her snow-puddled drive. He forbade his imagination to check whether or not Jules occupied the passenger seat.

Chapter Thirty-eight

Holly passed her ticket envelope to the baggage attendant at the curb, then glanced over her shoulder to where Jules arranged bags in a neat row before the check-in stand. Memory of the last time they'd been at the airport together nudged her. The day he'd left for Sri Lanka. Seven years ago, but it could have been last week, considering how distinctly her mind etched the scene. She appraised him in her peripheral vision. Familiar Hickey Freeman suit, ten-year-old skin shoes, a Polo button-down, collar frayed. Although she had always admired his flamboyant frugality, she made a mental note to retrieve from storage the boxes containing the clothing from his closet. How had he held on to today's clothing for seven down-and-out years in India?

"Pack these yourself?" Face florid in the nippy air, the attendant skewered her with kelp-colored eyes. She nodded. He droned on. "Anybody ask you to take anything on board for them?"

"No." Her eyes searched approaching traffic. She had held hope of Chess accompanying her until the last possible moment. Driving here, she'd even imagined him curbside as she arrived, checking in. Now her mind spun frantically, holding out hope for a gateside reprieve.

Jules closed the distance, assuming a possessive stance. He fished a tip from his pocket and placed the bills on the narrow stand. "I'll park the car. Be right back."

She accepted her ticket back, her thumb fingering the baggage checks stapled to the inside cover. "No. There's no reason for you to come in." That era had ended, leaving a memory more disturbing than poignant. He'd had no reason to drive her today other than needing the use of the Saab in her absence. He had vetoed her bid to take a cab.

Disappointment flicked across his gaze. He studied her, his scrutiny making her feel she had been mounted between glass slides and pushed under a microscope.

"Your flight doesn't leave for two hours." His observation pointed out her needless rush to leave the house. "I'll keep you company."

"I have calls to make. I'll go to the Red Carpet Club for coffee and use their phone." She bent for her hand luggage, adjusted the bag strap on her shoulder and clasped a new *Elle* to her breasts. Running out of avoidance tactics, she made herself meet his anxious gaze. "I want you out of the house by the time I get back, Jules. You've had three weeks to find an apartment."

He nodded, jamming his hands into his trouser pockets, rattling keys and change. She took advantage of the stance by milling into the crowd to ward off a farewell embrace.

A tenniscourt sized billboard boasting KENNETH FELD PRESENTS SIEGFRIED AND ROY AT THE MIRAGE gilded the entry of the hotel, an indoor tropical forest complete with waterfall. Holly observed her milieu while standing in a long registration line. Brass-tipped mahogany poles supported a dropped bamboo ceiling and tropically flowered carpet presented a take-me-to-the-casino trail through marble flooring. A mammoth aquarium lined with lava rock formed the wall behind car rental, safety-deposit and concierge desk. Hordes of garish-hued fish and one resembling the Goodyear blimp in ten-thou-sandth scale, fascinated a crowd lined up two-deep to stare and point.

When her turn came at registration, she canceled one of two reserved rooms, her voice revealing disappointment she now let herself acknowledge. She dashed her name on the registration slip. As she fished for her renewed corporate American Express card, she noted a clandestine discussion among check-in personnel behind the counter.

A gray-suited clerk with beehive hair and rhinestone glasses checked the computer, announcing, "Twenty-three's larger, but twenty-five has a corner view of the strip."

Holly made a listless decision. "The corner, please." At least a view might alleviate some of her loneliness.

The behind-the-counter conference, conducted to the background of clanging slot machines and raucous lounge music, slipped into hushed urgency.

"Is something wrong?"

"Nothing we can't take care of. Enjoy your stay."

She followed the bellman through a casino crowd of diversified ethnic cultures and dialects. Whether dressed in finery or grunge, all sought their fortunes at baccarat, poker, blackjack and slots. With this kind of competition, even if Chess had come with her, she might never have seen him.

Recalling their New York sojourn assured her differently.

Inside her room, the bellman placed her luggage on the bed, hastily unlocked the adjoining room and disappeared inside. As Holly unzipped bags he reappeared bearing two vases of flowers. Daisies, irises, marigolds, fuchsia, babies' breath.

"Where would you like these, ma'am?"

Curbing her curiosity, she pointed to the nightstands. "There and there, thank you."

He vanished again. Before she could search the blooms for a card, he reappeared with three more bouquets in vases clutched to his chest and stood silent, brows arched.

"Mmm….on the dresser, please."

He repeated his steps, this time bearing another vase of flowers and an armload of aromatic candles of various size, shape and color. She began to catch on. In the beginning, planning on coming with her, Chess had allotted her the bigger room.

"Are there more?" Her voice quavered.

He grinned. "No, ma'am."

She dug for a tip. "Anywhere is fine. I'll arrange them."

Once the door caught behind him, she searched every bouquet until she found a card disclosing something other than "Chess." She sagged onto the foot of the bed and read the message.

"I remember how you like flowers and candles." Her eyes stung. Sharp and bittersweet, a pang crowded her chest and her throat broadened. Sense of loss so overwhelmed her that her body seemed to have gone numb. "Your designs are awesome, partner. Break all sales records. Chess."

Feeling insignificant in the suddenly vast room, she pressed the note to her lips, envisioning his strength, his some-times tender touch, his poster-boy smile.

Again, she read a message any partner might send to another. Over the painful past few weeks she had accepted Chess's rejection, casting them at cross-purposes again. He had avoided her so blatantly, her pride forced her to follow suit, communicating by fax to avoid too-personal phone con-tact, handling their Xtreme functions in opposite shifts. She had begun to doubt she'd ever really heard him say he cared, he wanted her. The first line of this note, a reminder of what had transpired between them in New York, assured her differently.

That night in New York, within that circle of flowers and candles, she'd felt his love, as well as on the night they confronted Jules together. A man of principle, Chess was waiting for her to make a clean and final break with Jules. Meanwhile, she struggled to determine her moral obligations regarding Xtreme, praying Chess would continue to wait.

Chapter Thirty-nine

The day after Holly left for the ski show, Chess remained at the breakfast table after the boarders had gone. He needed extra coffee to recover from a sleepless night.

Long after the midmorning train had reminded him of Oklahoma wind whistling through his grandmother's warped windows, he had lain awake wishing he'd gone with Holly. Thinking of the candlelit hotel room in New York, he had invented an equally erotic scene for Las Vegas. Unleash a damn memory, and, like a Roman candle, it burst open and devised a thousand possibilities for creating more.

This morning, he made himself remember he hadn't gone with her because of Jules. Had Jules gone? Had he reaped the benefit of flowers and candles last night?

Chess rejected the thought.

Do Thi and her helper bustled about the long table collecting the accoutrements to corned beef hash and eggs. Chess kept glancing over the top of the *Denver Post* at the familiar scene, attempting to count his blessings. His castle was wavering on its foundation, but the threat was all on paper where he was trying his damndest to keep it.

He tried to concentrate on the *Post* business section.

Gates Rubber, held solely by the family for eighty-five years, had made a deal with the British company, Tompkins PLC. Chess made a mental note to sell a less promising stock and raise funds to take advantage of Gates's new public offering.

Coors was reporting an eleven percent increase over last quarter. No big surprise.

A proposed Aspen factory-outlet mall had been derailed when the developer's family accused him of wasting millions in family funds on the project. Chess toyed with a scenario in which the investor in question, assuming the role of financial warrior, was trying to increase the estate of a family with an expensive appetite but no balls for taking risks. His mind eased back to Xtreme. Confidence was sometimes hard to attain when naïve beneficiaries felt secure in the status quo. A beleaguered white knight often got no respect.

Beyond the window, Lance and Adam rounded the corner of the house where Adam's entry was located, Adam pulling a T-shirt over his head and stuffing it inside his beltless waistband. He sucked in his stomach to button his shrink-to-fit Levi's. He and Lance high-fived before Adam took off for the stable for his morning visit with Gigi. Lance crushed a cigarette with his heel, then headed for the house. Chess glanced at his watch as Lance strolled into the kitchen.

"Running a little late, aren't you?"

"I'm keeping boss's hours. That seems to work for you."

He pulled out an end chair, striking the antique pine table roughly, then sat and tilted back, hands gripping the table edge. Chess smelled cigarettes and leftover alcohol, attested by red-veined eyes. Lance grinned crookedly, his tone testy.

"Probably you're not eager to make the drive today. Since the wee witch has flown her cave, you've got no one to torture."

There'd been a time when the opposite was true, when Holly's presence had kept him away from Xtreme. He'd been staying away lately, but not because he didn't want to see her—make love to her—more than he wanted to draw his next breath.

He gave Lance a gauging look. "Well, I see you're in a piss-ass mood. Again." He folded the *Post* and picked up *The Wall Street Journal*, amused that Elaine Garzarelli, long separated from Lehman Brothers, could still roil the market with her predictions of a correction. Garzarelli, like Holly, was a woman capable of commanding respect and causing an upset. Garzarelli had leveled some sleepless nights on Chess. She and Holly had that in common, too.

"You're grinning like a peeping Tom. What's so funny, cuz?"

Chess shrugged, shuffling pages.

Lance reached in his pocket to where the Marlboro pack showed through his fine cotton dress shirt, but his hand came out with an inch-square foil packet. With expertise, he split the packet with his thumb, then popped gum into his mouth.

"Any chance of getting breakfast?"

Chess thumbed through the Journal, looking for the stock listings. "You know the rule. Pass on 6:30 breakfast and you wait for lunch."

"I won't be here for lunch. She's probably in the kitchen playing Mah Jong, anyway."

Chess's scalp tightened. "Do Thi is Vietnamese, Lance. Not Chinese. And she never has time to play games, so ease up."

"All those Nips look alike. Anyway, you'd think she'd offer me some coffee." He shoved back his chair, strode toward the kitchen door and set it swinging on its hinges.

The stock listings blurred as Chess listened to the kitchen discussion. Lance didn't want any damned corned beef hash. He wanted eggs. Sunny side up, runny. Bacon, crisp. Despite Do Thi's gentle acquiescence, Chess glued his rear to the chair, lips clamped, reminding himself of Lance's bloodshot eyes and a foil packet, of how his cousin catered to Adam. Of his contribution to Xtreme.

When Lance shuffled back through the door, carrying juice and a steaming mug, Chess spoke under his breath. "I said knock it off, Lance. She's not the enemy."

Lance shrugged, begrudging a grin. "No shit, Freud."

Ignoring him, Chess shared his *Journal* findings. "Remember that computer stock I gave you for your birthday? Compupac?" A thousand shares. "Do you still have it?"

"Hell, yeah. I kept thinking I'd sell, but I waited too long." An accusatory frown reminded Chess he had advised against selling. "It's in the tank. Who'd buy it now?"

"It just took a dead cat bounce."

"You're chock-full of that market lingo crap."

A rock formed in Chess's stomach. "Compupac fell like a dead cat being dropped off a building. But if you drop it far and fast enough, even a dead cat bounces back."

"Clever. Pretty soon I can start talking that jive. But talk's cheap, as my dead daddy used to say."

That took the edge off the good news of the recovering stock. "Yeah, well, just don't sell until I tell you to."

Mouth grim, Lance saluted, then launched a complaint about not getting the totals from shipping, which had prevented his completing the monthly bank report on time. He tabled his grievance when Do Thi ambled in and placed a plate before him.

He forked an egg center, smirked, and addressed her retreating back. "Hey, I said runny." She swiveled to see him lift a piece of bacon with his fingertips, drop the meat, and wipe his fingers on a napkin. "Is crisp too much to ask?"

She reached for the plate, but Chess's fingers gently circled her bony wrist to lower the plate back to the table. Head bowed, she returned to the kitchen. Glaring at Lance, Chess scraped his chair back, then followed Do Thi.

She stood at the sink, running steamy water. He pivoted her and clasped her in a bear hug, reaching to shut off the tap. Her dark, graying head came to the top of his rib cage. When Robyn had left, she tried to take Do Thi with her, but the old woman wouldn't budge. She'd stuck by Chess in those two crazy years when he had acted the way Lance was acting today.

"Don't let him get to you, Mama Woman. He's hung over and trying to quit smoking. Not a pretty sight."

She nodded and turned back to the sink, running a bony knuckle beneath one eye. Chess leaned his hips against the counter, hands braced on the ledge. He shoved his pride behind a gathering hunch. "You going to the store today?"

"Every day." She insisted Sol y Sombre's vegetables be fresh. Chess had tried to convince her that just because she bought them at Safeway daily didn't necessarily make them fresh, but she wouldn't accept that theory.

"Do me a favor." He pulled a horseshoe-shaped silver money clip from his Levi's and peeled off three twenties. "Buy me fifty quick-pick lottery tickets. Use the extra money to buy yours."

She looked up. Her face as lined and weathered as neglected tack, cracked a grin. "You're kidding, right? You always tell me not waste money on lottery."

"This jackpot's too vulgar to ignore."

Under her suspicious scrutiny, he reminded himself of the Gates stock being available for the first time. Compupac had bounced back close to his purchase price. The dollar hadn't rallied, but it had held steady for two days in a row. His Mexican bonds had stopped plunging, and Teléfonos was holding its own. A tingle rippling his spine resembled the one he got when dealt two-thirds of a hand that turned out to be blackjack. A positive hunch.

"I'd go for the tickets myself, but—"

"But you shamed to." Her smile turned sympathetic. "I do it for you. I got no shame."

His reluctance to go was more a case of pride than shame.

Chapter Forty

By mid-afternoon the first day of the show, Holly realized Xtreme had written no significant orders. Sales reps from around the country were on hand to greet their individual clients and take orders in the festive atmosphere. Chess had allocated a fortune for the new state-of-the-art booth, all tiers and columns of blond marbleized wood, cantilevered order tables outfitted with avant-garde chairs. Her latest zippered designs lined the back wall of the space, and order pads were conveniently placed.

The chairs remained virtually empty, never occupied for more than a few minutes. Clipboard in hand, reps took turns standing in the aisle in front of the booth to check off pre-scheduled appointments. The buyers loyal enough to show up either offered vague explanations of having already exhausted their budgets or remained secretive when cajoled about minuscule orders.

Between the token visits, Holly and the reps, all sporting pained expressions, stood shuffling their weight on aching feet while discussing the weather, the mammoth size of the convention center's exhibition hall, and private parties they had attended in conjunction with the show. Holly worked at warding off panic by taking a competitor-judging stroll through the exhibit hall.

Not knowing what to expect, her mind conjuring up one troublesome scenario after another, she approached a booth that shamed Xtreme's. A gathering crowd formed around the order desks. From a distance, Holly spotted a familiar appearing unisex jumpsuit, complete with a bold brass zipper. She stopped short, breath snagging. Coincidence? As she approached, she saw a bulky fleece sweatshirt, its hood unzipped to form an oversized collar. If the garment was lined with wind-stopping Gore-Tex, the design was no coincidence.

She skirted the crowd of buyers to a group of samples displayed for close-up inspection and fingered an exquisite jumpsuit, her hand gliding over tight-woven fabric. Her fabric expertise immediately identified a hardy wearability the silky texture denied. She examined the sweatshirt. Lined. Maybe not with Gore-Tex, but lined.

Flare-legged ski pants duplicated her own back-to-the-future design. Superior fabric and a minute letter M zipper-pull in place of Chess's beloved X, marked the only difference between this product and Xtreme's.

She lifted the sweatshirt sleeve to examine the manufacturer's label and the price tag pinned into the armpit. Motonaka Industries. Whoever they were, somehow they had stolen her designs and by utilizing far superior fabric and lower prices, they had obtained the orders Xtreme depended on every year. Chess was banking on the history of those past orders. The new accounts Holly's "awesome" designs were supposed to bring in were needed to put Xtreme securely in the black, paving the way to a public offering. In the clamorous midst of the hated booth, she faced the likelihood of Chess walking away from Xtreme now, rather than waiting until it was either solvent or sold.

Her hands grew slippery with sweat. The acrid taste of fear rose in her mouth. Motonaka. Her mind raced back to the fax she'd found in Lance's machine months ago. Unable to recall the sender's name, aware only of ethnic correlation, she thought of her tampered-with computer, the crushed cigarette butt in her Limoges bowl. Last week when returning from the clothing bin where she'd stashed copies of design disks, she had caught Lance watching her.

She felt dizzy, as if she had stood up too quickly.

Betty Hopkins, Xtreme's Idaho rep, stole up behind, her Midwestern twang invading Holly's dread. "What's going on here, Hol? How'd this happen?"

Not trusting her voice, she shook her head. She could tell no one before she told Chess. Oh, God. How could she ever tell him? He worshipped Lance. Relied on him. Trusted him.

Incensed, she marched to the front of the line and demanded to speak to Motonaka. The order takers rewarded her with dark-slitted stares. Holly asked for the person in charge. No one admitted to filling that role. She backed to the side and made herself watch the activity in the booth, the flourish of the Japanese reps showing the line—her line—while buyer's heads bent over order sheets and pencils raced.

The scene engraved on her mind, she bolted for a phone.

Chess wasn't at Xtreme, nor Sol y Sombre. She coaxed his whereabouts from Do Thi and wangled the Ruidoso number.

His voice mail disappointed her, but the sound of his voice jump-started her sagging heart. "Chess Baker here. Sorry I missed you. If you're interested in the racing stock I'm selling, or the vintage Corvette, leave your number and I'll get right back to you. Thanks for calling."

Selling his Corvette? Why was he—

The tone buzzed in her ear. "Chess, it's Holly. I have to talk to you—no—I have to see you. I'm catching an earlier flight home tomorrow as soon as I've seen to dismantling the booth." She closed her eyes, teethed her lip and humbled herself. "This has nothing to do with us. It's about the show. I know it's an inconvenience, and you're probably involved in something there…" She dodged thoughts of what that something might entail. Ransacking her bag, she found her ticket and read off the hand-written changes she'd made. "If you get this message, please meet me." *Please.*

She hung up, uncertain she had heard his greeting message correctly. He was selling racehorses? He loved every one of those horses. He had quoted the temperament and win records of each on the plane to New York. Selling them and the Corvette?

Something was going on with Chess. Something ominous.

At dawn she struggled out of tortured sleep to answer the phone. She held her breath, hoping it wasn't Jules, but the Second Coming couldn't roust Jules out of bed at dawn.

"It's Chess. What's going on, princess?"

His soft concern and soothing drawl started tears trickling like water from a leaky faucet. "Are you calling to say you can't meet me?" Where had he been all night? Someplace with someone that might keep him from granting her plea?

"I couldn't get a plane out of Ruidoso that would get me to DIA on time, so Wayne's driving me to the Albuquerque airport." She detected the tinny echo of country music before he said, "I'll meet you."

Static on the mobile line registered in her awareness. Some of her tension eased. "Thank you."

"How about a clue, Holly? It's a long time until tonight." He sounded hopeful, even though she'd told him her urgency had nothing to do with them. The two of them and Jules.

Her mind ricocheted. She could tell him about the show and Motonaka over the phone, but she could never tell him about Lance. She had to see him to cushion the blow, to have him soothe her own wounds and fears. "It's much too complicated."

"Come on, partner. With my sky-high IQ, I'll get it."

She pictured his cocky grin, wondering if she'd ever see it again once she shared her newfound knowledge. "I'm sorry, Chess. I'm not playing games."

"Neither am I, but the ball's in your end zone, huh darlin'?" A gentle reminder.

"I'll see you tonight."

He expelled breath. "Right. I'll be there."

"Chess?"

"What is it?"

She began crying, aghast that he might hear. "Where were you all night?" She had no right to know, wanted to not care. Damn him.

"Arabia Rose foaled a stillborn. I've been at the stables for two days helping the vet try to save her."

Save her? She visualized him in a muck-stained T-shirt, tight bloody Levi's, a hat crease marking his golden hair. In her imagination, his eyes stormed cloudy-sad. "The stillborn was a..." Her mind spun. "Mare?"

"Yeah, but Rose is dead, too." His voice fell flat, sorrowful like his imagined eyes.

"Oh." Finally she asked, "Were you selling her? Rose?"

Silence fell. Then, "I was trying."

Again, something tilted out of focus, something beyond the ski show, beyond Jules or Chess and her. It fell into the "personal" slot he guarded so rigidly. "I'm sorry, Chess."

"Thanks." Line static filled her ear. "I'll let you get back to sleep."

She risked, "I've missed you."

More, louder silence overrode the cracking background.

"The flowers are beautiful."

"Are you burning those candles?"

The wax cylinders stood dead except for their peachy smell. She had lacked the heart to burn them. "Every night."

"I have to go, Holly." His tone turned distant. "I see a McDonald's and we need coffee. I'll see you tonight."

"Chess—"

The line went dead. She sank into a bank of pillows, pressing the receiver to her breasts, wondering what she might've said if he hadn't broken the connection...that she was sorry for not confessing she loved him that night on her front porch? That lying here, troubled and lonely, surrounded by his flowers and cold candles, she agonized over the difference telling him might have made.

She summoned the strength to dial home and got her own voice mail. The third message was from Jules, his tone no longer solicitous. "I got an apartment. I'm out of our house like you wanted." She jotted down the number he gave as the message continued. "When I meet your flight, we'll have dinner and talk about Xtreme—about the stock split and how to get rid of Baker. I'm anxious to get this settled, so I can get back to work. Hope you've come to a conclusion."

Yes. She had only to detail the execution in her mind. Defying the trials facing her, she bounded from bed.

With plane announcements droning in the background, she called Jules from McCarron Field, assuming he'd be gone, relieved when her assumption proved true.

"Hi. I've made other arrangements for getting home from DIA, but we can still have dinner that night. Come at seven. I have matzo ball soup in the freezer, lox and bagels and cheesecake. I'm as eager as you to get things settled."

More eager.

Chapter Forty-one

Holly's gaze skimmed the crowd at DIA as she passed through the ramp door. Chess was not there. She repositioned her bag and purse and with leaded feet began the trek to the trains. In the crowded United corridor, she spotted him walking quickly toward her, a cell phone to his ear. He stopped, folded the phone and stowed it in his jacket. Shoving his hands in his back pockets, he watched her approach. She fought the urge to run to him, trying but failing to gauge his expression.

When he stepped forward and took her bag, she caught the scent of cigars, horses and day-old Bijan. His boots bore evidence of horse-stall grunge, sending her mind skidding back to the sanctity of Sol y Sombre.

"Welcome home, partner." Slate eyes mirrored his soft tone. His greeting blended into the din of passing travelers. He grinned stingily. "Xtreme's been hanging by a thread in your absence."

A renewed pang of regret for the show's outcome stabbed her, then turned to guilt. "I thought you weren't here."

"I told you I would be."

"Things don't always turn out the way we plan."

The furrow appeared between his pale brows. "I've noticed."

"Let's go in here." She nodded to double glass doors fronting the Red Carpet Club, her home away from home lately. "I'd like a drink." *Of strychnine.*

"What about your bags?"

"They'll keep."

She began walking and he moved in beside her as she rummaged in the big Louis Vuitton for her Red Carpet membership card. A woman at a curved mahogany desk waved them through. On the escalator, a step above Chess, Holly turned to him. His anxious expression caught her off guard, made her pivot to stare at the engraved frosted-glass walls banking the climbing staircase.

In the posh and subdued bar area, she found a table in an intimate corner. Beyond an expanse of glass, past the crowded runway, a pink and purple Denver sunset burgeoned beneath billowing clouds. Familiar. Comforting, normally.

Misery invaded her conscience, wearying her body.

Chess pitched the hat, one she hadn't seen before today, onto the granite table. "I'll get us a drink."

"I'll have Absolut vodka...on the rocks."

He grimaced, full lips pulling thin. When he returned he brought O'Doul's and a glass of white wine. Working up to the task at hand, she sampled the bitter wine without protest while staring at the expiring sunset in an abruptly oppressed sky.

"Thank you for coming," she murmured into her glass.

"No problem. But I'd like my payoff."

His face bore no smile, but her memory latched on to flowers and candles, a poignant note, his gentleness on the phone last night. She decided to approach from the back door. Dragging the carry bag toward her, she rifled through the briefcase portion.

"This was our largest order." She handed the legal-size

form to him. A new account had placed the substantial order early the first day, before Holly sensed anything amiss.

His brooding eyes skimmed down the page and back to the top. He thumped the paper with immaculate nails, looking up at her. "This order's worth less than the paper it's written on." She supposed her shocked, betraying reaction, made him explain, "Everyone knows Black Run won't pay."

"Not everyone."

"Yeah, well..." Eyes insistent, he measured her. "Take my word for it, they're notorious. Their credit's been shut off industry-wide. COD only." He pitched the paper back to her. "Sorry, sugar. There was a big article in *Ski Trade*. I assumed you'd seen it." While she shook her head, then gulped wine, he drawled tolerantly, "My theory is, worse than no business at all, is doing business and not getting paid."

Abruptly, the situation adopted the simplicity of a John Grisham plot. When Motonaka refused credit to Black Run, they had placed an order with Xtreme. Being from Japan hadn't stopped Motonaka from doing the homework Holly had neglected.

More guilt infiltrated the edges of her panic.

Chess laced his fingers through hers. She rejoiced in the stable feel of his callused palm. Fingers clinging, her gaze darted to their hands, then to his face, seeking solace.

"It's okay, Holly. You've been tied up lately. I should have shown you the article." Gently, he disentangled his hand. He poured more O'Doul's, but left the glass on the table. "Let's see the rest of the orders."

She pulled out a shaky too-thin file and wordlessly passed it to him. Only after he perused each order did he look up.

"This can't be all."

She nodded, eyes smarting. His disbelieving look chilled her blood.

"What the hell happened?"

She reached for the folder. He moved it out of her reach. "You're angry." Remembering her own reaction, she couldn't blame him. Would his response turn to panic, her predominant emotion when she had discovered the source of their dilemma?

He swiveled and shot his long legs out beside her chair, retrieved the Stetson and twirled it, staring as though waiting for it to change color. "Angry?" He seemed to taste the word. "You keep throwing these daggers at me, sooner or later you've got to expect me to bleed."

Her hair spiked. "Keep throwing?" Of course he referred to the invoices she'd mishandled, her reluctance to go public, desire not to sell nor to have him leave Xtreme. On top of all that, Jules. She felt as though she were attempting to carry water in a sieve. "I know. I'm sorry about...the daggers."

She postponed telling him about Lance, watching to see if he might implode, until he drew a long breath and released it in a slow, controlled way.

"Okay. According to the records, the same accounts have supported Xtreme for years. What's happened?"

Holly drew a breath that matched his and told him the story, day by day, blow by painful blow. "Somehow Motonaka stole our designs and featured them at the show."

"Who the hell are they? I've never heard of them."

The same curiosity had consumed her before it turned to fear. "Neither have I. This is their first Vegas show. People browse the booths before they buy, and they spotted Motonaka. They've duplicated our designs and used their superior fabric and merciless price cutting to get our business."

Her intended shrug failed to materialize.

He nodded with grudging comprehension. "How do you figure they came up with our same designs? Can it be a coincidence? Brilliant minds working alike?" He looked almost hopeful.

The urge to tell all tormented her as she measured him. Maybe she'd tell him tomorrow, after she planted hints tonight. More than she dreaded his reaction, she hated stabbing him again by voicing unsubstantiated suspicions. No matter who Motonaka was, or how cleverly Lance covered his tracks, sooner or later he'd tip his hand and make a slip he couldn't cover.

Chess might never have to hear from her of Lance's treason.

"It's no coincidence," she said at last. "They have every piece, cloned to the last...zipper."

He looked sick. Purposefully, he dug in his inside jacket pocket, producing a cigarette-size cigar and gold lighter. He held the cigar in one hand and turned the lighter reflectively in the other. His defeat in the battle to give up smoking, along with the No Smoking sign above the door nagged her.

"Is it as bad as you're leading me to believe, Chess? Did we need the orders that much?"

He suddenly looked as though he'd awakened from deep sleep. Then a mask slid over his eyes. He put the cigar and lighter back in his pocket, straightened in the chair and donned the Stetson, pulled it low on his forehead and assumed his white knight role. "I'm sorry if I'm scaring you, sugar. You did fine, but I should have been there to help you."

Revisited by loneliness, she nodded. "You should have."

Ignoring her agreement, he stood, shaking out his bad knee. "I'd have gotten to the bottom of it. I still will. I just need some time to work on it."

His hand assisting her from the low chair allowed her to recognize her exhaustion. Their connection had electrified her, then left her weak when he eased his hand away.

"Meantime, lock your computer and keep a close watch on the design disks." His smile looked forced. "Even though that's like locking the barn after the horses get out."

To tell him she'd been cautious, but apparently their culprit was a computer aficionado, would qualify as an excuse. "I think my key's been copied."

He arched a brow. "Order another key, or get the lock changed."

"Someone's been pilfering my computer," she ventured. If he took that news well...

"Who? Toby, maybe? Sally?" He looked skeptical.

"Neither of them can run the CAD system." She held out hope for his own conclusion.

Now he looked perplexed. "How about Janine? She told me she used CAD before she came to Xtreme."

She shook her head, looking up, attempting to convey a message she lacked courage to voice. "Janine turned in her building key when you—when she was terminated."

"She could have made a copy. The PC key, too. Maybe she anticipated a personnel shake-up early and acted out of spite."

"Janine's not like that."

Those stormy eyes drilled hers. "Who then, Holly? Me?"

She reeled a little. "Of course not. Why would you—"

A shrug elevated his shoulders, expanded his broad chest. "Maybe to expedite Chapter Eleven—bankruptcy. A legitimate reason to jump a sinking ship without ruining my reputation."

"You'd never do that." Her tone conveyed more confidence that she felt. Then she swallowed pride and confessed, "I saw evidence of tampering, but I couldn't convince myself anyone would steal from Xtreme, so I ignored it." A lie. "If I hadn't, I might have been able to stop the design theft. The whole thing is probably my fault."

"Bad judgment call, sugar. We're all capable."

His gentleness hurt more than soothed. His empathy prodded her incentive to come clean. But he'd had enough bad news for tonight. "I'll be more careful and keep you informed if I see signs of more pilfering."

He nodded, touched his hand lightly to her back and guided her toward the escalator. "I'd better get you home. Jules is waiting."

She stopped short, leaning back into his hand, forcing him to strengthen his hold. "Jules is not there."

He deftly fielded her masked invitation. "Then I'll get you home so you can take advantage of that and get some sleep."

She wrenched from his hold and led the way onto the escalator, too disillusioned to explain Jules's absence.

They drove in silence except for three calls Chess received. He talked to Adam, then someone he addressed alternately as Pete and Andrews, and his horse trainer, Wayne. By Chess's comments, she assumed Wayne had sold a horse named Apache. After hanging up, Chess brooded openly, drumming his fingers on the steering wheel, eyes fixed on Interstate 70. Troubled by his disquiet, she stared out the window, dreading the adjustments to be implemented at Xtreme. Beginning tomorrow.

When they reached her house, Chess left the Cherokee running, unloaded her bags and set them inside the front door, dredging up painful déjà vu he surely couldn't ignore.

"Good night." Hand on the doorknob, he stared at his boots.

She waited until he looked at her. "Don't you want me?"

Frustration, sorrow, then even more determination played on his face. He stared down the hall to her open bedroom door, took a chest-swelling breath and released it. Hands in his jacket pockets, he measured her with his gaze.

"I want you a whole hell of a lot, Holly. But if we're

going anywhere from here, the trip will be based on no gray areas. No doubts. No second-guessing. Remember that when Jules gets home."

Before she could tell him Jules was no longer staying in the house, he slipped out the door and across the porch, his boots pounding the steps. She sagged against the closed door. He'd yet to say he loved her, only that he wanted her. Did she feel his love? Was that what she saw in his eyes?

She pressed her hands to her ears to avoid hearing the Cherokee leave.

Chapter Forty-two

With Warrior snoring on his lap, Chess lounged on the sofa, hiding behind the *Rocky Mountain News*. Adam snuggled into the other sofa corner, one leg cast over the back, reading Elmore Leonard. To Chess, the *News* made no sense. Nothing he read upstaged what Holly had told him. When he'd seen her coming down the airport corridor, gotten a look at her wounded eyes, he knew his brief positive streak had ended.

Mentally he had folded his cards and left the game.

Now his mind darted down a list of things he could sell, besides the horses and the 'vette. The Rolex, maybe, and the Remington bronzes Robyn detested enough to leave. His wine collection could be auctioned and he could resign from Castle Pines Golf Club. Golf wasn't his game. He seldom went to the club, except for a meal of pepper steak and bread pudding now and then. The membership would net him fifty grand tops, and he'd still have to wait months for that. Compared to his obligations, his personal assets were as insignificant as his commemorative brick among the millions in Olympic Centennial Park.

He tried to get a grip on how Holly's news would affect

his plan to pledge the orders as collateral for a loan with which to order fabric for next season's line. Revenue from the show orders would have eliminated increasing his personal investment in Xtreme, money already allocated elsewhere, in anticipation of orders Holly failed to bring home.

He pictured the little sandstone building housing the bank in Okmulgee and his zeroed-out savings account. Grandma Chesney's disregarded wisdom, Aaron's ongoing reliance on him to pay off the bankruptcy debt, his boarders' need for food and a clean place to sleep, haunted him until his mind mucked over. His gut smarted like a canker raked with a currycomb.

"You want to play gin?" Adam asked from his end of the well-worn sofa. His voice held a sympathetic tinge for what he could only sense.

Chess folded the News and pitched it into a nearby rack. "Do bears pee in the woods?"

Adam swung around grinning, stowed his book and reached for the cards kept on the coffee table. "Dime a point?"

Eighteen months of gin with Adam had taught Chess the odds. "Toothpick a point, an extra for gin. I'm saving my money."

He shuffled while Adam went to search for Do Thi's hidden toothpicks. As he dealt, Adam reappeared with a conspiratorial smile, rattling the confiscated box of betting booty.

When Chess entered Xtreme the next day, Toby pounded the keyboard to whatever rhythm blared within her earphones. As he worked his messages off a spindle on the counter, her rolling eyes alerted him to something amiss. Inspection revealed an otherwise empty office. In the warehouse he discovered why.

In her stocking feet, red high heels on the floor, Holly

braced on a tall metal stool. A blank wall, which just yesterday had held zippered designs, formed her background. Xtreme's workforce comprised her audience. Chess spared a moment to regret not being present when she had mounted that stool in a miniskirt that fit her the way he'd like to. He dragged his mind away from that foregone pleasure to listen to the speech in progress.

"So...a lot of adjustments will have to be made, a lot of cost cutting, no overtime. Let no scrap of fabric go to waste."

One ski show in Las Vegas had changed all their lives. Sadness veiled her eyes. She was a scrapper, bucking up when she was scared and on the brink of crumbling. The last five months had proven her to be a fighter, but she wasn't street tough enough to keep her eyes from seeking out Lance where he braced against a far wall, arms folded, chewing like a cow with a stubborn cud. His cynical smile never altered. The way Lance was relishing the show strung hackles up Chess's spine, puckered his hairline.

The rest of the crowd, made up mostly of Dihn Quang's family and fellow expatriates, looked near tears.

Chess shifted his gaze to claim Holly's, conveying his disapproval. Her look implored him, yet her attitude warned that trying to interfere would do no damned good. She depicted a woman on a desperate mission.

"I know how unpleasant last winter's layoffs were...."

He frowned, made a cut sign by slashing a finger across his throat and mouthed an exaggerated "no." Her brief verbal falter was probably detectable only to him.

"But we'll have to take those same measures unless we economize."

Too much for Chess. He made his way through the gathering to her perch. Her chin shot up, her eyes widening like a mouse's facing an approaching cat. She raised her quivering voice. "So what I'd like to see—don't you dare, Chess Baker!"

Clinched fists went to her hips. Her eyes shot him a powerful warning.

With one hand, he scooped up her shoes while the other arm grasped her around the knees and slung her over his shoulder. She hung like a sack of feed until her temper snapped like a live wire in a downpour. Her feet, dangling at prime level, began to churn. He whirled toward the door, awkwardly bent over to avoid castration.

"Careful of the cojones, Holly."

She emitted some kind of indistinguishable growl, kicking harder as she jerked off his hat and flung it in his path. He swayed, stumbled and miraculously righted himself, but his heavy boot crushed the Stetson. On the surrounding faces, abashed humor blended with disbelief. He took in Sally's approving grin and Lance's undiscernible look, then kicked open the swinging door and bore Holly's pitching body down the hall.

Fists banging his back, she bellowed, "Damn it to bloody hell! Put me down, you son of a bitch!"

Inside their office, he plopped her rear on the crowded partner's desk. She struggled off and took a swing at him. He backed up, laughing, holding her at arm's length.

"Simmer down, sugar." His hands grasped her shoulders.

"Damn you," she gasped, eyes wild. "You made a fool of me."

"No, you made a fool of you. I saved your butt from creating a mutiny with your doomsday speech." Still holding on to her shoulders, he strained backward to kick the door shut. "Dihn Quang's people have been through enough. I don't want them worrying over something that'll never happen."

Chests heaved in unison. Eyes searched and held.

"The others—those who didn't grow up breathing Agent Orange—will desert this ship you claim is sinking, like rats with built-in life preservers. In layman's terms, they'll file for unemployment." He rushed on when she stopped squirming. "You've got to think, honey, before you go off half-cocked."

Her chin quivered. The wild-eyed, quest-oriented banshee disappeared, leaving a woman on the verge of ruin, struggling to hide her agony. Giant tears slipped down her cheeks. One dangled off her pert nose.

"Hey, what the hell? Don't do that."

She covered her mouth, trying to stifle a gulp.

Guilt pierced him like a heated ice pick. "Don't do that, Holly. No tears. Okay?"

The moment he let her go in an attempt to brush her wet face, she stood on tiptoe, curled into his chest and circled his neck. Her motive-filled gaze held his captive. She tilted her face, offering her petitioning mouth. Torn apart, fighting for control, he looked from her eyes to her plump wine lips and caught her face in his hands.

"Damn it, Holly." He touched his forehead to hers, rolled it back and forth. His hands cupped her tight little ass, lifting and molding her to him. Her smothered moan sucked him back to rationale. He eased her down, trying to smile. "We're veering from the subject here, darlin'."

She ran her fingertips across her cheekbones, her own vague smile forced. "Thanks for saving me from myself again, cowboy."

Her contrite expression ripped him. "No problem, princess. It'll be all right. I'll fix it." When she nodded, he rushed, "Let me take you to dinner. We need to talk, make a plan." He pushed away images of his overburdened credit card. For the first time ever, he'd made an interest-laden payment in lieu of remitting the full amount due. "A champagne celebration at The Palm. Seventy dollar steaks and Opus One."

She looked ill. "Celebrating what, for God's sake?"

"Finding out we've got adversaries other than each

other." He kept his tone light, cajoling. "We know where the real fight is now." At least he planned to find out.

Her eyes glowed, then clouded. "I'd like to, but I can't."

His insides roiled. The covetous bastard lurking behind his reasoning returned, intact. "Jules, right? Your own cele-bration on your first night back." He knew his smile was deri-sive, yet he couldn't desist. "Well, you've got your priorities straight. Guess I'll polish mine up." He pulled out his chair and snapped on the television and laptop. "Considering your stage performance, you'd better keep a low profile today, sugar."

A long silence brewed. Then, "Chess."

He cocked a brow, mocking surprise to see her still there.

"I'm working on the situation with Jules." When he nod-ded condescendingly, she urged, "Do you believe me?"

He definitely had doubts. "Sure, honey. Meanwhile, I could use a little cooperation. I'm starting to feel like the guy in the black hat, always having to say no to your come on. I need to see some results from your promises."

He gave her a mock smile just before she left him in the undersized, vacuous office. Alone.

Holly languished in the tub, herbal water floating beneath her chin, steam coating her face and kinking her hair. On the floor, Angel watched balefully, chin on paws. Holly closed her eyes and soaped her breasts with Anaïs. She moved a loofah sponge through the fold her right breast made on her rib cage, back again...back again. Drifting in thought, she reviewed the office scene and Chess's actions, carefully banishing the ware-house fiasco from her reverie.

Beneath Chess's boastful and pompous demeanor, he was selfless, a man pridefully trying to hide fear and apprehension, as she'd once done. He was a man with a task, a goal the same as hers, even though their means to accomplishment had differed from the start. Even as he'd steam-rolled over her, convinced he knew best, he'd tried to assuage her ego and meet her needs, sometimes making the path to their goals even rockier.

Chess was the most caring man she'd ever known. He loved Adam, loved Lance unconditionally, took care of them and his displaced boarders, while trying to guard the self-respect of the journeymen.

Caressing her other breast with the loofah, she thought of the concern her frustrated tears had unveiled in his eyes. His disappointment when she declined his dinner invitation had left her longing to be with him, and resentful of Jules.

She dribbled water over her chest and pulled the rubber plug. Angel raced forward to lick perfumed water from her mistress's calves. As Holly toweled her rose-splotched body, she fantasized being with Chess under normal conditions: gazing across a candlelit table into flinty eyes, challenging his phony arrogance, matching his honed good-old-boy wit, her eyes feasting on his lion-like beauty. And when the evening ended, going to his bed or taking him into hers.

In place of her fantasy, turmoil governed their lives.

What did his arrogance mask? Did his hurts stem from being rejected by Robyn, as Holly felt she had been by Jules? Were their wounds healable? Could they salvage each other?

She ran a brush through her hair. How wonderful it would be to rely on Chess to anticipate and head off her blunders, as he had at the design dinner, and today just before she broke down and sobbed before her followers. He had made them laugh, left them wanting more, bought time when she was too caught up in the war to plan the battle. What better components for partnership than his pragmatic calm and her creative energy? Yet in the beginning they had somehow gotten off on the wrong foot. She smiled into the mirror. He should never have called her darlin'.

Tonight she longed to hear that or any other endearment that fit his willingness to express affection. She longed for his guileless possessiveness. He was a man with needs, a desire to fill them and a desire to satisfy a woman.

But he wouldn't wait forever.

Ever sensitive, Angel whined, refocusing Holly on the enigma at hand. She swirled on chianti-colored lipstick, streaked blush on her cheeks, and pulled on a robe. In the kitchen, she stared out the window as she scratched Angel's warm head, the heady aroma of matzo filling the comforting space. When Jules pulled into the drive ten minutes early, she envisioned him being Chess, pretended to hear Chess's boots echo on the wooden steps and imagined his eager, unrestrained embrace.

This time he'd stay and fill the emptiness of her bed.

She listened to Jules's key being fitted into the lock. As she worked at opening the Far Niénté Chardonnay, she allowed a certainty to invade her fantasy.

Chess's tenderness will vanish when I tell him about Lance.

Chapter Forty-three

Tucked into a dark corner booth, Chess drew one leg up and planted his manure-crusted boot on the scarred wood bench. Across the way, a woman in baggy jeans and sandals fed the jukebox. Vince Gill's voice scarcely dented the noisy bar gab, but Chess knew "Under These Conditions" well. He understood every emotion expended in writing the song about two people in love, married to others and holding on to their principles. Which was worse? Both parties married and hurting, or lopsided hurting? Like his. Crap. He had slipped from self-pity into morbidity. But Holly could do that to him. She never did anything half-assed.

He took a cheap cigarillo from his pocket and used his Dunhill lighter. Spinning the thin gold cylinder on the gouged table, he speculated what he could get for it before wondering if he'd dropped over the edge to insanity.

Vince sang on.

Lloyd, the bartender, answered a jingling phone, then peered through the dimness, met his mark and shouted over the din, "Chess Baker." Two hours of Chess chasing Johnny Walker Red with Coors had lent familiarity to the beefy man's vexing grin.

Chess shook his head, glaring emphatically.

"Not here," Lloyd claimed, grin intact.

Grateful, Chess ambled to the bar, took a stool and ordered another Coors. Five minutes later, no more, he watched in the hazy mirror as Lance appeared in the doorway, framed by light from the grill section of Sedalia Bar and Grill. Balls.

Lance caught Chess's mirrored gaze and lurched forward, threading a path between chairs, stretched-out denim-clad legs, and jutting elbows. A drink went flying, ice bouncing, the glass tumbling across cheap dung-colored carpet.

If Lance were taking a navigation test, he'd just failed.

His grin matching Lloyd's, he climbed laboriously onto the stool next to Chess. "Whatcha doin' here, cuz?"

"Looking for privacy." He stared straight ahead, not liking what he saw in the dingy mirror, not wanting to look at his cousin, either. The way Lance had watched Holly today, close and satisfied, rested too heavily on Chess's mind. "You must've called from Bud's." Across the street, past the antique shop, down a crooked, small-town block. "You got here damn quick."

Lance pointed to the Coors on the counter, signaling Lloyd, then turned to Chess. "How'd you know?" He looked somewhere beyond Chess's shoulder. "You mad at Thurman, too?"

Chess caught the emphasis of too. "I was hungry for fries. Nothing personal."

Lance laughed, nudging and rocking him precariously. "You didn't want Thurman and Bud's gang to watch you ditch the wagon."

Lloyd's chuckle drowned out Chess's reply. "I alerted Bud's. Called the *Douglas County News*-Press, too. A preacher, and the BIA. Told 'em we had a soon-to-be-drunk Indian." He wiped the bar, grinning at the dingy rag. "Help's on the way."

Chess laughed instead of leaping over the bar and giving the man a shoulder block like he'd once used on murderous three-hundred-pound guards. Back in his glory days. "Don't worry. I'm pacing myself."

He worked his way off the stool and back to the booth, Lance on his heels, Coors in hand. Now Vince launched into "It'll Take Dying to Get It Done." God almighty.

He and Lance faced, knees colliding under the table before they adjusted in their seats. Chess slouched in the corner again. Lance propped on his elbows, hoisting beer to his mouth with slender fingers. He took out a crooked cigarette, slipped it between his lips, grinning, then wadded the thing, dropped it in the ashtray and fished his pocket for gum.

"Holly gave quite a show today, huh?" He popped the unwrapped gum in his mouth, tossed the square cellophane and foil pack in the ashtray. "Good thing Jules came back to have another go at her. She's too much woman for you, cuz."

"You think?" He'd like a chance to prove differently.

"Why so glum? You grieving over those hallowed show orders?" Lance leered, not quite focusing.

Chess wondered who'd drive the fabulous Baker boys home tonight. "I've seen things go better at a funeral. Cuz."

Sympathy ladened Lance's frown. "Buyer's remorse?" He signaled the waitress while he drained his beer.

"It's more complicated than that."

Lance rallied, like Geronimo when the bay mare, Full Moon, came on the scene. "How much more?"

In a fit of half-drunk self-pity, Chess related, "My fortune is being confiscated by an international conspiracy, and my stable of racers is disintegrating. Overnight, Xtreme's not saleable or fit for an IPO. The BIA—or some phantom witch woman—is threatening to take Adam. He's considering going, and I've got a new partner whom I thought was dead." He blew breath, feeling as if he'd unleashed poison in the room. "Otherwise, I'd have never put a dime in Xtreme." And he was in love with the former dead man's wife. He tried to smile around the jagged lump in his throat. "Other than that, things couldn't be better. How about yourself?"

Following a long, unfocused scrutiny, Lance commented, "Well, you had your fifteen minutes of fame, unlike some of the rest of us." As if remembering to, he grinned. "I knew she'd bring you to your knees."

Even in Chess's semidrunken condition, that statement rang odd, smacked of a set-up. He dismissed the thought.

Lance went on, "Too bad. You were a free spirit before she hid those invoices from you." Sarcasm glazed over his sympathy. "A rich free spirit."

"The invoices aren't important." Not when compared to her latest news about the orders and her story of a tampered-with computer and stolen designs. That gem of a confession had turned him instantly into a hack detective. And at this moment she was home with Jules, probably eating latkes and kugel, drinking Mums instead of the Dom he would have bought her with his close-to-maxed-out Gold Card.

Before Chess could get the Corvette situated beneath a budding maple tree beside the house—in hopes Lance would-n't side-swipe it—Do Thi shot through the door and raced across the greening yard, screaming, waving frantically.

"Mista Chess! Mista Chess!"

With Adam's face swirling behind Chess's eyes, he cracked his knee trying to clear the steering wheel. Was Adam sick? Gone? Chess stood weaving, holding on to the door as Do Thi closed in. She threw her scrawny arms around his waist, then danced backward, beaming. His fears about Adam eased, but what the hell was going on? Had Robyn tired of Rachel and Rita and shipped them home? Had Holly come to her senses and left Jules? Was she inside at this moment taking a bubble bath in Robyn's tub? What the hell was going on?

"You win lottery, Mista Chess," Do Thi announced as if she'd personally drawn his winning ticket. She grabbed his hand and plopped a severely crumpled ticket into it.

Sonovabitch! "How about that?" Mind-fog clearing, he bent unsteadily to read the ticket in the dash lights.

She beamed. "See there. You get three numba. You winna."

Yeah, right. Three numbers. Four dollars out of nine million. Some days it just didn't pay to saddle up.

Chapter Forty-four

Angel growled low and menacing when Jules entered the kitchen. He stepped gingerly, looking wary. When he saw Holly's clinging, velvet-piped-in-satin robe, satisfaction bordering on triumph replaced his wary expression.

"You're early," she greeted. "I haven't had time to dress." That should clear up any delusion concerning her attire.

He looked disappointed. "Don't change. Magenta's your best color. Brings back memories."

Stomach queasy, she tiptoed to an upper shelf for wineglasses. Jules stepped in quickly to assist, eliciting another warning from Angel. Holly held up a palm, backing Jules off, then busied herself pouring. He pitched a newspaper onto the counter. The format and size bespoke *Rocky Mountain News.*

"Seen this?" he grunted.

She handed him wine and peered at a folded-back article in the business section. "I only get the *Post.*" Before Jules's departure for places still unknown, they had subscribed to both Denver papers, plus *The Wall Street Journal.* On her own, Holly had neither money nor time for more than one paper.

"What is it?" Her heart beat arrhythmically when she glimpsed the headline. WUNDERKIND SALVAGES XTREME SKI.

It took only a few lines to know the lengthy article related to Chess's rumored success with Xtreme.

Only she and Chess knew the true story, which changed daily.

Jules scowled, gulping wine. "Nothing like banging your own gong. Or, in Baker's case, his own drum. Must be some ethnic thing."

Ethnic thing? Her spine stiffened as if she wore a whalebone corset. She forced a sip of wine before remarking, "I doubt Chess wrote this. He's diversified, but I've never detected a journalistic bent." Her tapping nail pointed out the article's byline.

Jules eyed her skeptically. "That's what PR people do, Holly. They're always touting their clients' talents in search of the next deal." Derision flavored his words.

His reminder of Chess's history of flitting from turn-around to turnaround disturbed her, while Xtreme's lack of solvency, regardless of what the News claimed, gave her false comfort.

Jules sipped and paced a little. His leather wingtips clicked on the brick floor, stirring déjà vu. As he stared out the window where she'd enjoyed her earlier fantasy, she glanced around the room, reliving the past. Her stomach twinged.

"Baker's quotes are overly complimentary to you and your designs." Jules addressed the darkness beyond the leaded glass. "Probably pitching for a bonus."

"Overly complimentary?" Someone had deemed the designs good enough to steal.

"You know what I mean." He looked more ruffled than apologetic. "It hacks me that he's taken my place. But at least he'll leave Xtreme in as good a shape as I left it."

"That doesn't compute, Jules. You left me owing every Abram, Caleb and Enoch you'd ever squeezed a dime from." Annoyed by his stare, she adjusted the robe's wide lapels across her chest and retied it. "Chess would never leave me in debt." Even though he had found her that way and had every right. He would leave only when he felt she could stand alone.

Jules shrugged. "You sound confident, but, then, you're intimate enough with him to know."

Holly ignored the innuendo.

"Can I do anything to help?" He glanced around the kitchen. "Set the table maybe?"

"You'd be lost. I've rearranged everything since you left." Wine and newspaper in hand, she moved toward the door, Angel nudging her thigh. "Watch Tom Brokaw while I get dressed."

Inside her bedroom, she bolted the door.

Dinner mimicked dancing in a minefield of unpleasant subjects while she tried not to appear disgruntled by Jules's tales of India. Anecdotes told with a smile, sometimes a chuckle, smothered her sympathy for his alleged amnesia. She pushed her half-empty plate away and folded her arms on the table. Angel bounded from the floor, anticipating her traditional token bite before the dishwasher devoured Holly's plate. Holly's not-yet look lowered the beggar back onto her haunches.

Eyes cast down, Jules spread cream cheese on a bagel, then layered on lox. He sprinkled that with onions, chopped eggs and capers, then took a bite while stretching for the wine housed in an insulated cooler.

He spoke tentatively, "I've been thinking, Holly. Now that I've moved out, we could date, start all over on our marriage."

She shoved back her chair, stood and scooped up his plate.

Neck reddening, he rose, too, and crossed to lean against the hutch front. She carried both their plates to the sink, squirted Ivory and ran hot water. She addressed her reflection in the window. "We're not married, Jules. We never will be again. I'm not the scared twenty-two-year-old who watched you board that plane." She swiveled to see him gazing at his feet as his hands rattled the change and keys in his pocket.

"The cheesecake is in the refrigerator. Would you slice it?" She painted tolerance into her tone. "It's from Las Vegas, the best in the world."

The cake had been frozen awhile, but she'd thawed and tested it, finding it still delicious. She had planned to bring Chess a reciprocal cake when she returned from the show, but her sojourn had turned frantic. Desire to talk to him, be with him, had commandeered rationale.

She refocused on the current dilemma. "I'll make coffee."

"I'm not hungry and coffee keeps me awake," Jules grumbled.

Apparently not in India. She offered him a begrudging smile. "Then cut me a piece. I'll make decaf. It's fail-safe."

He started toward the pantry.

"I keep dessert plates above the microwave now."

Preparation completed, she sat across from him again, taking tiny forced bites. Jules sipped coffee with an anxious air until she announced, "I've made a decision on Xtreme."

He straightened in the chair, drawing a resigned breath.

Before she could reconsider, she declared, "I'm going to give you half of my stock."

He sat straighter, paling, sweating. "That's only—"

She nodded. "Half of the forty-nine percent I hold. Two percent less than Chess holds."

His eyelids formed a slit. "How'd you let that happen?"

Memory roiled in her mind. "The only way he'd bail me

out was if he obtained controlling shares." He had been a different man then.

She had been a different woman.

"That was stupid, Holly. No wonder you jump to his tune."

She had been desperate. Jules wouldn't understand that. "Actually, I like dancing to Chess's music." She let him digest that. "You shouldn't take my gift lightly, Jules."

He flinched at the term *gift*. "How about Baker's stock? I deserve some of that."

She cocked a brow. "Why?"

"If not for me, he would've had no company to worm his way into—no one to take advantage of."

That truth made her smile. Painfully. "You can forget his stock. He operates with total control."

"Controlling bastard that he is." His eyes shot venom.

Chess's expertise was control. If she had only been wise enough to share her suspicions of design tampering, it might be a dead issue by now.

Checking her watch, she affected a pushed-for-time expression. "Your stock will be worth a great deal when Xtreme either sells or goes public." She watched his eyes gleam with new interest. "I've had Greg draw up an agreement between you and me, but it contains a stipulation."

His mouth pulled. "Greg's my lawyer."

"Not anymore." She forked a bigger, more assertive bite, chewed aggressively and washed it down with mint mocha decaf. "The agreement states you'll take no active part in Xtreme. You'll be a silent stockholder. You'll give me your irrevocable proxy to vote your shares."

"Goddammit, Holly, Xtreme is my company."

"Not anymore."

He blanched. "You can't blame me for having amnesia."

"I blame you for not calling me the minute you...woke

up." So much for not beating dead horses, but his story made no sense. That alleged third time he'd gone back to the embassy to get new papers, why hadn't they pulled up her missing-person report and contacted her? If she asked, he'd shrug and cite inefficiency in government, one of his favorite soapbox topics. "I spent seven years wondering if I was widowed or abandoned, Jules."

"Seven years to the day. You were eager."

She sipped coffee, eyes meeting his beyond the cup, and forced an unruffled tone. "Seven years, two weeks. I spent six and a half years struggling to overcome the debt you left, barely holding on, until Chess bailed me out."

He pounded the table, bringing Angel to her feet, ears flattened. "I want Baker out of Xtreme and out of my bed."

Chess didn't sleep in Jules's bed because he was more honorable than she suspected Jules of being.

"Chess and I are partners. Nothing can change that." Except Chess, once he salvaged, then left, Xtreme.

"Then the stock you're offering me is worthless."

She focused on maintaining some sense of control. Confronting Jules always resembled confronting her father, knowing she couldn't please him. Miraculously, failure to please either of them no longer mattered. "I have nothing else to offer," she advised. "Consider it a free ride to possible pay-off."

He pushed back from the table and stalked away. Angel followed to the dining room door and peered after, twisting repeatedly to eye Holly. As Holly collected the rest of the dishes, she listened to Jules on the phone. She was glad he couldn't see her hands trembling. If he believed her bluff and signed the agreement, his compliance would eliminate a disruptive court battle and prohibitive legal fees. Conscience had devised her offer. If activated, would the agreement satisfy Chess's ultimatum that she choose between him and Jules?

Again.

She heard Jules hang up the phone, then his strident foot-steps from the study and across the living room. She braced herself, holding on to the edge of the sink. Maybe Greg would take her case out of friendship, deferring payment until...until when? When did she expect a war chest to materialize?

From behind her, Jules spoke grimly. "I need a day or two to think about this."

"Fine." She turned with mock indifference, glancing at the wall clock. "Greg will finish drawing the agreement while you make your decision."

He fiddled in his pockets. "I'll get back to my place. You obviously have things to do. The curse of the working girl."

She leaned against the sink, hands massaging behind her back. Jules's eyes darted to her breasts; she brought her arms across her chest, gripping her shoulders. "Leave your key when you go."

Anger splotched his face. "Look here, Holly. This house—"

"If you'd rather, I'll have the locks changed and send you the bill."

The beautiful old house had been his when they married. On their first anniversary, he had deeded it to her, coinciding with his decision to put Xtreme solely in her name. She held the house together with glue and love, never neglecting its smallest needs, sometimes at the expense of hers.

"We're divorced. You can't have free access to my home."

He pitched the key on the table, metal echoing on wood. Holly grabbed Angel expediently. Jules pivoted, stomped across the living room and jerked the door open. A bell orna-ment in the spring wreath jingled frantically. When the door slammed, jarring its hinges, she felt the *t* had been crossed and the *i* dotted in the state of "almost finished."

Desperately wanting to talk to Chess, she made a move for the phone, then stopped short. Too soon.

One obstacle remained. Getting the agreement signed.

Chapter Forty-five

Wednesday morning Chess pointed the Cherokee away from Castle Rock Middle School and in the direction of Sol y Sombre. He glanced across the seat to where Adam sat rigid, coal-black eyes forward. A defiantly raised chin emphasized the hump on the bridge of his nose.

After miles of silence, Chess invited, "What're you thinking, Shallow River?"

Without turning, Adam reiterated his familiar Hollywood-redskin warning. "Bad spirits in white man's school."

Chess stabbed a remote device hanging on the visor, and Sol y Sombre's massive gate began a slow slide. The moment he had room, he darted the Cherokee through and reversed the gate mechanism, watched it close in his rearview mirror.

Another lonely day for Adam, another stress test for Chess. "You can bet your beads I'm not quitting because of what happened back there," Chess advised.

The boy's temple throbbed noticeably.

"For some reason, you're not giving me answers I need, so we're going on a tour of every Navajo rez within a thousand miles." He doubted the emaciated boy he'd found huddled

outside his gate could have walked or hitched beyond that distance. "Eventually someone will recognize you and give me
answers."

"If I am not Navajo, your trouble will be for nothing."

Like a Rottweiler defying a leash, futility tugged at
Chess. His head pounded like a triphammer, but he forced a
laugh, going for a bluff. "Oh, you're Dineh all right. I've been
reading up on you. I've heard your yei-bi-chai chant when you
think no one's listening. You tell the Navajo Emergence Myth
as good as I tell the Christmas story."

"You know I am Navajo, yet you want me to—"

"Get a universal education? You bet I do. I'm white
enough to know if I'd stayed in Tishomingo with my grandmother and gone to the Indian school the way she wanted, I'd
have learned Indian ways only." Times like today he questioned his decision. "I'd never have accomplished what I
have, never been able to help anybody, even Indians. I want to
give you the best of both worlds." He took his eyes off the
winding road, waited until his high-pressure stare turned the
boy's proud head. "You know why I want that for you,
Adam?"

"Because you have yellow hair, but an Indian heart."

Chess swallowed fiercely, sparing Adam a grin.

The boy's stern, chiseled face eased into leniency. "And
because I am the biggest prize—"

"Because I love you."

Adam rolled his sable gaze and grimaced, red-faced.

Chess clapped a hand on Adam's bony knee. "You put up
with my dictates and one of these days I'll push you out of the
nest just to watch how high you fly." Visualizing that made his
throat seize up, ache. "Deal, kemosabe?"

Adam clapped his hand over Chess's. "Shilt'áá'áo.
Deal."

Chapter Forty-six

Holly's head bolted up when Chess clumped into their office Wednesday noon, dressed to pose for *Esquire*, an unlit cigar clamped in his teeth. From her corner, Angel leaped to attention, tail flapping, ears peaked. Grinning, she crossed to Chess. The absence of his normally animated response surprised Holly. She peered through her reading glasses, vision foggy, as he banged his Coach briefcase onto the desk, ripped off the charcoal Armani jacket and pitched it over his chair back. Hands jammed in the pockets of his pleated pants, he stared at the wall of plaques the way he had that first day, then stalked over to straighten an errant tribute.

The absence of the Designer of the Year award heckled Holly. After eyeing him a moment, she folded her glasses, inserted one temple piece into the neck of her blouse, and rose quietly to hang his jacket on a guest chair. The wingback filled out the coat's shoulders. Unable to refrain, she caressed the fabric, barely resisting an urge to sniff his cologne residue. Their eyes met. Looking chagrined, he sank into his chair. Desire to comfort him led her to lean against his desk, their knees inches apart. Angel placed her snout on his leg, staring at him, forlorn.

His hand snaked out to caress Angel's sleek head.

"What's wrong, cowboy?" Today, he personified a highly agitated wunderkind, more than a cowboy.

"Long story." He flipped open the laptop, switched it on.

"I'm yours for the day. Use me."

His forehead furrowed, one brow jagging upward. His eyes revealed a fantasy that mirrored hers. Then he jerked himself back, leaving her to her sacred vision.

"It's Adam."

She waited.

"I took him to Castle Rock Middle School today to enroll him in summer school—early—to ask for practice assignments to get him acclimated." The disclosure lacked Chess's usual confidence. He fell silent. Throat moving, eyes glossy, he pecked laptop keys with one finger.

She nodded, plagued by his disquiet. "Mission accomplished?"

"He has no papers—school records, birth certificate—so I said we just moved in, that we're still unpacking and haven't run across the papers yet."

Uncharacteristically, he had lied. But for Adam, Chess would don a tutu and fight Mike Tyson. She smiled encouragement. "That story should have worked."

He took out his lighter, turned it in his hand, nimble fingers working unconsciously. Holly began to crave his touch. "It worked until the vice principal said she wanted Adam to answer some questions. First off, she asked where he lives. He said Sol y Sombre. The woman has lived in Sedalia all her life, knows more about Sol y Sombre than I do. Her uncle used to work at the ranch—groundskeeper. She sees Do Thi at Safeway, and she knows Dinh Quang and crew live on the ranch." His eyes stormed. "She thinks I'm running a rainbow coalition and made sure I knew she disapproved."

He placed the cigar and lighter on the desk, sank back in

the chair and crossed one ankle over his knee, foot twitching in agitation. "She raved about Sol y Sombre's beauty, about its history. While Adam puffed up with pride, out of the blue, she asked him how long he'd lived there."

Holly searched her memory, speculating the outcome. "He told her the truth." More than a year.

Chess nodded. "She turned her computer off and showed us the door. It took me months to convince him to enroll in school. It took that woman five minutes to derail my plans." He reached for the cigar and lighter. "I had no choice but to take Adam home."

His forlorn look, one she'd not been privileged to before, made her long to straddle his lap, hold and assure him. "Derail?" she ventured softly, liking the word's connotation.

"I'll get papers, somehow." She watched his mind race behind troubled eyes. "There are men—artists—who can falsify any document. Coming up with a birth certificate and a school record is a cinch."

"What will that teach Adam?"

He stood, bringing his body close to hers. She felt his beckoning heat, smelled Bijan, along with his disquiet. "I hated like hell to take him back to the ranch to sweat it alone..." His voice wavered. He looked disgusted. "No choice. I had a meeting I couldn't refuse with Phil Anchutze."

She had never seen him so unsettled. He seemed vulnerable, a curiously appealing trait. She grasped his hand. Eyes softening, he coiled his fingers around hers.

"Just what is Adam sweating out?"

"He's torn between his forsaken heritage—which involves not attending Indian school—and pleasing me. Doing the right thing."

He pulled her hand to his chest, flattened and pressed it there. She fought the gnawing need to move against him, to try to abolish his turmoil. Instead she spread her fingers, seeking his hard warmth.

"It will work out, Chess. You will find a way."

He eased her hand away, held it for a moment and let go, their fingers clinging for a delayed instant. "Adam won't tell me his family history, but I'm going to the rez and beg the Tribal Council to issue papers. He deserves the best, even if he doesn't recognize it. Somehow, I'll see he gets it."

"Have you ever considered that maybe the white schools aren't better? If you're set on him attending, then offer to tutor him in his own heritage." She paused, reading his reaction. The grave set of his mouth had eased. "If you want the best for him, why not give him the best of both worlds?"

His smile appeared hard to come by. "I'll do whatever it takes."

She returned to her chair, donned her glasses, shaking from their brief touch.

Angel stayed with Chess, reveling in more caresses.

—≈≈◈≈≈—

Late that afternoon, Chess's cellular phone rang. When he answered, Holly saw a wave of panic flood his face. He bolted from his chair, reaching for his jacket.

Anxiety gripped her, set her chest to thumping.

He spoke calmly, denying his frantic actions. "Settle down, Do Thi. Put one of those men on the line. Let him tell me that." He hurried into the jacket and crammed papers in his briefcase, the phone wedged between jaw and shoulder, his blond head cocked at a weird angle.

From the way his eyes narrowed and glazed over, Holly knew the man he'd demanded to speak to was now on the line. "The hell you are," Chess spewed. "You're not taking him anywhere." He listened, then warned, "You're making a mistake. If you take him, mark my words. Your ass'll be in a sling."

Holly removed her glasses and stowed them in a drawer.

As Chess listened again, he snapped the briefcase and searched a pocket, coming up with a single key. "I want to talk to him. The hell you can't. Put him on the goddamned phone."

Before Holly could circle the desk, his bluff turned to resignation. Then hope fired in his eyes.

"Put my housekeeper back on." With Do Thi apparently on the line, Chess's tone lowered into determination. "Stop crying and listen to me. Lock the gate with the house switch, but don't let them see you. Come hell or Democrats, don't unlock that gate and let the bastards out." He looked at Holly as though remembering her presence, then half whispered into the cellular, "Don't cry, Mama Woman. And don't worry. I'll fix it. Just don't open that gate before I get there."

He snapped the phone closed, stuck it in his pocket and grabbed the briefcase. At the door he whirled, nearly knocking Holly down. His hand darted behind her head, the key scraping her neck as he drew her face forward. He ducked to kiss her temple, his mouth cool and rigid, then pressed his forehead against hers. "I enjoyed our day, darlin', but I have to go."

His taking time to comfort her wrung her heart. "I'll go with you. I want to help."

He shook his head. "I'll call you, sugar. I promise."

In the wake of his long stride, she clopped down the hall in her platform heels and short, tight skirt, Angel taking up slack in the middle. An eerie quiet fell as office personnel viewed Chess's frantic departure. He left the door swinging, left Angel whining. Holly stood behind the barrier watching him unlock the Cherokee, climb inside, and engrave black marks on the asphalt.

Behind her, concern tempered Toby's normally sullen

voice. "Jeez, Hol. How can you fight with him when he's so nice?"

Apparently, she based her assumption on Chess's hasty exit, on their failure to say good-bye.

Angel glued to her thigh, Holly pressed her forehead against the glass, craving the simplicity of the feuds Toby addressed. "We weren't fighting this time."

The stakes were graver than their competitive natures. Something was going on in Chess's life that he chose not to share.

Not unlike Holly's lonely struggle with Jules and Lance.

Chapter Forty-seven

Chess hadn't prayed since his Sunday school days at the Indian Methodist Church in Tishomingo, but when the Sol y Sombre entrance came into view, the silent inner voice, a wordless, heartfelt plea, damn sure felt like prayer.

Inside the gate, a white government-issue van claimed the center of the road, blighting the landscape.

Heart knocking like an out-of-round wheel, he halted the Cherokee short of the arched entrance and weighed the situation. Two suits, one wearing brown, the other black, had been milling about the loamy lane when he arrived. They came to a halt now, gaping. Adam, a stoop-shouldered Indian in khakis, and the woman called Shimasani made up the entourage. The three squatted in the shade of the van like sheep awaiting slaughter.

Chess's plan fell into a more visceral than rational vein.

He took his foot off the brake and rolled forward while stabbing the remote device on the visor. The steel portal squeaked and groaned. A gap began forming. Chess inched the Jeep forward as the breach widened, angling the wheel right to clear the van.

The chocolate-skinned brother in brown sensed release

and yelled, "Everybody back in the van."

Satisfaction nudged Chess as he watched how torpidly Adam obeyed. When Chess jabbed the remote again, the gate stopped, half-way open, the Cherokee filling the gap. The other agent caught on to Chess's plan to block the gate, denying the van an opportunity to pull through, and raised his hand. Four intruders, plus a softly smiling Adam, halted their rush to freedom.

Chess shut off the engine, stepped out and locked the door. He dropped the keys into his pocket, attempting to read Adam as he ambled toward the van.

Brown suit fished a badge from his inside pocket and flashed it. Chess kept his eyes on the man's reproving face. "You're interfering with government business, mister. I order you to open that gate." Coal-colored eyes shifted to the pocket where Chess had stowed the key. The agent's dedication hinted reservation school. His surly dialect indicated Harvard or Yale after that, then a return to the reservation to ride herd on his brothers.

In Chess's side vision, the woman in buckskin and velvet and the old man, wearing Jesus sandals revealing dusty toes, moved in on his right. Adam appeared soundlessly on his left. Chess gave him a conspiratorial wink, before calmly addressing the agents. "I think we can work this out if you'll hear my plans for Adam and take them before the tribal council. I'm Choctaw. Adam has no family. Why not let—"

"His name is Nascha." Shimasani groused the correction. Chess's head jerked around.

Amused by his unmasked surprise, she bared her dingy teeth in a mocking smile. "He has family." She gripped the old man's shirtsleeve and tugged him closer. "This is Anaba, his uncle, his mother's brother. I am Nascha's shimasani."

He tried the name inside his head, tasting the bitterness of Adam's lies. Then truth rushed in. Grandmother; shimasani.

Adam had called her that, but Chess had confused the title with shaman, medicine woman. He'd been too busy playing savior to his boarders and trying to rescue Holly's pretty little butt to grasp the obvious.

Now he understood why Shimasani's visit haunted Adam.

"I want to talk to Adam." The words pained his parched, thickening throat.

"He has nothing to say to you. You fill his head with lies of becoming white in your white man's schools."

Anaba endorsed Shimasani's claim with a grunt.

The BIA agents folded their arms, enjoying the show. Adam kicked dirt, head down, hands in his back pockets. The all-American kid.

Chess cast around in his head for an argument. "I went to the white man's school. I came out okay."

Taking in his yellow hair and pale eyes, she scowled, then scoffed. "They chased the Indianness from you, as they would from him. They teach the young ones the hogan is dirty, their families are ignorant. They turn them to bleached Indians who never return to the reservation but are miserable in the city." She paused. Her white hair shimmered in the sun. Her eyes turned harsh. "They are not Anglo or Indian, but men filled with self-hate. I will not let that happen to Nascha Roaming Fox."

Self-hate? At the moment, her claim came too close to the truth. Chess suffered disgust, for sure, knowing he'd had an investigator looking for relatives named Tall Horse, while wallowing in self-pity over his shrinking wealth and lifestyle. He wheeled and grasped Adam's lanky arm.

"Hey!" The man who'd shown his badge jabbed inside his coat, rib cage high, kept his hand there, glaring at Chess.

Shimasani latched on to Chess's belt. Powerful fingers snaked inside the waist of his pants as she planted her moccasins in the dirt. Anaba stood flexed, awaiting her command. With his free hand, Chess disengaged the woman's hold, his eyes warning.

"I want to talk to Adam—to hear his version." If it didn't agree with hers, he'd find the money somewhere to hire an attorney—Jerry Spence, dammit—and fight the tribal council all the way to the Supreme Court. Provided the two courts did business together. How the hell would he, a bleached Indian, know? Maybe he needed to call a favor from a government echelon higher than the BIA. His mind raced to Senator Nickels' attempt to help him with Congress and Mexico. Defeat threatened.

Without waiting for Shimasani's blessing, he propelled Adam across the road to the far side of the Cherokee. "Let's hear it, kemosabe."

Adam's head didn't hang now. He looked Chess in the eye, his own glimmery, moist. "Please forgive me for lying."

"Done." Chess ruffled Adam's long, free-flowing hair. "You must have had a reason."

Reasons he apparently still felt disinclined to share, other than, "I left the night Kai—my mother—choked to death on her vomit as she gave birth to a baby boy. She was drunk."

"You have a brother." He filed that appealing fact under future projects.

Adam's gaze remained steady. "Yazhi. He died before Shimasani could cut the cord."

Getting the picture, Chess felt his gut clench. He thought of his father drinking until he lost everything, of Lance's father finally drinking enough to find courage to die. Chess nodded encouragement.

"I did not want to go back to—"

"Just where the hell is back, anyway?"

Adam looked past Chess's shoulder into the distance. "The reservation. Shiprock."

Based on hints he now knew Adam had planted, Chess had concentrated on the Navajo reservation in Arizona. He felt relief for knowing at last, not needing the investigator.

The dark eyes focused on Chess. "I want to go back now."

Abruptly Chess realized he had seen the dilemma from a different angle, considering them united in this quandary. Now that he knew differently, the fight left him like air spewing from a slashed tire. Reeling, he forced a placid tone, painted an indulgent smile on a paralyzed mouth. "I'll bet you have just as good a reason for going back as for leaving."

"Like you, I want to make a difference in the world."

Beyond Adam's shoulder, the agents sauntered to the gate, teamed up and yanked it. Chess figured he had little time before they ganged up on him and seized the truck key.

"And you've got a difference-making plan, I'll bet."

The stubborn chin tilted up. "I will go to the Indian schools and preserve my heritage, maybe skip some grades and graduate early. You have taught me well Hazk'e é...my father."

Adam's eyes welled up; Chess's watered on cue. An acid-like sensation burned his nose. Nodding again, he refrained from spitting out the metallic agony in his throat.

"After that I will attend Dr. Roessel's junior college in Shiprock." Chess had read the legend of the school. "I will learn something usable—it is the Navajo way—and earn credits to transfer to a university where my Indian ways will give me strength." Adam's proud head lifted, his aquiline nose a little red, eyes wistful and wet.

So this was what Adam had been pondering, deciding during those silent lapses when he declined to reveal his thoughts. Chess waited. His breath felt snagged by barbed wire.

"I want to be a doctor. A psychologist. If you will have

me back, I will go to any university you choose, but—"

"Deal." He clapped Adam's shoulder, jostling him. The boy was deferring to his grandmother, but not completely. Chess's pain eased enough for him to spare a grin.

Adam's mouth twitched. His pinched face relaxed somewhat. "You have not heard the rest."

"I heard the part I like. That's enough for now."

Light flashed, then faded in the moisture forming in Adam's obsidian eyes. Apparently sick of lies, he persisted. "After the university, I will take the white man's cures back to the reservation. Finally I will make a difference in the lives of my people."

Chess did a quick mental assessment. Providing Adam could skip a couple of grades, four years of waiting remained, four years of hell compared to the last year and half since he'd found the boy at this gate, half frozen.

"What about your...sickness?" Chess ventured. Not taking Adam for treatment, for fear they'd be found out, formed a guilt knot in Chess's belly. "Now that the slate's clean, we can get to the bottom of your aches and pains—the fever and chills."

"Shimasani will have the Blessing Way. It is a healing ceremony." Chess tried to douse a skeptical look, but Adam added, "My mind must be purified to overcome my ailments."

Beyond Adam's shoulder, Shimasani sat cross-legged in the shade, her purple skirt draped in abundant folds. Eyes closed, she chanted silently while fingering her feather necklace. Chess visualized her hiking from her hogan to a reservation store, hovering in a hot phone shell filled with broken glass, dog excrement and flies to call Adam—Nascha—and brainwash him.

"I damn sure hope her medicine's powerful enough to pull off the cure you need."

"The spirit is always with us. Medicine women only

introduce us. That way, we don't need Blue Cross or Medicare." A mischievous smile transformed the austere face, innate Navajo humor forced now for Chess's sake, he sensed.

As Chess groped in silence for a less terminal parting, Adam mumbled, "Maybe you could come to the rez...to see me." His throat worked painfully, his Adam's apple gyrating. Knowing the boy hurt doubled Chess's agony.

"How would your grandmother and Anaba take that?"

Adam raked a heel in the dirt, his eyes shifting to his family, then back. "If you bring cigars and candy, they will welcome you." He granted Chess a short-lived spastic smile. "Bring Warrior to play with the starving dogs." Unable to hold Chess's gaze, he stared down the sandy curving lane to infinity.

Chess drove back tears. "Maybe I'll bring dog food."

"Cool."

They were both dodging the bottom line: Adam had chosen to leave Sol y Sombre. Chess wouldn't be privileged to see him at Do Thi's breakfasts, nor to watch him struggle over too-advanced books, stuff himself with after-supper sandwiches. Or watch him sleep, snoring quietly, his black hair strung across a pillow.

Head cocked, Chess mulled a question he found his lips unable to squelch. "Why'd you chose the name Adam? You could have called yourself anything?"

"I thought it was safe. I don't eat apples." His consoling smile dimmed, eyes quickening, then glistening like buffed wood. "It was good to pretend to be the first man. Pretend I could make things different. Just as you do now."

Jesus. Nodding, Chess swallowed hard.

"Nascha means owl," Adam said solemnly.

And owl meant wisdom. At Adam's birth, how had his people known he'd be wise? "You've got to promise me something, Adam. If living on the rez is not all you're counting on, don't stand on pride. Come back here and we'll work it out." He swallowed hard. "Nascha."

Adam's arm jerked up and pressed against his eyes, then he moved into Chess's embrace, whispering his agreement. "Shil t'áá 'áko."

Behind them, Anaba choked back a rattly cough. Shimasani chanted aloud, a kind of wail.

"Back in the van," one of the agents called out.

Chess released Adam, circled the Cherokee with him, then unlocked the door and got in without watching him walk away. Craving air, he lowered the window, then unhooked the gate opener, swiveled in his seat and aimed the remote toward the rear of the truck. The gate thundered before easing open. Van doors slammed. The engine started. Chess's next thought was to back up, head for Sedalia and find oblivion in a Scotch bottle.

The van pulled through the enlarged opening, Adam's dark head against the window, raven hair flowing around his heaving shoulders. God damn. Knowing Adam grieved satisfied Chess in some demented way, but witnessing that grief tormented him. He stared into the rearview mirror until the van pulled onto the highway, then he dialed the phone. Four rings assured him of getting voice mail. He spoke after the greeting message.

"Hey, sugar. I promised I'd call." An image of Holly's anxious face, her plea to come with him, played inside his head. "Adam's gone." His voice threatened to break. He cleared his throat. "The BIA took him back to the reservation. Seems that's what he wanted." An ache shot past his throat into his chest. He shifted in the seat to view the van tracks in the dirt. "Maybe it's for the best. I've always heard that loving someone includes the willingness to let go." As if he had a choice with Adam. Or with her. "See you tomorrow, sugar."

He disconnected, punched in Washington DC information, asked for the Attorney General's office and scribbled down the number.

His fingers halted mid-dial as his words to Holly, "seems that's what he wanted," pricked his consciousness.

What was he planning to do? Pull political chains to force Adam back? The weighty conclusion of how much he loved the boy, depended on him to round out his life, give him a focus, someone to live for, to plan a future for, jolted him. How would he make it without Adam? Who would fill that void? The pain of giving Holly up doubled in the face of losing Adam.

Chess snapped the phone into its dash holder, lowered his forehead to the steering wheel and took the same refuge to which Adam had surrendered. Grief.

Chapter Forty-eight

Holly craned her neck to see into the partitioned areas of Xtreme's department heads. Lance was meeting with the payroll clerk, Ginger, in his glass box. A stack of spreadsheets covered the desktop. Lance tilted back in his chair, tie loosened, hands clasped behind his head. His expression wavered between a smirk and a skeptical scowl. According to office gossip, Lance was campaigning for a date with Ginger. A strung-out meeting was a safe bet. Holly headed for the warehouse.

She chanced a brief chat with Sally, congratulating her on Annie and the kids moving out, then continued to the far corner of the crowded warehouse where she dragged an aluminum table to a wall of shelves. She topped the table with a step stool, hoisted onto the table and climbed the stool until her shoulders aligned with the top shelf. She glanced over her shoulder. No audience.

The carton she sought sat far back on the shelf. She stretched to drag the box into inspection range, feeling a sharp prick on her instep before a feather-light object landed on the concrete floor. She glanced down, spotting nothing. The carton precariously balanced, she reversed her climb and knelt on the tabletop. She peeked over her shoulder before taking a box knife from her blazer pocket to slit the sealing tape.

Raising the flaps, she peered in at a bouquet of roses swaddled in tissue paper. Once rouge-red and plush, the blooms lay curled and faded. Putrid. Decayed.

Sudden sweat drenched her forehead and upper lip.

Damn it to bloody hell!

Wanting to disbelieve, she sank back on her buttocks and calves. She had made disks of her current designs, cleared her hard drive and hidden the disks, along with sketches she'd made for the upcoming catalog, in this box.

An ocean roared in her ears as a fist pummeled her chest.

Senselessly, she jerked the tissue-wrapped roses from the carton and flung them on the floor. A tinny echo led her to inspect the table surface. She found an empty Nicorette wrapper.

Her spine iced at the sound of footsteps.

"Need some help?"

She whirled, teetering on the table. Malice crawled worm-like over her skin.

Lance's gaze drifted from the carton to her thighs, exposed by her receding hemline. Her nerves snapped like whips. She hurled the empty gum casing at him and scrambled to the floor. He laughed as she dived beneath the table on her hands and knees, then rushed to her feet brandishing a second gum wrapper. Her eyes demanded the explanation her mouth couldn't. Tension hummed like electricity.

He stepped closer. Dim lighting cast his angular face in sharp relief. He spared a deferential smile, but with his brows pulled low over his eyes she felt the devil glared down at her.

"Seems like everybody's trying to quit smoking. Huh, boss?"

"But you're the only one too wimpy to quit cold turkey."

He laughed, his slime-green eyes glacial as an icy pond.

An inner sense told her she was taunting an uncaged tiger.

"Why not let me know how you really feel?" His sultry voice rasped over her nerve endings. He ran his hand along his conservative silk tie, smoothing it with a lover's caress. How could he manage to look like a disheveled GQ poster boy when he smelled of corruption?

She dipped to the floor to retrieve the wrapper she'd thrown. When she stood, he had moved closer.

"I want my disks and sketches back, Lance. Now, or I'll call the police."

His slack mouth formed a smile. Hands jammed into his pants pockets, he rocked on his heels, gauging her outburst with perverse interest. His gaze lingered on her mouth, fantasies mirrored in his eyes.

"Why don't we discuss all this over lunch? Or in bed, maybe."

Her stomach twisted around a hot lump of revulsion while her short and rapid breath hissed through clenched teeth.

"Your place or mine?" he taunted.

"Neither, you scummy bastard. There's nothing to discuss. I have the proof I need."

He advanced a step, then another, crowding her, flaunting physical superiority. Her heart hammered behind her breasts. She retreated, hips striking the table. He reached for her. She shoved him away. A chill pebbled her arms. Why did he continue turning the screw, forcing her to expose him, as though he wanted to get caught?

"You've gone too far," she ground out. "I'm telling Chess the moment I see him."

"Don't bother, babe. He won't—"

"He'll believe me, and he'll make you hand over the disks."

"Originals or copies?"

"You're fired, you bastard. Stay away from Xtreme or

suffer the consequences."   Consciously, she kept her voice lowered.

"You're a knockout when you're excited, babe—impulsive. I'll bet you scream when you come." He gave her that heinous smile. His low whisper turned her clammy.

"Get out of my sight, you son of a bitch!"   The order rebounded off the concrete walls.   On the other side of the warehouse, the hum of voices fell silent.

Still smiling, he ambled away, disappearing among steel shelves and conveyer tracks laden with clothing.   She stood shaking, gripping her waist, icy sweat rivering down her spine. Her lungs, incapable of drawing breath, turned to concrete and bulked up in her chest.   She choked back tears, preparing herself to meet the onslaught of curious employees edging through racks of last season's stolen designs, Sally in the lead.

Chapter Forty-nine

In U.S. Bank's private banking sector, nursing an emotional hangover, Chess sat across the desk from Dave Simmons. Adam's empty room weighted Chess's mind, stoking the nauseous cramp in his belly he'd had since he watched the van drive away. The first look at Dave's face had drained the hope out of Chess. He crossed a boot over the knee that ached on rainy days, the one that had kept him out of pro ball, putting him in this chair. He hung his camel-colored Stetson over the knee, swallowing a dose of humility connected to his prior cocky struts in and out of this office. U.S. Bank had backed him from the start, and his ventures had never disappointed them.

Change was a bitch. He hated this. When Do Thi's rooster woke him at dawn this morning, all he had wanted was to saddle Geronimo, put a lead rein on Gigi and ride until his grief-riddled mind numbed. Instead he had to contend with begging.

Pledging the ranch as loan collateral assured the bank a coveted shot at ownership if he failed to make timely mortgage payments. Historically, he paid cash for whims and worthwhile purchases. Thought of adding a mortgage to Aaron's bankruptcy payments curdled his insides. Paying interest kept people poor.

His fierce intent to hold on to Sol y Sombre had been for Adam, to give him a heritage aside from the one he tenaciously clung to. Where did that determination fit into the scheme of things now?

He felt like vomiting.

Dave closed the folder in front of him, tapped it, then opened it again. "You were dead right about the appraisal, Chess. With improvements, the ranch appraised right at a million."

He straightened in the chair, placing both feet on the floor. "That's good to hear." Hope rallied, urging him to ignore Dave's somber eyes and tone. A million just might do it, but if Congress and Mexico didn't get the hell off high center, these new funds could get sucked down the same tubes as the Okmulgee million.

He crammed that agonizing thought to the back of his mind. This was no time to expose a lousy hand.

"Unfortunately," Dave was saying, "we can loan you only fifty percent of equity."

To Chess, the word *you* sounded underlined. Dave's image wavered, but Chess tried to look indifferent. "Why's that?"

Dave closed the folder and rocked back, hands behind his head. His pinstriped coat fell open to expose a reptile belt boasting a gold and silver buckle. His eyes didn't quite line up with Chess's.

"Simple. Your cash flow—or potential cash flow—indicates a possible problem with repaying the loan."

Half a million, then. Hardly enough to warrant driving in from Sol y Sombre to fill out the application, something formerly accomplished with a phone call.

At least he could write off the interest.

Cold reality seized him. His thinking was definitely
screwed if he was fool enough to count on an interest deduc-
tion to pad cash flow.

Dave pitched forward and opened the folder again. He
fingered an oblong piece of ecru paper. "The check's ready if
you're agreeable to the terms."

"Sounds fair to me." He almost choked on the words.

Dave swiveled the folder and handed Chess a gold Mont
Blanc pen. Chess scrawled his signature in four different
places and extended his hand. Dave shook it, then handed him
the check.

Although he ached to see Holly, after the loan meeting he
felt too wretched to show up at Xtreme. Even National Public
Radio's timely announcement this morning that Congress had
voted to grant Mexico the loan they, and, he, had agonized
over, didn't change his mind.

Instead of turning right onto Sixth Avenue West, he kept
the Cherokee heading south on Broadway, toward the Valley
Highway on ramp and hightailed it back toward the mortgaged
ranch. Thirty miles down the interstate, as he cut cross-coun-
try on Route 85, he brooded over the latest oil rig to crown a
hill on Tweet Kimball's farm. Thoughts of Adam's hate for the
scourge on the countryside, the "stealing from Mother Earth,"
echoed in Chess's head. He had at one time wholly agreed, but
diminishing security had altered his attitude.

Today, he considered Tweet Kimball a blessed woman.

At home, he stood in the interior doorway to Adam's
room taking in the teenage trappings— Michael Jordan and
Dennis Rodman posters, CDs spilling out of their rack onto the
polished wooden floor, a rundown pair of Nikes at the foot of
the bed. The twelve-string guitar Adam was learning to play

leaned against a ladder-back rocking chair. An open dresser drawer and closet door indicated the hasty withdrawal of the sparse cache of clothing Chess had spotted in the back of the van. Why hadn't Adam taken the guitar? A feeling of unworthiness, or a quest for closure? The feel of absence, the eerie quiet, the sense of sterile cleanliness in the otherwise untouched room, turned him away to steal silently through the house to his own lonely quarters.

A small scrap of paper and a single bill decorated his pillow. He picked up the wobbly, pencil-written note, Do Thi's voice echoing in his head. "Have money lef ova, so buy you teekets. You nutha winna, Mista, Chess. Many hoppy return."

Chess shoved the twenty in his Levi's pocket and stared out the window where Gigi restlessly paced the dusty corral.

Chapter Fifty

Holly rang the ranch house from the Sol y Sombre gate. Do Thi answered and admitted her. Still fiercely angry at Lance, distraught over the missing disks, she rehearsed her disclosure to Chess once more, wallowing in self-recrimination for not having told him sooner. The perfect time had never materialized. Now was no better, considering Adam's defection, but this morning's encounter with Lance had stripped her of choices. Once she'd leveled with Chess, she would tell him about her stock proposal to Jules, her hope he would accept. She would even reveal the numbers in the proposed stock split and field Chess's protests, in order to assure him she wanted Jules gone. If he disclosed his personal problems in turn, those constantly clouding his eyes, the slate would be clean. They could build a relationship starting with post-New York status, when their tender lovemaking had revealed volumes to each of them.

Above her anxiety, she held hope and craved resolution.

She spotted Chess waiting for her atop the corral fence, his powerful outline sharpened by a sunset that would inspire an artist to scramble for paints. Holly ignored the ominous clouds drifting south to west, threatening the panorama.

Smile heavy, Chess jumped down and met her as she exited the car. "Welcome, princess."

He stood feet apart, boot heels pressing tender spring grass, hands shoved into his back pockets, measuring her. He smelled of the outdoors. Horses. Leather. She craved putting her arms around him, being able to replace the hurt she'd heard in his phone message about Adam with promises of better days.

Only her eyes caressed him. "I'm sorry about Adam."

His shoulders squared, his throat working furiously. "He'll be back."

"That's wonderful. When?"

She watched his mental calculation. "According to him, in about six years. He wants to get Navajo culture down pat, then come back here and let me send him to college."

She smiled, saddened by his grave tone and proud refusal to admit loss. "Could we go over there?" She nodded to a wooden, rope-strung swing hanging from a billowing maple. "I have to talk to you."

The furrow between his brows appeared, quick and deep, overworked as of late. "About what?"

She regarded the question as a ploy for time, felt she could actually see his mind gears shifting. Eyes on the swing, she reached for his hand. He kept it in his pocket.

"Tell me here, sugar. I like to take medicine standing up."

She sighed, wrapping her arms across her breasts, feeling chilled in the warm spring evening. Heavy silence fell like a blanket of humidity, until she couldn't hold back. "Lance has been stealing—Lance stole our designs. He sold us out."

Her words had the impact of an explosion. For seconds after, intense, pregnant silence held, forming the backdrop for the denial in his eyes, the tendons in his neck cording, the deep undulations of his chest. Profile grim, he glanced at Lance's cabin, then back to her.

"You're out of your mind."

She shook her head. "It's true. I have proof."

He cocked a brow. "Why are you telling me this now, when you've been worried about the designs for months?"

"I've suspected Lance all along." That bought her a derisive snort. "Every time I decided to tell you, something came up. Something I thought might be more important to you than my suspicions."

"That's no excuse." He crossed his arms, his rolled sleeves drawing her eyes to the silky gold hair covering his wrists. She gripped her own body more tightly, fortifying herself.

"I wanted to tell you after Las Vegas, but coming home with no orders, the news of Motonaka Industries showing our—"

"You say you have proof. What kind?" His eyes dared; deep brackets framed the corners of his mouth. "Why did you decide to tell me now?"

She closed her eyes for a moment, mind listing all the reasons. "That day I came to Sol y Sombre...that Saturday after the showroom..."

He nodded, eyes clouding.

"We agreed I'd be more tolerant of Lance, if you'd—"

"Not try to get you into bed."

"Yes." The word came out a whisper.

"We terminated that agreement in New York." His lips quashed a smile as soft as his voice.

"I suppose we did." Their eyes met and held.

"This is different, anyway, Holly. We're partners. If you knew something, you should have told me."

"At first it seemed I'd be reneging on our agreement. Whining. I decided I could handle the problem alone. But as my suspicions grew, you seemed..." She searched. "Troubled.

Preoccupied. The right time to tell you never came."

"Maybe because you weren't convinced about Lance."

She met his prying gaze. "I'm convinced now."

His tone hardened. "What kind of proof?"

No real proof. She told him about the sealed carton of rotten roses and an empty gum wrapper, about the second wrapper falling from the shelf to the floor. When disbelief tensed his features, she rushed backwards, spouting out of sequence the other times she'd encountered Lance, his attitude toward Chess and her, his lack of denial today. Fearing she would find no resolution, she said, "Lance has been...bothering me."

His gaze narrowed before it softened. "How?"

She outlined Lance's sexual affronts, word for word, each one an indelible stamp on her mind.

Aversion contorted his face, mirroring her own. He sifted her story for a moment before his eyes—charcoal now—turned savage. "The crude son of a bitch. I'll stop that." Then she felt him shift gears. He drew a long breath, mouth grim, eyes brooding. "On the other hand, since I've got no claim on you, maybe you should take it up with Jules."

Wanting to disbelieve her ears, she hugged herself tighter. If she let go, she'd fly apart. Just as Lance had predicted, Chess doubted her; yet the fierce look in his eyes countered her conclusion. She challenged him with a look he dismissed.

"I don't doubt he harassed you, Holly, and he'll pay for it, but that doesn't make him a thief."

"It's him. I'm sorry, but it's true. He hates me. He hates you more. He's sick, Chess. He wants to be caught."

Argument crowded his eyes before cognizance crept in. "You came all the way out here to—" His mulish words didn't match the leniency in his eyes, the way his mouth eased. He sucked in breath. "I don't need this, Holly. Not after giving Adam up. Not with all the other crap going on."

She waited, willing him to level with her, to reveal what had turned him into a caged, defensive animal. Unable to keep her heart out of a fight, it entered the fray, tender, brimming with raveled emotions. Resigned, she broke the silence. "I came all the way out here to be with you, because I'm scared and hurting. I came to ask for your help."

His shoulders sagged and he dropped onto the front fender of the Saab. "Help to send my cousin to jail, or help to find the real thief?"

He had her pegged a head case, twisting everything she said into a hysterical woman's lunacy. "Have it your way, cowboy." She spun around but had no fight left. Foregoing a go-to-hell stride, she crossed the yard without haste. The smell of wood smoke, supper cooking, the song of moaning pines, Warrior's bark, invaded her riddled senses.

When she reached the swing, she settled into a corner and launched crookedly with one foot, her eyes seeking the now stormy horizon. A brisk breeze lifted her collar, stirred her hair. Squinting, she watched Chess struggle in the distance, as she replayed his harsh, unfair suggestion that she take it up with Jules. Though the cousins' goals were poles apart, like Lance, Chess was capable of tightening screws to get what he wanted.

But what chance did they have if he chose Lance over her?

Chapter Fifty-one

Keeping a veiled watch on the swing, Chess began a slow migration around the eight-year-old Saab. He leaned on the fenders, bounced the body to check the play in the springs while being consumed by a blue-black vortex of pain.

He kicked tires, the swing's squeak and Holly's face filling his mind. God, he'd loved watching the Saab approach on the sandy lane, come to a stop at the yard edge. She had looked beautiful, frazzled and troubled. He could spot the look an acre away. Her stress only added to that air of vulnerability he liked. A combination of strength and neediness. He'd wanted to take her to the swing as she'd asked, hold her while she shared the latest disaster he saw engraved on her pretty face.

Briefly, his voracious need for her had let him believe he could forget he was cheating a man out of his company and his wife by forcing Holly to choose between him and Jules.

Goddammit, he wanted her to choose. Choose him. Stay with him tonight, ease some of the loneliness of Adam's absence. And then in the early morning, when that lonesome-as-hell train whistle blew, he'd hold her close enough, enter her deeply enough to drive his and her gut-gnawing demons away.

Watching her push that damn swing, he felt ripped in two. Her pity-filled concern about Adam had riled his pride, but when she accused Lance, the ground had shifted beneath his feet. For a moment he ventured onto the far side of furious, then along with his first twinge of belief, panic had fired his veins.

But his ability to mask panic with denial rated a ten.

In the twilight, he stooped to trace the tread of a rear tire. Damn Jules. Where was his head, letting Holly run around with threadbare tires and no shock absorbers.

The creak of the swing rode the air. Mesmerized by the even, rhythmic cadence, he peered over his shoulder. Never in his life had he pursued a debate with an out-of-line woman. Not even when Robyn ended their grievous marriage, nor when his grandmother disowned him for returning to his white father's house. Nevertheless, he now found his steps pointed robot-like toward Holly and a chance to resolve this chaos.

His grasp on the rope stilled the swing. One end pitched, jolting Holly. Her eyes searched his face as he propped a boot on the wooden seat, asking, "Come to your senses yet?"

"That's what you finally came over here to say?" Her words assured him she clung to conviction as tightly as to her exalted independence. Even as suspicion gnawed at him, he wanted to shake her, make her admit she could be wrong about Lance.

But who the hell else could be guilty, other than someone who had taken photos of the finished samples. And Holly had said the copies were so detailed they had to come from a computer. Had Lance duped him? Was he pursuing a sick kind of justice as payback for the hand life had dealt him, dragging Chess in? He tried to negate the thought.

"Look, Holly...." He drew a sharp breath and started over. "Lance has lots of anger to deal with—lots of garbage in his head. Maybe he's not the sharpest knife in the drawer, but he'd never betray me like—"

Her head jerked up.

"Betray us, like you've got it in your head."

"He said you'd believe him, not me." She stared into the darkness, her body giving off a kind of wrath-free resignation.

He settled into the swing, running his arm along the back. "Considering the stress you're under, honey, and your misconception that Lance and I tried to run a sting on you—to take over Xtreme—your misconception is understandable."

He felt her waiting for a more palatable argument.

Finally she said, "You're choosing Lance over me."

"No way." His arm snaked around her shoulder, tugged a bit. She didn't budge. "Whether or not I agree is a moot point, because you're wrong, sugar. You'll figure that out."

Stiffening, she folded her arms. "You're so damn cock-sure."

"I have good reason." He wished he could dredge one up.

"Fine." Still no pitched tone, no volatility. She left the swing gracefully, moved with more determination than haste across the yard, her body posture denoting unfinished business.

Chess fought an urge to tackle her. He craved to keep her here, hang a vulgar diamond on her finger, outfit her in Double-D suedes and custom-made Luccheses, take care of her better than Jules ever had or would.

But today's argument wasn't about Jules.

Headlights flashed the side of the house, then Lance's old Mercedes pulled up to the end cabin. Home for fresh clothes before tonight's erotic forage.

What the hell was wrong with him? He was a lot less sure about Lance than he claimed and acting like an asshole. In truth, he was pissed about Jules, and just being with Holly ignited his fury. But like a fool, he was bullying her instead of worshipping her.

He caught up with her as fat raindrops began to splatter the Saab's windshield. When he grasped her arm, she awarded him a "Well?" look.

His self-pitying thoughts raged into words that sickened him. "If you prove me wrong about Lance, I'll stay away from Xtreme, turn the company over to you and Jules. We'll go broke together." What was happening to him that he couldn't control his mouth? He had never acted so irrationally as to vie for self-destruction. Was it pride? Contempt for failure?

Was this the only way he could manage to give up Holly?

Challenge, lacking in her as of late, colored her reply. "You don't think I'm capable of running Xtreme without Jules?"

Helplessly, he opted for saving face over decency. "History speaks for itself, sugar."

She sighed. "Whether you believe me about Lance or trust me with Xtreme is irrelevant, cowboy. Proving you wrong—getting you out of my life—is the issue."

Grief smothered a retort. He could end the latest, worst nightmare of all by taking her in his arms, declaring himself a prideful fool, promising they'd work it out together. Instead, he spoke around his ache. "If getting rid of me's the goal, nothing's changed from day one. Huh, partner?"

She stepped out of his reach, grasping the Saab's door handle. When he covered her hand with his, she froze. He fished a key from his pocket. "Do me a favor. Drive the Cherokee. I'll take your car to Castle Rock tomorrow for new shocks and tires."

Her look said he'd lost his mind. She opened the door. He caught her hand and pressed a key into it. "For once, listen to me, Holly."

Indecision hung on the air until she wordlessly gathered her purse and briefcase from the passenger seat, crossed to the next parking spot and with difficulty climbed into the Cherokee. The headlights swung over him as she drove away. He lifted his face to the rain. The coolness on his forehead and cheeks felt good when compared to miserable loss. First Adam, which ate at him like a ferocious beast feasting on a carcass, and now Holly.

"Meeesta Che-uss." The call came from the house, a summons to supper. He felt more inclined to vomit than eat, but Do Thi had toiled over chicken-fried steak, mashed potatoes and gravy, hoping Lance would show up. She'd even made fry-bread.

He'd be damned if he would disappoint her.

Lance wandered in as supper was ending. Do Thi gave him a reproachful look, then dropped her head. He smirked. "Yeah, I missed dinner. I didn't want to risk Duck Do Thi."

Chess shot him a warning look, his gut festering like a boil. Holly's confession of Lance's treatment whirled in his head. He pitched onto the chair's rear legs and took a long appraisal of his cousin, weighing her accusations.

He ached to pummel him but lacked the proof to hang him.

"Was that Holly I saw on the swing?" Lance glanced down the hall to Chess's quarters. "She still here? I saw the Saab."

"She left it. It needs work. I told her I'd see to it."

"Ever chivalrous."

Before tonight, Chess would have labeled Lance's signature grin as mock malevolence.

"What did she want?"

"To talk." Their "talk" filled the screen of Chess's mind.

Lance arched a brow. "About what?"

"Business."

"Something I'd know nothing about." He grinned again.

Chess shrugged, pressing his fingertips on the table edge.

Lance copped a green bean from Chess's plate, sucked it down. "Seems like a tomb in here with Adam gone," he mumbled.

Chess's precise thoughts, but he chose not to honor the comment.

"Borrow the 'vette? I've got a hot one on the hook. She's waiting at Bud's."

"You'll be drinking."

"Bears piss in the woods, don't they?" His face sobered.

Chess tilted forward, exited the chair and crossed the family room to the sofa. When he tugged off his boots and propped his feet up, Warrior leapt into his lap and snuggled down. Chess massaged behind a tiny ear, sensing Lance's indulgent stare.

"You know Lance, maybe it's time to taper the drinking again."

Lance shoved away from leaning against the table and sauntered to a mirror above the buffet. Frowning, he smoothed his sandy blow-dried hair. "Is that a threat, cuz?"

Chess's fester worsened. "I'm concerned. No threat, yet."

"Hey!" He pivoted to face Chess, his grin nasty. "You're the Indian, cuz, not me. Better worry about your own drinking."

Chess seized a *Forbes* magazine and clicked on the television to *Money Line*. Lou Dobbs looked especially grave tonight.

"How about the 'vette? Anglos need a crutch with women."

"How do I know you won't wreck it?" Chess stared at the magazine, seeing nothing but a vivid image of the 'vette wrapped around a Colorado pine.

Lance seemed to hit on an idea. "When I get back to Bud's...from riding the little barrel racer...I'll leave it there and get a lift home. You can pick it up tomorrow."

What chance existed that Lance would be sober when he and his date left Bud's for— wherever? "I'll hold you to that."

On his way to the key-holder beside the back door, Lance pitched over his shoulder, "You're in a piss-poor mood since your little Indian buddy left. You know that, cuz?" He lifted the 'vette key and went out the door, letting the screen bang.

Warrior's ears pricked as he offered an empathetic growl.

Chess listened to the 'vette door slam, the throaty, mellow engine come to life, then fade in the distance. He tossed the magazine onto the coffee table, then took inventory. *Money Magazine*, the *Journal*, *Kiplinger's*, *Smart Money*. No literary classics in sight.

His life revolved around money. How to make it, how to hold on to it. Even Do Thi tried to gain his favor with winning lottery tickets. He sought comfort in riches, a trustworthy lover. Financial coups produced exhilaration, like a lengthy sexual climax, but in the past few months currency had adopted fickle traits. Wealth had proved worthless when it came to holding on to Adam. All the monetary favors he'd bestowed on Lance hadn't bought respect, and maybe not loyalty. Money scoffed hatefully while watching Chess turn Holly against him. Was real misfortune in losing his world-condoned wealth or losing the people he loved? If—when—he rebounded from the hovering havoc, he would take time to rethink his values.

Maybe the threat of poverty was fate's way of clueing him.

After the local news ended, he remained cemented to the sofa. He stared transfixed at commercials, hating them. Eventually, he would summon strength to turn the damn thing off. For now, his mind was a sieve. Inertia had the best of him.

Chapter Fifty-two

A glance at the Cherokee's dash clock assured Holly that early darkness stemmed from the rain. She still had time to get to Xtreme ahead of the clean-up crew and retrieve the rotten roses from the trash. While she and Chess held their standoff, rush-hour traffic had ended, but the spring rain slowed progress. She tried to relax, not to notice Chess's scent and paraphernalia surrounding her, embracing her. She struggled to block his hateful challenge from her mind.

The Cherokee and the cleaning van entered Xtreme's lot in unison. Holly leaped down from the truck, locking in her purse and the files Greg's courier had brought earlier. The unpleasant task of settling with Jules still lurked ahead of her tonight.

Xtreme's night shift kept the door locked to prevent unauthorized entry. Holly hustled past the clean-up crew unloading equipment, waved at them, and used her key. She went straight to the warehouse, harboring memories of the morning and her lingering revulsion.

Pricked by icy suspicion of being watched, she dug through barrels of production trash until she found the roses. She stowed them in a plastic bag pilfered from shipping, tied a knot and dangled the package away from her body as if it contained poison ivy.

Back in the office, she stopped to check Lance's cubicle. The space displayed the usual perfect order so incongruous with his character. Knowing Chess would halt the termination she had leveled, Lance had made no move to clear the space.

She dropped the roses on the floor, sank into his chair and tried the desk drawers. Locked. His computer, too. The empty fax machine tormented her. Lance dared her, mocked her, left her clues, while maniacally covering his tracks elsewhere. What was his game, other than acting out resentment toward Chess?

Weary, she leaned back in the chair, closing her eyes, a familiar image of Lance—thin hair, wan neck reclining on the headrest, a picture left over from his meeting with Ginger—prized her eyes open. She shot out of her repose.

To hell with musing. All she needed to remember was Lance's abusive temperament. Remember and fear.

In her own office, she perused the day's calls, her mind dwelling on the inevitable. Chess's callous demand for proof tangled with his controlling concern for the Saab's reliability and her safety. His challenge—or wager—cut like a diamond-edged knife, jagged, deep. So deep that even now she resisted the urge to buckle and curl into a protective ball. But as they had argued, his eyes belied his staunch conviction, and in the flash of Cherokee headlights she failed to detect the defiance his folded-arms and feet-apart stance conveyed. She rejected that notion.

He had chosen Lance over her.

Fate had dictated an unchallengeable course. She would show Chess, consequences be damned. As he maintained, she excelled in design, not finance. Greg would legally terminate Lance. With Lance and Jules gone, she'd hire a CFO on a profit-incentive basis, put Xtreme in the black, and give Chess proof all right. Proof he was wrong to ever doubt her.

Proof she didn't need him.

Chapter Fifty-three

Holly noted Jules's shock when he opened his apartment door. He stared at her, mouth gaping, then glanced briefly over his shoulder as he shifted his body between her and the interior.

"Did I know you were coming?"

She purposefully hadn't called, willing the element of surprise to lessen his resistance. "Greg got the stock transfer document to me today." She tapped her briefcase with her nails. "I see no reason to wait any longer to execute the agreement." The document lacked only their signatures to make it official.

He glanced behind him again. "I'll get my jacket. We'll have coffee. There's a Denny's just up the street."

She gave the door a nudge. "We can make coffee here. I don't want to go out in the rain again." When she increased her pressure, his hold eased. The door yawned open.

First, her consciousness absorbed a playpen in the far corner and scattered baby paraphernalia, then from a distance, soft, indistinguishable crooning. In her mind, shock and relief vied for top billing. Already wise, she leveled a questioning look on Jules.

"I have guests."

"I'd love to meet them." Clutching the briefcase to her breasts, she started toward the voice.

He caught her arm. "Don't go in there, Holly."

"I've earned it, Jules. I want to see proof at last."

She passed one room that held only a crib and a small, unpainted chest. In the bigger bedroom a dark-skinned woman, younger than Holly, rocked a fawn-haired, mocha-skinned infant. Seeing Holly, the woman's singing fell flat as her hold on the baby tightened. A red sari trimmed in gold lace, a head drape with a gold pendant hanging high center on her forehead labeled her foreign. Cherry-red toenails with polish as chipped as that on her fingers, protruded from scuffed sandals.

Convinced this woman was as deceived as she had been, Holly smiled. "I'm Holly."

Relief filled the dusky face and softened the fathomless black eyes, but she gave no show of recognizing the name.

Holly made a gesture toward the closet, offering a solicitous look. The woman's agreement propelled her across the floor. A row of colorful saris and pants and T-shirts bearing the Wal-Mart/Kathy Lee label filled half the undersized closet. More sandals and a pair of cheap sneakers neatly lined the floor. Her temples throbbed, vision blurring before relief ripped through her.

She was free.

Looking at the mussed double bed, envisioning Jules and the woman there, Holly felt thankful at last for the lack of intimacy in her and Jules's marriage, for her lack of guilt and regret.

The woman watched Holly anxiously as the baby stirred, its hands attacking the air, then drifted back to slumber against his mother's breasts. Giving her a smile, Holly crossed back to gently caress the baby's head before she left the room.

Jules buzzed about the living room, restoring order. At the sound of her footsteps, he looked up, feigning indifference. A familiar trait. "Savitri's the daughter of the woman who nursed me. She speaks only Sinhalese. You two probably couldn't—"

"Stop, Jules. Women don't need a common language."

He fell silent, statue still.

"You deserted me and cheated on me. Now you continue to lie. The charade is over."

Narrow-eyed, he watched her place the briefcase on a Formica-topped table, remove the documents, rip them in two and then in quarters. As they fluttered to the floor, she retrieved the case and strode to the door, back straight, head high.

He caught her. "Xtreme's my brainchild. I'll sue you."

With a derisive smile, she rummaged in the case, extracted Greg's card and handed it over. "Call my attorney. Bulldog, I think you used to call him. He'll look forward to hearing from you. He loves a good fight."

She held back her tears until she got outside. Once there, she turned her face up to the peppering rain and let it wash away her anger for having been naïve and the shame of being deceived. Then she raced to the car to call Greg and share her discovery.

Chapter Fifty-four

Chess shut off the television and stuck a cheap cigar in his mouth. From Do Thi's tool kit, he took a chisel, a cabinet-tipped screwdriver and a hammer and headed outside. The moment he stepped off the porch, he fired the stogie, puffing mightily, his hand sheltering it from the rain. Sucking bracing smoke into his lungs, he jogged across the spongy yard.

Inside Lance's cabin, Chess moved a pottery ashtray from bedside to desk and set to jimmying the desk lock, an intrusion he wouldn't have considered as recently as this morning. Lance's computer, left running, screen darkened, purred in the silence. Taking no precaution to conceal his effort, Chess abandoned the screwdriver for the hammer and chisel. The middle drawer sprang open. A compartmented tray held the key to the desk file drawer.

Not knowing what to search for, he thumbed through the labeled files. AUTO ACCIDENT. Lance had used the money from the settlement to buy the Mercedes. ADAM, filed out of sequence. Interest soaring, Chess eased the file up, peeked in. Photos. Adam the day he'd been given Gigi. Adam blowing out twelve candles on a homemade birthday cake. Adam reading from his upside-down sofa position. In another shot, taken at this year's stock show, Lance held the boy in a neck-lock while his other hand tugged the dark ponytail.

Lance, a masterpiece in contradiction.

Throat constricting, Chess questioned his sanity before reinserting the file and thumbing forward. An unlabeled file contained an unlabeled three by five disk. He removed the disk and placed it on the desk, then checked CORRESPON-DENCE/PERSONAL, which proved benign, other than one lusty love letter. He skimmed over INSURANCE, JUDO CLASS, K-FOUR, LOAN, MERCEDES 318. MIHATSU, KOICHI.

Heart thudding, he halted at NAKAMOTO INDUS-TRIES, Koichi Mihatsu's Japanese Corporation.

Nakamoto. Motonaka. Coincidence or scheme?

He reared back in the chair, feet on the desk, file in his lap and smoked the entire cigar before reaching the end of the file. Son of a bitch. He had treated Holly like a hysterical shrew when she was right on every frigging issue.

He felt like puking.

The disk caught his eye. Stomach roiling, he inserted it in the computer, tuned in the monitor and brought the file to the screen. His eyes hastily scanned downward as his mind spun into momentary denial, then adopted reality.

Anonymous letters, addressed to the BIA, dated as far back as last fall, as recently as four days ago, solved one more mystery for Chess. Lance had clued the Indian agency, bit by bit, as to Adam's location, proclaiming him a runaway, sug-gesting questionable treatment and that he was being held against his will. He scanned up the screen, read again the hints of mistreatment. What kind of mistreatment? Never. Not for a minute had it been so. A vision of Adam sobbing as the van pulled away, ate at Chess. Had Lance, too, been grieving, cry-ing out in some sick way—through these frigging BIA let-ters—for attention, for help?

Chess slammed the desk with his fist, sending the screen into brief chaos before it settled down to mock him. Goddamn it, Lance.

He shoved back and up, scattering the Nakamoto file and contents over the Navajo rug. He cast around for the Mercedes keys, praying he wasn't without transportation, then took off running for the extra set he demanded Lance leave on the kitchen peg board.

"Not here, Chess," Jerri announced as she popped open a Coor's and sailed it expertly to the end of the scarred bar. "He came in earlier." She glanced at the Miller Lite clock over the dartboard. "Couple a hours. He downed a Cutty Sark and blew Dodge."

Chess's pulse raced in his throat. "For where?"

She half laughed, half snorted. "Thank God, I'm no longer privileged to the intimate side of Lance's life." Empathy crept into her eyes. "He didn't say. Said he'd be back, would I take him home during my break." She grinned, eyes mischievous. "He promised I could drive the 'vette."

"Do me a favor, Jerri."

She raised a severely arched brow.

"Make him wait for the ride until you get off."

She looked stumped. "What's going on, doll?"

"Will you do that?"

"We'll run out of booze if he stays that long." Her grin faded when she caught Chess's gaze. She shrugged. "Whatever the fabulous Baker boys want—or in this case, only this Baker boy."

From Xtreme's night crew, Chess learned Holly had been there briefly. He found no sign of Lance having been in the building. Back outside he flagged a passing private security car.

"Seen any activity here tonight?"

The guard lit a cigarette, tossed the match into a puddle. Wipers slung wet diamonds off the windshield. "I saw your truck. Thought it was you till a woman got out. Little bitty thing. Musta been Miz Harper." Chess nodded and he went on. "Then this old Corvette pulls in while she's inside, but the guy don't go in. He walks round the building—I watched him—got back in and drove off. Seemed harmless. Maybe he went to take a leak."

Chess slapped the Escort door. "Thanks."

He had reached the Mercedes by the time the guard offered help. Shaking his head, he skidded the car backwards, reaching toward the dash to call Holly. Lance had no car phone. Chess pictured his cellular in the recharging unit on his desk at home. Goddamn it.

He floored the Mercedes.

Chapter Fifty-five

Holly left the pungent roses on the cocktail table and moved automaton-like into the kitchen. She turned Angel out into the back yard and locked the glass door, leaving the wooden door open. Nibbling a bagel, she gazed out. Showcased by a neighbor's security light, Angel cavorted, sniffed and scratched, glancing back at intervals for sanction. Mr. Coffee dripped and sputtered Jamaica Java for Greg's visit.

Holly sensed her world resettling, a world without Chess.

She concentrated on the way things had turned out with Jules, rejoiced in finding the evidence she had craved. She wanted to rehash what she'd seen—Savitri and the baby—carve it on her memory—her sometimes too-tender reasoning. She wanted to record the fresh emotions in her journal, so she could relive being deceived, now and then, guard against future dclusion.

She rummaged in a cabinet drawer for the recorder she kept there. Just as she slipped in an empty cassette and flipped the machine on, the doorbell disrupted her thoughts. She glanced at her watch. Greg had said an hour; only twenty minutes had elapsed. Relieved, she headed for the living room, placed the recorder on the cocktail table and peeked out the tiny eyehole in the door.

Pitch darkness revealed nothing. A switch beside the door indicated the porchlight was on. She flipped the toggle to OFF, then ON again. Burned out. She peered out the window.

Behind the Cherokee, her rain-cleansed drive lay barren.

"Greg?" She put her eye to the hole again.

A startling rap on the door led her to peer out a different window, this time toward the mailbox out front. Chess's Corvette was parked at the curb. Relieved, rash fantasies forming, she hurried to the door.

Mohammed had come to the mountain.

Outside the kitchen door, Angel barked and scratched. Whined. Barked again.

When Holly opened the door a slender form emerged from the shadows into the subdued light flowing from the entry. Her visitor tucked a warm lightbulb into her hand. He held the cut-glass light globe aloft, then let go. It shattered on the porch, echoing in the sound of soft rain.

Rapid breath stabbed her rib cage like shards of glass. Fear slicked her face and body with sweat. She shoved on the door, but a black shoe prevented its closing, then kicked it open. The intruder lunged into the entry. She hurled the bulb. It bounced off its target and imploded on the marble floor.

"Hey, babe." He grasped her arm and jerked her. Rib cage to rib cage. Wet, soured clothing steamed on his hot body. "Don't tell me you aren't glad to see me."

Liquor fumes gagged her as his slurred words took on meaning. She squirmed, kicked, gouged his hand with her nails. In the lamplight his eyes sparkled like pyrite, hard and cruel. Terror and disgust congealed in the pit of her stomach.

"What do you want?" she gritted out.

"A little romance. What else?" When he eased his grip on her arm, she scrambled backward, seeking space between them. He grinned maniacally. "It's time we settled accounts."

She struggled for courage. "Anything between us can be settled in Greg Friedman's office." Greg. Her head jerked around. The grandfather clock showed thirty-five minutes remained in Greg's allotted hour.

The phone rang four times, quieted. Angel howled.

"Expecting someone? Chess maybe?" Lance sneered. "Why waste time? Your biological clock is ticking and he's walking around with an empty pistol. Get a clue, babe."

He cupped a breast, thrusting his groin against her. She struggled violently. Primitive growls, frantic pawing, the solid sound of a massive head butting glass, filled the static air. Tonight's horror had begun six months ago when she had chosen Chess over Lance. Sickened by Chess's blindly confiding his sterility to a traitor, she seized Lance's hand, sank her teeth into the membrane between thumb and forefinger and held on.

"You friggin' bitch!" Venom flushed his voice.

Almost wrenching her arm out of its socket, he whirled her around, grasped her around the waist and hauled her back against his erection. Fresh adrenaline spurted in her veins. She twisted fiercely, jabbed back with her elbows. She tried to bolt, kick, stomp. Her heel connected with his shin. He uttered a feral grunt. Tightening his vise grip, he dragged her into the living room, wrestled her onto the sofa and stood gazing down.

From a foreign sphere, Angel's incessant protest wedged into Holly's mind. She screamed the dog's name.

Lance's backhand blow sent her head jolting side to side. She flailed, aiming for his bulging crotch. Sobering rapidly, he jumped back, eyes glaring his intent.

A chill slithered down her spine.

He may kill me, but he'll never rape me while I'm alive.

She screamed for Angel again. The dog's nails grated the glass door, the wooden frame. Face crimson, Lance sank to his knees, loosening his belt.

"Take your clothes off." Spittle showered her.

She drew her knees up, hugged her breasts and curled into a ball, sickened by his acrid smell and the proposed image. He hooked his fingers inside the neck of her blouse and yanked. Buttons flew; cold air assaulted her skin. He forced her skirt up and bent over her.

"You need your pump primed, bitch."

With icy hands, he tugged her pantyhose into a wad at her groin and ran the backs of his fingers inside the crotch of her panties. She squirmed, her hands circling his wrist, tugging.

"What's wrong? Hasn't Chess taught you to like this part?" He dipped his head.

With uncommon titan strength, she fought him off, kicking, screaming. "Angel! Kill, Angel! Kill!"

The thwarted beast howled pitifully.

Lance snarled, swinging at her from his kneeling stance. Miraculously, she ducked. In the kitchen—miles away—the door rattled mightily, then shattered onto the tile floor.

Tags clanked. Feet pounded.

Bloody hell! Like a passenger imprisoned by a vehicle sliding on ice, Holly anticipated the inevitable climax.

Angel took to the air and lit on Lance's curved back, bowling him over. The cocktail table flipped, crystal, rancid roses and tape recorder flying. Entranced, Holly watched a black, blood-splattered demon shred Lance's clothing. She rejoiced as jagged teeth sank into his thigh, released and sank again and again. Eternity dragged. Stuporous, she rose to seize Angel's rhinestone-studded harness, the backs of her fingers raking tiny imbedded glass shards.

"Angel, stay!"

The Doberman obeyed, body quivering, indecision of whether to kill or grant mercy burning in her onyx eyes.

Lance grasped the sofa arm and scrambled to his feet, his pants and shirtsleeve tattered, hands chewed. Blood streamed down his arm. Desire to release Angel rushed through Holly.

Instead she took aim and planted her foot in Lance's crotch. He wailed and bent over, clutching himself.

"Get out! I'm going to count to ten. Then I'm letting Angel go."

He glared, eyes mad. Holly eased her hold. Angel's forward plunge drove Lance to his knees. He came up with a shoe.

Holly's throat convulsed. "Leave the shoe. It's evidence you were here."

Eyes pleading, he wrestled with the shoe.

She tightened her grip. "Kill, Angel."

Angel growled, lunged, jerking Holly forward.

Shoe in hand, Lance raced for the door, pulling it to behind him but failing to engage the latch. A narrow gap formed. Angel broke from Holly's grasp, nuzzled the breach wider and slicked through. Lance's out-of-sync footsteps and the pursuing avenger's menacing bark bounced off the brick walk. A car door slammed. The 'vette fired on a second attempt. The sound of screeching tires swirled in Holly's head as reality of what she had escaped ripped her like daggers.

Kneeling amid the debris, she hid her face in her hands.

Chapter Fifty-six

Chess's adrenaline checked slightly when he turned onto Holly's street and saw no vehicles in her drive, other than the Cherokee. Then he sighted familiar taillights streaking around a corner a block away. When the Mercedes highlights showcased Angel turning circles in the street, his hairline pricked. His heart slammed into his throat. His foot wavered over the gas and the brake as Angel bolted toward him, then wheeled to race down the street again, her enraged bark echoing through the quiet neighborhood.

Holly's front door gaped; subdued light cast shadows on the porch. Chess jerked the Mercedes to the curb, jumped out and bolted across the lawn. On the porch, broken glass crunched beneath his feet.

The scent of sweat, evil, and fear hung in the entry.

"Holly!" He halted in the arched door to the living room. In the thundering silence, the skin on the back of his neck tightened as if hope had opened a door and walked out, abandoning him to whatever horror awaited.

A thin, buzzing sound drew him into the room. Flesh crawling, he took in the overturned table and scattered debris. A blinking, upside-down tape recorder accounted for the buzzing. The remainder of the room appeared untouched.

Terror thrust him around the sofa, his mind snatching, rejecting, then accepting his discovery.

Holly slumped on the floor against the front of the sofa, skirt bunched around her upper thighs, legs extended, round-toed clunky shoes housing her feet. Her head slumped to one side, eyes hollow, stuporous. Coagulated blood formed a line from the corner of her mouth to her chin, and a blotched, swelling cheek marred her face. Her hands rested palm-up on the carpet.

She resembled a broken dark-haired Raggedy Ann doll. Her stillness panicked him until his mind seized onto the tears streaming down her face, the palsied jerk of her shoulders. He sank to his knees, choking on a maelstrom of grief and rage. He wanted to drink her tears, ingest her sorrow, consume her. Never to let her hurt again.

She lifted her eyes. The confusion he saw mirrored that in his soul. After years of protecting Lance, Chess now wanted to kill him.

He touched her cheek, eased his hand into her hair, coiling his fingers into the rowdy tangles. His free hand pulled her gaping blouse together and fastened the one remaining button. Mysteriously, his lips formed words. "Did he rape you, Holly?"

She shook her head. As though she felt his furor, his desire to pursue, her small hand settled on his arm, holding him in place as effectively as an anchor.

"Angel stopped him," she whispered as if awed still.

He braced against the sofa and cradled her on his lap, rocked her, stroked her hair, kissed her temple. Sobs racked her body, making him acutely aware of her fragility.

"It'll be okay, sugar," he crooned. "It'll be okay." He squeezed his eyes shut, finding her bruised image printed on the backs of his eyelids.

So beautiful, so guileless, so unjustly doubted.

Eventually she quieted, curled up against him and opened her eyes. Instantly, she strained toward the floor debris, her mouth set. With a boot toe, he kicked the rotten roses away, then, guessing at her intention, raked the recorder within her reach. The insect-like buzzing droned on, signifying a used-up tape.

Eyes swollen, weighty, hands shaking, she fumbled with the buttons to reverse the tape. "I have it all." She sounded tipsy, tired but triumphant. "I was going to make a journal entry before Greg—Greg was coming over, but Lance..." She shuddered. "I have it all. I want you to listen."

Refusal slashed lightning-fast across his mind, but he nodded.

The rewinding stopped. She pushed another button. Silence, except for Angel's faint whine, Holly calling Greg's name, a sharp rap on the door and eventually, glass smashing.

Holly's face contorted. Chess imagined the horror that had accompanied the shattering sound, imagined it replaying behind her eyes. On the tape, he heard scuffling, more breaking glass, Lance's voice. "Hey, babe. Don't tell me you aren't glad to see me."

Sickened, Chess wrested the machine from her, stabbed the off button and tossed the metal box aside. Proof. The asinine wager haunted him. He had demanded proof of Lance's guilt and a sick, demented kind of fate had allowed Holly to attain it.

He had the ball now. Would he fumble?

"You have to listen to the tape." Her tone hinged on delirium. "Then you'll believe me."

He tilted her chin and softly settled his mouth on hers, more a bond than a kiss. "I don't need to listen," he murmured against her mangled lip. Blood oozed again. He swiped it away, then applied pressure to the abrasion with his tongue. "I believed you, darlin'—no matter how much I acted like an asshole—and I found a file that backs you up." His mind's eye dredged up the disk as well, Lance's backstabbing letters on the screen. "Every transaction with Motonaka was document-ed, including copies of deposits Lance made in the Castle Rock Bank."

Her eyes flashed relief.

"I'm sorry, Holly," he whispered against her hair.

One arm eased up to circle his neck.

"I'm so goddamned sorry," he moaned. "Can you forgive me?"

Her eyes closed again; her cheek barely moved as she nodded against him. "It's my fault," she whispered, regret sat-urating the words he hated hearing. "I should have...paid attention to the signs."

"I should have taken you at your word." Lance had offered so many cues along the way, clues Chess had ignored. Belief that he could save Lance had sacrificed Holly.

Her eyes opened, focused. He read weariness, and so much more. "I should have told you sooner. It's not your fault. I wasn't honest with you, the one thing you needed."

A tumbling boulder of guilt hit him. He had so much to tell her once his finances evened out and—no. He'd waited long enough for that dilemma to resolve. He determined to finish the damn puzzle dominating their lives.

Finish it tonight. After he'd finished with Lance.

He picked glass from Angel's back and swabbed her down with witch hazel while Holly watched from her perch on the bathroom vanity, her feet dangling. She sipped brandy from a glass she gripped with both hands. Her troubled eyes assured him she was mulling over details he'd filled in for her, trying to get her mind around the rancid triangle made up of Lance, Koichi Mihatsu, and Motonaka Industries.

"I should call Greg," she murmured. "I kept praying he'd come. I don't understand."

"He left a message—"

"That phone call," she whispered, shuddering.

He hadn't known about a phone call. "Something came up with a client. He said he'd call tomorrow."

She nodded, raising the glass to her mouth, sipping half-heartedly as she gazed into the middle distance. Chess looked away, pained by the disillusion in her eyes.

When he finished with Angel, he moved between Holly's parted legs while the Doberman pulled guard duty at his feet, ears peaked, throat rumbling a fixed growl. He tilted Holly's chin, kissed her tenderly. While he bathed her face and neck with a warm cloth, he surveyed the dimly lit room in the mirror. A wine velvet robe hung on a creamy-white door. Candles nested by the Jacuzzi tub and a bunch of past-their-prime flowers decorated the vanity. An imagined erotic scene involving him, Holly and the tub was quickly interrupted by memory of the actual scene he'd encountered tonight.

A bruised Holly. Trembling. Traumatized.

Rewetting the cloth, he dabbed the cut at the corner of her mouth. She jerked. He held the cotton balm to her eyes, then to her rapidly coloring, swollen cheek. Kissing her temple, he groaned in empathy. She hooked her heels behind his knees, drew him close enough to wrap her arms about his waist. He held her, his mind replaying the tape and all she had told him about Lance this afternoon. He had wanted so badly for her to be wrong. Reality of losing a false allegiance, loyalty Chess had relied on, reared its head to gnaw at him before hate snaked along his spine like flame on a dynamite trail.

"I'll put you to bed, sugar. I have to take care of something."

She pushed the cloth away, revealing reddened, knowing eyes. Attuned, Angel bolted to her feet and worked her way between Holly's and Chess's entangled legs.

"I'll be back, once I've seen Lance—settled some things."

Holly frowned. "What are you going to do?"

Stomp him. "Give Lance what he's needed for a long time—make up for what I've overlooked, what I've let him get away with." In the recesses of his mind, he had transferred grief for his uncle's suicide to fear of Lance's stability, then tied the whole warped package with barbed-wire-laced guilt.

"I'm going with you," Holly announced.

Angel pranced with wise anticipation.

Chess weighed Holly's claim, how she could be affected by what she'd witness. "You need to be in bed, sugar."

Boldly, she met his gaze. "We both need to be in bed."

She wriggled down from the sink, reached beneath her short rumpled skirt and agilely peeled off the riddled pantyhose. She cast them away, stepped back into her shoes, straightened her clothing and combed her nails through her hair. Then she disappeared into the closet and came out pulling an oversized cotton sweater over her head. Like the Phoenix rising from the ashes, she straightened to her minute, but regal, stature.

"He might come back. I'm going with you."

Chapter Fifty-seven

Silence filled the close confines of the Mercedes, except for Angel's clanking tags when she poked her head over the seat to lap periodic kisses on her mistress. Chess held Holly's hand, his thumb soothing, worrying, her palm. His agitated caress coincided with the brooding she sensed. When he abruptly turned to her, a traffic light painted a false blush on his face.

"I have to know something, sugar."

She nodded, one arm hugging her midsection tightly.

In the changing light, she watched him reconsider. "Relax," he said finally as the car shot forward. "Whatever you tell me won't change a damn thing."

She tried to smile. Her lip cracked again and she swabbed blood with a tissue. "Could you define 'damn thing'?"

"Why the hell wasn't Jules home? You must have told him about Lance if you told me."

Especially after he'd bullied her over telling Jules.

A sense of resolution washed over her. "Jules is no longer part of my life, Chess." When he opened his mouth, she raised an open palm. "That's over. Really over."

The way he waited, without offering his well-rehearsed arguments, fed her confidence. As the Mercedes turned onto C470 and sped west with purpose, she shared with him her never-dying suspicion that Jules had lied about amnesia, that he had returned only to claim Xtreme, even if it meant reinstating the marriage. Chess's eyes stayed fixed on the road as she related her plan to give Jules half her stock for his irrevocable proxy, thereby removing him from the picture. As she spoke of Savitri and the brown-haired baby, her throat caught. He turned to look at her. She knew that if not for the darkness, she would see the beloved furrow between his brows. Her pain eased with the story of ripping up the stock agreement and eradicating seven years of suspicion and guilt when she walked away a truly free woman.

"Jesus, Holly," Chess breathed, hands gripping the wheel. She felt compassion in his gaze as it touched her across the worn leather and dull chrome separating them.

"I know I should have told you what was going on between Jules and me, but..."

"The right time never came." Resignation colored his tone.

She gazed out the window until he spoke again.

"In the future, anytime will be right to tell me anything between here and hell, and I swear I'll like it. If not, I'll lump it." His dismal smile beseeched her. "I wish I'd been there, darlin', to cushion the hurt when you found out the truth about Jules."

"When I found proof of the truth, you mean." Her voice cut the memory-laden darkness. "Today, there was no hurt, Chess. I survived that long before you came into my life. Jules and I married for all the wrong reasons. He wanted me to make him young. I wanted him to be my father." Exhausted by the answers she still lacked, she sighed. "Either way, it's over. I could have confided more of my intentions to you, but freeing myself of Jules and my girlish illusions about him was something I had to do on my own. Something I accomplished." She turned her head to stare at her reflection in the window, her voice grieved. "I trust the outcome of my effort meets your high standard."

His hand covered her knee, moved up the inside of her thigh, warm and strong, but not quite coaxing. Still, recalling the malevolence in Lance's eyes, she trembled at the touch.

"I've been a bastard," he concluded quietly.

"Maybe it's more a matter of getting your way—not taking no for an answer."

"It's a matter of being a bastard." He eased his hand away from her leg and caught her hand, snaking his fingers between hers. "I couldn't face losing you, partner, so I pressured you, my typical way of doing business."

She tucked the confession into her heart, along with the irony of knowing she loved him so much she would have let him go.

⊰⊱⊰⊱⊰

Sedalia lay dark and, for the most part, shut for the night. They drove past Sedalia Bar and Grill, failing to spot the 'vette. As Chess eased the Mercedes past Bud's, they scanned the front parking strip, then the lot at Gabriel's, a lauded used-brick and gingerbread-trimmed gourmet restaurant across the street.

The Mercedes executed a quiet U-turn in front of the somber post office. Tags ajingle, Angel shifted her weight on the cargo seat as they swung into the alley between Bud's and a padlocked Jewel's Frozen Yogurt.

Holly ventured, "Maybe this isn't the time—"

Chess's stern stare deterred her. Spotting the 'vette parked behind Jewel's, he pounded the Mercedes wheel, his curse low and indiscernible. The car's classic tail end hung into the alley where a security light revealed a mangled fender.

Chess's breathing kicked up a notch, his anger pervading the car like water gorging a firehose. He shoved the Mercedes into park. "Lock the door behind me. Don't open it for anybody, for any reason." His hand jerked the door handle up. Light flooded the car.

She opened the door and scrambled out, commanding, "Angel, stay." In the mercury-vapor glow of the security light, Holly's eyes locked with Chess's across the car top. "Or should I bring her?" Memory of Angel's teeth piercing Lance's thigh made the suggestion palatable.

He thudded the door closed. "There's no way you're going in. You'll get hurt, sugar, sure as hell."

Only if he left her alone. "I'm going."

She rounded the car and waited at the back bumper until he joined her, mouth grim, eyes intent. A car passed on the street, radio blaring, then drifting into silence. Somewhere a dog barked, disturbing the cricket fiddling in the grass surrounding Jewel's souredmilk-smelling garbage.

Chess spread his feet, jamming his hands in his pockets. "For once, listen to me, Holly. I don't want you to see this."

For once? If she hadn't ached so, felt so dirty, so abused and discarded, she might have laughed. "You owe me this."

He grasped her shoulders, shook her gently, their eyes locking in the eerie light. Then he pressed his forehead to hers, running his palms up and down her arms with a soft groan.

Her fright escalated when she felt his hands quaking.

Chapter Fifty-eight

Pulse pumping, Chess entered Bud's through the back screen door off the alley, then held the door for Holly. A bulb in the ceiling revealed her anxious face. She hugged his heels wordlessly. He felt his pulse accelerate with each step until adrenaline pumped sour revenge through his bloodstream.

He held up in the shadows near the deserted dartboard, satisfying himself the near-midnight crowd was sparse. Only a heads-together couple in the back corner booth and two long-hairs in Rockies jackets at a table next to the silent jukebox.

Lance occupied the end barstool, two paces from Chess. Wearing a tattered, bloody shirt, loosened tie and ripped slacks, he hunkered over a half-empty glass, a bottle of Cutty alongside.

Behind the bar, Jerri glanced up, her gaze ricocheting from Chess to Holly to Lance. She punched Thurman, rousing him from a Rockies recap on the wall-hung TV.

Chess heard Holly's ragged breathing behind him. He shot a cautioning glance over his shoulder, then closed the distance between himself and his cousin. Mannequin-like, Jerri and Thurman looked on, Thurman gape-mouthed as a beached dead fish.

Lance seemed to sense an invading presence. His head bolted up, eyes meeting Chess's mirrored glare.

"Let's go outside." Chess kept his voice low.

Lance rotated slowly, eyes lighting on, then dodging, Holly where she hovered in the shadows. "You mad about the 'vette, cuz? Somebody passed me and clipped 'er. Hit-and-run. I swear."

"Get your ass off that stool or get it kicked right here."

Lance's glazed-green eyes darted to Holly, back to Chess. "What'd she tell you?"

Chess smelled Lance's fear.

"She's lying, whatever she said. You know I'm with you, cuz. All the way."

He spoke so convincingly that under different circumstances, Chess would have believed him. He caught Lance's sleek belt buckle and jerked him to his feet. Lance staggered back, clutching the bar.

Jerri called Chess's name, an ignored warning.

"Cut the crap, Lance. I've seen the Motonaka file and the disk. Now I want to know why. Why, you bastard?"

"I'm not quite a bastard, but just as well, compared to you." He knocked Chess's hand away, swayed, attempting to focus. "You fall in a sewer, you come up holding a silver dollar. I'm sick of you getting the breaks—sick of your miserly dole." Smirking, he cast around for support in the dead-quiet room. "You didn't get the breaks this time, though. With Xtreme or Adam."

Chess's gut lurched. "Tell me about Adam." His fingertips against Lance's chest, he gave him two jerky shoves, harassing moves left over from adolescence. Lance's photo collection got tangled along with the undeveloped pictures swirling in Chess's head. "How in the hell could you do that, Lance? When you loved him—Do you even know what you've done?"

A stupefied look answered the questions before satisfaction smeared Lance's slack face.

"I turned him in to keep you from demonstrating your almighty power to fix things. Hurts, don't it, cuz?"

"Yeah, it hurts." It hurt like hell. Like a festering snakebite. He hooked a finger in a belt loop and jerked Lance away from the bar. "Payback's a bitch, cuz, but it's here."

Cursing low, Jerri rounded the counter and maneuvered behind Lance, going to stand by Holly.

"I'm calling the law," Thurman gruffed, fumbling a cellular. Chess caught Lance's untucked shirt and twisted the front into a bull rider's grip. "Let's hear about Holly, you sonovabitch."

Panic honed Lance's face into razor-edged planes. "I didn't touch her." He glared at Holly, eyes wild, mouth quivering. "If she said I did—she's a slut, anyway. Who'd want her?"

Lance grabbed the Scotch bottle and wielded it, missing badly, throwing himself off balance. The bottle shattered on the wooden floor, glass flying, Scotch soaking Chess's boots. He stepped around Lance, grasped his arm, twisted it high behind and steered him toward the back door. Holly, Jerri, and Thurman brought up the flank. Chess shoved Lance once, twice, across the storeroom and through the door. He stumbled, recovered and whirled around, bobbing and weaving cobra like.

Chess launched himself like a rocket, hitting Lance waist-high, hanging on. He felt the wind whoosh from Lance's lungs as the two of them crashed to the ground. Crimson shards flashed before Chess's eyes. He heard his own heartbeat, felt heated blood pumping rage into his brain.

He reared up in a frenzy. With a mind picture of Holly's bruised cheek and cut lip shutting out reason, he swung with the strength of the possessed. His fist caught Lance's chin.

Blood spurted. Lance howled, tried to stand and failed. He pitched onto his side, adopting a fetal curl. Chess bounded to his feet. He stomped hair-close to Lance's face. Lance howled, rolled over and wrapped his head with his arms.

Chess's chest heaved as he stood over his cousin's quaking frame, fists clenched, listening to him weep. Rage gave way to disbelief, then pity as their family history filed behind his eyes, the question "why" reverberating in his mind.

From out of the hateful night, Holly moved close. Her hands gripped his arm, her jagged breath matching his. She hauled him backward and held on, exhibiting the courage of a lioness, the stature of a kitten. Turning, he looked into warm liquid eyes that saw straight into his soul. He caught her in his arms and buried his face in her hair, the sound of Lance's whimpers echoing in his ears.

"I called the cops." Apology hung in Thurman's claim. "Maybe you better go, Baker. We'll tell 'em it was hit and run."

Jerri touched his arm. "Go on. I'll take care of Lance."

He searched Lance's pockets for the 'vette key, then straightened and stared at his cousin's still form. Realization of no longer being responsible for Lance seeped into his mind. He drew a deep breath, filling his lungs with cool dry air, redolent with soured sweat, doused revenge, and losses dealt.

Chapter Fifty-nine

Holly hugged herself, trembling inwardly, as she braced in the door between Chess's bedroom and bath. By the filtered light from the bathroom, she watched him fold down one side of his feather bed and move two pillows into a single fat stack.

Passing back to the bath, he kissed her lightly, his hand caressing the back of her neck. Then he released her, turned on the tub faucets and sprinkled something pink into the water's wake. Gaze fixed, he adjusted the flow into the over-sized marble tub, his gestures heavy, trance-like.

His languid actions nagged some unlabeled sense in Holly. She thought of their day, the scene they'd just left, how his rage had slipped into near apathy. Passiveness resembling shock.

His smile tender, he lit the single candle taken from the storeroom where they'd bedded Angel down with Warrior, then placed a bouquet pilfered from the dining room table beside the tub and switched off the light.

He stood before her, candlelight outlining his form, cigar smoke, dried adrenaline-induced sweat, and hours-old cologne pervaded her senses. Suggestion of a sprouting beard pricked her fingertips when she reached up to caress his face.

He caught the bottom of her sweater and worked it up gently. She stopped his hands, pressed them to her breasts, glorying in the warmth against her chilled skin. In near darkness she sought his eyes, finding them as tender as his touch.

He worked his hands beneath the sweater, pushing it up, freeing her arms. The backs of his fingers feathered her skin as he deftly worked her bra loose, freeing her breasts.

She eyed the bed, smelled the peachy aroma of flourishing bath bubbles. "Is this bath and that bed meant to be a single, cowboy?"

He stripped off her sweater, dropped it on the floor, eased the bra straps off her shoulders and drew her against his blood-splattered shirtfront. "You've had a hellaceous day, sugar. You need rest."

His breath roused the hair at her temple; his words evoked disquiet. She worked his shirt buttons open and tugged the front loose from his belt, then circled his waist and pressed her wounded lips to his hot skin. His sprinkling of chest hair teased her mouth and memory. An ache oozed down, spread, then culminated in that cavern she wanted only him to fill.

"We've had the same kind of day. We need each other."

He slacked back. As he worked the side zipper of her skirt, she broke her embrace to undo his belt buckle. Eyes holding hers, the candle flame casting his face into cerise shadows, he pushed the skirt past her hips and let it pool around her feet. She unhooked the waist of his ripped Levi's. As she labored to free the metal buttons, his fingers glided inside the waistband of her bikini panties, then his splayed hands grasped her hips. "You need a warm bath and some sleep, darlin'." His words emerged strained, reticent. "We'll talk tomorrow."

The words reverberated in the sound of plunging, tumbling water, then swirled like rapids in her mind. She stepped back, arms crossed on her bare breasts. "I need you."

Seeming not to hear, he hooked his fingertips in the legs

of her panties, slipped them past her hips, then lowered her to the side of the tub. Kneeling, he peeled the garment down her legs, then held the soft satin for an instant before tossing it aside. Her legs pressed against cold marble as warm, soap-slick spray bathed her buttocks.

"Is it still Jules?"

"Jules is dead for me, too, Holly."

Hands behind his nape, fingers bound in a loose weave, she fastened his gaze with hers. "Then, why tomorrow?"

He sat back on his heels. "I want you. I need you." His voice stroked her, warmed her, almost assuring her. "But I love you too much to make love to you tonight."

Loved her? The words she had waited to hear.

Abruptly, she twisted to shut off the faucets. Deafening silence filled the shadowy surroundings. Somewhere, a clock struck; a wall settled. The wind had come up, rustling the branches of the maple outside the window, forecasting the next storm blowing in off the Rockies.

Cognizance rippled through Holly.

Regardless of his loss or guilt for doubting her, no matter what mystery hung over Lance's actions—regardless of her own trauma—sleeping in each other's arms tonight loomed paramount.

She turned back to face him. With her hands at his temples, she savored the feel of his hair, pure gold in the candle-light, spilling over her fingers. She drew his face to her breasts. "Lance didn't rape me, Chess. Don't you believe me?"

A rod shot up his spine. "I can't get the picture out of my head. I keep thinking how I should've—of Lance and you—

Her fingertip against his lip drew silence. "Somehow I would have found the strength and the means to kill him before I'd let him rape me." She whispered into his ear, "No matter what you did or didn't do, I forgive you. Give me a chance to prove it." Her hands cradled his head against her while she waited.

At last he parted her legs, moved between them to take her in his arms, drawing her against his quickening sex.

After a moment, he rose and removed his boots. Eyes voracious, she watched him take off his shirt, release the buttons at his fly and strip the remaining clothing off in one motion. She took his extended hand and he drew her into his arms, sealing their bodies, skin to skin. His mouth took hers in a kiss deeper, sweeter, more promising than her soul could ever have craved.

He guided her to the shower, turned on the dual heads, then drew her into the cool dark enclosure and beneath the warm torrent. Turning her, curling his front to her back, he splayed a hand across her breasts while the other delved between her thighs, sealing her to his searing erection. She toiled to press tightly enough to dissolve into him as his fingers massaged gently, sending tingling currents into the tender, intimate, hidden folds of her body.

He rocked her side to side beneath the pelting stream until she turned her face, straining for his mouth, then swiveled in his arms, seeking, hungering, unable to distinguish hands from water, his body from hers, craving from having.

"I love you," she half whimpered, crossing the last plateau. She tilted her face to wash away newly flowing blood his kiss had wrought. "I love you. I want only you."

He grasped her thighs. She sensed the harnessed strength in his hands as he lifted her and she clung with arms, mouth, being. Willfully, her legs circled his hips and he lowered their intertwined bodies to the shower bench lining one wall. He lowered her feet to the floor, helped her straddle his legs. Reverently, he tested her swollen cleft with his finger as he fixed his position on the edge of the bench. Hands at her waist, eyes penetrating hers, he guided her forward, then down in one fluid motion, gorging her with himself, with blissful, satiating pain until heat begat fire and she moistened to receive him, to cleave around him, stroke him.

Her head fell forward, seeking his mouth, then reeled backward when his hands on her hips churned her lower body, slowly, rhythmically. Seized by a sudden quest, she adopted the rhythm until she shattered. She soared, peaked, floated, spiraled down to reality, collapsing onto him, her body sagging, quaking.

"I love you, Holly." He drove the ragged whisper into her mouth, into her soul, as he rose, wrapped her legs around him, braced against the wall, and pursued his own completion.

His hot fluids filled her, seeped onto her inner thighs, mingled with shower water, leaving only sated longing.

Awakened by the baleful sound of a distant train whistle, Holly lay still in dark, unfamiliar surroundings. A breath next to her ear, an arm beneath her head, another looped across her to cup her breast, stirred her to awareness. She listened to the lonely whine of the train, the muted clatter of iron on iron, until the report grew faint, then died.

Chess spoke softly against her hair, no trace of sleep in the voice sliding deeply, smoothly into her ear. "She passes every night about this time." His arm tightened around her, his hand moving to her other breast. "Go back to sleep, sugar."

His husky, whispered directive tweaked an awakening she attempted to ignore before wondering why she should.

His hair smelled vaguely of shampoo and the cigar he'd smoked after their shower, alone in the dark on the porch. But he smelled of sex, too. Their sex. She curled her hand beneath the corner of the pillow to lift and cushion her bruised cheek, tracking her sensual awareness through a stirring phase, into that familiar sharp pang at her innermost core.

Gently, his hand eased from her breast to her waist, one finger finding her navel, rimming the indention so lightly she knew she had only wished it. His touch trailed across her stomach, down her thigh, up, back to her breast. She shifted her back to him, elongating her body in a futile attempt to align with his, then lay witnessing him coming alive against the backs of her thighs. The greedy cavity between her legs throbbed. Willfully, her back curved, a foot caressing his hard shin.

"Can't you sleep, darlin'?"

Moaning, she revolved in his arms, arched her back, her leg looping his hip, and sought his mouth in the dark.

His body vibrated with gentle laughter as he drew her beneath him, spread her legs with one hand and entered her with the same cocksure control with which he had entered her life.

Chapter Sixty

Dawn faded in, infusing the horizon, slowly replacing the misty gray of a May morning. Beyond the undraped bedroom windows, Geronimo, Gigi, and Jamilah, a pregnant Arabian, moved about the corral, dark silhouettes against a sluggish dawn. Cushioned by the feather bed, Chess lay absorbing the peaceful sound of rain falling on his shrinking kingdom. His eyes roamed the room, recalling the night before, Holly's persistence, his helpless, and wise, compliance.

He propped on his elbows and stared out at the row of cabins, all lighted, except for Lance's. A jolt like a drill hitting a nerve raced through him, aggravating a briefly forgotten, well-honed insecurity.

As if aware of his angst, Holly stirred beside him, sighing. Her gentle-as-the-rain protest enhanced the morning quiet.

He turned on his side to enjoy an unguarded appraisal.

She smelled of sleep, his shampoo, and sweet sex. Her bruised cheeks, one purple blotched with yellow, the other shaded with cobalt, seared his conscience. He resisted imparting a healing kiss that might wake her.

Free of the tangled covers, her breasts graced the plane of

her dusky body like rounded dunes, radiating warmth, as though kissed by the sun. One foot had escaped the covers. The gold ankle bracelet gleamed in the dawn. A novel gesture for an on-the-surface conventional woman. A voluntary smile tugged his lips. Always full of surprises, Holly kept him on constant guard, a slave to anticipation.

Her eyelids clenched, then opened, revealing sleepy, raisin-dark eyes that sucked him in, nudged his heart. The truth of her presence rocked him, then whispered that this was not a moment to take for granted.

"It's raining, sugar," he murmured, the backs of his fingers feathering her cheek.

She nodded and stretched with a hushed moan.

"I've thought of waking up with you here," he confessed, "but I forgot to paint rain into my wish."

"Wish?" She smiled, tugging on the sheet, smile widening when his grip prevented modesty.

"My dream, actually." His fingertip traced a wispy, gray-blue vein that rivered to her nipple. Then he eased his hand beneath the sheet, across her rib cage, down her body. Her skin, oiled satin, supple and soothing, conjured memory of her filling the contours and hollows of his body like melted wax. He peeled the cover back, tossed it aside gently, winning another smile when his fingers invaded her thatch of crisp curls, teased, explored tentatively, then withdrew. Tenderly, he kissed the unscabbed but dry cut on her mouth. "I love you, Holly."

"I love you." Her eyes sobered. "Since the day I first saw this bed, I've longed to wake up beside you."

Not confessing their love sooner had been a lonely waste.

"Now you know the magic words, sugar, so you can come anytime."

Her eyes sparked as a blush softened her bruises. She caressed his face, nails raking his beard, reminding him of her tender skin, proof he shouldn't persist in his wake-up greeting.

"How about that bath now, princess?"

His breath tripped when she sat up to eye the tub, baring her upper body. Her mouth dipped at the corners. "Not alone."

His gaze traveled the plane of her back, the rounded corners of her hips, caressed the firm contour of her backside. "Not if you don't want to, sugar. You made a believer of me last night."

⟶⟵

They reclined at opposite ends of the tub. Bubbles, the fruit of Robyn's cast-off Boucheron bath gel, crackled over his chest like June bugs on an Oklahoma summer night, teased Holly's chin and the hair straggling out of her pinned bun. His foot massaged the warm, plump folds between her thighs. One knee protruding from the bubbles, the other extended, her toes teased and stroked the gentle erection he hoped to curtail until they had talked, revealed, and, hopefully resolved yet untouched subjects.

Looking pleased, yet surprised, she observed, "You have my picture on your desk. The one taken at the designer awards banquet."

"Guilty." He'd gotten a copy from *Powder Magazine*. The last couple of months her silver-framed likeness had comforted as well as tortured him.

"I'm flattered, cowboy."

"I doubt that, but if you are, I'm glad."

"I have pictures of you I've cut from the *Post*." She hiked an eyebrow. "From the business section, of course."

"Before Xtreme, I was a regular in the *Post* human interest section. Ask Do Thi. She made a scrapbook." His neck prickled, heated. He grinned contritely. "One for herself, not me."

"Ever humble." Her toes squeezed beneath his scrotum, lifted, probed. He flinched, making her laugh. Then she sobered. "Your life was different before Xtreme. Before me."

"Not better," he realized. "Just easier." Before and after differences reeled across the screen of his mind. "I'm not that wealthy bastard who walked into your office that first day. Not today, anyway."

"That chauvinist who tried to scare me into submission?"

"That one." His lips sketched a thin smile. "Because I had too much pride to admit my money problems, for months you've watched me wrestle the going-broke demons without a clue."

Cognizance and what he hoped was relief crowded her eyes. "I knew something was wrong. Sometimes I thought it was me, and other times I believed it had nothing to do with me."

"Only indirectly. It started with discovering I had bought into Xtreme with wrong expectations." Her frown made him rush on. "We've been over that, sugar. I stopped blaming you the minute you explained it. I wanted Xtreme so much I didn't do my homework—at least not as thoroughly as usual." He'd wanted it worse after tangling with her that first day. "I was highly leveraged, always am. That's the way I do business."

"Why?" Quietly, without challenge.

"Lots of reasons. I like a gamble, the thrill of knowing the dice can turn up any number. I committed just enough money to get Xtreme up and going, figuring hard work would take care of the rest. By the time I discovered the discrepancy in the figures my cash was tied up. I had to borrow money to cover Xtreme's deficit. Just asking for the loan left a rotten taste in my mouth."

He paused to read her reaction, finding her look supportive. "Before Xtreme, I was debt free. Clipping bond coupons kept me in day money—" A sweeping arm gesture indicated their surroundings as his mind checked off obligations he chose not to elaborate on. "Bonds, plus the interest on a once-sacred million-dollar CD in the Okmulgee bank."

The last torqued her brows with curiosity.

"Right after I got the loan and plowed it into Xtreme, the Mexican crisis came up." She opened her mouth to speak and he threw in, "Right. The U.S. bailed them out, but it took a while. The dollar lost its edge on the international market, and when the dust cleared, my empire had toppled like a house of cards. Nothing I tried worked."

"Like what?" Her voice was husky and soft. Her hand stole beneath the water to caress his foot, press it against her.

"Like when you balked at selling to America Ice."

Her eyes fogged with memory mirroring his, of that ecstatic, chaotic trip to New York.

"I came around," she reminded him.

"Yeah, but I loved you too much to keep bullying you."

"You loved me then?"

"Couldn't you tell?"

"I wanted to believe that."

"I loved you. That's for damned sure." With his eyes, he apologized for making love to her, then leaving her to wake up alone as she'd been doing for seven years. "Because the AI sale didn't happen, I took the money from the Okmulgee bank—"

"You stole money?"

She bolted to a sitting position, her wet breasts glowing in the muted light. Water glided, dripped from her nipples, making the bubbles sizzle.

"No way, sugar." He was too wise to steal or to laugh at her alarm. "The Okmulgee money was inheritance. Estate planning I promised I'd never touch."

Lena Chesney's grooved face, sturdy stature and abhorrence for risk ran through his mind. When she'd added the million to what she'd already given him, he'd been married and horny for his wife. He rubbed the signet ring with his thumb. It had belonged to his grandfather and his grandmother had held it, passed it on to Chess to give to his firstborn. If she were alive today, she still wouldn't accept his sterility.

"I took that money and doubled my risk in a down market." He shrugged. "I'm waiting for that gamble to pay off." Or not.

She eased back into the water, sinking down, finding his foot again, reinstating hers. Her eyes underlined her words. "Money means nothing to me. I've told you that."

She'd told him that all right, in the heat of battle, when she accused him of selling her down the river to America Ice. He wanted to clean the slate, clear up any ambiguities.

"Money means everything to me—or it has in the past," he said, just in case she'd missed that trait in his cocky, swaggering white knight role. The portrayal of a warrior who'd now lost his weapons. "My obsession to make money comes from my family background. A craving, I guess, to offset my dad and Lance's going broke."

She nodded, eyes like black silk. "Sally told me."

His hairline tightened before he evolved from pissed to pleased. "How much did she tell you?"

"Everything you told her." She named his father's drinking, the changes the bankruptcy made in his life, his uncle's suicide, how he'd stuck by Lance, trying to make it up to him. And Adam. She fell reticent for a moment, then said tenderly, "All that only made me admire and love you more."

His mind backtracked to the tell-all drink he'd had with Sally, only weeks into the partnership. "You loved me back then?"

"I think I loved you that first day."

He looked skeptical. "Jesus, how could you?"

She shrugged. "The challenge of impossible odds?"

"I equated money with self worth. How appealing is that?"

She smiled. "About as appealing as my obsession to hold on to Xtreme?"

Memory dredged up a soft laugh. "We're a pair, all right."

"If you'd told me about your financial difficulties, made me understand, I could've helped maybe." She raked her lip with her teeth. "God, when I think of what I spent on that show booth, only to be shot down by Motonaka. That's one expense we could have foregone."

His gaze drifted to his desk in the adjacent study. The begging-for-attention clutter was insignificant when compared to all the last eighteen hours had unveiled.

"Pride kept me from telling you, sugar." He'd kept quiet, believing revelation, in life, like in the Bible, to be inexplicably linked with apocalypse. "I'd have gone to debtors' prison mute, leaving you to wonder how you got free of your tyrannical partner."

She smiled. "Holding on to you, rather than getting rid of you, has been my biggest goal. Surely you noticed."

"Hell, no wonder we didn't get along." Using past tense made him feel absolved, but the need to dig another issue out of his gut and get it onto the table needled him. "Tell me something, sweetheart." Her elevated chin invited him to elaborate. "Something that relates to my promise to leave Xtreme if you proved me wrong about Lance."

"I didn't consider that a promise. To me it was more of a challenge."

"A wager," he corrected. "Your proof against my exit."

"You were angry. Upset."

"Were you?" Or had she been honest when she adamantly accepted his challenge? She might love him but still prefer that he live up to the wager he'd lost.

A dark, damp brow quirked. "Angry when I said my goal was to get you out of my life?"

"That's what I mean, darlin'."

After a moment she said, "I was hurt—stunned—when you chose Lance over me. Like you, I'm not above saving face. That's all behind us."

He waited for more, wanting the slate rubbed clean.

She found the soap, ran it over her chest. Shielding bubbles began to dissipate, granting him a veiled view of her perfect, petite body.

"I want you to stay, Chess, but if you..."

She raked her lip again; it whitened. Worried about the cut, he frowned, shaking his head. She released her lip and swiveled the soap in her hands thoughtfully.

"If you don't, I'll make it. I have a plan. I'll survive."

Though he hated the drift of the conversation, he believed her. She was even stronger now, more determined than when they'd met. That challenged his bent-on-control mania while triggering his admiration, his pride in her. The gist of her statement, her wanting him with her, filtered in, latched on. He took the soap, lathered his chest, then rinsed. More bubbles disintegrated.

"What do you want from this partnership, Holly?"

She studied the clearing water, then the disheveled bed, her tongue flicking out to moisten her lips. Her eyes, windows on her wishes and needs, sought his. "I want us to be a team. To have common goals, no matter what they are."

He held out his hand. She took it. Drawing her forward, he turned her and snuggled her backside into the well of his legs. He glided the soap over, in and out of her most intimate secrets. "I'll stay, Holly. I love you too much not to," he murmured against her ear, feeling her taut nerves run smooth.

She languished in his arms like a trusting kitten while he pondered what would have to take place. "I can stop the design thievery, but..." His mind dived into corners, caverns of possibility.

"How?" she murmured.

He chuckled. "Maybe I'll ask a favor of an influential friend. I've been holding off till the right time."

She twisted her head, her smile humoring.

He might have to make that call to Washington after all, but not until he'd tried his own hand at righting Lance's wrong. "Motonaka is launched now, with plenty of money to hire superb designers. They'll be tough competitors, but we'll try to hold our market share—ride out Xtreme together. If we go broke, we'll go aiming for the same goal, just like you want, sugar."

Her slick body spun in his arms, her eyes declaring she'd heard only his concession to stay. "You won't be sorry, cowboy." Her smile wicked, she ran the tip of her tongue across his mouth, invading the corner.

His groin kicked like a randy racehorse.

"You mean women tycoons still have to resort to those tactics?" He sank against the tub back.

"We don't have to, but we enjoy letting men think we do."

He stood, drawing her up with him, stepped out and lifted her over the side of the tub. Their bodies dripped onto the thick mat. He damp-dried her firm, delicately sculpted body with a luxurious bath sheet, then draped it around her and tucked it at her silky breasts. He kissed her brow while reaching for a second towel. She sat on the side of the tub, hands pressed at her sides, staring at her water-withered feet where the ankle bracelet sparked against rosy skin. Then, as he rubbed his own body, their eyes ricocheted, locked, skittered off again as though executing a curious dance.

Finally she spoke soberly. "Remember me telling America Ice about my idea to launch an aprés-ski line?" He nodded. "That didn't come off the top of my head to impress AI. Phillips Philadelphia has approached me... They want to license me to design and Xtreme to manufacture and distribute a new line under the Phillips label."

"Why didn't they contact me?"

"I'm not sure they knew about you. The letter said they'd been following my design history from the beginning. You know how hot Phillips is. I felt I'd pulled a coup."

And back then, she probably felt she needed any advantage she could get. He didn't know much about women's clothing, but he nodded encouragingly, anticipating where she was headed.

"We'd not only distribute to the ski shops but to Phillips's established retail markets. Nordstrom, Saks, Bloomingdales." Her face lit like that of a child presenting an excellent report card. "Phillips proposed to do the marketing, but with your international connections and the reps we've hired in South America, I thought we..." She stopped, eyes clouding before she dropped her chin to gaze at her feet again. "Actually, I didn't consider this part when Phillips first contacted me. Knowing you planned to abandon—to leave—Xtreme, I was holding the offer like an ace in the hole, for when I was on my own again."

"Thought what, sugar?" He wrapped his waist with the towel.

Her tone hinged on excitement. "Using our reps to extend Phillips' market internationally would be a cinch. Signing with them could put Xtreme back in the black."

As recently as yesterday afternoon, he would have complimented her on the Phillips offer, promised her he'd think about it, then agonized over the money needed. Today, he opted for honesty. "We don't have the money to buy more machines, hire more people, and buy fabrics for a new line. Nor a way to honor the lease for additional space we'd need."

In the sudden quiet, her disappointment was palpable.

Chess heard water running on the second floor of the old house. Outside the bedroom door, Warrior whined, then yelped. Angel barked once, a sharp, no-nonsense demand.

At last Holly spoke. "I trust your judgment. We'll gamble that Phillips wants Xtreme enough to wait."

Her compliance assured Chess she wanted him now, not just what his money could do for Xtreme. Rising, she wrapped her arms about his waist, tiptoeing, mouth pursed. He ducked his head to kiss her, relief lining up alongside gratitude.

From a bank of built-in drawers, he came up with a T-shirt, which he shook out and held by the back hem. "Put this on, sweetheart." Catching her dubious look, he coaxed, "It's heavy. You won't need a bra, and the logo'll help. I'll ask Do Thi to wash your things."

He eased the shirt over her tousled head, protecting her bruises. It fell to just above her knees, longer than the pin-striped, suit-skirt she'd worn last night, but, somehow, more erotic. The OU ATHLETIC DEPARTMENT logo masked her breasts. His name stamped boldly across her back gave him the sense of putting his brand on her.

He produced a pair of man's black bikini briefs, drawing her wry smile. "A gift from Robyn," he said, kneeling, holding them for her.

She eyed the garment, leaned to size up his hips and butt, then held onto his shoulders and stepped into the briefs, then gathered the shirt around her waist and performed a pirouette.

"She had perfect taste." She pecked his lips. "Until she left you."

Grinning, his throat tight, Chess pulled on shorts and a T-shirt. "Hungry?" Judging by the rumbling in his own stomach, she must be. He doubted she'd found time to eat, considering her trip to see Jules last night and having to fend off Lance. He fought down new outrage, determined to put Lance out of their lives as she had Jules. "Everyone else has eaten, probably, but let's scavenge the leftovers."

Her cheeks warmed, lighting bruises from behind, mellowing them. "What will Do Thi think?" Palms splayed on her breasts, she glanced at her bare feet. "She'll know we..." Shrugging, she smiled prettily. "Made love."

"Do Thi's the least judgmental person I know."

He extended his hand to lead Holly from their sanctuary.

Chapter Sixty-one

Holly united with Angel outside the bedroom door, then Angel and Warrior, who had been camping there, tagged mistress and master into the dining room. Chess seated Holly to the right of his head-of-the-table position; Angel took her usual post at Holly's feet. Warrior raced around Chess's chair like movie Indians circling pale-face wagons, then bounded onto the sofa and curled into a ball, ears peaked.

Holly observed the dining room, all warm wood and subdued lighting. The unpretentious family room offered comfortable seating and a wagon-wheel coffee table. Firewood crammed a washtub and magazines overflowed a wicker basket. An Indian rug draping the sofa contrasted with the stark modern living room where she'd waited for Chess on her first visit, a room she somehow connected with Robyn.

A large, undraped window overlooked the yard, the cabins, the barn and corrals. The wrecked 'vette was parked next to where she'd left the ailing Saab yesterday.

Bare feet hugging the chair rung, Holly sipped coffee served by Do Thi's helper. Chess chose the *Journal* from a stack of newspapers next to his plate, scanning headlines as he balanced his chair on its back legs. The fingertips of one hand pressed the table edge for equilibrium. Holly's eyes feasted on the hard, well-defined thigh muscles exposed by brief runner's shorts before she forced her gaze to the window again.

"It looks as if you're collecting wrecked and under-the-weather cars." She smiled consolingly.

He lowered the paper, gazing out somberly. "It's starting to resemble the rez."

"You miss Adam terribly, don't you?"

He stared at his hands. "Breakfast was one of our best times of the day. It had a family feel." He lifted his glistening eyes. "Having you here damn sure helps, sugar."

"Especially with Lance missing."

"Lance doesn't—didn't—always make breakfast." His voice turned raspy and hard.

Her hand slipped into his at the moment Do Thi hustled in from the kitchen, smiling, clutching her ruffled apron. Her eyes appraised Holly's cheeks openly, saddening before her troubled gaze shifted to Chess, her mouth austere. He nodded, puckering his chin and dragging his lips down. His mimed sadness seemed to temper Do Thi's agitation. Dark eyes crinkling in a smile, she sucked in breath that elevated her shoulders before they settled into appeased posture.

"Congratulation, Mista Chess," she beamed. "Look like you win lottery at last."

In the middle of French toast Chess had touted as a Saturday ritual, he lifted and cocked his head to listen, then turned to look out the window. Holly's gaze followed his. The Mercedes pulled up to Lance's cabin.

Her heart skipped irrationally before she recognized Jerri as the lone occupant. Swiveling to face Chess, she found his face bleak, his mouth forming a somber slash.

Questions charged her mind before he said, "Wait here.

I'll see what's up."

He tousled her curly crown, then left the house. She watched him cross the yard, hug Jerri's shoulders, converse gravely for a moment, then enter the cabin with her.

An antique mantle clock ticked off twenty minutes in which Holly watched them cart out armloads of clothing, a computer, and various personal items. They stood eyeing the stuffed-to-the-roof Mercedes, then closed the trunk and passenger door.

Hands on hips, Chess watched the car pull away. After a listless wave, he moved with a purposeful stride in the opposite direction, down a footpath that twisted around the barn and out of sight. More surprised than curious, Holly finished her coffee, appetite suddenly nonexistent. Still shoeless, she left the house, heading the way Chess had gone.

The rain had ended, leaving everything dripping. Sunlight transposed random droplets to new rhinestones. A breeze rustled satin-like in the maples and set the pines to murmuring. The loamy smell of nearby woods and the fragrance of a spring morning announced winter's end and the advent of a more promising season.

Favoring her bare feet, she picked her way along the path to a log shed behind the barn, a slouching, slant-roofed appendage too worn out not to be an original structure. When she reached the sagging door, she spotted Chess in a dim corner, squatted facing the wall. His T-shirt hugged his lean, muscled back. A wisp of consciousness introduced her to the wasted times of her life. She forced her eyes away, enjoying the evocative smell of hay bales stacked from earth floor to sod-and-log ceiling.

She stepped inside and dragged the door closed behind her.

The sound of iron grating iron split the quiet when she engaged the crude latch. Chess started a bit, then threw her an over-the-shoulder glance. A welcoming smile replaced his surprise before he turned back to whatever held his attention. Sensing something profound, yet unrelated to Jerri's visit, she approached gingerly and peered over his shoulder.

She had no comprehension of the tawny critter lying on a black CCB monogrammed towel, other than its being a three-legged feline starring in a maternal role. Two dun-colored, crop-tailed fur balls worked at the mother's tits while three slit-eyed siblings rooted around, cheeping like foundling robins. Chess held a sixth baby in one hand as his other coaxed milk from the mother's nipple to tempt a minuscule mouth. The baby latched on. Chess held the nipple in place until a faint sucking, smacking noise filled the quiet as tiny jaws pulsed rhythmically.

Holly sank to the earth. One hand on Chess's knee, she watched him repeat the action with a different kitten.

"She's a bobcat." His voice held quiet homage. "Shideezhi. Little Sister."

"Isn't she wild?" She resisted the urge to explore.

"Not anymore. Adam found her in the woods, caught in a trap. She had given birth after getting snagged. She couldn't get food, so they were all half-starved and nearly frozen. Adam was healing them." Voice gravelly, he added, "I inherited the job." Smokey velvet eyes smiling suddenly, he nodded to the scene at their feet. "Sweet, huh?"

His guileless emotion created an awareness in her, a stirring encouraged by the suckling mouths, contented gurgles and Chess's thorough gentleness. She grieved for past hurtful words she'd leveled on him, prior schemes and distrust, for wasted days and nights when they could have found solace. The victory in his agreement to stay with Xtreme, with her, paled in the light of this moment, this true portrait of Chess Baker.

"They're beautiful," she breathed, moving to kneel

before him, arms circling his neck.

His eyes cognizant, he situated the infant cat, folding a corner of the towel to bind mouth to body, then switched to a cross-legged position and enfolded Holly in his embrace. He rasped against the pulse in her throat. "I've been god-awful lonesome for so long. If I had my kingdom back, I'd trade it all for you."

Her chest tightened into an ache. As she kissed his temple, his closed eyes, her thoughts gave birth to words. "If you'd told Robyn that, she wouldn't have left you. You never had to be lonely."

He eased back to see her eyes.

"If I'd told her that, it would have been a lie."

⸻⋇⸻

When the train moaned, then wailed, in the middle of their second night, Chess reached for Holly, tucking her into the folds of his body, molding them together.

"You're awake." She sounded as if she'd drawn a black-jack. She eased out of his arms and propped against the head-board, knees drawn to her chin. "Good. I've been thinking."

Habitual tension pricked his hairline. "About what, sugar?"

"What you said about Xtreme's financial status. About Lance and Koichi Mihatsu, about Mihatsu's connection to Motonaka."

He urged her back down, hating how this fiasco was affecting her when all he wanted was to absorb it himself, protect and nurture her, never see those beautiful eyes cloud with worry.

He whispered, "Never mind, princess. I'll fix it."

Her tongue caressed his ear as she whispered back, "You damn sure will, cowboy. I've got it all figured out."

Chapter Sixty-two

Early Monday morning, Holly and Chess watched two men from the warehouse clear Lance's former office of personal effects to be stored until he came for them. After seeing the project to completion, Chess kicked back in Lance's chair, hands steepled under his chin, Luccheses propped on the desk, ankles crossed.

Holly entertained memory of an earlier morning scene: Chess's face lathered up, the towel around his waist inching up to expose his tight buttocks while he leaned over the sink, razor in one hand, his cellular in the other. She had hugged his waist and nuzzled his silky, granite-hard back, then withdrawn in deference to the gravity of the conversation.

She perched on a desk corner now, the backs of her hands tucked beneath her thighs, dangling her feet while she attempted to gauge his closed expression. "Chess?"

His brows elevated, eyes a bit remote.

"I forgot to tell you that while you were on the phone to Washington this morning, I heard something interesting on the financial channel." At least she hoped it would interest him. Catching his anticipatory look, she finished with a flourish. "Those bonds you talked about—Banomex?"

He nodded, one brow torqued.

"They've bounced."

His eyes danced. "A dead cat bounce by any chance?"

She smiled. "That's good, I assume?"

"Right as rain, princess. Thanks for spotting that." Appearing less tense, he resumed his studious posture.

She murmured a warning. "No solitary plotting."

He rallied, swinging his feet down. "No way. I'm just thinking how brilliant you are, honey, how you never give up."

He spun his lighter on the desktop, grinning. She hadn't seen him smoke since he'd gone out to the rain-drenched porch last Friday night.

She'd come to think of the lighter as a pacifier.

"I'm also thinking how your idea can't help but work." His tone held conviction.

Her heart skipped. "You're all set, then? Everything's in go mode?" She couldn't bring herself to ask if Lance was still around and still willing to comply with the plan.

"I'm chompin' at the bit, partner."

Rising, he splayed hands on hips, rolled his shoulders forward then back. He snapped his briefcase and donned his doing-business black hat, eyeing her from beneath the brim. "You're sure you won't come with me?"

"A showdown is man's work." Her throat swelled at the thought of his absence. "I'll just mind the ranch, mend a few fences, maybe."

His eyes turned solemn. "You're welcome to come, Holly."

"I know," she rushed. "But you and Lance need time alone."

That time might start Chess's healing.

She needed time to begin forgetting.

⊰⊱⊰⊱

Aboard United's Denver to LA flight, Chess scrunched in an aisle seat, his laptop perched on the pull-down tray, connected to his cellular phone. His thighs elevated the makeshift desk, setting the monitor screen at an odd angle.

Twice, the market report had filed by. His heart had surged each time TMX, symbolizing Teléfonos de Méjico, appeared, each time the stock crept up another point. At nineteen now, it had gained three points since the morning's bell, four points higher than when he'd gone crazy and bought the last half-million-dollar batch at fifteen. Over the months, he'd watched the stock plunge to a record-low twelve before shaking loose last Friday to gain a point.

Banomex Bonds had soared an astronomical three points this morning. Any spot on the board, other than the cellar, encouraged his gut to gradually uncoil. As he'd predicted and hoped when Peder Andrews challenged him to swim deeper into shark-infested water with his last dollar, that tough old broad, Mexico, was rebounding. Thanks to a benevolent U.S. government. From here on, if luck held, his only decision was whether to convert bonds to stock, a roll-of-the-dice, no-lose choice.

He rested his head against the seat back, seeing Holly's sympathetic expression when she'd faced him over a mound of bubbles, two mornings ago. His confession that he and Xtreme were going broke had proven to be an aphrodisiac for his love life. And the way the cards were turning in his favor, if Holly's plan worked, too, Xtreme could turn out to be his biggest turnaround to date.

Across the aisle, Lance slept fitfully, seat reclined, head slumped to the side, mouth ajar. When Chess had picked him up at Jerri's house mid-morning, he'd been sullen, his Misonni suit rumpled, reeking of cigarettes and beer. Chess thought he'd seen hope of reconciliation in Lance's eyes. Or was it triumph? Although myriad topics needed ironing out, he was grateful he'd booked opposite-aisle seats, thereby forestalling conversation. He was not yet ready to cross that bridge.

The cab slugged along the 405 Freeway from the LA airport, headed for the inner city. Elbow on the armrest, chin in palm, Lance stared out the window in stony silence as though memorizing every nuance of the smoggy, sun-blotched landscape.

Chess noted the deep scuff marks on Lance's Bally loafers. Lance always depended on Do Thi to keep them shined. Had today's circumstances been different, just another of those out-for-a-lark excursions from their past, he would be taking his cousin shopping later, for whatever he needed or took a shine to.

Sympathy edged into Chess's ruminating. Senseless, asinine pity he struggled against.

Bitter knowledge of Lance's seventeen-year resentment that hadn't stopped him from taking everything offered to him, counteracted Chess's compassion. What kind of ego rendered a man as blind as he'd been? As assuming? As trusting? He jerked his mind back to the task at hand and stared out a different window than Lance, determined to let sleeping dogs lie.

Holly faced Greg across a table in Caper's Bistro, the posh pink marble and fake foliage eatery in the Stapleton Plaza Hotel. She picked at her lunch, consulting her watch. Twelve-forty—Chess would have landed half an hour ago. With no luggage to claim and barring airport congestion, he should now be on the second leg of his mission.

Her palms moistened into clamminess. She wiped them

on her napkin, half listening to Greg's incensed listing of damages she should have inflicted on Lance three nights ago. Sipping house Chenin Blanc, she awaited her turn to assure Greg she'd landed the last blow, and in a strategic spot. While Greg talked, she tracked a tentative schedule for Chess, concluding she couldn't expect to hear from him for several hours.

She wiped her sweaty palms again and sipped more wine.

Chapter Sixty-three

The cab stopped at the curb fronting the Arco Towers, next door to the Bonaventure Hotel, where they had overnight reservations, should that prove necessary. Inside the Tower, Chess consulted a building directory, then crossed to the elevators servicing floors twenty through thirty. Lance barely squeezed through the no-nonsense elevator doors before they wheezed shut. An ugly fantasy of Lance avoiding the door—wheeling, running—of chasing him down Figueroa Street and through downtown Los Angeles, made Chess grateful that dependence on his cousin would soon end.

His hands grasping a brass rail, stance wide, Lance gazed out the soaring glass cubicle to the congested street below. In the harsh light, Chess took in Lance's wasted condition: sallow complexion, sandy hair combed forward to disguise a receding hairline, a shallow pocket of flesh beneath his chin.

Delicate Baker genes dominated Lance's anatomy. Aunt Sibyl, Lance's mother, had been frail and peaked, a follower like her son, including the day she followed an Oklahoma City news anchor to Memphis and never returned. Having no siblings, Chess had enjoyed Jerri calling him and Lance "the fabulous Baker boys," liked the connotation. Today, the unresolved question of what his cousin had to do with Adam leaving usurped all tender emotion involving Lance.

A pretty Japanese receptionist acknowledged their presence, her dark, heavy-lashed eyes shielded by small oval glasses with frames wrapped in pseudo snakeskin. Her tiny hands scrawled notes in Japanese on a pad as she continued speaking softly into the mouthpiece of a set of headphones. Ironically, the ultramodern decor and austere furnishings resembled Sol y Sombre's living room, including the same lack of welcome. From his stance, Chess could see into a large partitioned space filled with a bevy of metal desks and Japanese females—young, and for the most part, attractive—manning phones. Computer keyboards clattered softly in the otherwise perfect quiet. All business.

He recognized the receptionist's good-bye tones and pivoted to face her over the high partition surrounding her desk.

"Mornin'. Lance Baker to see Mr. Mihatsu." He handed her Lance's confiscated business card. "We have an appointment."

Expression benign, her gaze shifted to Lance.

"My assistant," Chess said quietly, avoiding a name.

Beside him, Lance flinched, sucked in breath, blew it out.

"We have a one-thirty appointment," Chess added.

She nodded, spoke soft Japanese into the headset, then nodded again to Chess and Lance. Chess asked permission to store their carry-on luggage behind her desk. In flawless English she agreed. With a tiny, tastefully manicured finger, she directed them down an art-strewn corridor that separated administrative hierarchy from clerical.

Chess turned a second corner and spotted Mihatsu in an open doorway. Mihatsu recognized him and blanched, his mouth gaping atypically. His heels snapped a Hitleresque salute. Coal-black eyes narrowed, his gaze riveting on Lance as they drew nearer. Mihatsu bowed, then shot his hand toward Lance when the two men stood shoulder to mid-chest.

Lance's acceptance of the hand, even though he shook it listlessly, pissed Chess. Lance might no longer be in Mithatsu's camp, but he was sure as hell riding the fence. His neglecting to bow got Chess's attention. He curbed his resentment, disappointed at not having an irresistible reason to finish what he'd started at Bud's by mopping up the Nakamoto offices with his traitorous cousin.

Mihatsu offered Chess a handshake.

Chess shoved his hands into his back pockets. If Mihatsu wanted to out-finesse him, he hoped he would serve lunch and supper because they'd be here awhile.

Noticeably flustered, Mihatsu addressed him. "To what do I owe this..." He paused as if searching for a term. "This unexpected pleasure, Mr. Baker?"

Chess gave Lance the eye, then strode past Mihatsu into an office so dimly lit it reminded him of Holly's soft-light fetish. Uninvited, he took a chair before the desk. Lance followed suit.

Mihatsu moved into the hallway and glanced both ways. Was the little man planning to run or call an arbitrator? Eventually, he stepped inside, closed the door, and went behind his desk, where he switched on a lamp on the credenza. The lamp produced a warm honey glow and kept the light behind him and in Chess's face. The guy knew stagecraft. Mihatsu pushed a button on the phone and spoke Japanese.

The office was informal enough to be friendly, yet traditional enough to bear no relation to the outer space. A nearby library table held stacks of files and books. Chess grudgingly admired the lithographs depicting ducks swimming in serene water and noted the baseball trophies crowding a large shelf. No photographs graced the walls or Mihatsu's desk.

His voice wavered between mock politeness and uncertainty when he addressed Lance. "It is good to see you, my friend. How have you been?"

Grimacing, Lance shoved out of the chair, mumbling, "Not so damned good." He strode to the wide window and stared down twenty-seven floors to the street.

During the ride to the Denver airport, Chess had learned that stealing the designs had been Mihatsu's idea. Lance had been paid ten thousand dollars for the design disks, plus another fifteen percent of the total show orders.

According to Lance, he hadn't done it for the money.

Now Chess eyed the window, gauging its stability, worrying whether Lance could seize something to shatter it and jump before he could stop him.

Old habits remained alive, but they were losing ground.

He took off his hat, crossed an ankle over his football knee and hung the hat on the toe of his boot. "How was the ski show?"

"Our skis sold well, as always, thank you."

"What about ski apparel?"

Mihatsu's head jerked like the head on one of those toy dogs Okies placed in the back windows of Chevy Impalas. His glossy brows shot up. "I am very sorry to say it was not convenient for me to attend the show. I regret not being able to view Xtreme's current line. I am sure your sales were excellent. As always."

"Cut the crap. You and Lance stole Holly's designs, Nakamoto produced them and you exhibited them with the Motonaka label." Peripherally, he saw Lance turn from the window and felt his body heat when he settled back into his chair.

Resignation outweighed shock in Mihatsu's expression, as though he'd known but hadn't cared that only a matter of time governed the theft's discovery. After checking the copyright laws, Chess had found nothing that labeled Mihatsu guilty. Copying underpinned the clothing industry. Robyn had bitched constantly about paying a grand for a Chanel bag, then seeing a less discriminating or less affluent peer sporting a three-hundred-dollar clone.

Nevertheless, Chess launched his bluff on Mihatsu. "In exchange for clemency, Lance has agreed to be a witness."

Lips curling, Mihatsu eyed Lance. He reclined his chair, hands forming a slightly palsied triangle beneath his chin. "Witness to what, if I may ask?"

"To what I said. Stealing, manufacturing, and marketing Xtreme designs." Chess steepled his own rock-steady hands, which in no way reflected his racing heart, and yawed sideways, getting comfortable. "But you went a step further by cutting prices to the quick to steal any orders we might have gotten."

Mihatsu shrugged. "Capitalism, I believe you call it."

To keep from leaping over the desk and choking the life out of the evil little bastard, Chess rejected his relaxed pose to grip the chair arms. Sweat bathed his back as he stared at the phone. Surreptitiously he checked the clock on the credenza.

Timing was getting screwed.

"Capitalism, huh?" He pretended to roll the words through his mind. "Maybe so. We'll see what the media calls it."

Mihatsu's brow beetled. His peaked fingers twitched.

"If things don't go the way I want this afternoon, Lance and I will keep our appointment with a syndicated journalist who'll expose your thievery to the international marketplace. Tomorrow morning, we're meeting with the Justice Department. By noon, Nakamoto will be ordered to cease and desist importing skis as well as Motonaka apparel into the U.S."

Mihatsu spared them a laugh. "You are bluffing. You are a very small fish trying to swim in a very big pond—playing out of your league, I believe you Americans say." He scrunched forward, elbows on his chair, warming to the ridicule. "Your claim will make a dent in the evening news. Then all will be forgotten."

Pretty much the way Chess saw it, too, if miracles didn't start happening quicker than he could draw his next few breaths. "Lance is my ace in the hole. The right media connections can change lack of interest to frenzy feeding. Once Lance tells them that you, personally, approached him, your ass is feathers."

Lance shuffled his feet, leaned to balance elbows on knees and dropped his head into his hands. Then, shocking hell out of Chess, he looked Mihatsu in the eye. "You bet your butt."

Mihatsu's face pinched. He moved even closer to the desk, forearms resting there, hands clasped as though awaiting dinner. Or maybe he was praying.

"If you carry out your threat—"

"No threat, Mihatsu. A promise." Chess managed to smile.

"If so, I will sue you for libel."

Just what he didn't need. Chess snuck a glance at Lance's watch. "You can sue. I've got a battery of lawyers rearing to go." Yeah, right. Greg Friedman, if he wasn't too pissed over Holly spending the last three nights at Sol y Sombre. Considering the small fortune Chess owed his compadres, Karsh and Fulton, P.C., he wouldn't be inviting them to the Nakamoto/Xtreme shootout.

"Nakamoto retains the most superior attorneys in America, Mr. Baker." Mihatsu shrugged. "However, as CEO I do not favor bad publicity. Perhaps we can come to some agreement, although I feel I owe you nothing. Only from the goodness of my heart will I listen."

Chess placed both feet on the floor; his hat plopped onto the carpet. He took a file folder from his briefcase. "Your thievery is documented. Lance may not be selective in who he deals with, but he's thorough. I'm taking this file to the Justice Department tomorrow morning, if we don't reach an agreement today."

Mihatsu arched caterpillar brows. "Which would be?"

"Nakamoto agreeing to purchase Xtreme at a price that would make a lawsuit infeasible."

Mihatsu pursed thin lips, then screwed up his mouth in contemplation. "What kind of price do you suggest?"

Chess hoped his fortifying indrawn breath went unnoticed. "Twice the profit I projected had I taken Xtreme public which was my goal before your thievery pushed me off target."

Mihatsu scoffed. "Insanity. I will listen to no such blackmail."

Chess tapped the file against his thighs, his gaze riveting Mihatsu's dark, fathomless eyes. "I'll also expect you to assume the ten-year lease I signed for new facilities for Xtreme, which computes to a couple million."

Mihatsu popped from the chair like a bagel from a toaster. He pounded the desk. "I will not listen to this bullshit!"

A real cross-culture response. Chess would have laughed if his palms weren't sweating and his pulse wasn't keeping time to *Jaws* background music.

"Fine." He shoved the file into his briefcase and reached for his hat. Feeling Lance's stare, he wondered if it held triumph or concern. "I'll catch you on television tomorrow night, Koichi. Wear black. It suits you."

A soft buzzing sound dented the tense surroundings. Mihatsu snatched the phone receiver to bark, "I said no calls."

His irate expression slipped into confusion, turning to consternation. Chess's heart omitted a couple of beats, then rocked his chest.

Mihatsu leaned across the desk to pass him the phone.

"Chess Baker." He mentally crossed his fingers, then

calmed a bit when he heard the caller's voice. Involuntarily, he smiled. "Yes, ma'am, it's really me. Thanks for chasing me down to return my call." He caught Mihatsu's unguarded stare and deduced he'd been told the caller's identity.

Beside Chess, Lance's interest grew palpable.

"How's Kevin? Twin boys? That's great, Ms. Richardson." Her answer had taunted his envy demons. He avoided the image forming in his mind to answer a question. "No, ma'am, I don't have any. Not yet, anyway." Not ever, now that Adam was gone.

He regrouped. Focused. "I know you're busy, so I'll be brief. I called regarding a little problem I've run into." Her interruption coaxed another smile. "Yes, ma'am, you did tell me to call anytime, and I appreciate it. I may still be able to work this out myself, but if not, I'll have to ask you to turn the dogs loose."

Mihatsu's brows hiked, a nearly imperceptible frown surfacing. Chess checked the time for a different reason now, running possible plane schedules through his mind, twisting his ring, thinking of Holly.

"Just in case things go sour here, could I have a number where you can be located for the next twenty-four hours?" He used Mihatsu's gold pen to dash off the number on a desk pad. "Thank you, ma'am—Ms. Richardson. I'm much obliged. If you don't hear from me, you'll know I made out all right." He waited out her insistence that he call either way. "Yes, ma'am. I'll call tomorrow for sure. Give Kevin and Jennifer my best. Congratulations on those twins. Nice talking to you." A grin in his tone, he gave her the customary Okie farewell. "Bye-bye."

He passed the phone back to Mihatsu.

"The U.S. Attorney General." Chess watched Mihatsu pale. "Her son and I co-captained the Oklahoma Sooners awhile back. Hell of a nice lady, doin' a hell of a job." His voice held steady while an ocean pounded in his ears.

Mihatsu mopped his brow with a starch-stiffened sleeve, chancing a glance at Lance. Apparently finding no support in Lance's eyes, he stabbed a phone button with a nicotine-stained finger.

He growled into the line. "Come to my office. Bring coffee and a blank letter of intent."

Chess settled in his chair. His heart danced a two-step.

Chapter Sixty-four

At a window table in the rooftop lounge in the Bonaventure Hotel, Chess and Lance faced over two O'Doul's. Beyond Lance's hunched shoulders lay a smog-blotched view of merchant ships moored in the gray-blue water edging San Pedro's Harbor.

Chess switched his gaze to the LA skyline. Jagged marble towers stabbed a low, brooding sky. His mind ricocheted from Jimmy Buffett's reference to brown-yellow haze, then to Sol y Sombre. He drew mental pictures of a vintage ranch house, indigo skies above rolling plains. Amber dawns. Terracotta sunsets. A wave of homesickness washed over him.

He couldn't resist a peek at his watch to gauge the time. "So." A brilliant lead-in to a painful exit.

"Great performance you gave in there," Lance begrudged. He swigged O'Douls, squinting through cigarette smoke.

"I majored in communications, remember? Running a bluff's my specialty."

"Still, I thought you had the chance of a whore at a tea dance." Chess recognized Lance's sucking-up smile.

"I can't take credit. It was Holly's idea and Anita

Richardson came through for me." Speaking Holly's name in
Lance's presence felt like sacrilege. "Women can be a hellaceous asset to a man, if he can swallow his pride."

Eyes hollow, Lance signaled the waiter without comment.

Chess placed a stack of hundred dollar bills banded by a
currency wrapper on the table. Lance's gaze, contrite but
greedy, fastened there. Chess dug a set of papers out of the
briefcase and placed them beside the money. Lance's brow
creased, his eyes shifting back to the document. Chess
allowed him time to glean the contents.

"You never should have touched Holly, Lance."

Lance's verdant eyes grabbed his, then took on a hot, wet
glow before they shifted to Chess's middle shirt button.

With one finger, Chess tapped the pack of bills. "You and
I are finished, so here's your choice. You can use this for walk-
ing-around money, one bar to the next." Did Lance realize his
tongue had flicked out to wet his lips? "If you get a cheap
room, or hook up with a lonely woman, the money'll buy you
a history-making binge." The imaginary scene turned to bile
in his stomach. He tapped the document. "On the other hand
the rehab center's paid for. You can dry out, again, maybe for
keeps this time, and use the cash as future seed money. It's not
a lot—"

"It's more than I deserve."

Chess swallowed, eyes smarting. "That's for damn sure."

Lance sank back in the chair, somehow managing to look
even frailer.

"If you were trying to hurt me, Lance, you succeeded."
In rapid mind glimpses, he examined their relationship from
inception to this moment, ending with an acquiescent gesture.
"Maybe I deserved it, maybe not." Their eyes locked. "I bent
like hell, but I didn't break. Along with my Indian blood, I got
resilience from the Chesneys." His smile left an acrid taste in

his mouth. Stomach churning, trying to deny Lance's pathetic expression, he prodded, "Tell me. When did you turn on me? And why? How'd you get Adam to pull up stakes and go back to the rez? Or did you?"

Lance dropped his head, shook it, mouth grim. His hands snaked to the money. "Why bother to give you answers you wouldn't believe? Ask Adam."

"Trust me, cuz. I will."

He shoved to his feet, collected his bag and briefcase and took one last, indelible look before walking away.

Chapter Sixty-five

Holly lounged in a warm bubble bath, sipping peppermint schnapps, willing the libation to calm her frantic nerves. She checked the clock on the vanity. Five-forty. Four-forty LA time.

She should have gone with him, as he'd asked her to. She should have shared his task, thereby honoring her request they share goals, work together, no matter what the project. But she'd had some weird, god-awful idea of using this mission to prove she trusted him, believed he had her interests at heart, that he'd come through for her. For them. For the partnership.

She loved him, cared about his damned, cocksure ego.

She checked the wall mirror to make sure she was Holly.

When the phone rang, she lunged for the tub-side extension, dumping schnapps everywhere. "Chess?"

"How's it goin', sugar? Get those fences mended?"

She closed her eyes, slipping down into the now-tepid water. Weariness, resolve, and triumph resonated in his caressing voice. "When are you coming home, cowboy?"

"I'm in the boarding line as we speak, be there in a couple of hours."

"What happened? I've imagined all kinds—" No. His knowing the horror of what she'd imagined would do nothing to assure him of her new determination to trust him. "I'm dying to hear."

"I'll tell you all about it at dinner." His buoyant tone lessened the stress of not knowing. "I want to buy you that ninety-dollar lobster at The Palm and order their most expensive wine from that snooty steward. I want to play footsies under the table and..." He lowered his voice. An unidentifiable cracking noise on the line led her to envision his hand shielding the provocative words from fellow passengers. "I want to see your lips straddle the edge of a cut-crystal wineglass, and watch your nipples harden when I talk dirty."

"Oh, God." Fiery response raced into anticipation.

"Most of all, I want to spend two hours not being able to touch you, but knowing we're leaving that restaurant together." He fell silent, allowing her to fantasize what would follow. "How about it, sweetheart? Interested?"

More like seduced. "I'll meet you there. That way, we'll move the climax of this indecent proposal an hour closer."

She judged his laughter more genuine than she'd heard lately. "Now that's a good partner, partner."

"I'm aiming to please."

"See you soon, princess."

She rolled the conversation around in her mind, along with the riddle-filled outcome of his mission. Ambivalence jammed her reasoning. If Mihatsu actually had buckled to Chess's demands, she and Chess had won. Yet Xtreme, their child, their bond, was gone. Their partnership was over.

Did the possibility of a new and different union exist?

Chapter Sixty-six

The chic restaurant, Denver's current favorite, teemed with life. Local celebrities, whose framed caricatures papered the walls, stood two deep in the bar shouting to be heard. Plates rattled, glasses and flatware clinked as waiters hustled to serve an unusually large Monday night crowd. In a special-request back booth, Holly sipped Ferrari Carano Reserve and toyed with an Australian lobster glazed in drawn butter.

She shut out the surrounding din by focusing on Chess's storm-cloud eyes and cushiony lips, his classic face.

"Was Mihatsu horrible to deal with?" Though she knew differently from Chess's description of their adversary, she couldn't help picturing a Sumo wrestler stalking his prey.

Chess cocked back and grinned. "When it came right down to it, Koichi Mihatsu was all hat and no cattle."

She laughed. "No match for Chess Baker, you mean."

"I've got the letter of intent to prove it."

She liked seeing a bit of arrogance reinstated. "I want to hear about it. Leave nothing out."

In his easy but articulate way, he talked about the estranged plane ride to LA, hinting at market news he'd discovered en route and promising to share details later. He described the stone-silent cab ride, his lonely panic in Mihatsu's office, how he'd thrown his bluff on the table while praying for a phone call. His voice gravelly, he related how at mid-meeting, Lance had come around to support him. With gestures more animated than usual, he acted out Anita Richardson's phone call and Mihatsu caving in. Eyes somber, he shared his and Lance's parting, the pain of not knowing Lance's plans, the futility of trying not to care.

He took a long drink of water, his throat dry, she imagined, from talking more than was his custom. His socked foot caressed her calf. "The perfect conclusion to the trip was boarding the plane with a post-phone-call erection."

Easily recalling her own aroused state when she'd hung up, she slipped off her shoe and caressed him back, working her toes inside his pants leg, voicing her thoughts. "I'm surprised you demanded twice your projected return on Xtreme. I'd have never..." But then she'd chosen not to accompany him, chosen to trust him and his judgment. "How did you decide to do that?"

He shrugged, cutting into his T-bone steak, swabbed a bite in red-brown residue, then lowered his fork. "I had a hunch, probably based on the kind of day I was having in the market."

Her eyes invited elaboration.

"Demanding twice as much was like doubling down in blackjack. Twice the risk, twice the gain. This time it paid."

A born gambler for sure, a trait both perturbing and appealing. "That's remarkable. You brought about a miracle, more than I could ever hope for." Smiling, she added, "Except for being unemployed, we have no more problems."

"I've got one. I want to know if Adam got wind of Lance's scheme. If he left Sol y Sombre to keep the BIA off my back." He inched his plate back, placing his napkin beside it. "Not knowing how much Lance affected Adam's choice bothers the hell out of me."

"Did you ask Lance?" She recalled his stupefied look when Chess had questioned him in Bud's. "What did he say?"

"He said to ask Adam."

"Are you?"

"Will you come with me to the rez this weekend?"

She looked into his eyes. "Is the rez the end of the earth?"

"Some people think so."

Her hand covered his, pressed. "That's as far as I'll go with you, cowboy."

He shifted, strained a little to touch his foot to her thigh. Glancing at his lap, he eased the napkin back in place.

"Nice, sugar. Real nice." His gaze penetrated hers as he drew his plate forward and began to eat again. "Well, here's the story on the market. Mexico is coming out of the crisis, so the whole market is bullish. The convertible price of Banomex bonds is less than Banomex stock, so if I convert I score a fortune. I can pay off the Sol y Sombre mortgage and get back to breeding thoroughbreds and racing year-round."

This back-on-top Chess frightened her a little, although he seemed to have no reluctance to share information. But would he shut her out if future financial problems occurred? Then she remembered the partnership was ending. "I don't care what you do with the money, Chess."

His head jerked up. "Sure you do, sweetheart."

She sipped more wine, not sure who would drive her ailing Saab home. "I fell in love with you when you started going broke, although I had no idea your newfound poverty was the lure." Her teasing smile camouflaged the seriousness of the statement. "Truthfully, money's not important to me."

He studied her, mouth toying with a smile, eyes skeptical. "Making money is a hallowed Jewish trait. You have to care."

"I like accomplishment, not payoffs."

"Money is a way of keeping score, Holly. Market coups, turnarounds, winning horses would mean nothing without you. Especially now that I know what having you entails."

She drew a foot into the booth and beneath her. Taller now, she leaned to stroke his already stubbled cheek. "I guess I was fishing for assurance." Her honesty surprised yet freed her.

He kissed her palm, grinning. "I'll make you a tape to play when you get skittish." He cut another bite of steak, chewed leisurely, washed it down with a blood-red burgundy he'd been ordering by the glass for himself. "What if I told you this windfall allows me to guarantee Do Thi's sister-in-law's cousin a job at Sol y Sombre. With a job, he can get a visa."

She smiled, more comfortable with this Chess. "That's different." She swirled her wine and stared through it to his distorted face, jerking back to reality when he spoke.

"We need to talk about our partnership."

Heart clattering, she beat him to the punch. "I'm not sure we're cut out for partnership. You're a global thinker, jumping all over the place. I'm more concrete. A ponderer, but tenacious once I make a decision. The traits don't mix."

He grinned, appraising her tolerantly. "How the hell did you come up with that?"

"I read it in Barnes and Noble."

She watched him examine the theory in his intricate mind. "You're right, sugar, but if my way of doing business bothers you, I could tighten the reins. No problem."

The vise-grip on her heart eased. "I could be a little more lenient, speculate, even gamble, a little more."

He nodded, smiling, signaling for coffee.

"Decaf," Holly told the waiter.

Chess winked at the man. "Bring her the real stuff. After this we're headed for a rodeo."

She leaned back, smiling, folded her arms and shook her head, taking her turn at smiling indulgently. "Shameless."

He discarded the napkin.   "What are your current thoughts on taking up Phillips Philadelphia on that offer?"

His question surprised her into silence.

"You had your heart set on it, and I made it damned clear to Mihatsu that neither of us would sign a noncompete clause."

Again, her mind raced, seeking his meaning. He had protected her by refusing the noncompete clause in Mihatsu's letter of intent, granting her the legal freedom to accept the Phillips offer if she still desired. Her design reputation would sustain her marketwise. Her part of the price he had wrangled from Mihatsu would guarantee her the funds to start over, maybe even on the present premises, once Xtreme had taken up the new lease.

She spoke carefully. "The offer still appeals to me."

"I'm glad, sugar. I've gotten attached to the apparel business. It's a bigger gamble than the stock market."

Near cognizance settled on her. "Then you meant, what would I think of the two of us taking them up on the offer?"

Smiling tenderly, he reached for her hand. "You bet your pretty ass." He brought her hand to his mouth and kissed her palm, then tucked it into both of his. "Ever hear the story about the snapping turtle, Holly?"

She shook her head. "How did I miss that one?"

"When he bites, he won't let go till it thunders."

She nodded, scarcely breathing.

"I'm in this for the duration. I hope you are, too."

"The duration can be short or long, Chess. Depending on how many thunderstorms we encounter."

Eyes showing concern mixed with mischief, he signaled for the check. "Let's talk about this lying down. You're much more rational in that position."

The customary ripple moved through her. "I'll leave my

car here and ride with you to the ranch."

He shook his head as he peeled bills onto the table. "Not this time, sugar. We're headed for your house."

In the Cherokee, his face illuminated by dash lights, he took time to check his messages. Holly turned sideways, drawing her legs into the seat, content within the sound of his voice, satisfied to observe his masculine body language, to track his expression changes, message by message.

Finally, he disconnected. "Adam called. He sounds great, glad to be back on the rez."

"That's wonderful." She noted his posture had stiffened. "Isn't it?"

His shrug seemed feeble. "Maybe I was hoping that Lance had—I guess I wanted Adam to miss me more. Need me." His hands massaged the wheel at ten and two.

Holly's throat tightened. "Maybe he does, but doesn't want you to worry about him."

He glanced over. "Actually, I'd rather have him happy than missing or needing me. Maybe someday..." He clamped his lips, holding in the words.

She conjured up an assuring smile. "Sounds like the mystery in our trip to the reservation is gone. Strictly pleasure now."

He rallied. "We'll hit the stores for candy and cigars before we go."

She nodded, as if she understood.

Gazing onto the almost-empty freeway, he asked, "How do you feel about children, Holly? About the fact I'm sterile?"

Caught off guard, remembering children had never been a choice in her marriage, she searched for an answer. "I hurt for you, Chess, because having them means so much to you."

He turned to seek her eyes in the near darkness. "I'm thinking of trying to adopt, going through legitimate channels this time."

She mulled over the changes a child would bring to his life. And hers. "An Indian baby? A little Chess?"

He smiled. She knew if she could see his eyes, they'd be tender. "Maybe something more authentic, like a little version of Adam. Or maybe a girl. What do you think, sugar?"

"That would be wonderful. You have so much love to give."

His hand stroked her knee. "So do you, Holly. You'll see."

The moment her front door closed behind them, he folded her to him and kissed her deeply, tapping her responses, then led her down the hallway to her bedroom. When he began tossing back covers, she helped. On opposite sides of the bed, they undressed hastily, heedlessly casting clothing onto the floor.

They met in the center of the big bed.

"Why here, Chess, instead of me going home with you?"

His hand glided down her body, homing in to stoke her, ready her. "This is Jules's bed. The last demon we have to get rid of, darlin'. I don't want anything left either of us can ever question."

He turned onto his back and drew her onto him.

Holly wakened from the sweet aftermath of making love to find Chess waiting for her. He kissed her, welcoming her back and then with a satisfied smile, he worked the ring off his hand and held it between his thumb and forefinger.

Intrigued, she sat up against the headboard, tugging the sheet over her breasts. "What's going on here, cowboy?"

His hand cupped her cheek as he drew her to him and kissed her tenderly. "I want you to know, you're the best partner I've had."

She eyed him skeptically. "That's no real commendation, since you've never had another partner."

His eyes clouded. "If I had, I'd damn sure want her to be you."

She smiled. "What can I say? Women do it better. It's a new world order."

He crossed his legs and drew her, facing him, into the well, wrapping her legs around him. His gaze locked hers in. "I want to propose a different kind of union." He caught her hand, kissed her palm, and slipped his ruby signet ring onto her hand. Her finger drooped and the ring shifted, sagging to the side. Eyes somber, he righted it, clinching her fingers to hold the offering in place.

"Marry me, Holly."

Her breath snagged, then soughed past her throat. "Is that an edict, or a request?"

His eyes on the ring, gaze pensive, he twisted it as she'd seen him do so often on his own finger. "A plea." He gathered her close, his kiss a pledge complementing his entreaty. "Will you, marry me, partner?"

Her mind raced to a loveless past, examined the chaotic present and imagined a testy future with Chandler Chesney Baker.

"I will," she whispered. "Under one condition."

His eyes burned like clear, clean smoke. "Name it, princess."

"This time we'll go fifty-fifty."